Alice Cary

Pictures of Country Life

Alice Cary

Pictures of Country Life

ISBN/EAN: 9783337227661

Printed in Europe, USA, Canada, Australia, Japan

Cover: Foto ©Andreas Hilbeck / pixelio.de

More available books at **www.hansebooks.com**

PICTURES OF COUNTRY LIFE.

By ALICE CARY,

AUTHOR OF "CLOVERNOOK," "MARRIED NOT MATED," ETC., ETC.

NEW YORK:
PUBLISHED BY HURD AND HOUGHTON.
1866.

CONTENTS.

iii

LEM LYON.

———◆———

THE rain had fallen slowly and continuously since midnight —and it was now about noon, though a long controversy among the hands had decided the time, finally to be three o'clock : no one among the dozen of them had a watch, except Lem Lyon, the most ill-natured, the least accommodating of all the work-hands on the farm, and no man ventured to inquire of him, for he was more than ordinarily unamiable to-day, and lay on the barn-floor apart from his work-mates, with a bundle of oat-straw for his pillow, and his hat pulled over his eyes, taking no part in the discussion about the time, and affecting to hear nothing of it.

One after another stepped forth, and essayed to see his shadow, but in vain—one after another looked up at the sky, and guessed at the whereabouts of the sun, but it was only guessing, for many a day has looked brighter after sunset than did that one at high moon.

There was a half-holiday among the men, and as it had happened to fall the day after Sunday, it was less welcome than as if it had brought a log-rolling, brush-burning, or stone quarrying with it, for people little used to leisure are apt to find it lying heavily on their hands.

There had been some coarse jesting in the morning, which

had gradually subsided into more sober talk, and ultimately to silence, broken only by yawns and wonders about the time of day. The cattle turning their faces from the rain and cowering beneath the sheds, had been, in imagination, severally slaughtered, and divided into hide, hoof and horns—the amount of money each one might be turned into reckoned up, and there was nothing more interesting to be said about them. Corncobs had been thrown successively at the daring roosters that ventured out from beneath the barn-sill, and they were done with, having been fain, after a little scanty picking, to settle back in their dusty hollows, and wait with shut eyes for their dripping plumage to recover its wonted brilliancy.

"By thunder !" exclaimed Bill Franklin, dashing a pitchfork at a colt that had ventured to put his fore feet on to the barn-floor, partly to shelter himself from the storm, and partly to steal from the mow a mouthful of hay—"I, for my part bleve I'll roll up my sleeves and go to grubbing stumps, it's a darnation sight easier than this ere kind of a way of worryin' out the time—what d'you say, boys ?"

"I'm with you," said Jake Wilkinson, "guess we can stand it long as the rain can, can't we, Bill ?" And having shouldered crowbars and grubbing hoes, amid a good deal of laughter, the two men took their way resolutely to the clearing.

Joseph Barnet presently climbed to the hay-mow to read over his first love-letter for the twentieth time—muse on it in secret, and endeavor to compose an answer, which he did after his own crude fashion. But what matters the fashion of the speech, the sweet meaning is all the same whether the words be, "I dreamed of you last night," or "I will buy you a calico frock to-morrow."

Others followed the two energetic leaders before long, and at length only four of the hands were left in the barn. Joseph Barnet, cutting the initial letters of his sweetheart's name on the weather-boards, with many flourishes ; Lem Lyon, with hat over his face, and wrapped in less pleasant contemplations ; and Peter and Dan Wright, brothers, and the oldest hands on the farm. They had been farm-hands all their lives, and neither had ever owned or expected ever to own a foot of land —they were contented with hard work, did not know there was anything better, and I am not sure that there is. Peter was shelling corn very quietly in the trough of the weaned calf, that was tied in the stable adjoining the open barn-floor, and Dan had taken off his shoes and sat on the door-sill—the slowly dripping rain falling upon his naked feet, when a sound like a stifled sob caused them both to look round—there lay Lem with his hat over his eyes, and nothing else was to be seen.

"What was that noise ?" asked Peter, putting his arm about the calf's neck.

"I don't know," answered Dan, as he drew one foot up beneath him, "I thought I heard a kind of crying, but I reckon it was an optical imagination—do you bleve in such things ?"

Lem Lyon began to snore very loud, and the two brothers innocently concluded that their previous impression was wrong, for both had at first supposed the noise proceeded from him— a more suspicious nature might have thought the sleep an affectation.

"Well," said Peter, leaving the calf munching at his corn, and seating himself beside his younger brother on the sill of the barn, "I thought t'other night, the time we had the husking bee, that I see one of them ere ghostly critters you talk about."

" You don't say !" inquired Dan, " where mought she a-been ? and did you feel skeery ?"

" Well, as to being skeered, I ginerally wait till I'm hurt, 'cause you know there's no use wasting material of no kind— but to own the truth, I did sort a hisitate."

" You don't say ?" ejaculated Dan, again.

" It was getting well on toward midnight, I reckon, a moughty moonshiny night, if you mind ; I had taken the cider jug to go to the house and tip a leetle might of whisky into it —the dry cornblades was rustling on both sides of the lane, and the owls in old Dick Wolverton's woods were howling kind of lonesome like, but I was more listening to Lem than to the owls—for he was husking up on the highest scaffold, you mind, and singing a melancholy ditty to himself like—it was as good to hear as a novel, coming over the noises of the winds—so I walked slow along, thinking of the times when my hair was black as yourn, Dan, and I could leap a six-barred gate with the best of them, for there was something in Lem's song that carried me away back and back, I didn't hardly know where— walking slow along, I was, and just as I got so near to the bars that I mought have touched them a'most with my hand, what do you 'spose I saw ?"

" One of the critters, I reckon, for a lively imagination like yourn, Pete, is dreadful oucertain to be depended on, especially after drinking cider."

" No ! it wasn't a critter—that is, it was no animal critter, so to speak. It wasn't white, and it wasn't black ; it was kind of grey like, so to speak ; but the first I see, and the most I see was two bright shining eyes, and then gradually the operition took shape like, and I see it was a human critter."

"You don't say! Who mought she a been?"

"That ere now is just what I want you for to find out. She don't belong no whar in this section—'cause I never see her till that ere time I tell you of. She was apparently carried away by Lem's singing, and forgotful, so to speak, of things in gineral, and when I come of a suddent, her face turned as red as a rosy—and she said something in moughty purty words, I can't string 'em up as she did, but it was, so to speak, like as if she had said she hoped she was not doing any harm. I told her 'no, mem,' as soon as I see that she wasn't a ghost; but says I to her, at first, says I, 'I thought, mem, you was a ghost,' and then it was after that that I says to her, says I, 'no, mem, your doing no harm, fur as I see.' And then says she to me, says she, 'you see all the harm I'm doing, just listening here to that man sing,' and then she says, says she, 'it kind of sounds like a voice I used to hear,' and then she hesitated like, and then she hugged her baby up moughty close, and turned and went away kind of moaning to it like."

"Why didn't you follor her, and see whar she mought a gone to?" asked Dan, eagerly.

Lem was now wide awake, and with his head propped on his hand, listening attentively.

"I did foller her, 'cause thinks says I to myself, nobody knows what nobody else is till they have found 'em out by close watching—so I follered along kind a sly like, she never moustrusting that I was anywhar a-near, and when she got along just in the ege of old Wolverton's big woods, she sot right down on the ground, and I reckon you mought a-heard her a crying clar hur!"

"What business had you to pursue a woman as if she was

game?" exclaimed Lem, coming forward with menacing ges-
tures.   "I hate such idle curiosity—but what became of her at
last?"

The brothers did not remark that his last question contradicted his assertion, and Pete, who was used to subserviency
to Lemuel, proceeded good naturedly to tell all he knew about
the woman, which, in truth, was little more.   It contained one
or two hints, however, upon which Lemuel seized with avidity.

It appeared like she never would have done crying, Peter
said, but at last her baby, it sot up, and then she apparently
forgot whatever it mought have been that was troubling herself, and hugging it with such noises as birds make to their
little ones, she took off right through the woods toward old
Dick Wolverton's house, where, to the best of Peter's belief,
she had been spinning part of the past summer.   He remembered to have seen a baby tied in a high chair, paddling against
one of the garret windows of old Dick's house, and of hearing
a wheel at the same time, and he knew Mrs. Wolverton's
youngest son was big enough to go sparking.   Old Wolverton's, he said, was a moughty hard place for the gal, whatever kind of a lark she mought be.

"What need you care who or what the woman is?" said
Lemuel; "I don't see as she is anything to you."

"You speak like as if she mought be to you, peers to me,"
remarked Peter, quietly.

"I do?"   And Lem went on to say he did not see how that
could have been, for that as all knew, he hated women even
more than men, if that were possible; and he carelessly added
that she probably was a relative of the Wolvertons.

"No, she arn't that," said Peter, "she arn't of their turn,

no ways—she was pleasant and soft spoke, so to speak, and if you mind, the Wolvertons are red-haired, the whole tribe of them, and her hair was as black as a raven."

Lem moved uneasily, and Peter went on to say that he should not be surprised if he yet found out something about the stray lark, for that he had picked up a handkerchief where she sot so long on the ground, "and I see by the moonshine," he concluded, "that it was marked with sampler letters in one corner."

Lem listened with painful interest now, and Dan inquired with a more stupid curiosity, "What mought the sampler letters a been, Pete, do you mind?"

Peter could not make out the letters by the moonlight, he said, but he had put the handkerchief in his Sunday hat, and if he did not disremember, he would look at it before he went to bed.

Lem drew his hat suddenly over his face, and muttering a curse upon the weather, concluded, as he glanced towards the house, with the wish that women and children had a world made especially for themselves.

In vain the two brothers defended the gentler sex with eloquent eulogies. Lem was unmoved—grew in fact more denunciatory, and ended by heaping profanity on denunciation.

"Well," said Dan, "I've got no woman, and I never calculate I shall have, but the good it does me to go whar women folks are is immense. To see them in meeting, bright as a row of pinks a sitting on the benches, does me more good than the preaching."

"Their smiling," said Pete, "iles up a man's heart, like, so to speak," and having laid this cap-sheaf upon the stack of his previous eloquence, he turned his pale, little eyes upon Lemuel's dark ones almost compassionately.

"Well, God bless the whole race of women, and all the babies to boot," cried Lem, in a tone which indicated anything but a blessing mood, and buttoning his coat hastily, he went down the lane with such strides as would soon have taken him across the continent.

"That is a curious chap," said Dan, when Lem was out of hearing. "I'll be blamed if I don't bleve that some gal has some time give him the mitten, and that's why he hates 'em so."

"If I mought be allowed to say just what I think," mused Peter, smoothing his grey hair, "I should say that that ere same Lemuel Lyon had not allers done what was right by women. Didn't you mind how he chewed his beard and frowned when he said God bless 'em ; mind, I tell you, he is a man, proud and handsome as he is, that is onsatisfied with himself."

"Shaw ! Pete, you're getting childish," replied Dan, who was younger than his brother by seven years, and running up the ladder, he joined Joseph Barnet on the hay-mow, where he was still musing on his love-letter, and composing an answer which did but imperfect justice to his feelings. He had told his beloved that her letter was received, and that he had taken his pen in hand to reply—that he was well at present—that all the hands were well at present, and that he had no news that could interest her at present, when Peter joined him, and inquiring whether there were any hens' nests on the mow, dragged him down to the dead level of ordinary life. Ah, Joseph, it is only for stolen moments that we are permitted to flourish the initials of our sweethearts upon the weather-boards of our barns, or otherwhere—for the most part, we must work and be tired and heart-sick.

Toward night the clouds lifted in the west, and left a breadth of blue sky above the wet tree tops ; and the winds made noises in the woods, especially in Dick Wolverton's woods, that were indicative of coming winter. The hands were chilled through and through, and, impatient of supper time, hurried toward the barn when first the sunset held up its red signal. They had not reached it, however, when the tin horn sounded its welcome summons. There was a good deal of pretended detention, and when the chores were done, a good deal more idle lingering about the barn doors ; so that the chickens were crowding the roosts, and the windows of the farmhouse all a-blaze (they had been close shut the preceding night, and darkened all the day past), when Peter, a wise smile playing among the wrinkles of his cheeks, led thither the rough troop, shy and bashful as so many girls—Joseph in the rear, most shy and bashful of all. The supper was laid in holiday style, and the walls decorated with red and yellow maple boughs, in honor of the little immortal that had that day taken up her inheritance of mortality.

There was whisky as well as tea—plumcake as well as bread, and the good Mr. Mayfield, master of the house and hands, broke through social distinctions, and spiced the entertainment with many a pleasant story. Peter proposed the health of the new-comer, and on glancing down the table to see whether he had unanimous sympathy, discovered that Lem was absent. There was a general expression of wonder, and of uneasiness on the part of Mr. Mayfield, for he was used to consider Lemuel his best hand, notwithstanding his surly moods.

The horn was blown again, so loud that the hills sent back the echoes, but no echo did Lemuel return—he had not partaken of food since breakfast, and no one could imagine what could detain him, unless he had been overtaken by a fit, or some other terrible accident. The table broke up in confusion, and the hands dispersed in different directions about the farm in search of the missing man.

Peter instinctively took the path which led to the Wolverton woods, and he it was who found the lost man. Nothing had happened—he had heard the horn, he said, and should have gone to the house if he had required anything to eat—he was sorry the hands were such a set of fools as to waste their strength in looking after him—for his part he did not care a darn where any of them went, and did not wish them to care for him any more—he hoped he could take care of himself.

"I wish that ere young man was not so kind of onsartin like," said Peter, when he found himself among the hands again. "Sometimes I think his heart is froze, so to speak, and if something could only thaw it out, it would be as good as any of our hearts."

"Whar mought he a been?—why, it's as cold as thunder!" said Dan, shivering and buttoning his coat.

Then Peter told how he was found sitting like as if he was moonstruck, so to speak, on a pile of dry stones that had once been a lime-kiln—his hat on the ground beside him, and no sign of a coat on. "Whatever mought have made him so," concluded Peter, "I don't know, but he was right onsociable with me, so to speak—never see him more onclined to be to himself."

The spirit of hilarity which had been subdued by the fear that some evil had befallen him, now arose with redoubled buoyancy; and there was wrestling and racing, swapping of knives and trading of hats—rude jesting, some of it upon women, I am sorry to say, profanity, rising more from recklessness than wickedness I am glad to say ; and when at a late hour the hands went to bed, each one felt himself considerably richer than when he got up in the morning.

"I say, Pete," whispered Dan, as the brothers were about retiring, "whars that handkerchief you was talking about to day ?"

Peter took down the Sunday hat from its peg in the wall, looked inside of it—uttered an exclamation of surprise—turned it round and over, thumping it on the sides and top, but nothing except a Bible, hymn-book, pocket-book, red silk handkerchief, and two or three cigars fell out of it.

"I'm sartin," he said, at last, slowly and soberly, moving his eyes searchingly about the room, and holding up the empty hat, "that I put that ere little squar of linen in thar, and no whar else !"

Notwithstanding this conviction, he prolonged the search for half an hour, but without success—at the end of that time he hung up the Sunday hat in its proper place, and with a soliloquy on the onsartainty of human evidence, went to bed— no suspicion linked with Lem's curiosity finding any room to harbor in his innocent soul.

For some days after the events recorded, Lem was unusually silent and moody. If he spoke at all it was sourly and sarcastically—he selected the work that was hardest, and in fact seemed to take pleasure in imposing tasks upon himself that nobody else could or would perform. Often in the chill rainy days he would work all day long without his coat, and at night, instead of joining the circle about the kitchen fire, he would stray away by himself, and it was noticed that he generally took the path toward the Wolverton woods. Peter said he must be fond of coon hunting—what else could take him thar of nights that were cold enough to freeze a bar, so to speak. And Peter, chiefly owing to his wrinkles and grey hair, was conceded to be the wisest of all the hands, so it was settled that Lem was fond of coon hunting, and there was no more speculation or wonderment about it.

It was the pleasant custom of Mr. Mayfield to give a frolic to his hands two or three times in the year, and the season was now come, the corn being gathered, for one of these happy occasions. There was to be a fine supper, and dancing—all the young women for seven miles round were invited, and Bill Franklin, Jake Wilkinson and Jo Barnet had "been at charges" for new white cotton shirts, and "fine dancing pumps," and some of the other hands had provided themselves with new boots, and other articles, specially designed for the occasion; but Lem made never a call upon shoemaker or tailor—frolics might do well enough for women and children, but for his part he hated them.

Since the conversation which took place on the barn-sill, he had manifested a consideration for Peter, relieving him of hard chores sometimes, and had indicated a disposition to cultivate his acquaintance never shown before. He had inquired of Peter, on one occasion, if he knew where he would be likely to get some flax-thread, he wanted some to mend his saddle-girth, and he could not find any strong enough at the stores.

It might be had, Peter thought, of some of the neighbor-women, and Lemuel then suggested that if Peter would be so good as to make inquiry he would be doing a great favor, and he named Mrs. Wolverton as the person likeliest of all he knew, to have the thread.

Peter did the errand willingly, for not one of the hands but was glad to oblige Lemuel—all felt with Peter that his heart was frozen, and if it could only be thawed it would be a very good sort of heart. When Peter returned he found Lem sitting on a log in the edge of the woods, and would have thought he was waiting for him, had not he said expressly that he just happened to be there—his first inquiry was, not whether Peter had got the thread, but whom he had seen, and when informed that he had only seen Mrs. Wolverton, he was further inquisitive to know whether she had mentioned anybody ; Peter thought not, and Lemuel then remarked, carelessly, that he did not know but that she might have said something about that ghostly woman that lived with her.

No, he neither saw the woman nor heard mention of her. Upon hearing this, Lemuel laughed confusedly, and said, that since Peter told the ghost story, he had not thought of her till now. It occurred to Peter that it was a little strange Lemuel never once thought of the thread.

Once or twice on Peter's return from church, Lemuel had met him by the merest accident, and inquired, simply for the sake of saying something, Peter supposed, whom he had seen at meeting, and whether any one who looked like a ghost. After these manifestations of humanity and familiarity, it is no wonder Peter was disappointed at Lemuel's behavior in view of the grand frolic.

" Of course you will outshine them all !" he ventured to say, one day, "for the girls will look their prettiest, and all have their eyes upon you." "I wonder if all men are fools and dupes to the last?" soliloquized Lemuel, and he made no other answer.

He had a habit of looking about him in a startled way, as if in expectation of some unwelcome visitor, and this peculiarity grew upon him of late, so much that Peter said Lem reminded him of a wild beast that had once been in a trap, and was "afeared of it again, so to speak."

"I think," said Lemuel, approaching Mr. Mayfield, a day or two before the frolic, "that I will go to some other part of the country, if you are satisfied to have it so."

Mr. Mayfield was not satisfied—had he not done all that was right, and if so what objection could Lemuel have to remain— the season of hard-work was over, and there would be comparatively easy times, for awhile—nevertheless he was willing to increase the wages a little to his best hands. Lemuel said he was not begging for an increase of wages—as to that he did not care a curse whether he earned a cent or not, he had always done his duty, pay or no pay—he laid great stress upon having done his duty, and glared upon Mr. Mayfield as though he had asserted the contrary, and finally he ended with the declaration, covered all round with profanity, that nobody on the farm could understand him, and he would see if there was any place where they could. Argument, entreaty, were useless. Mr. Mayfield saw it, and informed him that he would make arrangements to settle with him that day. When he was making up his knapsack in the cold red light of that evening, there was a little tap on the door, and Mrs. Mayfield's nurse-girl informed him that her mistress desired to speak with him.

Lemuel said at first he was too busy to go, but after a little, shame for such rudeness subdued him, and having thrust his fingers through his long black hair, and pulled his wrinkled shirt collar about his chin, he descended.

"Ah, how kind of you !" cried Mrs. Mayfield, running forward and shaking both his hands.

"What did you want with me, madam !" asked Lemuel, withdrawing his hands, and standing erect.

"Why, to see you, to be sure," she answered, pulling him forward by the coat-sleeve, and almost forcing him to sit in the best chair.

His startled eyes swept the room with a glance, and seeing nothing but the cradle he gave himself passively up, resolved to suffer it out, if it must be so. Mrs. Mayfield talked of the late frost, of the apple-crop, of the prospect of snow, and then she told Lemuel she should look to him to see to it that she did not freeze to death during the winter—he must provide the best hickory in unlimited quantities, that was her royal command. Lemuel smiled a grim smile ; perhaps he found it not disagreeable to be softly ordered by so pretty a woman. He replied, however, that he had made up his mind to go away. Not till the winter was past, certainly ! Mrs. Mayfield could not hear of it—in the spring he might go if he chose. Why what would become of her poor baby, if Lemuel did not stay to make the fires —nobody but he knew how to make a fire at all. "By the way," she concluded, drawing the cradle close to Lemuel's side, " you have never seen the baby !"

"Humph !" said he. She did not hear him, but with a countenance beaming with pride and tenderness folded the blanket, oh, so softly, from the little face. Lemuel looked another way, but she playfully caught him by the button-hole, and forced him to see her darling.

He said nothing even then, and a frown, as he looked, knitted up his handsome forehead into positive ugliness.

" Why, you don't like my baby, Lemuel," she said, in a tone made up of grief and tenderness, as she looked up reproach-fully.

" Oh, yes, I do," he answered, his own heart condemning him, " God bless all the babies, I say."

But there was no blessing in his tone or manner, and Mrs. Mayfield turned away to conceal her disappointment. Just then the little creature opened its blue eyes and looked up to Lemuel for the protection and comfort it was used to receive—the hard man felt the appeal, and unawares, perhaps, extended his rough, brown hand. The baby caught it in its delicate fingers, and held it with so soft, yet firm a grasp, that Lemuel could not for the life of him resist the appeal, and began shaking the cradle about after the only fashion of rocking he was acquainted with. When the baby smiled in his face he smiled back again. Mrs. Mayfield smiled too, nay, laughed outright when she heard him chirping to her darling as he had heard the wood birds to their little ones.

" I think," said Lemuel, as he softly touched the rosy little cheeks with his rough palms, " that more fire is needed here," I'll think of what you said. The next morning he went to cutting and splitting wood with right good will—he had made up his mind to remain a month longer and lay in the winter wood for Mrs. Mayfield. On the farm and among the men his behavior was no whit gentler than formerly, but when at night he filled his brawny arms with hickory wood and heaped it against the jamb, the hard expressions of the day fell off like a mask, and he was sure before leaving the room to give the cradle a jog and shake hands with the baby.

With the frolic Lemuel would have nothing to do, and while the other hands were making ready, he was observed to take his way alone toward the Wolverton woods.

It was "clar and sartin, to his mind," Peter said, that Lem liked coon hunting better than any other fun. That simple-hearted old man was drawing water at the well, when near midnight Lemuel returned.

"Well, how many simpletons have come to the dance?" he said, stopping and taking a drink of water.

Peter was enthusiastic as to the number and beauty of the young women who graced the occasion. "When I see them smiling so, and looking so pretty," said he, "I can't help wishing I was young, and here are you, so young and so hand-some, who would rather go coon hunting than stay at home where they are blushing like a hedge of roses—how strange !"

Lemuel replied that he had always been just so, that at no time of his life would he have preferred the society of any woman to the winds and woods, and his own thoughts. Peter was right, he said, to infer that he had been hunting—it was a sport of which he never tired. As they walked together toward the house, he repeated over two or three times that he had never cared a straw for any woman, and that he had always cared a great deal about hunting coons. "By the way," he said, when they reached the door, "is that ghost-woman that you are always talking of, at your merry-making?"

"Oh, no," replied Peter, and instinctively stumbling on the truth, he added, eagerly, "you need not be afeard of seeing her! Come in, Lem, jest a leetle bit—do!" Lemuel gave Peter's shoulder so violent a jerk as to jar the water he was carrying over the pail, and answered with a round oath that he was not afraid of ghosts—much less of women, and that he would go in and show the whole of them that he was not afraid of them, nor ashamed of himself. And so saying he rushed rudely past Peter, and with his red woollen shirt-collar thrown open, and brawny bosom bare, entered the gay assemblage, where he became at once the pointed object of attention—nay, of admiration, notwithstanding his rough manners and rougher costume. His eyes were dark and beaming with intelligence—his hair and beard of massy luxuriance of growth, and his tawny cheeks sufficiently bright with angry excitement to make him as handsome a specimen of rustic nobility as may anywhere be found.

He was too proud to manifest any interest in what was going forward, if he felt any, and sat with an abstracted air, paying no heed to the many soft glances that invited him to dance as plainly as glances could invite him.

"Pray, Lemuel, what has happened?" asked Mrs. Mayfield, joining him in the obscure corner where he sat.

"Nothing," he answered, without glancing toward her.

"Why, you look as if you had lost your sweetheart," she continued, gaily.

Lemuel reddened with anger, and said women were always thinking of love—always talking of sweethearts, and turning everything into sentiment, which he hated. He had never had a sweetheart, and of course could not have lost her. Mrs. Mayfield was determined not to be angry with him, and answered playfully that for her foolish talk to so grave and wise a man, she was in the dust of humiliation and repentance, and she begged that he would forgive her, and as a mark of his reconciliation dance with her. No, Lemuel never danced—he would as soon be caught stealing a sheep—he hoped Mrs. Mayfield would find a more interesting partner.

The good-natured little woman called him an ugly bear—said she would try to find a more interesting partner, and meantime if he would not use his feet, she would compel him to turn his hands to good account, and placing her baby on his knees as she said so, she skipped lightly away.

It was an awkward position for Lemuel, and he was at first half inclined to let the child fall off his lap, but when he found it tipping one way and the other, he caught it in his arm, and having once caught it, he could not let it go. The soft, little hands found the way to his face, and the stubborn man presently found himself leaning down his head so they might tear his whiskers and eyes just as they chose.

When it grew tired and fell asleep to the music of the violin, he tenderly carried it away to its cradle, and rocked and kept the fire bright till long after midnight.

When the spring came round, and the nurse would carry the baby out on the south porch, Lemuel would stop as he passed that way to attend his work—smooth its silken curls beneath his rough hand, and perhaps give it some bright flower which he had brought from a distant field. Sometimes one or two of the other hands would join him on the porch, for the baby was gradually becoming a central object of interest to them all, and it was curious to see how the manners and voices of those rude men softened as they approached the little creature. The greatest change imaginable was being wrought in Lemuel—he was less sullen than he used to be—isolated himself less from the other hands during the day, and at night went rarely to the Wolverton woods. Before the summer was gone, little Blossom, for by that name she was known among the hands, had learned to know who loved her, and to clap her hands and shout when she saw Lemuel coming, and reach up her little arms with a tender appeal that brought his neck right down to her—then he would seat her on his shoulder, and as she clung tightly to his ears, hair or beard, as it happened, carry her up and down the door-yard till she was tired out. Sometimes, when Mrs. Mayfield rocked her darling to sleep on the moonlit porch, Lemuel would busy himself with chores that kept him near about, not knowing himself perhaps what influence was secretly at work in his heart. In the autumn, and before she could hold one of them in her tiny hand, Blossom's little lap was filled every day with bright apples, and when the old mare was brought to the well to drink at night, Lemuel's great coat was doubled up into a cushion and laid across her neck, and little Blossom, in her soft, white cloak and cap, was handed up, and rode sometimes to see the cattle, sometimes to see the sheep, but it was always Lemuel that protected her so softly, and brought her back so safely.

In one corner of the door-yard was a maple tree, beneath which was a rude bench, where often in the early evening Lemuel sat trotting the baby on one knee, and singing old ditties for her that he never sang at other times. Sometimes he would tell her long stories, and the pathos and the power of his voice at those times, not unfrequently frightened the little listener, and when she would cling to his bosom in strange alarm, he would tell her very softly that what he had been saying was all a great story—that no such people ever lived as he had been talking of, and when by the tenderness of his tones she was soothed, for she understood nothing of what he said, he would carry her up and down the door-yard until she fell asleep, for she loved him now as well as she loved her mother, almost, and her first faltering steps were towards him.

When her birth-day came round, the farm house was lighted up, the hands wore their best clothes, and Lemuel danced with her on his shoulder, to the great delight and amusement of the young women, whose admiration he was sure to win, no matter what he did.

It was about the middle of June, and little Blossom, who was now a year and a half old, could run about the door-yard and pick flowers for herself. She was become the pet and plaything of all the hands, and even upon the most careless there fell a silence when it was mentioned at dinner-time one day that she was not well. That evening, when Lemuel took her on his shoulder, she did not laugh and clap her hands as usual, but put her arms around his neck very quietly, and leaned her cheek down upon his head. He carried her longer than usual, and told her over all the pretty stories she had been used to listen to with delight, but her cheek grew hot as it rested heavily upon his head, the arms clung more and more tightly to his neck, and she moaned and fretted, not noisily, but piteously, and to herself, as it were.

When he had exhausted all resources, he carried her back to the porch and placed her on her mother's knees, thinking that all would now be well, but when she moaned and fretted piteously as before, he went to his old seat beneath the maple tree and watched the stars as they flew away from the clouds. Two or three times he came to the porch-side to ask whether she were any better, and when he learned at length that her katydids had sung her to sleep, he went to bed saying no doubt she would be better in the morning, but not altogether believing it.

At daybreak he was astir—he did not know why he could not sleep, he said, he thought it was owing to the heat—poor man, he was ashamed to say it was his love for a baby that could not yet speak plainly that kept him awake.

The hands were all silent at breakfast that morning, for they missed the prattle of little Blossom, and the fear that they should never hear it again was making its way to their hearts.

At noontime Lemuel brought the oxen close to the door, and when the baby, pleased for a little while, put her hands on their heads, as they bent them down to her gentle touches, he deceived himself with the hope that she was better. It was strange to see the rough man parting her silken hair—rocking the cradle so softly, and leaning over it with such tenderness— his heart was more than touched.

The third day of the illness of little Blossom, the hands walked softly along the porch-side when they came to dinner, for they saw standing under the cherry tree at the gate the old white faced horse of the village doctor. Lemuel left the table long before the other hands that day—he did not feel very well, he said. Soon after this the usual order of the work was suspended, the hands loitered about the barns and sheds, some of them, and some found their own work.

One evening, as Peter sat on the wood-pile cutting sticks with his penknife to divert his thoughts, Lemuel joined him and inquired if he knew whether little Blossom was any bet- ter.

"Better!" Peter exclaimed, "why, no, sartainly she never will be any better," and he procceded to say without circumlocution or softening, that in his opinion she was struck with death the midnight past. For a few moments he cut his stick in silence, and then, as if in pursuance of some train of thought, inquired of Lemuel whether he had brought the spade and grubbing-hoe from the hollow where he had been ditching.

A cold chill crept over Lemuel as he replied irritably, "No! why should I bring them? We shall be using them again to-morrow."

"I know we shall use them to-morrow," answered Peter, "but not there—I will go and fetch them."

"Oh, no, no!" cried Lemuel, "for Heaven's sake don't go;" and seizing his arm, he pulled Peter back to the log from which he had half risen. While the two men talked together, several neighbors passed along, and each one stopped to inquire how the baby was, and to suggest some remedy or proffer sympathy. Among the rest was Mr. Wolverton. Lemuel had never liked him, for he was a hard, money-loving man, but leaning over the fence he shook hands with him, and entered with unaffected interest into all his affairs.

"Sartainly," said Peter, joining the "work-girl" at the kitchen door, "that Lem Lyon is the most onreasonable critter I ever see—he was angry just now because I wanted to go to the field and bring home the grubbing-hoe—'cause I see it would be needed, you know, and then he seemed mournful-like, more than mad, so to speak, and all at once he goes and begins to talk with old Wolverton, whom we all know he never could bar—a strange nater he's got."

Ah, Peter, you hit the truth there, it *was* a strange nature that Lemuel had—one that he could not himself understand, much less you.

Trial and tribulation are to trivial natures always hard to bear, and the "work-girl," glad of any pretext, said the Mayfields were a queer set. She was tired of being among them—afraid, in fact, of catching the baby's fever, and would, she believed, tie up her bundle and go home.

She gave no other intimation of her intention, to any one, but without more ado carried it at once into execution, throwing upon poor Mrs. Mayfield a burden of domestic care and responsibility to which at that time she was unequal.

The morning was cloudy with prospects of rain, and on rising Lemuel saw with alarm the doctor's horse standing beneath the cherry tree, and he judged by the circle of turf pawed away, that he had been there a long time. He knocked at Mrs. Mayfield's door, and was bidden in a low voice to come in. The inquiry, "How is little Blossom?" died on his lips—he saw how it all was. The mother vainly hoped that her darling might recognize the voice of Lemuel and look up once more. He was not ashamed now of showing that he loved her—he took the little hands in his, but they would not grow warm—kissed the blue eyelids and called her by her pet name, but though at last she looked up, she did not know her good friend any more. There fell the last hardness, the last unworthy pride from the heart of Lemuel Lyon. Just as the candle flickered in the whitening light of day, the little life went out.

Peter saddled the old mare and rode away to the village to bespeak a coffin ; and Dan, who never lost sight of his personal comfort, took upon himself the overseeing of the housework, and having directed one man to make a fire, and another to fill the tea-kettle, took the coffee-mill between his knees, and fancied he was doing an efficient work, albeit he was turning the crank the wrong way. About sunset Lemuel set out from home in Mr. Mayfield's covered wagon, for what purpose none of the hands could imagine ; the rain was falling pretty fast, and there were indications of violent winds, which would make the roads through the woods dangerous to travel.

We will pass over the funeral, saying only that when the service was over, the coffin was placed under the maple tree in the corner of the dooryard, and that the hands, when they had seen the little face for the last time, followed Peter who, with tear-wet cheeks, carried the coffin in his arms to the burial ground. From all the sad ceremony, we will pass to the time of Lemuel's return.

It was just after sunset—the birds whistling and chirping among the branches of the trees, along the topmost fence-rails, and here and there from the ground, as if there had never been a cloud nor a sorrow in the world ; the bereaved mother stood at the window, gazing steadily one way—the only way she cared to look, now, when her attention was arrested by a noise at the gate—there stood the farm wagon, splashed with mud, and the farm horses, their tails knotted up, their heads down, and a cloud of steam rising above them—and there was Lemuel, and by his side a woman, not handsome nor young, but with a good heart shining in her face, and a bright-eyed boy of three years old in her arms.

Lemuel, seeing that he was observed, hesitated slightly, and a deep flush brightened the bronze of his cheek, but he mastered the weakness, and taking the child in his own arms, said with emotion, that might have been shame—might have been tenderness, or was made up of both, perhaps, "What do you call him, Lydia?"

"Lemuel,—what else should I call him?" replied the woman, in a tone that was exceedingly soft and gentle. The boy turned his bright face bashfully aside from Lemuel, and with one hand clinging tightly to his mother's shawl, they came down the walk together.

Mrs. Mayfield met them on the porch, and covering the boy with kisses, said, perhaps to save Lemuel the embarrassment of an introduction, "how very much he resembles your wife, Lemuel," and shaking hands with the woman, she led her into the house, where she sunk into a seat and burst into a flood of tears—the result of mingled emotions—pride in Lemuel—pride in her beautiful boy—shame for herself.

When Peter had completed the chores and was coming towards the house to supper, he saw the strange child at play in the door yard—trying to cover a butterfly with a white handkerchief. At sight of him the boy ran away, leaving the handkerchief behind him, which Peter picked up, and idly examined. All at once there came a glow of curious wonder into Peter's face, and turning back in the path and joining Dan who was a few steps behind, he exclaimed, "I b'lieve my soul this is the very handkerchief I found and hid in my Sunday hat, the one that vanished away, so to speak, and here's the name in the corner, in sampler letters, 'Lydia;' the whole affair is a great mystery," and a mystery it always remained, for Mrs. Mayfield kept faithfully the secret that Lemuel had only now made the woman who had been the mother of his boy so long, his true and honorable wife. Once indeed, Peter remarked to

Dan that if Lem's wife had all the roses and the sunshine took out of her face she would look 'amost like the gal what took that cryin'-spell in old Wolverton's woods.

Innocence and beauty win their own way, and little Lemuel was soon the light of the house—the favorite of everybody, Lydia was installed housekeeper and mistress of the kitchen, and Lemuel, now Mr. Lyon, became manager of the farm, and as much beloved by the hands as he had formerly been feared.

MARRIED LIFE OF ELEANOR .HOMES.

A GOOD many years ago I fell in love and was married.

"How did it happen ?"

Why, how does it ever happen ? "I doubt if the sagest philosopher of them all could explain how the like happened unto him, and therefore it were presumptuous to expect a woman to make luminous so great a mystery."

"You think a woman might understand her own heart, even though a philosopher might fail to ?"

"Audacious ! Don't you know that women shine faintly at best, and by reflection ?"

"Really, I don't know. I never thought about it."

"Many women never do, and pass through life without ever being sufficiently grateful for the blessings they are permitted to enjoy. However, I believe the minds of the sexes are wholly dissimilar, even when of an equal power. Women *know* more, but *acquire* less than men ; they do not investigate and analyze, and infer and conclude—their inferences and conclusions are

34

independent of any process of reasoning. Since the beginning of time nature has said of every one of them—

"This child I to myself will take ;
She shall be mine, and I will make
A lady of my own."

And if each were permitted to follow her instincts, and rely upon her intuitions, there would not be among us so many miserable bewailings. All women have more or less genius— which, after all, is simply power of suspending the reasoning and reflecting faculties, and suffering the light which, whatever it be, is neither external nor secondary, to flow in. But I proposed to tell a story, and repeat, I fell in love, and was married.

"Did I really love ?"

I suppose so ; indeed I am quite certain, from intimations now and then received, that it was one phase of that capability which lives under wrinkles and grey hairs, in all the freshness of youth. But it is difficult to define the exact limit of positive love—it shades itself by such fine gradations into pity and passion, friendship and frenzy. The state of feeling I fell into was none of these latter, I am quite sure, and yet I should be loth to affirm it was that condition of self-abnegation which admits of no consideration aside from the happiness of the object beloved ; for, if I remember rightly, there came to me at rare intervals some visions of my own personal interests and pleasures. And yet I had no hesitancy in pledging·myself to love, honor, and obey, because I had no idea that these pledges conflicted with the widest liberty. Was not he to whom I should make these pledges a most excellent and honorable gentleman, who would have no requirement to prefer at variance with my wishes ? To be sure he was. Did he not always prefer my pleasure to his own, or rather have no pleasure but mine ? So he was pleased to say, and for my part, I never doubted it.

We took long moonlight walks together—talked sentiment, of course—read poetry, and now and then quarrelled prettily about the shade of a rose, or the pencilling of a tulip, and interspersed our discourse with allusions to our cottage that was to be. Should it be smothered in trees or open to the sun ?

"Just as you prefer, my dear."

" Oh, no, darling ! it shall all be just as you say."

Could I have a pot of geraniums and a canary bird to brighten my cottage window ?

" A thousand of them," if I chose ; but my own self would be the grace that graced all other graces—the beautifier of every beauty beside.

What should our recreations be ? That was an absurd question, and soon dismissed. The introduction of a foreign element would never be necessary into society so perfect as we two should compose.

So we were married—never having exchanged a single thought concerning the great duties and responsibilities of life —I, for my part, having no slightest conception of the homely cares and ingenious planning ; of the fearing and hoping, patience, forbearance, and endurance, that must needs make a part of life's drama, wherever enacted.

The bridal veil was never looked through after the bridal day ; consequently the world took another coloring before very long. I must be allowed to say I was not yet twenty, as some extenuation of the follies I should have been ashamed of, even then, and must also relate some little incidents and particulars of my married life that gave ineffaceable colors to my maturer mind and character.

My husband's name was Henry Doughty—Harry, I used to call him, partly because the designation pleased him, and partly because I entertained a special dislike for the name of Doughty. I gave a much better one away for it, however.

My maiden name was Homes—Eleanor Homes—Nellie, they called me among my friends, before I was married ; afterward, when the novelty of calling me *Mrs.* Doughty was over, they said *poor* Nell.

We had not been an hour from church—my bridemaids were about me, among them my haughty sister Katharine, who had not very cordially received her new relative. Some one rallied me on my promise to obey, and asked Mr. Doughty how he proposed to enforcé my obligation.

" Oh, after this sort," he replied gaily, brandishing the little switch-cane he was playing with about my shoulder. I turned carelessly, and the point of it struck my eye.

" It was your own fault ?" was his first exclamation. The pain of the wound was intense, but it was the harsh words that made the tears come. I was frightened when I saw them, for I felt that it was an awful impropriety to cry then and there, and putting by all proffered remedies as though the little accident were quite unworthy of attention, I smiled, nay, even affected to laugh, and said it was solely and entirely my own foolish fault, and moreover, that I always cried on like occasions —not, of course, on account of any suffering, but owing to a nervous susceptibility I could not overcome.

Katharine, meantime, to augment the criminality of the offence, was proffering various medicines ; among them, she brought me at this juncture, a towel, wet with I know not what.

"Take it away again," said Mr. Doughty; "nothing I so much dislike as nervous susceptibility—pray don't encourage it."

Katharine would not speak, but she replied by a very significant look, and, to conciliate both, I accepted the towel, but did not apply it to the wounded eye—swollen and red by this time to an unsightly degree ; in truth, I was afraid to do so. My sensations were certainly new, as I thus trifled with my afflictions, forcing myself even to make pitiable advances toward my offender, in the hope of winning him to some little display of tenderness, for the sake of appearances wholly, for I was not in the mood to receive them appreciatively just then. I was singularly unfortunate, however, and might have spared myself the humiliation.

I had succeeded, in some sort, in reviving my spirits, for it is hard to dampen the ardor of a young woman on her wedding-day, when my enthusiasm received another check. I was sitting at the window, that I might find some excuse for my occasional abstraction in observation, and also to keep the wounded eye away from the company. Happening once to change my position, my husband said to me : "Keep your face to the window, my dear madam ; your ridiculous applications have made your eye really shocking !"

"Why, Harry !" I said—if I had taken time to think, I would not have said anything ; but the unkindness was so obvious it induced the involuntary exclamation, and everybody saw that I felt myself injured.

By some sisterly subterfuge, Kate decoyed me into her own room, where my husband did not take occasion to seek me very soon. When he did so, he patted my cheek and said half-playfully, " I have come to scold you, Nell."

My heart beat fast. He had felt my absence, then, and was come with some tender reproach. I began to excuse myself, when he interrupted me with an exclamation of impatience. He was sorry to find me so impetuous and *womanish*—exhibitions of any emotion, but more especially of tender emotion, were in bad taste. I must manage in some way to control my impulses, and also to discriminate—he was always pleased to be called Harry, when we were alone, but in miscellaneous company a little more formality was usual !

" Your name is not so beautiful," I replied, angrily, " that you should want to hear it unnecessarily."

He elevated his eyebrows a little, and smiled one of his peculiar smiles, never too sweet to be scornful.

I hid my face in my sister's pillow, and almost wished I might never lift it up.

Seeing me shaken with suppressed sobs, he bent over me and kissed my forehead, much as we give a child a sugar-plum after having whipped it, and left me with the hope that I would compose myself, and not wrong my beauty by such ill-timed tears !

Excellent advice, but not very well calculated to aid me in its execution. Many times after that I wronged such poor beauty as I brought to him, by my ill-timed tears.

The story of the accident, and of my crying on my wedding-day, went abroad with many exaggerations, and my husband gave me to understand, without any direct reference to anything that had taken place, that I had unnecessarily brought reproach

upon him.   It had been arranged that we were to live at home
a year ; my parents—foolish old folks ! could not bear the
thought of giving me up at once—as if the hope to make all
things as they were, were not utterly useless, after I had once
given myself up.

The experiment proved a delusion—empty of comfort to all
parties concerned ; and here let me say, that if two persons,
when they are once married, cannot find happiness with each
other, no third party can in any wise mend the matter.

I think now if there had been no one to strengthen my
obstinacy, and hinder such little conciliations as, unobserved, I
might have proffered, our early differences might have been
healed over without any permanent alienation.

However well two persons may have known each other
before marriage, the new relation develops new characteristics,
and necessitates a process of assimilation, difficult under the
most genial circumstances.

Of course my family took my part, whether or not I was in the
right, and thus sustained I took larger liberties, sometimes, than
it was wise to take—trifled and played with all my husband's
predilections—called them whimsies, if I noticed them, but for the
most part affected an unconsciousness of their existence.   For
instance, I had a foolish habit of turning through books and
papers in a noisy way, which I persevered in rather in consequence of his admonitions than in spite of them.

One night he did not come home at the usual time.   I grew
impatient, uneasy, and at last, in spite of Kate's sneer, took my
station at the window to watch for him : in a minute or two
thereafter he came up the walk.   I opened the door and my
arms at the same time, crying, "How glad I am !"

"What for?" he said, gliding past me in his quiet way.

"Are you not glad?" I inquired, determined not to be put out of humor for once; my best feelings had been really stirred.

"Certainly," he answered, seating himself in the corner opposite to me, and opening the evening paper. "I am glad to get home. I am very tired."

He did not once look at me as he said this, and Kate completed my discomfort by saying—

"Well, I suppose Nell is blessed enough to be permitted to look upon you, even in the distance. She used to have a little spirit, but I believe marriage has crushed even that out of her."

"Humph!" said my husband.

"What do you find interesting in the paper to-night?" I said, determined to enforce some attention by way of triumph over Kate. He made a motion which deprecated interruption, and taking a new novel from his pocket, threw it into my lap.

"Milk for babes!" said Kate, sarcastically. I said nothing, and she went on provokingly: "Take your plaything away, child, and don't make a bit of noise with it."

Here was a happy suggestion. I had failed in my effort to be agreeable. I would be disagreeable now to my heart's content. I was at some pains to find an old pair of jagged scissors, and having found them, I seated myself at my husband's elbow, and began to saw open the leaves of my book, with the double purpose of annoying him and convincing Kate that I had some spirit left yet.

Now and then I glanced towards him to see if his brows were not knitting, and the angry spot rising in his cheek, but to my surprise and vexation I saw no manifestation of annoyance—he read on apparently completely absorbed, and wearing a smile on his face—a little too fixed, perhaps, to be quite spontaneous.

So I went on to the last leaf, cutting and ruffling as noisily as I could, but I had only my trouble for my pains—he did not lift his eyes towards me for an instant.

When Kate left us alone, I felt exceedingly uncomfortable—for I had felt my behavior countenanced by her presence. After all, I thought, presently, my husband is perhaps quite unconscious of any effort on my part to annoy him; but whether he were so or not, my best course, I concluded, would be to affect unconsciousness of it myself. Thus resolved, I yawned, naturally I thought, and, as if impulsively, threw down the book—took the paper from his hand with a wifely privilege, and seated myself on his knee. He suffered me to sit there, but neither smiled nor spoke.

"Why don't you say something to me?" I was reduced to ask at length.

"What shall I say?"

"Why, something sweet, to be sure."

"Well, sugar-candy—is that sweet enough?"

"What a provoking wretch you are!" I cried, flying out of the room in hot haste.

I hoped he would forbid my going, or call me back, but he did neither.

After some tears and a confidential interview with Kate, that made me more angry with her and with myself than with my husband, I returned, and found him quietly lolling in the easy-chair, and eating an apple!

As time went by, Kate's arrogance and insolence towards Mr. Doughty became insupportable—twenty times I quarrelled with her, taking his part stoutly against her accusations. One evening, after one of these accustomed disputations, my husband said to me—

"Nell, we must take a house of our own ; I can't live in this atmosphere any longer."

"Why can't you ?" I knew why, well enough.

"I don't like your sister Kate."

"Does she poison the atmosphere, my dainty sir ?"

"Yes."

Of course I flew into a rage and defended Kate with all my powers. She was my own good sister then, and had done every thing to make the house pleasant which it was possible for her ~~to do~~—I would like to know who would please him.

"You, my dear," he replied.

The end of the matter was, I refused to go away from my father's house with him ; said I would not be deprived of the little comfort I now had in the sympathy of, and association with, my family ; he had agreed, I reminded him, before our marriage, to my remaining at home one year at least—his promises might pass for nothing with himself, they would not with me ; if he chose to take a house he might do so, but his housekeeping would be done independently of me ; if my wishes were never to be consulted by him, I should have to consult them myself—that was all.

I never gave him greater pleasure, he replied provokiugly, than when I consulted my own wishes ; for his part, he could have none in which I did not heartily concur.

He admitted that he had cordially agreed to my remaining

at home a year after marriage, but that late experience had slightly modified his views ; he was not infallible, however, and probably erred in judgment—indeed, he was quite sure he did, since I differed from him ; he hoped I would pardon his unkind suggestion, and believe him what he really was, the most faithful and devoted of husbands.

Amongst my weaknesses was a passion for emeralds. Mr. Doughty had heard me express my admiration for them many a time. The day following our little rencounter he came home an hour earlier than usual, seated himself on the sofa beside me, and taking two little parcels from his pocket and concealing them beneath his hand, said playfully—

" Which one will you have, Nell ?"

" The best one !" I replied, reaching out my hand.

" The better one," he rejoined quickly ; " the best of the two is not elegant—at least it was not till you made it so."

I withdrew my hand and averted my face. If he and I had been alone, I might have taken the reproof more kindly ; but Kate heard it all, as it seemed to me she always did every thing that was disagreeable. I might have made some angry retort, but a visitor was just then announced—an old classmate of Mr. Doughty's, whom I had never seen.

" He is come specially to pay his respects to you," my husband said as he rose to join him. " You will see him, of course."

" If it is my lord's pleasure," I replied ; " bring him to me when it suits you."

Involuntarily he put his hand on my hair, and smoothed it away, glancing over me at the same time from head to foot. The motion and the glance implied a doubt of my observance of external proprieties, and also I felt at the moment, personal dissatisfaction with myself.   The interview was embarrassed and restrained ; I was self-conscious every moment, and crippled completely by the knowledge, that in my husband's eyes I was appearing very badly.

I misquoted a familiar line from Shakspeare ; expressed admiration for a popular author, and when asked which of his works I read with most delight, could not remember the name of anything I had read.

My discomfiture was completed when my husband said apologetically, " I dare say that wiser heads than my little Nellie's have been confused by similar questions—in truth, she is not quite well to-day."

The old classmate related some very amusing blunders of his own, calculated to soothe, but rasping my wounded feelings only into deeper soreness, and presently the conversation fell into the hands of the gentlemen altogether ; and I am sure it was felt to be a relief, by all parties, when our guest announced the expiration of the time to which he was *unfortunately* limited.   My husband walked down street with him, and during his brief absence I wrought myself into a state of unwomanly ugliness, including dissatisfaction with everything and everybody.

The words " my little Nellie," which my husband had used, rung offensively in my ears.   *My* little Nellie, indeed !   What implied ownership and what tender disparagement !

When my husband returned he took no notice of my ill-humor, but proceeded to his reading as usual.   It was never his habit to read aloud ; on this occasion I chose to fancy he had, in his own estimation, selected a work above my appreciation.

"There, Nell, I forgot!" he exclaimed after a few moments of silent reading, and he threw into my lap the little box which I had declined to receive. I did not open it immediately, and when I did so I expressed neither surprise nor pleasure, though it contained what I had so much desired to possess—a pin set with emeralds.

"Very pretty," I said carelessly, "for those who can wear such ornaments; as for myself it would only make my plainness seem the plainer by contrast." And before the eyes of my husband, who had thought to make everything right by its purchase, I transferred it to my sister Kate. From that time forth it glittered in the faces of both of us daily, but we neither of us ever mentioned it.

It was not many days after this occurrence that Mr. Doughty informed me that he was called suddenly, by matters of some importance to him, to a neighboring State. He did not say *us*, but limited the interest entirely to himself—nor did he intimate by word or act that the necessity of absence involved any regret. I inquired how long he proposed to remain away—not when should *I* expect him.

He was not definitely advised—from one to three months. We parted without any awakening of tender emotion. Our letters were brief and formal—containing no hints, on either side, of a vacuum in life which nothing but the presence of the other could supply.

I was informed from time to time that affairs protracted themselves beyond his expectation, but the nature of the affairs I was left in ignorance of. The prospect of staying at home a year added nothing to my happiness. Kate and I agreed no better now that we were alone than before. I secretly

blamed her for my unfortunate alienation from my husband :
it was not the importunate nature of his business that detained
him, I was quite sure. I grew uneasy, and irritable, wished to
have him back, not for any need my nature had, that he alone
could answer. I wanted him to want to come back—that was all.

Kate accused me of unfilial and unsisterly preference for a
vulgar and heartless man, to my own family.

"The dear old Nell was completely merged in the selfish
Doughty," she said, "and she might just as well have no sister
for all the comfort I was to her."

So we kept apart a good deal, and by keeping apart, soon
grew apart pretty thoroughly. In truth our natures had never
been cast in the same mould, and it was impossible that they
should more than touch at some single point now and then.

At the end of six months a portion of my fret and worry
had worked itself into my face. My hair had fallen off and
was beginning to have a faded and neglected look. I was
careless about dress, and suffered my whole outer and inner
person to fall into ruins. By fits I resolved to project my general discontent into some one of the reforms, I hardly knew
which, when after a day of unusual irksomeness and personal
neglect, my husband unexpectedly returned.

He was in perfect health, and rejoiced in the possession of
affluent beard and spirits—he was really quite handsome. I
looked at him with wonder, admiration, and some pride—kissed
him and said I was very glad ; but there was no thrill in my
heart—no tremor in my voice—the old fires of anger had left
the best part of my nature in ashes, I found. He was sorry to
find me looking so badly—I must go with him on his next adventure and get back my beauty again ! If I could only see

his smiling, blushing cousin Jane, it would shame my melancholy and sallow face into some bloom ! And by the way, I must know her—he was sure I would love her just as he did—she had done so much to make his banishment from me delightful—no, not delightful—but bearable. He would defy any one to be very miserable where she was. She kept about her under all circumstances such an atmosphere of cheerfulness and comfort ; was so self-sustained and womanly, and yet as capable of receiving pleasure as a child ; as an example of a beautiful and child-like trait in her disposition, he told with what almost pious care she preserved every little trinket he ever gave her. She would clap her hands and laugh like a very baby over the least trifle bestowed upon her.

I thought of the emerald pin, and of (as doubtless he did) the contrast my whole character presented to his charming wonder.

" Ah, me !" he concluded, and fell into a fit of musing. I did not interrupt him by any poor attempt at cheerfulness I did not feel.

Before long I succeeded in coaxing upon myself a headache—slighted the advice proposed, and at nightfall had my pillows brought to the sofa, and gave up altogether.

I was almost glad to be sick—it would revive in my husband some of the old tenderness perhaps ; but what was my disappointment when he took up his hat to leave the house.

" What, you are not going out to night ?" I inquired in surprise.

" Why, yes, my dear, why not ?"

" If you ask why not, I suppose there is no reason."

" Is there anything I can do, or shall I send the doctor ?"

"No, there is nothing special I need, but I thought you would stay at home to-night—I am unhappy every way."

"I am very sorry, but my engagement to-night is imperative—I promised Jenny I would immediately see some friends of hers, here."

I hid my face in my pillows and cried, and I confess there was some method in my tears—I did not think he would leave me under such circumstances. I was mistaken—he did.

"Have you seen any house that you thought would suit us?" I ventured to ask him before long.

"No, I have not been looking for a house."

He did not follow up my suggestion, and I added, as if I had but to intimate my wishes to have them carried out, though the hollowness of the sham was appalling—"I really wish you would look." He still was silent, and I continued—"Won't you?"

He replied, evidently without the slightest interest in the matter, "Why, yes, when I have time." He paid no further attention to my request, however, and when I reminded him of it again, he said he had forgotten it.

It seemed to me I could not live from one day to another—change would be a relief, at any rate, and my husband's indifference to my wishes made me importunate ; but from week to week he put me off with promises and excuses, both of which I felt were alike false.

He could not see any places. "Inquire of your friends." He had, and could not hear of any.

"Why, I saw plenty of houses to let, and was sure I could secure one any day—would he go with me some time?"

"Yes, certainly at his earliest convenience.'

I awaited his convenience, but it did not come. In very desperation, I set out myself ; but searching without having fixed upon any locality, size of house, or price to be paid, was only a waste of time, I felt, and accordingly I wandered about the streets, looking at the outsides of houses, and now and then inquiring the terms at the door, but declining in all instances to examine the premises, or take the slightest step towards the securing of a house.

"Had you not better consider it a little ?" Mr. Doughty said at length, as if I had not been considering it for six months !

He feared I would find it lonesome—he might be from home a good deal, such was the unfortunate nature of his prospects. Where was he going and what for ?

He was not going at all that he positively knew of, but his affairs were in such a state that contingencies might arise at any time, that would demand his absence for a few weeks or months.

"A happy state of affairs !" I said with womanish spite ; "I suppose one of the contingencies is your charming cousin Jenny !"

He would only reply to my foolish accusation by saying it was quite unworthy of my generous nature—I wronged myself and him, and also the sweetest and most innocent little creature in the world.

For some days nothing was said about the house ; but I was a woman, and could not maintain silence on a disagreeable subject, so I renewed it with the importunate demand to know, once for all, whether or not we were ever to keep house. Thus urged, he consented to go with me in search of a house.

The air was biting on the day we set out—the streets

slippery with ice, and gusts of sharp snow now and then caused women to walk backward, and bury their faces in their muffs.

We turned into streets and out of streets, just as it happened —Mr. Doughty did not care where he looked—anywhere I chose ;—sometimes we passed whole blocks of houses that seemed eligible, without once ringing a bell : he did not suggest looking here or there, made no objection to terms, and suggested no proposals. Now we turned into a by-street and examined some dilapidated tenement, and now sought a fashionable quarter, and went over some grand mansion to be let for six months only, and furnished !—an exorbitant rent demanded, of course.

The whole thing was so evidently a sham, that I at last burst into tears and proposed to go home. Mr. Doughty assented, and with my face swollen and shining with the cold, my hands aching and my feet numb, I arrived there in a condition of outraged and indignant feeling that could go no further.

I comforted myself as I best could, for nobody comforted me, and my husband, monopolizing the easy-chair and a great part of the fire, opened the letters that awaited him.

When he had concluded the reading of the first one— addressed, as I observed, in a woman's hand—he said suddenly, " Come here, Nell, and sit on my knee."

I did so.

" What should you think of taking the house in —— street ?"

" I should like it very well."

" I think that would suit us—room for ourselves, and a visitor now and then, perhaps."

I did not sit on his knee any longer ; I felt instinctively that the letter he had just read was from the charming cousin, and that the prospect of having her for a guest had changed the aspect of affairs.

The house was taken at once, and Mr. Doughty informed me before long that I had a great happiness in prospect—that of knowing the little cousin I had heard him speak of.

She came almost before we were settled ; impossible, thought I, that I should be jealous; the idea of affinity between her and Mr. Doughty was so ridiculous. She was white, short, and fat as a worm in a chestnut, and almost as incapable of thought. The flax-like hair was so thin you could see her head beneath it all the time ; her cheeks and chin trembled with fatness ; her eyes were of the faintest blue, and cloudy with vague apprehen·sion ; her arms hung stiff and round as two rolling pins, and her pink and blue silk dresses were pinned up and fringed out, and greasy : but she was amiable—too simple-hearted and indolent to be otherwise, indeed.

“ She is a child, you see,” said my husband, “ and I bespeak for her childish indulgences ; you must not be surprised to find her arms around my neck any time—playful little kitten, that she is.”

I was not so much surprised to find her big arms about his neck, as by the fact which gradually broke in upon me, that they had power to detain him from the most important duties.

Towards her he was gentle and indulgent to the tenderest degree—towards me exacting, severe, and unyielding.

If I fretted, he was surprised that I could do so with so patient an example before me ; if I forbore complaint, he gave me no praise ; I had done nothing more than I ought to do. If I slighted or blamed Jenny, as I was sometimes driven to do, he was surprised and indignant that I, a reasonable woman, should treat a mere child, quite incapable of defence or retaliation, so cruelly.

By turns, I resorted to every device : grave and reserved dignity, playful badinage, affected indifference, rivalry in dress and manner, pouting, positive anger, threats of divorce and separate maintenance—all would not do. I ruined thereby the slender stock of amiability and fair looks I began with, and gained nothing. Now I went home for a few days, and now I affected illness ; but I gained nothing, for of all lost things most difficult to be regained, lost affection is the most hopeless.

This state of feeling could not last always ; the nerves of sensibility could not be laid bare and left bare without becoming indurated, and by degrees I became incapable of receiving or of giving enjoyment. In our treatment of one another, my husband and I fell into a kind of civility which was the result of indifference. Before folks we said " my dear ;" and when we were alone— but we never were alone—we had ceased to have any of those momentous nothings to communicate which require to be done without observation. I had no longer any motive in life—duty was tiresome, and pleasure a mask that smothered me ; love was a fable, and religion, I knew not what—nothing that comforted me, for it can only enter the heart that is open to the sweet influences of love.

In a fit of the most abject depression I swallowed poison, and lying down on my sofa awaited death with more interest in the process of its approaches than I had felt for months. The pain and the burning were easier to bear than I had borne many and many a time ; gradually the world receded, my eyes closed, and a struggle shook my whole frame—death had indeed got hold of me. A terrible noise filled my ears ; my dead and stiffening body seemed to drop away ; I sat upright and saw about me all familiar and household things. On the floor beside me lay the picture of Mr. Doughty which I had been holding in my hand when I fell asleep—the noise of its falling had waked me.

"Then it had been only a dream, after all ?"

"Why, to be sure ; did you not see all along that such things could not have really happened ?"

THE OUTCAST.

Saturday night has come, and the last sunstreaks have drawn themselves down the snowy hills of Clovernook, and where they lately shone, the darkness is fallen and unfolding very fast. The chickens are gone to roost among the cold, comfortless boughs of the trees nearest the barn ; the cows are milked, and in most places the work-horses, feeding in the stable, have had an extra currying, preparatory to Sunday morning, when they are expected to walk soberly and straightly to the village church, drawing after them, in the newly-washed and tar-smelling wagon, father and mother, and all the children, from the eldest son— as proud of his darkening beard, and " boughten" coat and hat, as he will be in years to come of more stylish appareling or senatorial honors ; and the little girl on her mother's knee, more pleased with the brass buttons on her father's coat, and her own red shoes, than she will be, perhaps, with her point lace and shining brocade, when a few years hence she shall dance at the president's ball.

Another week has gone ; great, in its little events, to the unambitious people who are now done with its hopes and fears, its working and planning—with their tending of sick beds, and making of wedding gowns—as great to them as the largest experience to the largest mind ; and who knows but that in the final summing up of good and evil, the highest glory will be set down to the account of those who have thought always of the pride and place of this world, as the child does of the marvels of the fairy story ; for what, after all, can be got out of this life but usefulness ? With all our racking of the soul, we cannot solve the problem of fore-ordination and free will, of good and evil, of life and death. I am not sure that they are not wisest, as well as best, who are " contented if they may enjoy the things which others understand," and let alone the mysteries which all effort to unfold but folds anew.

It was about the middle of February, and along the northern slopes of the hills, at the roots of big trees, and close in the shadow of the fences, lay the skeleton of the great winter snow. For all their searching, the sheep had not found a single patch of green grass as yet, and the mother cow had brought home to the stable her young calf, without waiting to be invited, so sharply went the winds along woods and meadows.

The smoke issued briskly from chimney-tops, and the heaps of dry wood near the doors, and the lights shining pleasantly out along the frozen ground, told of quiet and comfort within. Here and there an axe was busy at the woodpile, or a lantern shone over the dry sunflower stocks by the garden fence, as some less orderly farmer than the rest went from house to barn, to attend some little chore forgotton or neglected.

Mostly, however, it was quiet, and cold, and dark, except at one or two windows of each house, and the snow and frozen earth, ground together, powdered the lonesome road before the late travellers. Of these there was, on the night I write of, not more than one to be seen ; at any rate, it is with one only my story has to do. If you had seen him you would not have noticed him much, I suppose, they who saw him did not ; and yet he seemed very tired, and bent under the bundle hung across his shoulder, as if he had trudged a long way ; for this bundle was not large, and it could not have been the weight of it that so crooked his shoulders. You would have thought him old, doubtless, for his face was browned and careworn, and a slouched hat and tangly hair and beard gave him the air of years. You would probably have said, if you had chanced to look out of your own room, and observed him shuffling his tired way through the grey chilly moonlight, "there goes a man with a sack on his back ; I wonder if he knows where he is going and what after ?" for so we see our fellows, brothers and friends, going burdened and bent, past our warm hearths every day, and to us they are only as men with sacks on their backs.

Once or twice he stopped where the lights shone brightest, as if he would go in ; but having cut the air with his disengaged hand, as if he were done with some vagary, went on, his feet leaving a trail in the snow and dust, crooked as if he were purposeless. And so, alas, he was ; and wondered, as much as any one, as he pulled his hat lower and turned thought introspective, where he was going, and what for. Ah, that was the worst of it ! footsore and burdened as he was, he had no object, not even a shapeless outline for his future. He might be going into the lap of the best fortune in the world : such things have been done, so he has heard, and he smiles at the bright suggestion ; but reduce it to a where, and when, and how, and the possibility loses all probability ; it is not at all likely any good luck will happen to him ; everybody says he deserves no better fate than he has, and he supposes he does not. He had an object once, which was to get away from everybody that knew him—from his mother who sometimes cried and sometimes scolded about him ! from his father, who said he was going down hill as fast as he could, and the sooner he got to the bottom the better for his family and himself too ; and from the black eyes that looked scornfully upon him the last time he dared look up into their searching brightness.

This last humiliation, more perhaps than anything else, made him rise in the middle of the night, some weeks ago, bundle together a few necessary effects, and steal like a thief away from the house where he was born—unblest of his mother, and with no " God-speed you," from his honest old father. But back of the scorn of the black eyes, the complaining of the mother, and the sentence of the father, there are intemperance, and idleness, and profligacy, that brought all about ; why these should have been he doesn't know, he did not mean to be a bad son nor an untrue lover ; he doesn't say he was ; he doesn't really think he was ; but he knows other folks say so, and so, trying to be indifferent to what men and women think of him, to all the past and all the future, he changes the load on his shoulder, and trudges on.

About half a mile down a narrow lane, that turns out from the main road, he sees a house, small and apparently rude, but with light shining so brightly and cheerfully through all the windows, he is almost persuaded to turn that way ; he doesn't know why nor what for, only it seems for a moment that he has got home. The watch dog sees him from his post at the gate, and sends him forward with a suspicious and unfriendly growl. He fancies he hears a song in the cottage, it may be the wind in the treetops ; he won't stop to see, for what are songs or lights to him ! He is half disposed to lie down on the frozen ground, at the wayside ; but it is cold and hard ; and he has always known the comfort of a warm bed—he cannot quite do that yet. He passes a good many snug farmhouses, but the front doors are close shut, and he feels just as if they had been closed to keep him out. But by and by he is very tired, and his diffidence grows less and less under the necessity of rest; he doesn't much care where it is, nor who accords it, but he must have rest, somewhere ; that is the strongest feeling he has. The wind blows against him harder and colder all the time, and he concludes *that* has become his enemy too, as long ago he settled into a conviction that mankind were leagued against him. 'Tis a pity that he himself is his own worst enemy ; but he cannot see it, and that is a pity too. Presently he sees a commodious house, brightly painted, and with lights streaming from the front windows, right before him ; the curtain is drawn aside, and he discovers a man in black and goodly apparel, reading in a large book, it is the Bible, he thinks ; he is very tired and hungry and must have food and rest. Without more ado he approaches the door and thumps with his stick confidently and boldly. No hearty voice answers, " Come in !" and as he crouches, in dim expectancy, he hears the crackling of the wood in the fireplace, and the prattling of children. The door opens soon, carefully and narrowly, and the man in the black coat looks out distrustfully and asks, " What do you want ?"

" I want to stay all night," answers the traveller.

The door is pushed round a little and the man in the black coat says, " We have no accommodation for travellers."

" But I am tired and hungry," urges the stranger.

" We are sorry," says the man in the black coat, speaking for himself and all the house ; and so closes the door.

The tired man thinks he hears the key turn, but he is not quite sure. His senses are bewildered, and he hardly knows whether or not he saw a dish of apples, and another of cakes, on the table before the fire, but he thinks he did, and that he also saw a prim-looking woman, in a silk gown, shaking her head at the man in the black coat, while he held the door so cautiously open.

The house was not like a farmhouse, and he is almost sure it is the parsonage ; but he is not quite sure about anything, poor fellow. He is sure enough, however, to anathematize all piety as hypocrisy, and he says with an oath he doesn't care for all the preachers in the world ; he will get to heaven as soon as any of them ; and he wishes the white neckcloth of the man in the black coat might choak him that very instant. And then he imagines how he would take possession of the parsonage, and sit by the warm fire and eat apples and cakes, and never pay one cent for preaching as long as he lived. One thing he would do, he knows, he would entertain poor travellers.

He has climbed a long hill, and gone over a hollow, where there is a one-arched wooden bridge, and where he hears no tinkling of water ; even that has shut itself away from him, under ice ; he almost expected a murderer to come out from beneath the dark arch, but there did not ; and now he ascends another hill, abrupt and high ; and as he nears the summit he sees a good many lights shining, and presently becomes aware that he is entering a village. A number of covered wagons almost block up the road before him ; each is loaded with boxes, and barrels, and farming implements, full as it can be, and from among them, or from under each wagon, looks out a huge dog— the faithful guardian while the teamster sleeps. Immediately

overhead creaks the sign of entertainment ; he has found a
door open at last. He is so glad to throw down his budget,
and seat himself at the fire, that he heeds little the fumes of
whisky and tobacco with which the room is reeking. The
idlers there make him welcome, and offer him cigars and punch,
and in return for their kindness, he grows merry and talks
freely and indiscreetly ; sometimes profanely ; and so the night
wears into midnight, and the merry-making has become a ca-
rousal. We will not linger over it, it is too sad to see manhood
so debasing itself ; intellect burning itself out in evil passion,
and the likeness of the angel becoming more grovelling than
the brute.

Sunday morning comes ; the heavens are full of clouds, and
of winds ; very rough and cold they are blowing everywhere ;
but roughest and coldest through the leafless locust trees that
grow along the fence of the Clovernook graveyard ; so thinks
the poor fellow who lies beneath one of them, his stick by his
side, and his bundle for a pillow—all the wild merriment that
filled the tavern last night, dwarfed to a drunken dreaming.
The people ride by to church, one wagon load after another,
and now and then some one says, " There is a drunken man ;"
but many pass without seeing him at all, and no one stops to
see whether he is alive or dead. He is lying nearly opposite
the narrow lane, where he paused last evening, seeing the light
in the rude house, half a mile away. If he were roused up he
would not know how nor why he came to be where he is, nor
do I myself know, unless it were that Providence directed his
staggering, when he was found to be inebriate and penniless,
and driven away from the tavern where he had paid his last
sixpence for his present imbecility.

Heavy and mournful through the dull air sounds the church bell, like a summons to penance rather than a cheerful call to thanksgiving ; the troubled sleeper hears it and thinks doomsday has come, and groans and turns on his comfortless pillow. A stout grey horse, with an eye that looks kinder and nobler than has been given to some reasonable creatures, climbs steadily the steep hill in the lane, and trots briskly forward, the neat little wagon behind him rattling in a loud and lively key ; out into the main road he comes, and turns toward the call of the bell ; but as he passes the graveyard he looks round as if seeing the man lying there and pitying him.

"Dear me !" exclaims the woman who is driving the grey horse ; and she draws up the reins and is on the ground in a moment ; so is the young woman who'sat beside her, and she indeed is the first to climb the clay bank and reach the dead man, as she thinks he is ; and truly he is dead—to all that a man should be alive for.

"Oh, mother, mother," she cries, clapping her hands joyously, "he is only asleep, after all ! I am so glad ! What makes him lie here, mother ?"

"I don't know, my poor child," answers the ·good woman, wiping her eyes ; "I am afraid he has been drinking at the tavern ;" and stooping over him, she shakes him by the shoulder.

"Yes, mother, I will get up in a minute," he answers, without opening his eyes.

"How funny," says the young girl, laughing aloud ; "he thinks you are his mother."

"Mercy," says the deacon, peeping from the front of his dearborn, "if there is not Mrs. Goforth and her daughter Elsy, talking with a drunken man ; don't children, don't any of you look at her." And he touches his horse smartly on the flauk, and does not apparently hear Mrs. Goforth call to him.

She is at a loss what to do, and well she may be ; for though she has tugged and lifted the man to a sitting posture, he cannot retain it for a moment, unsupported by her ; how then is he to stand or walk ? The air is bitter cold, and he may freeze to death if she leaves him. She asks him who he is, and how he came there ? but he says he does not know ; and pulls at her shawl, and looks in her face like a bewildered child ; and repeats that he will go as soon as he can walk, that he is sure he is not harming anybody.

"But you are harming yourself, my son," says the good woman ; " that is the trouble."

" Why, it is not any trouble to you," replies the young man, " because what I do ain't nothing to nobody ;" and he relapses again into his horrible unconsciousness.

The bells were already done ringing ; but Mrs. Goforth was not a woman to go to church and leave a man freezing to death by the roadside ; she could not, to use her own words, have any comfort of the meeting whatever ; and though she did not like to stay away from her place, she thought it was right to do so under the circumstances ; so, having turned about her grey horse, she brought the little wagon as close to the clay bank as she could, and she and Elsy, half dragging and half lifting the poor outcast, got him into it, in some way.

It had come to the ears of the parson, before the hour for service, that a man was lying drunken by the road-side ; and the fact afforded a text for the severest denunciation of sinners, especially of this sort. He did not once reflect, let us hope, how large a share he had in bringing his fellow-mortal, and fellow-sinner too, to the condition and exhibition of infamy which he so unmercifully condemned.

The meaning of the vacant seat of Mrs. Goforth was hardly construed, for in the preacher's mind, when taken in connection with other absences of late, it argued conclusively a growing indifference to the Lord's sanctuary. This was wrong, and uncharitable, as the reader sees ; but none of the congregation saw it then, or felt it then. Good Mrs. Goforth was casting her bread upon the waters, with no thought of future reward ; but after many days, as we shall see, reward came.

Monday morning it was still cloudy, and not only so, but snowing—a little fine icy snow, that struck sharply like sand against Mrs. Goforth's small windows ; for she lived in a small house, and the windows were not much larger than a lady's pocket handkerchief. It was but a cabin, indeed, built of logs, very rudely ; and humble as it was, and small as it was, Mrs. Goforth would have thought herself rich to own it. Yet she did not own the house, nor the meadow, nor the wood adjacent, nor much in all the world, except a heart that was large, and truthful, and loving. She did not complain, however, that she did not own a great house and a hundred or more acres of land, like most of her neighbors ; she was cheerful, under the necessity of hiring a small lot, and milking her own cow, and feeding her own chickens, and working in the garden. Now and then she procured a few days' work, but for the most part she and Elsy managed to get along alone. And very comfortably they did get along ; no young woman in the neighbor-hood looked tidier than the widow's daughter, and surely none was prettier ; in summer, no dress in all the church was whiter than hers, and no hat was so nice and so tasteful, albeit it lacked the flowers and the rich ribbons of some there. She was a dreadfully giddy young girl, to be sure, and her mother had often to recall her eyes to her hymn-book from a new dress or shawl which for the first time had made its appearance in a neighboring pew; perhaps sometimes from casting upon some young man an admiring glance; so the older and more staid young ladies said, at least, though Elsy stoutly denied it. She did not care whether the young men saw her or not, she often said, but that she could not help seeing them when they were in the same house with her. And anybody who saw her blue laughing eyes, would have readily believed she could not help it.

Jacob Holcom, for that was the name of our purposeless traveller, awoke to self-consciousness early on Monday morning —perhaps with the tinkling of the snow on the window-panes, perhaps with the remorseful stirrings of his own mind, and the dreamy memory of a face that looked kindly upon him.

First, he saw the whitewashed joists above him, and felt that he was not at home in his own chamber, which was large and substantial; and as he sunk back on his pillow, his eye caught the neat stitching in the pillow-case, he wondered whose hand did it, and involuntarily linked it with one he had dreamed of as loosening something that choked him, when he lay on a very cold hard bed somewhere : he could not tell when or where. He could not tell much better where he was now; that he was in the flesh he was sure, for his hands had the mark of the axe and the hoe-handle ; but the room was new to him, and how he came there passed all his recollection. Raising himself on one elbow, he peeped curiously about, pleased as a child with a new baby-house.

The second thought was of his unfitness for the place—all was so neat—there was such an atmosphere of purity about him—and the bed itself was so sweet and so white—what business had he in it? There was mud on his face and in his hair, that had come from some sorry resting-place, of which he had but a faint recollection now.

He could not do much in the way of personal renovation; but all he could do, he did, brushing his soiled garments and hair, and drawing upon his small bundle for such clean articles as it contained. This done, he felt quite at a loss, and looking out into the snow-storm, half wished he were in it, rather than in a place of which he was so unworthy.

Mrs. Goforth and Elsy had been an hour astir; the cow was milked, the fire burning on the hearth, the table spread near it, and the coffee sending up its pleasant steam with the smoke, when the footsteps of the unknown traveller arrested their attention; and a soft rap on the door and the announcement that breakfast was waiting, fell strangely enough on the ears of the bewildered Jacob; it was just as if his own mother had called him, except that she had not spoken his name.

More ashamed than he had ever been in his life, he obeyed the call, and with downcast eyes and a blushing cheek, presented himself, expecting, notwithstanding the mild call, to receive summary dismissal, with severe reproof. But a cordial good-morning, and an invitation to partake of the breakfast that awaited, almost caused him to think he was still dreaming, and in his hesitation, he behaved so awkwardly that Elsy would have laughed in spite of herself another time, but now, she felt not only pity for the stranger, but in some sort responsible for him. He did not look like an evil-disposed person to her; she did not believe he was one; and she did not care what anybody said, she would not believe it. Now no one had said anything about the young man that Elsy knew of, and it was strange her thoughts should run before and suppose an accusation, and take up a defence; but such was the fact, and such are often the curious facts with which love begins his impregnable masonry.

As Jacob partook of the breakfast (without much appetite we may suppose) he kept inventing stories, one after another, with which to make himself appear better than he was, in the event of being questioned by his hostess in reference to his past life, which questioning he momently expected.

At first he thought he would say he was turned out of his father's house for a supposed fault, of which he was guiltless, and that he had travelled till quite exhausted by cold and hunger, when, in a fit of temporary delirium, he had lain down by the road-side, and that that was the last he knew; he would offer to pay for his entertainment after breakfast, and affect surprise at finding his money gone; and say that it had been stolen from him during his insane sleep. But Mrs. Goforth talked of the late storm, and of her fears that the apples and peaches would have been killed—of her plans for gardening and farming—in short, of her own affairs altogether; so the lies Jacob had invented died in his heart. If she had breathed one word of blame of him, they would have come out, black as they were.

His next plan was to modify the story somewhat; he would

blame himself a little more, his parents a little less ; and he would say he laid down, because he was too tired to go on, and growing numb with the cold, had fallen asleep ; that he discovered that morning his money was all gone, though how he had lost it, he did not know. This gave him a little more satisfaction, and he was just on the point of commencing an exculpation, unasked, when Elsy brought to the table some warm cakes she had been baking, and offered him ; he felt obliged to refuse : and when with her own hand she laid one on his plate, he felt the second story all going to pieces.

He now wished heartily the meal was concluded, and resolved to steal away the first moment he could do so, without saying a word. He had no money with which to pay for his entertainment, and what were apologies and thanks ? Nothing ; he would steal away unobserved, and somewhere, and some time, try to amend.

He did not know when nor where, nor once ask himself, why then and there would not be as good a time and place as there would ever be.

When the breakfast was done, Mrs. Goforth gave him the best chair and the warmest corner ; and having told Elsy to run over to farmer Hill's, and see if he could not spare his son John to chop for them that afternoon, she went herself to the "milk-house," a little cellar that lay under a mound of snow, a few steps from the door.

The opportunity Jacob had longed for was come ; he stole back for the bundle he had left, took it up, and there was nothing in the way of escape, nothing but a natural nobility of soul that was not all gone yet. There was the white bed, Elsy's own bed, he knew, which she had given to him ; and there was the pot of winter-flowers, blooming bright in his face ; and there was the Bible on the snowy cover of the table ; all mute, to be sure, but they seemed to rebuke the purposes he had formed, nevertheless. No, he would not, and conld not, steal away like a thief, which he was not. Was not the house, and all that was in it, trusted in his hands? If there had been any suspicion manifested toward him, it would be easy to go ; but he could not return basely the frankness and confidence he had met. He would see Mrs. Goforth—tell her truly his destitute condition, nothing else—give her his thanks, which was all he could give, and somewhere seek for honest employment.

So resolving, and wishing the resolutions were executed, he sat, when his hostess returned, followed almost immediately by Elsy, her cheeks blushing red with the rough kisses of the wind, and her eyes sparkling, notwithstanding the disappointment she had met. John Hill had gone to town an hour before, and who was to chop their wood she conld not tell ; but she looked at Jacob when she said so in a way that implied a sns-picion of his ability to solve the problem.

Jacob ventured to say he would like to work long enough to pay for his entertainment, if he dare ask such a favor ; it would not be asking, but doing a favor, Mrs. Goforth said ; and, throwing down his bundle, the yonng man took up the axe.

The old dog that had kept a suspicious eye on him all the morning, arose now, and with some hesitation followed him to the woodpile, whence the sturdy strokes, issuing presently, made agreeable music in the widow's honse. That day, and the next, and the next, he kept at work, and that weck, and the next, faithfully he performed all the duties intrusted to him ; but he spoke uo word concerning his past life.

Many of the neighbors expressed surprise that Mrs. Goforth should pick up a man in the high road, and hire him to do her work ; they could not account for it, except by saying she was a strange woman ; they hoped she might not be paid for her foolishness by finding her horse gone some morning, and her hired man with it. But when she was seen going to church, and this hired man riding in the wagon with her own daughter, there was such commotion in the congregation as had not been known there for many a year. Some of the women, indeed, passed by the pew where the widow and daughter sat, pretending not to see them, and such sayings as that "birds of a feather flock together," and "a woman is known by the company she keeps," and the like, were whispered from one to another, all having reference to Mrs. Goforth and the drunken man, as everybody called Jacob. But the good woman had little regard for what her neighbors thought, so long as her own heart did not accuse her, for "what have I done," she said, "except practice what they preach ?"

All the truth about the young man, after his arrival in the neighborhood, was speedily bruited about and lost nothing as it went. Elsy believed not one word of it, for a nicer or a smarter person than Jacob Holcom she had never seen in her life. If she could believe it was true she would not talk with Jacob so freely ; but she knew better ; and even if it were true, she thinks those who talk of it might find some faults nearer home to attend to.

It was about the middle of the sugar-making season—night and raining. Jacob had been busy in the sugar camp two or three days, so busy that he had scarcely been at the house except for the doing of necessary chores. The day we write of he had not been at home since morning ; he must be very tired, and very hungry, and very lonesome, Elsy thinks ; and she goes to the window often, to see whether he is coming, but she does not see anything of the torchlight gleaming over the hill—and Jacob is used to make a torch of hickory bark to light him on his way home at night—so she keeps standing and looking out into the dark, and the rain, hoping her mother will say, "You had better run across the meadow, Elsy, and see whether some accident has not happened to Jacob ;" but her mother keeps at her knitting, by the fireside, and doesn't say anything of the sort; *her* heart has not fluttered her steady common sense into unnatural fears. At last she can bear the darkness and rain no longer ; who knows she thinks, but that Jacob may have had another of those dreadful fits, and so fallen into the fire, or the boiling water. "Mother," she says, "it is not raining much now : I think I will take Carlo, and run over the hill and see if I can tell whether Jacob is in the sugar camp ; if I see him from the hill top I will come straight back."

"Very well, my child," replies Mrs. Goforth ; "but I don't think anything has happened to him."

Elsy was not long in tossing a shawl over her head, nor long in reaching the hill-top ; she did not once think of darkness and rain ; one moment she paused and stood on tiptoe, looking earnestly into the great red light that shone against the trees, and flickered along the ground of the sugar-camp. She did not see Jacob, and therefore sped on faster than the wind.

Before the stone furnace, where the sugar water was boiling, a rude hut had been constructed, which afforded protection from the storm ; and here, seated on a low bench, watching the jets of flame as they broke from the main body of fire quivered a moment, and went out, sat Jacob Holcom, when Elsy, her hair dripping with rain, and her face pale with fright, presented herself before him.

"What can have happened?" he asked in surprise, taking her hand and drawing her to a seat before the fire.

Elsy's cheek grew red when she found that she was come of a foolish errand, and she stammered the truth—her fears for him—as the best excuse she could make. It was Jacob's turn to be confused now, and taking up a handful of the straw that carpeted his rude hut, he pulled it to pieces, his eyes bent on the ground, stepping aside till he was quite out of the shelter.

"Oh, don't stay in the rain," said Elsy, "sit here by me, there is room enough."

Jacob sat down, but kept his face averted from the gentle, confidant eyes of his companion. "I am sure you have not told me true," said Elsy, "and that you are not well. Oh, if you should have another of those dreadful fits!"

Well might she have thought, poor simple-hearted child, from the strange behavior of the young man, that a fit was about to seize him, for as she looked up in his face, he covered it with his hands, and she presently saw the tears coming out between his fingers.

All at once she divined the truth, she thought she had wounded him by speaking of the fit, for people said it was a drunken fit, and Jacob might fancy she believed it.

How to begin she did not know, but to sit in silence and see Jacob weeping like a child, was not to be thought of, so she stammered in some way that she did not know as anybody had said anything against him, and if they had she did not believe it, she did not care what it was. And the more she said she did not care what was spoken against him, and that she believed he was all that was good and true, the more discomforted the young man seemed. If she had joined her denunciations to the rest, he could have denied their justice perhaps ; but to be thought so much better than he was, made him more sadly humble, more truly good, than he had ever been in his life.

He assured Elsy, in a broken voice, that he was quite well, but that he was not worthy of the interest she had taken in him, though he thanked her for it.

"Poor Jacob," thought she, "I am sure his mind is wandering ; *he* not worthy, indeed ! then I don't know who is." And she went herself out into the rain to mend the fire, and afterward arranged her shawl against the crevices of the wall by which Jacob sat, so that the wind and rain should not blow against him.

"Sit here yourself," said the sugar-maker, rising from the seat, and drawing Elsy toward it ; "do, I pray, for I cannot ; I would rather stand out in the rain."

"O Jacob, what do you mean ?" she asked in affright ; "sit down beside me ; the bench is long enough, and tell me what it is troubles you." And there, the rain beating around them, and the fire brightening, and fading, and brightening again, Jacob told all the story of his life, sparing himself no whit.

But if he has done wrong sometimes, thought Elsy, what of that ? I suppose every one has some faults, and if everybody has turned against him I am sure there is the more need I should not. In fact, she believed he made his vices greatly larger than they were ; but even if he did not, it was so magnanimous to confess them, and to come back to virtue. Verily, she admired and loved Jacob more than ever before. When he came to tell of the black eyes that had made all the woods about his home brighter than the May sunshine, and how their loving beams changed into sharp arrows, and pierced him through and through, Elsy's little foot tapped smartly on the ground, and her own eyes looked as indignant as it was in their power to do, for in her heart she felt that the woman who could scorn Jacob, no matter what the provocation, did not deserve to have a lover. It is to be supposed that Jacob saw all this, for such thoughts shine right in one's face as plainly as written words ; nevertheless, to make assurance doubly sure, no doubt, he said, " and you, Elsy, would have spurned me just as she did, if I had been a lover of yours !"

"How can you say so, Jacob?" she replied, " I should have felt that you needed me most when that you were not strong enough in yourself to resist temptation."

"Dear Elsy !" he said, and the bench, which a little while before was not big enough for two, might have accommodated three very well as he spoke. But there is no need to repeat what more they said ; suffice it, they forgot to make a torch to light them home, each confidently believing the full moon was shining in all her splendor, they saw the way so well.

When Jacob rapped next at the parsonage, it was not to entreat a night's lodging, and the door opened so wide, and the parson smiled so blandly, he could hardly believe it was the same house or the same man he had seen before ; and when he sat next in the pew, at church, with Mrs. Goforth and Elsy, not Elsy Goforth any more, there was nobody in all the house that did not see them, and smile, and shake hands.

Jacob never had another fit, and the manly dignity and propriety of his conduct soon won for him, not only the esteem and admiration of all the neighborhood, but led the people to believe they had wronged him in their first accusation ; and they bestowed upon Mrs. Goforth the reputation of having a gift for curing fits, and many were the applications for advice she received in consequence. When she assured them that she practised no art, and that simply doing as she would be done by, was all her wisdom, there was invariably disappointment and sorrow, so hard is it to understand the hardest of human possibilities, and the most wonder-working. Five years after the mysterious cure, Jacob Holcom owned one of the prettiest little farms about Clovernook, and in all that time Elsy and he had never had any disagreement, except when he affirmed that she was an angel, which she always stoutly denied ; but she was a good and true wife, and that is but a little lower than an angel.

HASTY WORDS, AND THEIR APOLOGY.

"GET out of my way!" said Luther Brisbane, pushing the gate against the little girl whose face was pressed on it. He was just coming home from school, two miles away, and in no very amiable humor—having made bad recitations that day, and failed of receiving his customary honors.

"I thought the gate opened the other way," answered the child, modestly, and stepping confusedly aside.

"There is but one right way to do anything," replied the boy, "and this is the right way to open the gate ; and shoving it roughly against the little girl, he went hastily down the smoothly-gravelled walk, without once again turning his eyes towards her.

She looked after him, feeling sorry for the offence she had given, but quite at a loss what to say ; and when he disappeared round the corner of the house, her slim little fingers were pulling at one another, and her brown eyes slowly filling with tears.

"Well, my son," said Mrs. Brisbane, looking up from her work, and smiling, as he entered the room where she sat, and dashed himself into a chair, sachel in hand, and hat lowered over his brows.

He made no reply to her pleasant salutation ; but fixed his

grey eyes sharply and demandingly upon her. Mrs. Brisbane was well used to that ungracious demand, but she was Luther's mother, and humored the selfish caprices of her son, as fond mothers are likely to do.

She put down her work at once, and slipping the sachel from Luther's arm, hung it in its proper place, and then removing his hat, smoothed away the heavy black hair from his forehead, and said she would have the supper prepared at once, she was sure he must be very tired and hungry. "Yes, as tired and hungry as I can be," said Luther, lopping his head heavily against his mother, and never once thinking she might be tired too. He was the only son, and his parents, not a little proud of him (and indeed there was a good deal in him to be proud of), had given way to his natural strong will, till it had grown to stubbornness, a stubbornness quite too hard to melt, and which, if subdued at all, must needs be broken by some terribly sharp blow. Perhaps those little fingers, in their workings, were gathering strength for such a blow—we shall see.

Luther saw that it was a little girl's dress his mother was sewing on ; but he was too proud to seem interested in little things, and without appearing to notice her occupation, threw himself at full length on the sofa, and taking up book after book, went over the day's studies in good earnest. But it was not his nature to forget himself long, or allow others to forget him ; and suddenly, without regard to his mother's preoccupation, he took off his waistcoat, and throwing it at her feet, said, "That must have two buttons sewed on," which meant, of course, "You, my mother, who should have nothing to do but attend to my wants, must sew them on."

For once she did not allow herself to be interrupted, but kept on steadily stitching the ruffle to the short sleeve of the blue dress she was making.

"I say, mother, did you hear?" said Luther, holding his book aside, and fixing his grey eyes upon her after the old fashion.

"Yes, my son," she replied, "but I can't do it just now."

"Why can't you?"

Mrs. Brisbane said simply that she was busy—perhaps Luther thought she would explain what she was busy about, and why the work was urgent; but she did not, and pushing the curtain back, further and further, as the light grew dim, and lifting the sewing a little closer to her eyes, kept on. Luther would not for the world ask his mother what she was doing—he was quite above such trifling interests, or wished to be thought so; but try as he would, he could not suppress the wonder as to whether the dress was for the little girl he had seen at the gate; and, if so, why it was for her; and why indeed, she was there. With every shadow that crossed the door he glanced aside from the page, but he saw not the little girl he looked to see.

Presently he might have been seen coming round the corner of the house, whistling carelessly, and looking for nothing in particular—certainly not for the little girl, for scarcely did he turn his head towards her.

She was sitting on the border of grass at the edge of the walk close by the gate, where Luther had left her, and with one hand was pulling the curl out of her brown hair, while the other rested on the head of the big watch-dog that lay with his speckled nose half buried in the turf at her feet.

Luther mounted the steps of the portico, and looking in all directions but where the dog was, whistled for him loudly—perhaps to arrest the attention of the little girl ; but her brown eyes looked steadily at the ground ; and when the dog, slipping his head from beneath her hand, trotted down the walk, she remained quiet, looking on the ground all the same, only betraying that she felt herself observed, by pulling her scanty skirts over her bare feet.

Luther petted and scolded the dog by turns, but without eliciting any notice from the child ; he then took his play-fellow's ear in one hand, and raced up and down the walk, close to her feet, but she, turning slightly aside, picked out the grass, spear by spear, never once lifting her brown eyes.

She had gone to the gate to meet and welcome him home ; he had given her the unceremonious greeting recorded, and no second friendly overture would she make. Luther had found his match : half way down the walk he stopped suddenly, exclaiming, " Oh, I have found something beautiful ; whoever comes for it may have it." Now, there was no one to come except the child at the gate ; but he had not called directly to her, and she would not go. Luther now sat down on the bank and fixed his grey eyes on the little girl (for he was not used to be so disregarded), but in vain were all his looks of displeasure when she would not see them.

He was sorry in his heart for what he had said, but he would not openly acknowledge it ; and modulating his voice to something like entreaty, he said, " Come here and see what I have found."

" It is nothing that belongs to me," the child answered, for the first time lifting up her eyes.

Encouraged by the mildness of her voice, he added, authoritatively, " I tell you to come and see."

"I will not," answered the little girl, tossing the curls from her bare brown shoulders, and returning his gaze.

"Well," said Luther, "if you won't come for it, you shan't have it—that's all;" and he affected to put something in his pocket.

"I don't want what is not mine," she replied.

"But how do you know that it is not yours?"

"Because," said the child, wiping her eyes with her hand, "I had nothing to lose."

Luther regarded her more attentively now, and saw that she did not look as if she had much to lose—her dress was faded and outgrown so much, that, try as she would, she could not make the scanty skirt stay over her bare brown feet. One by one the tears fell from her eyes slowly down her cheeks, and with each that fell the boy took a step towards her. He had not spoken as yet, however, when the gate opened, and Mr. Brisbane entered. He brushed aside the brown tangles that had fallen down the little girl's cheeks, gave her a flower which he had in his hand, and led her down the walk towards the house, saying to Luther as they came where he was standing, "This is to be your playmate hereafter, my son;" and as he spoke he joined the hands of the two little folks, telling the girl that that was his son, and his name was Luther; and the boy, that the girl's name was Almira Curtiss.

"Myrie—my mother called me Myrie," said the little girl.

"But it is not right, for all that," said the boy.

Myrie spoke not; but her fingers loosened their hold of the boy's hand; and though they entered the house side by side, it was in dissatisfied silence on the part of both.

Thus much of the first acquaintance of the lover and lady, as they were to be hereafter.　Not far away from the substantial and comfortable home of good Mr. Brisbane (for he was a good and exceedingly benevolent man), there had lived—and the day previous to the opening of our story, died—a widow, whose only wealth was her virtues and her little Myrie.　When Mr. Brisbane had prayed at her dying bed-side, she had said, " What shepherd will take care of my little lamb till the heavenly shepherd calls her?" and he had laid his hand on the drooping head of the little girl, and comforted the mother with the assurance that the orphan should not be forgotten.

And the funeral was over, and the mother laid to rest—to that deep, deep rest, to which she had gone gladly—the promise had been kept ; and Myrie had opened her brown eyes wonderingly to feel the kiss of a stranger on her cheek.

The door of the empty and poor little house where she was born, and where all the nine years of her life had been passed, was closed behind her ; and in a pretty carriage, drawn by gay sleek horses, she was carried to a new home—a very fine one as she then thought.　So came the meeting of the littte folks— the poor orphan and the rich man's son.

When Myrie had been living two years at Mr. Brisbane's, she went one day to pick berries a good way from the house. When she came near the hedge where the blackberries grew, she saw on the next side-hill a boy not much older that herself, binding sheaves of wheat in the sunshine.　Sometimes he stopped to·pick the briers from his fingers or his feet, for he wore no shoes, and was indeed in all respects poorly clad.　He did not sing or whistle as he bound up the bundles, but stooped along the hill-side as though work was his doom.　Myrie stopped quite still to look at him—his patched trousers, and

4*

torn hat, and tanned and bleeding feet, drew her sympathy; and if she had done as her heart inclined, she would have put down her basket and assisted him for an hour or two at his tiresome work.

It was so cool and pleasant where she was, for the wild grape-vines were looped from limb to limb along the hedge where the briers grew, that she every now and then turned to observe the poor tired worker in the hot sunshine.

Her basket was not yet half full when the twittering and fluttering in the leaves overhead were greatly increased, a sudden gust of wind turned the leaves all wrong-side out, and a heavy black shadow ran along the hill, chasing the sunshine away. She ran out of the hedge to see if the sun was going down, it was so dark; and taking off her hood, turned her face towards the sky, where the blackness was becoming dense. There was a flash of blinding light and a thunder-peal that seemed for a moment crashing the sky, and then went rumbling and muttering into silence.

Plash, plash in her face came the heavy rain drops.

The little boy threw down the bundle he was binding, and bending forward as he ran, came towards the hedge.

"Here, little girl," he said, as he parted the heavy tangles of leafy vines that roofed a scrubby tree, and drooped around it almost to the ground: "come in here, and the rain will never touch you."

She was quick to avail herself of the offered shelter, and in a moment the two children were sitting side by side on a mound of turf, listening half afraid and half delighted, to the music of the rain on the broad green leaves above them.

"Don't be afraid," the boy would say, again and again, after the subsiding of the sharp thunder and lightning : but though he said so often, " Dou't be afraid," he was greatly awed, if not fearful, and with every flash uplifted his hands—appealing involuntarily for protection.

Presently the rain found its way through the leafy roof, and the curls of Myrie were full of it ; but the violence of the storm was past now, and little cared the children for the plashing of the bright drops on their heads, or in their faces. It was natural they should begin to talk about going home as the storm subsided, and then it was that the homes, and afterward the names of the strangers, became known to each other. Charles Robinson was the name of the lad—he had no father, nor mother, nor other friend, he said—he was lately come to the neighborhood to seek his fortune, and chanced to be at the time in the employ of the farmer who owned the adjoining wheat field. He brushed the rain drops carefully from his worn hat, saying, half sadly though jocularly, that he should be very sorry to have it spoiled.

Myrie told how poor she had been, and how poor she was then, except for the kindness of the good man with whom she lived, for she felt that her pretty bright dress contrasted with the old soiled clothes of the boy, and she knew that he felt it too, and in the gentle goodness of her heart, tried to make their positions as nearly equal as she could—for Myrie was not proud or willful, except to those who towards her were proud and self-willed.

Charley smiled, for he felt the kindness, and for a moment the dew came to his eyes ; but having twisted off a handful of grass that grew up pale and tender in that shady bower, by way of diverting his thoughts, he brushed the rain drops from the thick curls that fell along his forehead, and parting the viny curtains, stepped resolutely out into the sunshine—for the clouds were breaking up, and hedge and wheat field, and the wet woods close by, were all shining in a flood of splendor. The birds were singing in full chorus, hopping from ground to tree, and from limb to limb, for their exuberance of joy would not let them remain quiet. "Come, Myrie," called Charley, "and I will help you fill your basket before I go back to my work."

"But you will lose the time," answered Myrie, glad of companionship, yet at the same time mindful of the lad's interest.

"Oh, no matter, I can work by the moonlight—I meant to do so, at any rate."

"What for?" asked Myrie.

Charley laughed gayly, and said, "To finish the field's work, to be sure—what else should I do it for?"

"I thought, perhaps," said Myrie, half ashamed to place the sordid calculation beside the generous impulse of the boy—"I thought perhaps, you would get more money."

Charley laughed again, and said, "that some way or other money slipped right through his hands when he had it, and that he believed he was just as well off without a cent as with it;" and treading carefully, for the briers were sharp, and his feet bare, he made his way to where the berries were thickest, and Myrie's basket was presently heaped almost up to the handle.

On the hill-side, opposite the wheat field, she turned as she went towards home and saw Charley bending along the stubble; he looked up and, with a wave of his old hat, bade her a second and genial good bye.

"Only see, Lu, what beautiful berries!" and taking the

leafy covering from her basket, Myrie ran down the walk toward the portico, where sat Luther, with a book before his eyes.

"Very beautiful!" he replied, scarcely glancing aside from the page.

"Where have you been!" asked Myrie, in good-natured surprise, bending one knee on the step at his feet, for she saw that his shoes, generally so polished, were positively muddy, and that the hems of his white trowsers were almost dripping wet, while the usually prim collar lopped, damp and limberly.

Luther did not so much as lift his eyes this time, but in answer to the question of where he had been, replied concisely, "in the rain."

Myrie said not another word, but having adjusted the leaves that covered her basket, skipped round the corner of the house, provokingly indifferent.

"Did you see Luther?" asked Mrs. Brisbane, as Myrie came in ; "he has been watching for you this half-hour."

"I did not think he was watching for me," she replied ; "he would hardly speak."

"Well, poor boy," said the mother, "he is a little vexed, I suppose, and no wonder ; he went out with the umbrella to bring you home, and could not find you ; and besides that, was caught in the rain, and soiled his clean clothes, as you saw."

"Oh how sorry I am !" said Myrie, and filling the cup with the berries, she hastened to offer them to Luther, with the expression of her sympathy and regret.

"Where were you?" asked he, setting down the cup as though for his part he cared nothing about blackberries.

Myrie said where she was, and with whom, adding that

Charley Robinson was the nicest and best little boy she ever saw.

"Dear me," said Luther, tartly, "if I had known you were so well protected, I might have spared myself much trouble, and the danger of getting cold and dying, perhaps."

Myric laughed a little derisively, and replied, "that the warmth of his temper would be likely to keep off a chill;" and sitting down on the portico, opposite him, amused herself by humming a tune. Perhaps she thought that Luther would speak to her; but he did not, and directly, as though the tune interrupted his studies, closed the volume and retired to his own room, leaving the berries untouched.

"It would not be Charley Robinson that would ever be so sullen, I know," thought Myric; and as if the thought were some retaliation upon Luther, she recalled all the pleasant interview of the afternoon, and at last ended in a dreamy musing, forgetting Luther altogether.

With now and then some such ruffling of the current as we have described, the lives of the little folks ran on. Many a spring they gathered flowers together along the fields and in the woods—many a morning they planned and planted the garden—and many a time picked together the white nuts from the ground, and the red apples from the trees; and so they stepped up the years, one after another, into manhood and womanhood, and the blushes many a time shone between Myric's curls, when Luther found place for some tender sentiment, as he instructed her in French, or drawing, or music.

And during these years, Charley Robinson went tossing about the world, drifting every now and then into his boyhood's harbor, by chance as it seemed—perhaps it was so, nevertheless he was sure to come first and last to see Myric—she always joyously, demonstratively glad to see him—he always bashfully, silently, more than glad to see her.

Sometimes his pockets were well lined, and his coat glossy and new ; and at other times his feet were badly shod, and the brim of his hat not much less torn than of old.   Poor Charley ! fortune played all games with him.

He had seen many countries, and a number of the great cities of the world, picking up some knowledge, but not much wisdom ; enlarging experience, but reaping small profit ; now on the sea as a common sailor, now as a traveller with money and leisure ; sometimes prying stones from the hard quarry, for the sake of daily necessities, and then again coining money by this or that chance speculation : but his hands had still the old trick—the money slipped through them—no poor man nor woman crossed his path who was not the richer for it, and often his last shilling went with the rest.

It was nothing Charley said—he would get more some way; and so he did, but it was often some very hard way.   But he seemed rather to like bad fortune, and put his shoulder to the wheel with the same desperate energy, no matter how small the benefit accruing to himself, or if, indeed, the advantage were all another's—poor Charley ! there was no method in his nature—all was just as it chanced.

Up and down the world were scores of people who had enjoyed his liberality, and said, " What a good, careless fellow he is !" and forgotten him, for though a genial companion, the impression he left was generally evanescent.   There was not in his character strength and power enough to leave its impress on others fixed and well-defined.

Luther never, with all the advantages of education and manners, prospective wealth and respectability of position, and beloved, as he knew himself to be, felt quite easy in the presence of the self-cultured and really noble-hearted Charley. He invariably spoke of him as one so much his inferior as by no possibility to come in competition with him, but when they met, Charley compelled from him an acknowledgment of social equality. For it is hard to frown in the face that smiles upon us confidingly, or to draw back our hand from a cordial grasp. But he was careful to repeat to Myrie whatever stories of Charley's improvidence he could hear, doubtless with no intention to exaggerate, and yet the character of Charley never shone the brighter for his handling.

If he had ever said, "My dear Myrie, I am ashamed of the weakness ; but I am pained, jealous if you will, when I see you so much entertained by the adventurous tales of Charley Robinson, for I fear the glow of his really generous nature makes my selfishness seem all the darker." If he had said this, or anything like this, Myrie would have told him frankly and truly that Charley was to her like some poor brother who had shared all the hardships of her cabin-home, and with whom her sympathy, in consequence of shared pain and poverty, was very close ; that it seemed her duty as well as pleasure to be to him strength and comfort—to make, as it were, a dewy morning in the weary workday of his life ; for lightly as he talked, and gayly as he laughed over the struggles he had had with adversity, she knew that it was not in human nature to be insensible to suffering—that "the flesh will quiver where the pincers tear," however the martyr may suppress the groans.

But such was not the course of Luther Brisbane ; he would

not confess the weakness of fearing any man, but strove to make void his real fear by pretence of its non-existence ; and by the frequent assertion of supremacy and declaration of his dislike of Charley, he called out defences from Myrie, which she would never otherwise have made ; and whatever woman is required to defend, she speedily learns to love ; so, whatever, coolness Luther showed the young man, she atoned for by a double warmth.

When Luther went away to college it was with a heart quite at rest. Charley was gone, Heaven only knew where. When he came to say good bye to Luther that young man had treated him with unusual cordiality—he quite received him into friendship, even to confidence ; it is to be hoped he did not know the full extent of the harm he was doing, that he was in truth but softening a heart that he might press the thorn down deep.

As they sat under the summer trees together, the young collegian unfolded to his pleased listener the plan of his future life, the crowning bliss of which was, of course, to be his marriage with Myrie, to whom he was already betrothed.

The next day Charley was gone from the neighborhood, no one knew why nor where. The full moon that had shone so brightly over the lovers the night past had lighted his lonesome steps—anywhere he cared not, so it was to new scenes and new adventures ; yet every step that divided him from Myrie, stirred the thorn that was in his heart, and made it bleed afresh. Poor, poor Charley !

There is a sort of love, if love it may be called, that only lives upon opposition—it will break down every barrier, climb to every height, and descend to every depth, to obtain its object, or in other words to triumph—it is like the boy's passion for the butterfly, prompting the chase through brier and bush, up steep places, and over rough grounds—but when the treasure is captured, the passion dies—the pretty wings, handled roughly, lose all their beauty ; and feeble and spiritless, the insect is let go to creep and flutter as it can, admired of its captor never more. It is, perhaps, wrong to call what is only love of power, love—but I have called it so, because it is a counterfeit that passes current in most places. Selfish natures, wishing to subdue all things to their own interests, are apt, I think, to deceive themselves ; and it is not that those men are hypocrites beyond all others who smile, and smile, and murder while they smile, but simply more ambitious of subjugating others to themselves. It may be that Luther so deceived himself.

After the first sorrow of separation, no bird in the meadows was so happy as Myrie ; you might hear her singing under the trees, and skipping nimbly about the garden, now telling the dog about his absent master ; sometimes, indeed, she would sit in her chamber for an hour or more ; but if you could have peeped over her shoulder, you would have seen that she was writing and rewriting letter after letter, and yet all the same letter ; for one and all began with " Luther, dear Luther," and ended with " Luther, dear Luther." She was trying to maker her letter good enough to send to him—poor, sweet child !

He had not gone three days, when she began to watch anxiously for Mr. Brisbane as he returned evenings from the village where the post-office was ; he might bring a letter, she thought ; indeed it was the most likely thing in the world, that

Luther would seize the first spare moment, and, perhaps, from the first inn at which he should stop send back a line to say how he thought of her every waking moment, and dreamed of her every sleeping one, and pined to be back in the past, or away in the reunion of the distant future. She was more troubled for Luther than for herself—she had so many comforts of which he was deprived. Could she not sit in the shade of the very tree where they had sat so often—read the poems they had read together ; and were not these things the accessories of a closer spiritual communion than he could have ? Ah, yes ! Luther had the hardest—had, indeed, all the suffering. She had flowers, and books and walks, and a thousand things to assure her and reassure her ; but Luther, poor Luther, could see no evidence of the blessed past out of his own heart. That, she knew, was filled to aching fullness with its honied sweets ; and she saw that the pleasure of new sensations and new experiences were his—that his zest of mere animal life was much keener than hers—that he had, too, the sustaining stimulus of prospective endeavor and triumph ; but with all, and for all, Luther, poor Luther, had the worst of it.

After the few first evenings, Myrie prolonged her watches by beginning them an hour too soon ; and when in the distance she saw her guardian approaching, she could not stay within doors any longer, but would go out to meet him—at first only to the gate, then to the next hill, and so further and further as the nights went by and no letter came.

She never said she had come for anything, or expected any thing ; but the smile and eager look with which she always met Luther's father would presently fade away, and, taking his hand, she would walk beside him, looking on the ground, and speaking not a word. If asked what the matter was, she would say, " Nothing," and that was all.

The color began to fade in her cheeks, except now and then when they flushed with the old brightness at the thought of Luther's constancy, or with her own shame for indulging a doubt. Were there not a thousand reasons for his silence—the hurry and confusion of settlement, and all the engrossing occupations of a new life's beginning. She had been foolishly exacting, and would wait her lover's leisure and pleasure more patiently. Then the fearful thought would come that he might be ill, for love is of all passions most tormenting ; and in measuring the strength of his attachment by her own, she could not by any possibility reconcile herself to the silence. She could not have thus kept *him* waiting, if life and liberty were hers, no matter what else intervened. Then would come the thought of forgetfulness and desertion, and the mental and bodily prostration would be followed by the bitter energy of reacting despair ; but this came at moments and at intervals, and for the most part she felt that some dreadful calamity had befallen her darling ; for, underlying all possibilities and probabilities, was the deep-seated conviction that, whatever her sufferings, he had the worst of it.

One week—two weeks—ten days—nearly two weeks were gone. The caty-dids in the top of the high pear-tree that grew near the door were noisily welcoming in the early autumn, and in the distant woods the winds were making that moaning murmur that comes when the glory of summer is gone : the sunshine was lessening on the hills, and the gladness in Myrie's heart was lessening like it. She had scarcely spoken all day, and yet she was not ill, she said, nor sad ; and to every inquiry as to her disaffection, the reply was, " Nothing, nothing."

Mrs. Brisbane, kind, motherly soul, put down her sewing more than once, and laying her cool, moist hands on the girl's forehead, besought her to lie down for a little while—to taste of cordial, or to walk among the late garden flowers, and try to steal from their beauty some color for her cheeks.

Myrie's eyes would fill with tears ; but she would say she was very well and very happy, and remain quietly gazing away across the fading woods and hill-tops—she herself knew not where. It was not the cordial, nor the walk, nor the bodily rest she required. Poor Myrie !

She thought now, as the sun went down, she was watching the fading light, and the motion of the leaves, and the darting hither and thither of the night-hawks, that were come out an hour before their time ; but all the time her eyes kept gazing in one direction ; and if the look fixed itself nowhere, it took in nearly all the dusty length of the road till it wound down among the hills beyond the village, where the one spire, beautifully white, held up its glittering cross. She wondered how Mrs. Brisbane smiled so cheerfully, and went about the house possessing her soul in peace—how could she be so calm and fearless of harm, saying lightly, when she spoke of Luther, that it was enough, like the boy, to remember them only when he needed them.

The sun went down, and the owl hooted dismally, as if in mockery of all gayer sounds, and still Myrie kept the old position. She would not go to the gate even to meet her guardian that night ; she was trying to believe she was no longer hopefully expectant, as if she could shut her heart from her heart.

Foolish girl ! Many hills were yet between them when she saw him, and though, to fortify herself against disappointment, she told her soul over and over that he would not have any letter —and if he had, it would not be for her—the first approaching footfalls made her heart beat the brightest color up to her cheek that had been there for days and days.

She would not turn her eyes towards her guardian as he came in ; but when he said, "here is a letter from Lu," there was an involuntary reaching out of her hand, and such an exclamation of joy as one might make if the dead were brought to life. It was a very little sheet of note-paper, folded neatly, and addressed simply, "For Myrie." "How did you get it !" and "could it come to me this way?" were Myrie's first happy exclamations ; and when she learned from her guardian that it had been inclosed in the envelope containing one to himself, the first enthusiasm was gone. She hardly knew why, but she would rather have broken the seal, and that the superscription had been all to herself.

"And how does he excuse himself for not having written till this late day ?" inquired the mother, still evenly drawing up the threads of her sewing work.

"Let me see what he does say," replied the father, and, adjusting his spectacles, he unfolded the letter, and placing the candle between it and himself, read aloud slowly :—"'Dear parents, I have been too busy and too happy to write.'"

"There, Myrie," exclaimed Mrs. Brisbane, interrupting the reading, "I told you so !"

"I know it," replied the girl, and, crushing the letter she held, glided out of the house, the bitter waters that had been stirring in her heart, brimming over her eyes.

The moon came out of the lonesome woods, and looked down on her tenderly and sadly, and climbed higher and higher to the middle of the great quiet sky before she arose from the seat she had taken under the low apple tree—the same on which she sat when Charlie stooped over her, and with one kiss turned heavy-hearted away—how heavy-hearted she felt now for the first time, for she suffered now with a kindred pang. It was as if her tears, watering a hitherto unnoticed bud, caused it to burst open, and she saw what manner of flower it might have been.

Then, as she smoothed out the as yet unopened note, and with a step steadier than that with which she came, turned towards the house, came the thought that had come to her once before, when she was a little girl. "Charley would not have done so." But where was he? She could not tell; but in her heart she wished heaven would keep him and guide him back some time, and with no conscious significance, she sang, as she walked under the moonlight, "Jamie's on the stormy Sea." Who shall say that thoughts go not like arrows to their marks, and leave their impress more or less deep, as spirits are kindred or impressible.

Luther did not say to Myrie he had been too busy and too happy to write—he did not intimate any thought of her expectation of a letter earlier, or of one at all indeed. True, he began with "Dear Myrie;" but to the reader the words seemed dead, as it were—there was no earnest and deep meaning in them. He expressed no fear of her unfaithfulness—there was nothing to be faithful to, as the letter suggested—no concern lest she might be unhappy—of course she was happy—why should she not be? Life was before her, and the choice of her own way—thus implying freedom from any obligation to him. He did not say he thought of the old walks, or repeated the old poems ; but the entire letter was in a light, flippant strain, and chiefly about himself, his occupations, plans, and prospects, with some allusion to the weather, an attempted description of the scenery about his new residence, ending in an elaborate account of one of his professors, meant to be exceedingly funny.

He hoped Myrie would write at her leisure and inclination, and tell him all the news of her little world ; and if she found herself oppressed with any superfluous amount of tenderness, after duly caring for Brave (the dog), her birds and flowers, she might bestow it upon him if she could so far forget his unworthiness, and so oblige her devoted friend and humble servant—Luther Brisbane. No abbreviation from, nor addition to, the full and simple name—just as he would have written to any one else. The butterfly had opened its wings wide before him—had nestled close in his bosom—he had counted all its rings of gold and brown, and was willing, nay, glad, to toss it off his hand.

Strong in health and strong in hope, selfish, proud, and ambitious, we must let him alone ; he will learn, perhaps, by and by, that affection has taken deeper root in his heart than as yet he is aware of.

Sometimes Myrie thought she would not write at all—then she would make bitter accusations, and by showing him how desolate and broken, and altogether helpless her heart was, make him, perforce, take it up tenderly, as of old. Then again she resolved to affect indifference, and reply to his careless and flippant letter in a tone as careless and flippant as his own.

Hope and despair, and much suffering, doubtless, ran through all this unsteadiness of purpose, and whether she in the end adopted a middle course—now silent, and now speaking, half coldness and half fondness—I know not, but think this course likeliest; one thing, however, is certain, the less strength Luther gave her to lean upon, the more she leaned upon herself. Choke up the fountain in one direction, and it will make itself a channel in another; and unless the living waters of love be dried up at their source, as sometimes happens, they will flow over something, not unlikely over weeds as well as flowers.

More than a year had passed since Luther went away, and Myrie was coming at sunset along the dusty path by the roadside, looking thoughtfully and walking slowly—perhaps she dreaded to say at home that she had no letter from Luther— and this was the ninth week since the last one came.

Hard struck the hoofs of a fast rider on the clay of the beaten and sunbaked road—nearer and nearer they sounded, and the shadows of the gay horse and hasty rider were just before her, she turned into the deep dusty weeds and thick shadows of the low elms that grew by the road-side. The hands that lay on her bosom, one on the other were suddenly unclasped, and a voice to which joy lent so solemn and so deep a music that she scarcely recognized it for Charley's, said "Myrie!"—how often we turn aside like her and so meet our fate!

When Myrie wrote next to Luther she told him (who shall say why or wherefore?) that the social enjoyments of the neighborhood had been greatly quickened by the unexpected return of Charles Robinson; and she added, as a pleasant bit of information, perhaps, that his growth of manly beauty and mental stature were alike remarkable. This was all or nearly all, she said about Charley ; nevertheless, it was sufficient to rouse the old jealousy, and make Luther himself again. The return mail brought a long letter, assuming all the old authority, if less than the old love.

Night and morning Myrie was heard singing again in her chamber, in the garden, up and down the dooryard walks. The leaves faded and fell, and the sun rose and set in the dull glory that comes duly with the dying year ; but the winds were now pleasant companions to the heart that thought them so lonesome the year past.

Not unfrequently Charley sat at the supper-table and told stories, less perhaps, for the good old folks than for Myrie, and often in the moonlight, under the trees at the door, he sat with her alone, telling stories still ; and under all, felt by both, but spoken not, was the one story which he did not tell.

Suddenly, without intimation or excuse, Luther appeared at the old homestead. Without excuse, I said, though *he* said he was suffering from ill health, and required relaxation and quietude. Whether in ill health or not, it is quite certain he came in ill humor, and that poor Myrie was from the first the recipient of it. He had grown handsome, grave, and reserved ; but there was one subject which darkened all the beauty of his face with frowns, and swept away his reserve with a torrent of angry denunciation—nothing connected with Charles Robinson would he suffer to be mentioned in his presence, and yet himself made the most constant allusions to him. He was astonished that his mother should find entertainment in the inflated inventions which the vagabond Charley was in the habit of passing off as experiences. It was quite proper, to be sure, to show a certain civility to inferiors ; but when they presumed upon it as did this vulgar person, it was time to put some protecting restraint upon politeness ; he could plainly see, though no one else could, a pitiful deterioration in the morality of the neighborhood within the year past, and who so blind as not to know to whom to trace it all. Why, nobody could be so blind ; he was very sure Myrie could not, she was quite too sensible, too capable of higher appreciation ; he was not in the least afraid of her being misled by the pleasantries of a mere adventurer—by what he was sure she knew was but the shining of rottenness. Oh no, it was not for her he feared ; but for the artless and unsuspecting village girls, not one of whom would be suffered to escape the serpent's fascinations. He had one sure hope, however—doubtless the spendthrift would soon find himself reduced to his customary shameful poverty, and have perforce, to make another recruiting expedition, and relieve the neighborhood of his presence, while he pursued his trade of begging, borrowing, or stealing. Luther was not certain whether to one or to all the said makeshifts Charles Robinson was addicted.

Some such tirade as this he concluded one day by saying, " Perhaps Myrie can tell."

Myrie smiled quietly, and replied, " that as it did not especially concern her to know in what particular manner Charley possessed himself of money, she had never made it a subject of speculation much less of inquiry ; she doubted not that it was fairly won ; for one thing she had admiringly observed of Charley, and that was that when he could not speak of man or woman in honest approval, he was always generously silent."

" And so you own to me," said Luther, biting his lip, " that you admire this profligate who calls himself Robinson ?"

"I admire his abstinence from evil speaking;" and seeing the frown gathering darker and darker in the face of Luther, she continued, perhaps with the perverseness and daring of which we all have our share, "he has many noble and generous qualities which I admire, and which I wish were more common." She hesitated a little on the close of the sentence, and Luther taking it up, said sneeringly, "which you wish I possessed—thank you, Miss Almira."

Now Luther had never once said Almira, much less *Miss* Almira, since the day of their first acquaintance, and she smiled again at the meaning formality. She made no other reply, and Luther continued, in deepening anger, "Perhaps you would have me say Miss Curtiss—I will endeavor to gratify you, though the associations are anything but agreeable to me." Myrie's eyes flashed with fiery indignation; but the thought of her sweet, patient, dead mother, who in all the trial of her hard life had never dishonored that name, put out the fires with moisture, if not with tears, and she answered with a slow speech, that showed she weighed the words as she uttered them; "As to what you shall call me, please yourself—hereafter you can neither please nor displease me." As she finished speaking, she arose and turned to leave him.

"One moment, Myrie," said Luther, startled into something like earnestness, "one moment, till I explain—truly I did not intend to convey the meaning you have received." Myrie turned half round and said, "One moment would not serve to explain away the bitter meaning of your words—I will give you a year; yes, twenty of them, if I live so long, to devise an apology."

"I wonder" said Mrs. Brisbane, who had come to the door

to thread her needle, and smiling on Myrie as she passed, " I wonder what can be burning ; there is such a great smoke across the fields, and it seems to me just about where your mother's house used to stand. I hope no accident has happened."

Glad of an excuse to be alone, Myrie said she would go and see.

There are times in life when the saddest memories are comforting ; from the aching of some present grief they draw us away, and casting a shadow over all our life, make the cloud and the night less gloomily visible. So as Myrie walked on and on, she tried to define distinctly the almost forgotten memories of her childish life ; but it was only some isolated experience here and there, which had been deepened she knew not how, that she could bring distinctly out of the almost forgotten past of early childhood. Gradually she could make the picture more clear—so clear that she trod softly, lest the rough stubbly way should hurt her feet, for she seemed a little girl again, a poor bare-footed little girl, and almost believed herself going home with the scanty earnings of her mother's hard week's work. She could almost see the pale, anxious face at the window, the narrow, hard-beaten path leading up to the door, the hearth-stones and the fire, the one better chair than the rest, the floor so white and so nice, the whitewashed wall, and her own two or three faded dresses hanging against it. Quite unconscious of time and distance, she kept on walking and musing as she walked, till the summit of the slope, on which stood the little house where she was born, was reached.

A look of bewilderment displaced the one of sorrow that had been deepening in her face all the way. Could she be mistaken ?   No ! surely that was the hill, that was the very clump of trees, under which she remembered to have played many a time, while her mother sat by and sewed ; the very trees under which that mother's coffin had rested, when she for the last time looked upon her ; there was the little house itself, the same, yet not the same. New porches, and new roof, and new blinds, and new paint had so completely changed it, that had she seen it elsewhere, it would scarcely have reminded her of her birthplace. The trees were newly trimmed, the briers removed from the rear grounds, and these it was which made the smoke that showed so far away. The sod was shaven smooth, and the old rose-bushes, carefully pruned and tied together. She was not yet done surveying the scene in astonishment when, as her eyes ran down the walk, she saw Charley Robinson coming forth to meet and welcome her.

"Come in," he said, a smile of joy illuminating all his face, while Myrie was yet in the midst of delighted exclamations that her poor old home could be made to look like such a paradise. "Come in and see how you like my style of furnishing."

How pretty it all was ! just as she would have done it herself.   Curtains so fine and so white, chairs and tables so small and so neat, just as if they had been made for the very cottage they adorned ; and the carpet ! what a pattern of beauty —a green ground, dotted with bright red roses ! Who could have chosen it ? Was it Charley, and simply to please himself ?

"No, dear Myrie, it was to please you. I thought you would like to see the old place looking bright and comfortable, and that you would perhaps come and see me sometimes, for I am going to live here, and be a sober farmer hereafter."

There was a mingling of sad and joyful sensations in Myrie's, heart as she walked home, for it had been a long while that the love had been lessening for Luther, the liking increasing for Charley ; and she could not help saying over and over, as she remembered what seemed—whether it were so or not—the taunt of her early poverty, " Charley would not have done so !" and had he not now given her living proof of his kinder and nobler disposition ? How much tenderness and poetry were concealed in his careless and seemingly unsusceptible nature, after all.

It was after midnight when she went to sleep, and then with a confused image in her mind that was neither Luther nor Charley—partly one and partly the other ; for so sometimes it seems as if we surrendered to fate, and as for ourselves had no choice in the matter. To us all there come seasons when one thing seems little better than another ; when there is nothing that seems very bright, or very much worth having.

And so, says the reader, they were married, Myrie and Charley, and lived very happy, and Luther remained a discontented old bachelor all his life as he deserved to. You may as well say so at once, for I see that will be the end.

Now, dear reader, I am not a story-*maker* ; if I were I should perhaps shape fortunes more smoothly sometimes ; often what would seem to me more equitably just ; but I am simply the writer of stories life has made for me, and life's stories or life's histories do not always run as we would suppose they would, or as we would have them. Now in shadow, now in sunshine ; now where it is extremely rough, and then, for a little while, along smooth ground, we go on and on, and lose ourselves in the silent sea.

Myrie's life was not very different from the rest, nor was Charley's, though his ran faster, and was sooner lost to the windings and shadows of time than are some others ; perhaps, however, he had his share of the sunshine—who shall tell ?

A letter from Luther's 'mother was laid one day on his table where he sat composing what he hoped to be a graduating honor. The letter was superscribed in the usually clear and steady hand of his mother, which seemed to say, plainly enough, that all at home was well. That was all Luther cared to know ; so he thought, and so the letter lay till he penned sentence after sentence. Coming to the foot of a page, he glanced along it with a satisfied smile, tossed it aside, leaned back in his chair for a little respite, and broke the seal of his mother's letter. For a moment he thought he saw this great, shining world dizzily drifting away from him ; he involuntarily reached out his hand and caught at nothing ; there was nothing left to catch hold of—aching, empty darkness, that was all ! He might not be Luther Brisbane, and that fair writing before him might not be a prize essay : it was nonsense—nothing : himself was nothing for all he knew. With one hand he swept letters and papers together, locked them in the desk and walked out, perhaps to see if the world were really gone, and himself and his little dusty room all that were left.

Luther did not know—none of us know—what a great hope

is to us until it is dead. Not till we take it up and find how cold it is, and how heavy it is, and that we have nothing to do but to bury it, do we, or can we know.

He learned then how much all his future life had been colored by the dream of his love ; he saw for what all his strife had been ; now there was nothing for which to strive. Notwithstanding the estrangement, he had never thought of home disconnected from Myrie ; she was not there, and his mother said she rejoiced while she mourned—rejoiced that Myrie was so happily mated, and living so near, and yet sad for the breaking up of the different future she had planned for her. She did not say what that future was. Luther's own heart told him what it was. "I cannot be sad," the letter concluded, "when I see our darling the crowning beauty of her beautiful home."

Here, then, was something to catch hold of. When Luther re-read the letter, he lingered a long time upon those closing words. "So, then," thought he, "Myrie is happy ; I wonder if it will not send a shadow across her threshold when she hears of what honors I am come to," and he carefully adjusted the papers containing what was to be the prize essay. "And this is the strength of woman's attachment, is it ?" he went on ; "they are all artful and fickle alike—not worth regretting—in fact, I consider myself a fortunate man."

And as the disappointed student mused, he tore his mother's letter into little slips and scattered it to the winds, saying, "so perish my boyish fancy, and now for a career of ambition, of manly effort—now for a life that *is* a life ;" and he concluded with a flat contradiction of all he had said by exclaiming, "I'll see if she can forget me ! I'll be a man yet, she might have been proud of ! I'll make her see, and make the world see, that I am sufficient to myself ! Men shall not think of naming me in the same breath—not in the same day—with Charley Robinson."

So Luther resumed his pen, and a vehement and nervous energy mortised the words one to another, as all his artistic ability could not previously have done.

If we could see the influences that sometimes work out fine results, we should be sadly taken aback. It is not best, perhaps, to inquire too far, but to enjoy the shadow without having first pryed into the tree's heart, to see if that be sound. The blackest cloud gives out the brightest lightning ; the grass grows greenest and highest where the carcass lay. The thought of the applause of men may have mingled with the most beautiful charities, and stimulated the missionary to do his work, the martyr to do his.

Certain it is, Luther Brisbane made a fine speech on the sufficiency of the mind to itself, showing very clearly, and to the satisfaction of most who heard him, that the bitterest experiences and sharpest disappointments of life are but the steps by which it goes up and on—the breaking of the heart's idol but the breaking of a child's toy—suffering, all privation, of whatever sort, but the process of education towards higher and wider knowledge.

Many faint-hearted striplings went home that day, built up in hope and encouraged in faith ; with cheeks glowing, and eyes resting on some bright Eden in the future, between which and themselves they were determined, just then, nothing should intervene.

Luther, meantime, victor where all were honored, with con-

gratulations ringing in his ears, and the smile of a proud satisfaction shining on him from his parents, shut himself away from
all who sought his company, buried his face in his pillow, and—
shall I say to the honor or the shame of manhood?—wet it
with his tears. On the whole, I think it were better said, to
manhood's honor, he wept; for it is the weaknesses of our
fellows more than their strength that endears them to us; we
love those who need our help more than those who need no
support.

Myrie sat at the window of her pretty cottage, glancing from
her sewing work now and then down the walk; it was time
for Charley to come home from the village. She had not
waited long (for Charley was a good husband, and never
kept her waiting long) when she heard his quick step
coming.

"I have kept you waiting, Myrie," he said, shaking back his
curly hair; "but never mind, I have brought you something
that will more than pay you. I waited for the mail, and here
is Luther Brisbane's prize-essay."

He threw it in her lap, and went on: "Put down your work,
my dear, and read it; everybody is praising Luther, and I
almost feared to bring you this, for it throws me all in the
shadow; indeed, Myrie, I don't know how it was you ever saw
anything in me to admire!" He spoke lightly, but the moisture
came to his eyes, and affirmed that he was not idly depreciating
himself.

"O Charley," said Myrie, putting the grand essay aside, and
her arm about his neck, "I should love you for your generosity,
if you had not one of your other thousand good and admirable
qualities." After a moment she added, "Luther is not great

enough to praise *you;* but no matter about him at all ; let us go water the flowers while the tea is making."

And in their cheerful and healthful occupation they presently forgot all about Luther Brisbane ; and when, the following evening, Charley read the prize-essay aloud, Myrie said she had not thought of it since he brought it home.

If Luther could have heard her say s o, he would have taken another upward step, perhaps, in his long and bright progress.

When Mrs. Brisbane came to drink tea with Myrie she said she had hoped to bring Luther with her, but that he had been complaining all the day of headache, and did not look a bit well, poor boy—and besides, he had taken a long walk in the morning, and felt quite overcome.   Had he seen Myrie's white curtains gleaming through the roses, and heard the music of her voice as she called across the hill to the good and loving Charley ?   Perhaps so.

The next day—not when Charley saw her, however—Myrie gathered the prettiest bunch of flowers she could cull from all her choice collection, and sent it to the indisposed Luther. Was it in the hope they would wake " disagreeable associations ?" or was it to show him that she had so far outgrown her childish fancy as to regard him only as a sick neighbor, whom she would fain do kindly by ?

Why should we pry into what it does not concern us to know ?   Let us for once leave vulgar curiosity, and receive simply that " Mrs. Robinson sends Mr. Brisbane some flowers, with her very kind regards."   So the errand-boy said, and that is all we have to do with it.   Daily, Luther made long walks about the neighborhood, and on each return his mother inquired whether he had been to see Myrie ; and again and again he replied that it was too late or too early, or that his walk had been in a different direction ; and perhaps these answers were all made in good faith—at any rate, it does not concern us to know.

His stay at home was brief, and his visit confined chiefly to his parents, avoiding all society in as far as was possible. The momentary enthusiasm created by his prize-essay went down wonderfully during that brief visit. He was grown so unsocial, the villagers said—too proud to recognize them any more. What else could they infer, seeing not the heart of the young man, and how indifferent it was become to all things.

One young lady of the village, who had admiringly read the essay half a dozen times, growing enthusiastic at each reading, and essaying her own powers on some too ambitious theme— which, alas ! only showed how insufficient, as yet, her mind was for her task—resolved that Luther should be brought within the magic circle of female influence ; and, after a great deal of coaxing of the old folks, leave for a little merry-making was obtained. But vain are all human calculations, as the ambitious young woman found ; for after all the preparation, and all the expectation, there came at the latest hour, and when hope was weary with standing tiptoe—not Luther, but a message from his mother, saying that increasing debility had hurried his departure beyond his design. She was only comforted for his absence—for he was gone, perhaps, for years—in the hope of his restoration to health.

Poor young man ! said one and another; and while they talked of him other young men came, and thought turned back into light and lively channels, and Luther Brisbane was forgotten. He might have left deeper impressions if he had chosen to do so ; but easy acquisitions were not among the things he valued ; and nothing would so surely have kept him away from the little festival as the knowledge that he was anxiously expected there. The hearts of the best of us are sadly perverse, I am afraid.

December was come, the seventh one since Myric was married, and far out over the sunset-snow gleamed the bright, warm light through her windows. The maid was busy preparing the tea-table, stopping now and then to give the cradle a tip, or to slap together her strong brown hands in the face of the baby, that was old enough now to sit up and look about and smile—and she did look about almost constantly, seemingly to be all the time wondering what manner of world she was come into. Her brown eyes were browner than her mother's, as it were with melancholy shadows ; and her hair, thick and dark, hung a hand's breadth over her neck, or shoulders rather, for it was not much of a neck that little Lucy had. She sat up in the cradle, not looking in the fire, as she often did, but keeping her eyes steadily towards the door, and her white fingers working one with another, as if she were anxiously looking for her father to come. The maid might slap her hands merrily as she would, pull her hair, or shake the cradle like a playful storm, the child would not laugh, scarcely smile ; nor could any device turn her for more than a moment from her watching at the door. Once or twice, when the wind rattled the shutters, and drifted from the eave a light cloud of snow, a shudder passed over her, and she looked beseechingly at her mother, who, talking through her to the maid, kept watch beside her. Warm and bright, and cheerful the room was, and nothing was wanting to make it a perfect picture of a happy home but the coming of Charley, who had been away all day. Myrie looked often down the snow-path, and seeing him not, stitched on with nervous energy, and looked again, and stitched again faster than before.

Shadows crept over the snow where the sunshine had been, and the wind calmed itself down into keen and biting stillness—deeper grew the shadows, and deeper, and it was night. The sewing had been changed to the book, and the book had been opened and closed a dozen times, and was at last laid on the shelf; and stooping over the cradle, the young mother, perhaps to strengthen herself, told the baby again and again that father was coming—now he was almost come to Mr. Brisbane's house, and now he was past it—now he was on such a hill, and now riding beneath such a tree—now just in sight and now coming up the path; and so she would lift the baby up to see him; but no, he was not there—all was still and cold, and white. Presently there was a stamping at the door. Myrie hurried to open it, and the baby reached out its hands; but it was not the husband and father. Neighbor Brisbane was come to talk with him about some proposed improvement in the village—that was all: for Charles Robinson was looked upon as the most public-spirited and liberal of the people among whom he lived; and it was largely owing to his generous encouragement and aid that the new school-house was built, and the meeting-house, and the Lyceum-hall, and the turnpike-road; in fact, and in short, that the village was the pretty, and populous and thrifty village it was. Mr. Brisbane said he had heard of the failure of a great bank in town, and he feared it was business connected with that which kept Charley so late. Any excuse was a relief to Myrie, and she felt for a moment that if that were all she should not care, even though every cent were gone with the bank. Mr. Brisbane said, too, that it was reported that Peter Mendenhall had run away, but that he hoped it was not true. Myrie said she hoped not ; but just then she cared very little whether or not Peter Mendenhall had run away with the thousand dollars Charley had lent him. Once or twice neighbor Brisbane arose to go ; but Myrie said so earnestly, " Won't you wait a little longer ? I am sure he will come "—that he stayed more for her sake than to talk with Charley.

At last they sat by the fire very still, for it is hard for one to keep up talk where there are two, and for her life Myrie could not say anything but, " Why doesn't Charley come ? Oh ! why doesn't he come ?"

The baby was wide awake, quietly watching the door, when the gate-latch made a joyful sound ; then came a quick step, the door opened, and a stranger stood before them ; his clothes frozen stiff about him, and his words frozen too. He was come to tell the saddest news that ever can be told. Charley was dead. When he had ended the story the baby left its watching towards the door, and with lips curling and trembling with the bitter cry it did not make aloud, hid its face in the cradle-pillow and would not be comforted.

Poor Charley ! he had gone bravely, generously—just as he had lived.

As he was riding homeward, he saw a boy who was skating on the ice suddenly slip under, and springing to the ground, he plunged in, brought him up, bore him almost ashore, and with the effort that lodged him on safe ground, slipped himself, went down under, and was lost !

Poor, poor Charley !

"When the deep gives up its dead you will see him," said good Mr. Brisbane, and he laid his trembling hands on Myrie's head, stricken down with that sorrow which will not know hope ; for across the valley of the shadow of death hope travels slowly.

Misfortune comes not singly, it is often said, and I think there is truth in the saying. So it is with good fortune—an agreeable thing rarely comes to us isolated ; there is, perhaps, attractive power in a good thing for its kind, and in a bad thing for its kind, and so it comes that if we slip, our neighbor gives us a push ; and "if we have a sheep and a cow, everybody gives us good-morrow."

Mr. Brisbane's fears were not without foundation ; it was true that Peter Mendenhall had run away, and that the bank where Charley Robinson had put his money for safe keeping (and so done what everybody said was a very wise thing in Charley Robinson) was gone to ruin, and Mrs. Robinson saw herself a widow, with poverty, if not actually at the door, coming thither very fast. She knew nothing about self-reliance, and it is not easy to stretch one's self up to an equality with fate, especially when there is a great sorrow dragging us down. We are more likely to sit and nurse our woes, most of us, till necessity says, "arise or perish," than to gather up our courage and press on alone. So sat poor Myrie, a long, long time.

The ring which Luther had given her on the day of betrothal she had always worn on the finger with the wedding ring ; but now, as if it were a wrong to poor Charley, she took it off, and wore only the wedding-ring. Every book he had liked was preserved with scrupulous care, every flower he had planted tended better than the rest, and her best comfort was in telling the little Lucy what a good father she had had, and how many things he would have done for her if he had lived, and in asking her over and over if she remembered how he looked, or any word he had ever said to her ; and whether it were from hearing it so often, I know not, but the child learned to say father long before she could say mother.

When the little girl could run about, she looked like another Myrie. Her faded dresses and bare feet looked like hers too ; her brown eyes only had more sadness and less sparkle than her mother's had at the same time of life.

We are soon forgotten when we cease to minister to the happiness of others, and a great deal of beauty is reflected in the face sometimes from a costly dress ; certain it is, Myrie was never praised any more except for her nice needle-work, which was more in demand than her company, when the table that used to be so bountifully spread was left against the wall, and nothing more than bread and butter on it.

The pretty cottage and the grounds went out of repair, and one room was let, and then another, till finally there was but one poor chamber left for Myrie and her little girl.

And the village grew and flourished, and children grew to " fair women and brave men." Lucy grew with the rest in beauty as well as height, but nobody thought of calling Lucy beautiful. Laurie Morton, who had a rough red face and an impudent stare, was thought to be a great beauty ; everybody saw her big costly ear-rings, and nobody saw her big ugly ears ; her father was a very rich man, and of course Laurie's beauty could not be questioned.

Annie Clough, too, a white-haired pale-faced, slim young woman, with no particular expression in her grey eyes, but with a great deal of money prospectively in her purse, was thought to be of quite an elegant order of beauty, and a dozen children of the town were named Annie Clough, and lifted up to kiss the pale cheek of the young woman as often as possible. But Lucy Robinson had no namesakes, and only the winds kissed her fair cheeks. She was only the daughter of a widow, and a seamstress.

In the free-school and the Sunday-school she could say as good lessons as any of them ; but it *happened* she never won the first prize, nor the second. Her quiet manner, and wealth of hair and soft and wondrous eyes, were not so striking to the vulgar gaze as the broad bright stripes of Laurie Morton's dresses, or the dead pallor of Annie Clough.

The day Lucy was fifteen years old, she came home from school with her eyes more filled with shadows than their wont, and, turning her face from her mother, bent low over her open book. Bending at her weary task sat the mother, as she had sat all day long. At length, drawing a long breath of relief, and breaking her thread, she said, " What is the matter, my child ?"

Lucy replied that she had studied hard that day and knew her lessons quite perfectly, and yet had received more bad marks than good ones.

" Well, never mind," said the mother ; " but tie on your bonnet and carry home this bundle of work, for you know how badly the money is needed—indeed, we have no tea nor bread to-night."

It was a pretty collar for Annie Clough, and a gay skirt

for Laurie Morton, that Mrs. Robinson had just finished ; and half smiling and half crying, Lucy took the parcel and did as she was directed ; but when she returned, half an hour later, the smile was wholly gone—she was crying outright. Mrs. Morton had said nothing about paying for the work, and Miss Clough was not at home. "I met her, though," said Lucy, " walking with Laurie Morton, and neither of them noticed me at all." Mother and daughter went supperless to bed that night, and sad enough.

A night or two after this, Lucy brought home most of her books—there would not be any school the next day—there would be a great meeting of citizens in the afternoon, and a dinner, in honor of some distinguished gentleman and traveller who had just arrived. " Mrs. Morton, don't you think," continued Lucy, " is to give a fine ball ; and that is what you made the lace capes and things for, mother."

After a moment she added, pettishly, " Well, they may have their fine ball and their fine traveller too ; don't you say so, mother ?"

" Certainly, my child," replied Mrs. Robinson—and directly she asked Lucy if she knew who it was that was come ? " You read so much, you perhaps know something of him," she said.

Lucy tossed back her curls, quite contrary to her usual method of softly brushing them away, and replied that she never heard of him in her life, and that his name was Brisby, she believed. The quickened beating of Mrs. Robinson's heart caused the work to drop from her hands, and a bright, warm blush clouded the settled pallor of her cheek. She turned away, seeming to search for her lost needle, and asked Lucy again what she said the stranger's name was.

"Bushby," answered the girl, "I did not call it right before, did I ?"

Mrs. Robinson drew a long sigh—half of regret and half of relief, and presently putting down her work, unlocked a drawer, opened a miniature case, kissed the poor semblance of what was once Charley, and when she returned to her seat the quiet and the customary paleness were back again. But she did not work any more for a long while, and sat silent, rocking to and fro till the shadows had deepened into night, and till long after that.

Lucy brought her stool to her mother's feet presently, leaned her cheek on her knee, and with her long hair dropping down her neck and shoulder, and almost to the floor, fell asleep, quite unconscious of the strange tumult her careless words had awakened and stilled.

While they sat so, mother and child, in their dark little room, Mrs. Morton's fine house was full of lights and merriment. Laurie choked on the tea, and was obliged to leave the table in convulsions of laughter. "Dear Annie Clough," she exclaimed at length, "did you ever hear anything so preposterous ?" But that white little person had turned aside, and was concluding her laughter with a violent cough. Still holding both her sides, Laurie resumed her seat, and as soon as she could calm herself sufficiently, said, "Seriously, mother, it is not possible you thought of asking old widow Robinson and her girl ; a pretty figure they would make at our ball, wouldn't they. Why the widow is forty years old, ain't she ?"

"No, my dear ; not much more than thirty," answered Mrs. Morton, who was really a good and kind-hearted woman ; and she added, " when you young girls are thirty you will find your hearts feeling just as young as they do now, perhaps ; and besides, Mrs. Robinson and Mr. Brisbane were thought to be lovers once."

"Oh mother !" cried Laurie, and "Oh, Mrs. Morton, !" cried Annie ; "it is not possible !"

"Why, Mr. Brisbane is just in his prime, young enough for either of us, and Mrs. Robinson is an old woman."

Mrs. Morton repeated again that Mrs. Robinson could not be much beyond thirty, and going back to the time Lucy was born guessed at how old Myrie was then, and so guessed again at what Lucy's age must then be, and assured the laughing young ladies that Myrie Robinson could not be more than thirty-three.

"At any rate," said Laurie, "it would be an absurdity to ask her to our house to meet Mr. Brisbane. Why, he is the handsomest man I ever saw, and rich too, it is said, and she a poor old sewing woman—ridiculous !"

Mrs. Morton was half ashamed of her suggestion, and said she had not really thought of inviting Mrs. Robinson ; and to smoothe over, in some sort, the terrible absurdity of the thing, she related to the young ladies what she knew, and the much more she had heard, respecting the relations existing long ago between the handsome Mr. Brisbane and the widow.

They, however, could not believe there had ever been any serious attachment between them ; they knew, indeed, there could have been none on Mr. Brisbane's part. In short, they concluded the girl Myrie, as any other presuming dependent might foolishly do, had fallen in love with the elegant student, and probably married at last to cover the mortification of defeat.

Mrs. Morton said it was not unlikely, but she said it with an ill grace, and had evidently her own thoughts in the matter ; and when she arose from her nicely spread tea-table, she said, with some heartiness, she would go and see Myrie Robinson before a week, and her manner seemed to say, "Laugh as you will you cannot keep me from doing that."

Lively and busy times there were in the village, but Mrs. Robinson's little room was as still and as lonesome as usual. Lucy selected the poems in her school-books, and read them to her mother again and again ; sometimes she even ventured upon a song, but it generally ended in a sigh, for poor Lucy had no mates and no joys but her duties, and such reflective silences as were little suited to her years.

It was a sunshiny day of about the middle of August, that they saw, mother and child, through the dusty vines at the window, the many people hurrying to the grand reception, for which the school had given its recess, and for which so many preparations had been making the week past ; they saw as if they saw not, for it was not for them, poor and unmirthful, to have to do with festivals.

"Dear mother," spoke Lucy at last, "don't sew any more to-day ;" and with gentle force she took the work from her weary hands and folded it away. "No, no, my child," said the mother ; "what will become of us if I leave off working ?"

Lucy opened the hymn-book, one of the few books they had, and read :

> " Judge not the Lord by feeble sense,
> But trust him for his grace;
> Behind a frowning providence
> He hides a smiling face."

She added nothing, but the mother saw the beautiful and trusting light in her face, and suffered the work to be laid away.

"Dear good mother?" exclaimed the happy child, and pulling down her long hair, she combed and curled it as she saw it in the picture that was laid away. There was a gentle protest against the curls, but the mother yielded in that too, though when they were made she pushed them back half carelessly and half conscientiously, for she had worn her hair all put plainly away since Charley died. Lucy declared that her mother had actually added to the beautiful effect of the curls, and in her strangely playful and sunny mood brought forth from the drawer the white dress she so liked to see her mother wear. "Really," she said, standing apart and looking at her in loving admiration when she was dressed, "nobody would believe you were my mother, you look so young, and oh, so pretty !" and, indeed, they did look more like sisters than like mother and child. She tied on her hood directly, and, concealing a small basket under her apron, went out, saying only that she would be back in an hour or two. It was her habit to wander often about the woods and fields ; but it was not simply her own pleasure she was seeking that day. She saw everybody having a holiday, and, after her own fashion, she was trying to make one too, and the concealed basket she hoped to bring home full of berries—an addition to the supper which would happily surprise her mother ; but little did she then dream of *all* the happy surprise she was preparing for her. She knew well where the vines were, and that the berries were ripe to blackness ; but she turned her feet away from them, and hurried towards Mr. Brisbane's house, to ask the liberty which she knew would be cordially accorded. She did not see the old family carriage moving up the road, and Mrs. Brisbane, in her best black silk dress, seated so comfortably and so respectably beside her husband ; she was thinking where the ripest berries were, and of the nice supper they would have at home, and lightly crossing the porch, tapped on the door of the parlor, which stood ajar. "I have come to ask you, Mr. Brisbane," she said, stepping within the room, "if I might go to the hedge for berries."

Luther Brisbane—for it was he who was reading by the window—dropped the paper he held, and in his bewilderment said nothing.

Astonished at his silence, Lucy, rubbing her sunblinded eyes, drew nearer, saying, "Dear father (for she often called Mr. Brisbane so), what is the matter ?"

"My pretty child," he said, in tones tremulous with emotion, "you have mistaken me, I fear. I have no right to the name you call me." Blushing and ashamed, Lucy explained and apologized as well as she could, and having obtained leave to pick the berries, hurried away, scarcely in her confusion, having noticed the many questions the stranger asked in reference to her home and her mother. She reached the hedge and filled her basket before she was aware, so full of thoughts was her heart, and hastened home to relate her little adventure.

"Yes, yes," said Mrs. Robinson, "he came directly here and told me all about it ; he is an old friend of your mother's ; we were playmates you know ;" and she added, after a moment, that he had partly engaged to come back and drink tea with them ; but she hardly thought he would do so, he would receive so many better invitations. However, the supper was arranged for three, and not in vain ; that little room, with its loved inhabitants, was to Luther the brightest spot he had ever found.

Mrs. Morton's guests waited wearily for the most honored guest of all. At last he came, so late as to make necessary an apology. Laurie's bright flounces seemed to drop suddenly from their wide flaunting, and Miss Clough's white cheek grew still whiter, if possible, when they knew it was Mrs. Robinson who had come between them and their crowning pleasure.

" I told you so, young ladies," exclaimed Mrs. Morton, lifting one finger in sly exultation ; but Laurie stoutly maintained that she was the first to suggest the propriety of inviting Mrs. Robinson, and Annie Clough was quite sure she had seconded the proposal.

It was December again, the snow lay white and cold over all the ground ; the wind blew roughly, now and then scuding the flame down the chimney, and almost to the feet of Myrie and Luther, for we may call them so again, rattling the shutters, and sometimes driving quite through the broken pane. Myrie's hands were clasped together, and her eyes rested on the ground; but Luther's eyes were resting on her lovingly, tenderly, and his hands moving uneasily, as if they sought something. At length she raised her eyes and asked Luther—for woman is apt to be impatient of such silences—whether it was the rough night he was thinking of ?

" Myrie," said he, taking both her little hands in his, clasped together as they were, " do you remember once when I said— no matter what I said—something that was rash, boyish, foolish—wicked, I am afraid—and you gave me twenty years to frame an apology ?"

The trembling of Myrie's hands showed that she·remembered, but she said nothing, and he went on : " All those twenty years I have tried to frame that apology, and now I have only to throw myself on your goodness, your generosity ; for what I said there can be no apology made. Can you forgive me ?" The tears were in Myrie's eyes ; the deep humility of the strong, proud man had touched her heart, and, in a voice sweet and unsteady, she answered she had nothing to forgive, just as she would have answered twenty years before if he could only have bent his stubborn will to speak those simple words. How it ended the reader sees well enough, and I will only add that Lucy stammered and blushed anew when, an hour after the *apology*, Mr. Brisbane awoke her with a kiss—for with cheek resting on her arm she had been asleep all the evening—awoke her, and asking if she remembered calling him father by mistake when they first met, said that for the future it would be a mistake if she called him anything else, and that he hoped to merit at least some part of the affection and respect belonging to that name.

The ring of betrothal took its old place again, but the wedding-ring—Charley's, ring was never removed. Happy as mortals may expect to be, their lives glided on ; but in spite of all the brightness around her, in spite of all efforts to the contrary, some days were full of clouds and shadows to Myrie, and at such times she was sure to say Charley instead of Luther—*he* had spoken no word to her that it was not sweet to remember, and held to the last the purest place in her heart—let us not be curious to know whether the deepest or not, or if the glitter of gratified ambition and pride did not dissolve itself into a vain and foolish thing when set against the memory of a heartfelt smile. Of course Mrs. Brisbane became the pet and admiration of the people among whom she lived, especially among those who had been least conscious of her existence previously to her second marriage ; but " she had learned the world's cold wisdom " now, she had learned to pause and fear ; and doubtless it was well, else might her heart have been made vain by the constant adulation, and her life have been rather a strife to be great than good. As it was, she never forgot the instability of earthly things, or ceased from laying up treasures were moth and rust doth not corrupt. So we leave her with her wealth ; her husband, hospitable and stately ; her daughter, beautiful and dewy as a rose-bud ; her sacred memory, and her heavenly hope.

SARAH MORRIS.

Sᴀʀᴀʜ Mᴏʀʀɪs was termed a *smart* girl by everybody who knew her, and her acquaintance was only limited by the number of people in the neighborhood. And with all she was a favorite, as she deserved to be, for she was blessed with a large share of plain, common sense ; and beneath the fun and frolic that always sparkled on the surface of her nature there was a quick intelligence, a singularly happy tact, and a generous amiability.

She was not pretty, but there was a heartiness in the grasp of her little black hand, and a cordiality in the brightness that illuminated her little, dark face, when it approached you, that made you forget her plainness ; for plain she certainly would have been to critical, or indifferent eyes, if such could have looked upon her.

There was a rough honesty in her nature that no refined instinct counteracted the expression of, and that ears polite would have required to be toned down ; but with the uncultivated people among whom she dwelt, it was, perhaps her most potent charm. Wherever there was funeral, or church, or quilting, wedding or sickness, there came a sprightly little body, black-handed, and black-haired, and black-eyed, laughing or weeping, as the case might require, active with words and works, or coquettish with nods and becks—tossing of ribbons and flirting with parasol and fan—rustling and stirring, and winning all eyes from their tears or their devotions—and that was Sarah Morris.

Her horse was the gayest and the best groomed of any one in the neighborhood, the cushion of her saddle of the deepest crimson, and its stirrup of the most elaborate silver plate. No sober filly for her ! and many a time her scorn and derision came in the shape of a cut across the flank of the more gentle and unsuspecting one her neighbor rode.

But when the offender was discovered nobody was ever offended, and the quick spring of the animal and the jolt of the startled rider were sure to be followed by a laugh and a good-humored exclamation.

She might catch the chair from beneath her grandmother and send her headlong to the floor, but nothing was thought of it by anybody, except that it was Sally Morris's way. She might laugh in meeting so loud as to make half the heads in the congregation turn towards her, but still it was Sally's way, and no face was so rigedly solemnized that it would not relax when it saw the black eyes of Sally twinkling above her fan.

How lightly she used to spring upon the back of her dapple-grey, spurning the assistance of the many hands reached out to assist her, and how proudly she galloped away, sending a cloud of dust in the faces of her admirers, for their worshipful pains !

"Touch us gently, gentle time," was a song that Sarah had no inward prompting to sing. She was equal, she felt, to all changes and to all chances ; and, in truth, her little black hands, with the assistance of her shining black eyes, could well make their way through opposing combinations.

There was nothing to which she could not turn her talents, from raking in the hay-field and dropping corn, to the braiding of a straw bonnet and the fashioning of a silk gown ; and a good deal of broad, brilliant taste had Sarah, as was always manifested in the gay colors and striking contrasts she wore.

The black hair under her red ribbons, the bright blue petti-coat, and the flaunting rainbow sash gave her quite the air of some half-civilized Indian queen, as, on her gallant grey, she leaped fences and divided hedges and underbrush as lightly as the rye-stalks.

The glee of the children was doubled when they saw her, and breathlessly they hurried into the house to communicate the fact of her having ridden past as a piece of most stirring news. The young men paused from their occupations in the wayside fields as she rode by, and were ready to throw off their enthu-siasm by shouts and hurrahs for anything, at any moment, for hours thereafter.

Doubtless they would have sighed many a time, if they had not felt the utter futility of such an expenditure of breath, as she disappeared behind the next hill, or as the woods shut her in.

No love-lorn maiden dare show her pining cheek in Sarah's presence, for her laugh of scorn and derision was never done ringing from one to another of her young acquaintances.

"What fools you are," she would say, " to put your hearts out of your own keeping, and then cry to have them back ; just as if any bear of a man would take as good care of them as yourselves !

"I wish some of your charmers would steal my heart," she used to say ; " I'd show you how long they would keep it in torment. Catch me crying for the best man alive, and you may expect the sky to fall next.

"Just as if all the goodness in the world could be in any one man, supposing him even to be 'all your fancy's painted him.' Why, bless me, the least atom of common sense will teach you what dunces you are !

"Let me tell you, a feather bed, and a blanket, and a good dinner are decidedly more cheerful to think about than that little dark place you will get into soon enough. Come, pluck up a little courage, and show the poor, vain coxcomb that roses can grow in your cheeks independent of his planting."

This was her softest manifestation of sympathy and comfort, and if the disease yielded not to this method she was apt to resort to severer applications.

She would offer to gather willows, and speak in solemnly low and affected tones of her friends' grievances, treading on tiptoe and carefully shutting out the light—singing hymns of awful dolor, and in all ways possible exaggerating into the ludicrous the miserable suffering of which she had no conception ; healthful, light-hearted creature that she was.

Sarah's mother was a common-sense, common-place, hard-working, hard-feeling old woman, out of whose nature the sweetness of human sympathy seemed to have died. A countless number of wrinkles in her cheeks and forehead cradled an everlasting expression of care, and her little stumpy feet, trotted up and down, and down and up, and in and out, and out and in, from morning till night, and from year's end to year's end. She never went from home and never stopped toiling long enough to contemplate the accumulations of her industry.

There was no holiday for her, and no rest except in the variations of her work. She seldom spoke, except it were to Job, her husband, and never to him unless to scold.

She had probably married because four hands could do more work than two.

But why Job had married her was still more questionable— he had been crazy at one time of his life, and it may have been during that malady, or induced by it ; for certain it is, no mortal ever saw any manifestation of love for the other on the part of either of them ; but though it would be curious to inquire into the origin of their relation, our story leads us forward, not backward, and our interest in the latter direction must be sacrificed.

Enough that Sarah's father was a hardy, hen-pecked old man, who did the drudgery, and was kept, or kept himself, mostly out of sight.

Whether he was ever quite sane, nobody could determine, as he was never heard to say enough, and never seen sufficiently to warrant a conclusive judgment. If he appeared at all, it was only in dodging from one concealment to another ; and if he spoke at all, it was merely in reply to some order from Sarah or Sarah's mother.

Sarah herself has been known to say, in her wildest moods, that he had *vacant rooms in the garret.*

No one ever thought of saying Mr. Morris ; it was all old Job, and the old man Morris ; and the greatest deference he ever received was to be called Sarah Morris's father, as, by some of her more favored admirers, he has been know to be. Even his house was not his own, nor his grounds ; both were considered and designated as Sarah Morris's, and in truth, and notwithstanding the shrew-tongue of her mother, she was mistress of all.

There remains yet another individual, who, together with her parents and herself, comprised all the household—this was a youth named Elijah Burbank. In his boyhood he had been indentured to Job Morris, and in his young manhood, as he always had been, was known by the opprobrious epithet of Sarah's bound boy.

He was slight and delicate, with hands as small as those of his mistress, and much fairer; a face of extreme refinement, and a mouth of that peculiarly sensitive expression that is apt to awaken the tenderest sympathies in the opposite sex—and the derision of men. His blue eyes and soft flaxen hair completed the effeminacy of his appearance, and made his manhood seem farther away by some years than it really was.

It was the evening of the day that Lije was twenty-one years old that Sarah sat alone on the high south porch, known as the two-story porch. There was no look-out from it except towards a near and thick wood, and, moreover, it was pretty closely curtained by trumpet flower and creeper vines; so the view, such as it was, was considerably obstructed: and why she chose this retired position was perhaps hardly known to herself, for her custom was to recreate of evenings on the steps of the front portico—a position commanding a mile-length view of the high road.

Out upon this porch opened the door of Elijah's room, and presently out of Elijah's room came with a soft step Elijah himself.

He was dressed in his new freedom suit; and as he stood blushing in the moonlight, with one hand hiding itself in his yellow curls, there came to the heart of Sarah a feeling of bashfulness and tremor that she could in no wise account for. " What do you want, Lije ?" she said directly. She meant by her tone to demand why he was there, but somehow it yielded concession and solicited confidence.

" I want you," Elijah answered timidly, and looking down.

Sarah laughed a little foolishly, but recovered herself quickly, and answered, playfully extending her hand, " Well, here I am, take me."

Elijah took the hand in earnest thus offered him in jest, and bent his head so low over it that his lips more than touched it.

" Nonsense !" cried Sarah, withdrawing her hand, " if you are very hungry, Lije, you will find something in the cupboard more eatable than my hand."

Poor Lije ! abashed and trembling for what he had done, dropped on one knee and said, " I only wished, Miss Sarah, to thank you for all your goodness to me, and if I—if I kissed your hand, it was because I could not help it."

" And if I box your ears," replied Sarah, " it is because I can't help it ;" so saying she affected to slap his face, but it was done so softly with the tips of her fingers that Lije did not suffer any physical pain. " Besides," continued Sarah, " what do you want to thank me for ? I have done nothing to deserve your thanks that I know of."

" Why, Miss Sarah, do you forget these nice new clothes, and then your goodness to me all the while for so many years ?"

" No, Lije, I don't forget that as my bound boy I was bound to give you a freedom suit ; and, by the by, I suppose you have come to remind me that you are free."

"No Sarah, not that ; I am not free—I am your slave, and always shall be." He bent over the unresisting hand again and kissed it again ; but Sarah's pride, which as yet was the strongest feeling of her nature, was aroused by this time, and rising she said, " I am glad to know I have a slave ; but how do you think you will like Mr. Hilton for a master ?"

Poor Lije said he did not know, and went despondently away.

The Mr. Hilton alluded to was an old admirer of Sarah's ; and though it was suspected by Elijah that she had refused him more than once, he was none the less annoyed by the intimation she threw out. So, as I said, he went moping away, and putting his hand in a cutting-box designed to chop oats for cattle, made as if he would cut it off, almost hoping that by accident he might do so, and that Sarah would then at least pity him. He felt as if his brain had undergone some fearful shattering, and for his life he could not tell whether Mr. Hilton owned a thousand or fifteen hundred acres of land, nor could he determine whether he owned two flouring mills and a saw mill, or two saw mills and a flouring mill ; but he was fully conscious that in whatever shape his riches lay, he was a rich man, and that the black shadow of his big stone dwelling-house fell right over him, and would not even suffer him to see the sunshine. His heart received a most thrilling telegraph presently in the voice of Sarah calling him in a tone softer than its wont. She had spread the table with unusual care, and was herself waiting to serve the tea.

The little that was said during the meal had no reference to what both were thinking of. Sarah praised the new clothes at length, and intimated that Elijah would be leaving her for some better place

Elijah remembered that she had called him her bound boy, and, drawing his manhood up to its full height, replied that he should try to find some place to live where he was not despised, and that the farm of his mistress, big as it was, did not comprise the whole world.

Sarah replied, with a proud toss of her head, that she hoped he would not only find a nice place to live, but that he would get just such a wife as he desired, and she supposed that would be some one very unlike herself.

"Unlike you in some respects, certainly," replied Elijah, rising from the supper of which he had partaken very sparingly.

Sarah began to sing gaily as she tossed the dishes together,

> " I çare for nobody, no, not I,
> Since nobody cares for me."

Elijah whistled his way to his own room, but returning directly, threw a letter into Sarah's lap, saying he had forgotten to deliver it sooner, and was especially sorry for it, as it was probably from her lover, Mr. Hilton.

Sarah replied that she hoped so, though nothing was farther from probabilities, and she knew it. It was addressed to her mother, and in the writing of her mother's only sister, announcing her severe and protracted illness, and begging her sister to come and see her. Sarah did not that night go through the formality of making the reception of the letter known to her mother, but having broken the seal and read it, retired to her own room, whether to think of Elijah or of her far-away relative was known only to herself.

Sometime in the course of the following day Mrs. Morris was

made acquainted with her sister's illness, and shortly afterwards fifty dollars were demanded of Job, and in a humor of especial courtesy, Sarah informed him that she was going to visit aunt Ruth, and that her return was uncertain.

When it became known to Elijah that she was actually going from home, and for an indefinite time, the little pride that had been developed in him wilted away, and he drooped like a plant that lacks its proper nutriment. "If you are going away," he said one day to Sarah, "I will remain here till you come back, for what would become of Job if both of us were away?"

"Very well," said Sarah, "don't let the old man suffer;" but she was much more particular and earnest in her directions for the care of her favorite riding horse. She need not to have given any orders about anything that was hers, and Elijah in a trembling voice could not help telling her so. Sarah tried to laugh, but it was sorrowful laughter, and turning her face away asked him—she had always ordered him till them—if he would bring from the harvest-field a nice bundle of rye straw. An hour had not elapsed when it was laid at her feet.

Sarah made no parting calls, and left no messages for her friends—"if I die," she said, "what good will it have done that they smiled over me when I went away ; and if I live to come back, why we shall be just as glad to see each other as if we had a formal parting."

Up to the last moment of her remaining at home, poor Elijah had promised his trembling heart one more interview with her, and what was his disappointment and humiliation to find, as he sought to join her on the portico the evening previous to her departure, that she was already engaged in conversation with

the rich miller, Mr. Hilton ! All that night there was a rumbling in his head as of mill-wheels, and all that night he
dreamed one dream over and over, which was that Sarah had
lost all her proud spirit and was a pale-cheeked prisoner of Mr.
Hilton's gloomy old stone house.

The miller had been married once, and report said the
gloomy old·stone house had chilled the lost wife to death ; but
Sarah only laughed when this was told her, and replied that if
she were born to be chilled to death she would not die any othei
way ; to the miller himself she was capricious as an April day,
now shining upon him in smiles, now frowning like a thunder-
cloud ; but he was an obstinate prosecutor of his purposes, and
in no wise awed by a cloud, never so black though it were. It
was a matter of interesting speculation among Sarah's acquaintance whether or not she would ever marry the miller ; but it
was the opinion of the shrewdest of them that she was merely
dallying with him as the cat does with the mouse, and that
when the mood suited she would toss him aside contemptuously
and forever.

Probably such was her purpose ; but she loved power, and as
almost all her young friends would have been proud of his
attentions, she exercised through him a pretty extensive
supremacy.

To Elijah, the big, silent house of Job Morris was desolate
enough when Sarah was gone—it seemed that the noon would
never come, and when it was noon that it would never be night.
Job worked silently on the same, and Sarah's mother scolded
and worked the same, but Sarah's wheel was still and Sarah's
busy feet were not to be seen, and so to Elijah there was
nothing worth listening to in the world.

All the first evening long he sat on the stoop and talked with Sarah's mother, albeit she scolded incessantly ; it was now and then about Sarah that she scolded, and to hear Sarah's name pronounced in any way was a sort of miserable happiness to the poor young man. He could not prevent himself from speaking of the time when she would come back, as if it brought it any nearer, and of talking of places greatly more distant, as though that brought her nearer.

She had bidden him adieu with some careless jest about the pain of parting, and he could not avoid recalling the tone and the manner over and over, and of trying to find some latent meaning that no one else could have found. Who but one who is famishing for hope, can judge of his surprise and joy, when on entering his room for the night, he discovered lying on his bed, where Sarah had laid it, the new rye-straw hat she had braided for him. It was trimmed with a bright blue ribbon, and lined daintily with silk of the same color, and with this slight and perishable foundation to rest all his future upon, we will leave him till such time as he shall again cross the path of our story.

The husband of the aunt Ruth, at whose door Sarah found herself one morning in June, was a man of considerable cultivation and some wealth. He was a dealer in furs, and employed, in one way and another, a good many men, in one of whom only we are particularly interested—this person's name was Rodney Hampton. He was exceedingly handsome, and Sarah thought his full auburn beard, penetrating blue eyes, and polished manners contrasted with every one she had known so as to throw them altogether in the shade. Aunt Ruth's home was a comfortable and even pretty one, situated in one

of the frontier towns of the West; but there was a refinement
and nicety about it that, to Sarah's uncultivated ideas, appeared
the height of style and elegance. Aunt Ruth was an invalid,
delighted with the sprightly companionship of her niece, and
rendered doubly dependent by the absence of her husband.
Rodney Hampton was this man's most confidential clerk, and
necessarily a good deal at his house—oftener still from choice,
after the arrival of the romping niece. She was speedily
known to half the inhabitants of the town, and a universal
favorite, as she was at home.

Is it any wonder if an impulsive, careless girl, as was Sarah,
should never have stopped to inquire who Rodney was, nor
whence he came, and how, more and more, the interest
awakened by her first introduction to him was settling down
into her heart? or if it be a wonder, why it must remain so?
for certain it is she did not inquire till she awoke one day to
find that only within the circle of his influence was there any
world for her. They rode together into the country, and came
home under the starlight and by the light of their own imagin-
ations; they walked together in the suburbs of the town, and
found interest in every ragged urchin or thorny shrub in their
path; they sat together in Aunt Ruth's pretty parlor and
smiled unutterable things.

By degrees the ruder portion of Sarah's rusticity became
toned down, and her extravagant taste subdued itself to a more
artistic fashion, so that when she had been with Aunt Ruth six
months she was regarded as quite the belle of the little city of
which she was an inhabitant.

And as the fall came on, not an evening passed that did not
find Rodney conversing with his gay-hearted favorite in tones

that insinuated more than they said, and lingering and lingering in such fond way as certainly contradicted indifference. And to Sarah's credulous belief indifference was not only contradicted, but admiration, respect, love—all proclaimed with more than trumpet-tongued assurance.

He was a fine singer, and many a romantic song made sweet promises to her heart, and many a meaning glance confirmed the promises.

Every pretty cottage in the neighborhood had, at one time and another, been selected as the future home of our lovers, when there came one day to Sarah a letter, written in the trembling and unpracticed hand of the almost forgotten Elijah.

It told her how much her mother wished her to come home; how much, indeed, she needed her, and enlarged pathetically on the miserable way the good woman was wearing off her feet; it told, too, how much everybody wanted to see her, and said how dreary and desolate the neighborhood was without her; it even hinted that Mr. Hilton was pining away, and for sake of pity of him, if for nothing else, she must come.

"The old house here seems lonesome as the barn," urged Elijah, but he did not say whether it were thus lonesome to him, or to whom. "Your beautiful grey," he concluded, "is looking handsome, and is impatient to bear you about as he used to do. Oh, Miss Sarah, for everybody's sake you must come!"

The funds for defraying the expenditure of the homeward journey were inclosed, and when Sarah had finished reading she was more sorrowful than she had been for a long while.

The door of an old and less enchanting world was again open, and she saw that she must leave her soft dreams for hard realities, for she had been used to hard work and hard fare at home, for the most part, and if she felt less tenderness than a child should feel for its parents, why, they had felt less for her than parents should feel for their child.

In reference to again meeting Elijah, she could not herself understand the nature of her feelings—there was so much of pity and tenderness, so much of protection on her part, and of servitude on his, and, above all, so much love for Rodney, it is no wonder Sarah could only cry, and wish she had never gone away from home.

The letter was lying open in her lap, and the tears dropping silently down her cheeks, red as roses still, when Rodney joined her, and with a tenderness that seemed real, inquired the nature of her sorrow.

She would have spoken, but grief choked her voice, and she could only indicate the letter.

"From some lover ?" asked Rodney, half angrily and half reproachfully. Sarah shook her head, and he proceeded to read it, saying, " Then of course you have no secrets from me ?" thus implying a right he had never asked for.

As he read he laughed many times in a sneering fashion that Sarah did not like, and would have resented when her heart was less softened than now, indicating, as he laughed, the numerous blunders in the manuscript before him.

" Every one has not had your advantages, remember," pleaded Sarah ; for Rodney was a ready, correct, and graceful writer.

" I knew this fellow was your lover," replied the dissatisfied young man, and he mockingly placed the letter upon the heart of the weeping girl.

" And what if he were my lover ?" said Sarah, with something of her old ironical manner, smiling as she dried her eyes.

"Nothing, nothing," replied Rodney, dropping the hand he had been demurely coquetting with, and speaking in the tone of one vitally injured. "But," he added, "you must have known, Sarah, you must have seen, you must have felt [here he pressed his hand against his heart, as though, if possible, to prevent its breaking then and there], that you were cherishing hopes never, never to be realized. O Sarah ! may heaven deal gently with your conscience, and never suffer it to reproach you, as mine would me under a similar accusation." He ceased speaking, and hiding his face in his hands, seemed to be weeping. Sarah put her arms about his neck, for she loved him, and love is not ashamed of such demonstrations, and said artfully :

" And if Elijah were not my lover, dear Rodney, why, what then !"

" Can you wrong me so cruelly as to ask ?" spoke Rodney, still hiding his face from her. " You know that to make you my wife was a hope dearer than life to me." And he went on with a pitiful deceit men are fond of practising upon credulous women, to speak of a predisposition to early death in his family, and to say it mattered not ; nobody would grieve for him, and least of all, Sarah.

Sarah affirmed that his death would break her heart, and especially if she knew that by a single moment she had hastened it, and she gave him abundant proof of what her grief would be, in the passionate outburst of tears which even the suggestion of so melancholy an event produced.

" No tears for me," said Rodney, " I am not worth them. You are so good, so pure—I would not have been worthy of you, dear Sarah, and it is better as it is. I must try to forget you—try to live on; and you—you will soon forget me with him."

He hid his face in his hands again, as if to hide from himself the terrible truth; for it is astonishing to what sacrifices of truth men will resort in order to appear true.

Blinded by her love, and bewildered by his pathetic appeals, Sarah told him in the honesty of her full soul, that Elijah was not her lover, or if he were, that she did not love him in turn; that only himself was dear to her, and that if it were true he loved her as he said, there was nothing between them and happiness.

Rodney kissed her cheek, and said he was blessed; but the voice seemed devoid of meaning, and the kiss more like the farewell to a dead friend then the betrothing to a living love.

When they parted it was under a positive engagement of marriage—even the day was arranged that he was to come to her father's house and " bear her away, his bride."

Many times he sought to drag poor Elijah forward, and to make him an insurmountable obstacle in the way of the fulfillment of his dearest hope, as he called his engagement; but Sarah saw in this the jealousy, and not the weariness of love; and would not suffer the happiness of her life, and of her dear Rodney's life, to be thus idly thwarted. So they parted betrothed lovers. Aunt Ruth was better, and with the prospect of so soon again seeing her niece, smiled her benediction, and Sarah went away; the bloom in her cheek softened to the tenderest glow, and the flashing of her dark eyes subdued to the gentlest radiation.

Rumor runs faster than the wind, and the report that

Sarah was coming home to get married preceded her, and curiosity was on tiptoe to know who the intended husband was.

She made no denial of her engagement when her young friends came round her with playful banter and laughing congratulations. The general impression prevailed, that the rich miller was the happy man ; and that the engagement was of old standing—an impression that Sarah did not discourage. There was one who did not come to offer congratulations, to entreat pity, or to breathe reproach—and this was Elijah Burbank. With the intelligence that Sarah was coming home only to get married, he had gone, no one knew why or whither. Sarah's mother could divine no motive for his sudden resolution. All at once, she said he had seemed to droop like a motherless kitten, and scold hard as she would, she could get no spunk into him. It seemed, she said, as though he had no interest in any thing but Sarah's horse and Sarah's garden, and that by the hour he would talk with the dumb critter, and the flowers, as if they had been sensible beings—that his last visit was to the garden, and that he had gone away with a rose from Sarah's favorite tree in his hand.

Tears came to the eyes of the young girl when she heard this ; but they were speedily dried in the sunny happiness that awaited her, for when we are very happy it is hard to believe there is any great misery in the world.

And the wedding-day came near, and the wedding-people were all invited ; but who the bridegroom was, was still a secret. The miller was observed to be repairing his old house about this time, and the fact gave credence to the rumor that he was to carry off the prize.

How proud and happy Sarah was as she half admitted the

correctness of the suspicion, in the thought of the brilliant
undeceiving that awaited ! What a triumph it would be to
have her friends look up expecting to see the miller, and
behold Rodney—the handsome, accomplished, and elegant
Rodney !

And the wedding-dress was made ; and the wedding-veil was
ready ; and the wedding-heart was beating with joyous expec-
tations, when there lacked three days of the marriage-day. It
was an evening of the late November that Sarah sat among
her myrtle pots on the portico watching the gloomy gathering
of the clouds, and the last yellow leaves as they fluttered on the
almost bare branches, and dropped now and then on her head
or at her feet. It would not rain—she was quite sure it would
not rain. She thought the clouds were breaking and drifting
away, though any one else would have seen them closing more
darkly and darkly, and any one but she would have heard in
the sound of the wind the prophecy of the long November storm.

She wore a dress of red and black stripes, and a little gay
shawl coquettishly twisted about her neck, some bright scarlet
flowers among her black hair, for Rodney had oftentimes admired the contrast of scarlet blossoms in her dark hair, and it
was for him she was watching, as her quick vision swept the
long distance again and again.

At length, as the last daylight lost itself in shadow, her
heart beat so quick and so loud as almost to choke her. She
had heard hoof-strokes in the distance, and who should be coming but Rodney !

Nearer they came and nearer. She could see the horseman
more and more plainly—fear completed what hope began, and
she sank down almost fainting.

The miller—for it was he—attributed her emotion to the delight she felt in seeing him ; and his spirits rose, and his tender attentions and soft insinuations were doubled.

Every moment Sarah hoped Rodney would come and rid her of his disagreeable presence ; but he came not.

Across the field, half a mile away, lights were seen and voices heard. They were near the road-side, and as Sarah's imagination linked everything with Rodney, she proposed going to see what was doing, for she feared that some accident might have happened to him—he might be dying perhaps within sight of her.

Silently she went along, leaving the breathless miller tugging after as he could, till she reached a little knoll that overlooked what was going forward. A glance convinced her that Rodney was not there ; and in the reaction of mind she experienced, she laughed joyously, and running back to meet the miller, told him in a lively tone what she had seen.

The lights were the fires of a camp made for a night's rest by some people who were moving from one part of the country to another. As they descended the slope together, they could see two women preparing supper, by a fire of sticks and logs, while one man was busy chopping wood, and another with some children lay on the slope in the light of the blazing fire Beneath a low oak tree, yet full of dry rustling leaves, a rude tent was spread, within which voices of women in low and earnest conference were heard.

" Seeing your lights," said the miller, addressing the man at the fire, " we crossed the field from our home, which is just over the hill, in the hope that we might be able to serve you ;

this is my good lady who is with me, and indeed it was her
kindly heart that drew us this way."

Sarah smiled her acquiescence in what the miller said, and
the delight he felt in being for half an hour believed to be her
husband, even by a few strangers whom he might never meet
again, manifested itself in a thousand exuberant antics. He
quite made himself master of their little camp, and pressed
their own hospitalities upon them with a generous kindness
that was amusing to witness.

Meantime the women and children hastened to do reverence to
Sarah by offering her a mat to sit upon, and insisting that she
should remain and partake of their fare. They seemed to be
poor people, scantily enough provided with necessaries, to say
nothing of comforts. The children were barefoot, and most
untidily dressed and combed, but they seemed healthful, and
were noisily frolicsome. The women who were preparing supper looked pale, and seemed discouraged, but patiently endur-
ing. What they were going to they knew not ; but they had
come from poverty and suffering, and they were willing to go
forward even faintly hoping for something better. Recognizing instinctively, perhaps, the presence of strangers, a gossiping
old crone emerged from the tent, and pulling Sarah by the
sleeve, began to address her in whispers. She appeared to be
the mother of part of the campers, and affected or had mater-
nal feelings for all.

" You see," she said, " we would get along well enough, my
sons and daughters and me, though I am ninety, but for one
we have in there—she don't belong to us, though—she is sick,
and I'm afraid she will never live to get to him, though if resolution could keep a body up, it will keep her up, for I never

saw so much soul, as you may say, in one poor little body.
Her baby was born after we were on the road, and that de-
layed us a week a'most ; but it was her, and not ourselves, that
we cared most about : poor young woman, maybe it will
brighten her up like to see your face—it looks cheery and
good : suppose you just step inside and see the baby, and encourage her a little ;" and as she spoke she took Sarah by the
hand and led her into the tent, while the wistful eyes of the
miller followed her.

It was a pitiful picture that presented itself : on a rude bed
of straw that was spread on the ground, and with the light of
a tallow candle falling upon her face, lay a young and beautiful woman. One hand lay on the quilt of patch-work that
covered her ; and Sarah could not but remark the extreme
delicacy and smallness of it, while the other rested on the head
of her baby. Her voice was low and sweet ; but when she
spoke of the baby's father, whom she said she was soon to join,
it grew strong and full of enthusiasm and courage. By extreme
necessity, she said, and no fault of his, she had become separated from him ; and when the old woman alluded to the suffering she had endured, she said, with an entreating earnestness
again and again, that it was not the fault of the baby's father.

She seemed so well-bred, and so continually ignored any
endurance on her part, that poor Sarah, whose sympathies were
all interested, was at a loss how to behave, or in what way to
offer such charities as she felt to be required.

She was not without a woman's tact, however, and by praising the baby won her way to the heart of the mother—for
the child she would accept some milk—nothing for herself.
She was comfortably, nay more than comfortably provided.

She held up the child for Sarah to kiss as she was about going away, and as she did so her own enthusiasm was awakened anew—the eyes, the hands, the hair, were all so like the father of the dear baby—"If you could only see him," she exclaimed, "I am sure you would not wonder that I love him!"

"Show the young lady his picture, won't you?" interposed the old woman.

"Oh, she would not care to see it," replied the loving wife; and she added, pressing the hand of Sarah, "pray, pardon me for talking of him so much; but then he has never seen the baby, nor me for so long—dear Rodney, how much it must have grieved him!"

Sarah's eyes fixed themselves with a new and terrible interest on the baby, as it lay asleep in its smiling innocence and beauty—the blood settled back to her heart—a faintness came over her and she sunk to the ground.

The old woman dashed a cup of water in her face, and she recovered enough to say it was nothing; she was used to fainting fits, and would presently be quite well.

"Show the picture, it will revive her like," insisted the old nurse.

"Yes, yes," gasped Sarah, "I must see the picture!"

The young mother took it from her bosom, with some apology for its not looking so well as the original, and presented it, to complete, with its fair familiar smile, the undoing of a too trustful heart. Her eyes in one long stony stare fixed themselves upon it, as though she would fain look away the horrid lie, that in some fearful way had obscured the truth of her betrothed. Catching at the shadow of a hope, she whispered to herself, "I see, I see how it is, it is the brother of my Rodney."

"Can there be another in the world," cried the sick lady, "who resembles Rodney Hampton? Where did you meet the person you speak of? not surely in —— ?" She named the place where Sarah had met Rodney—where she had loved him, and where she had promised to be his wife.

"No, not there—not there," replied Sarah ; "the person I know, you have never seen ;" and pressing a kiss on the white hand of the startled invalid, she went away with an unsteady and hurried step.

Heavily she leaned on the arm of the miller as she slowly returned homeward. "I suppose those people took you for my wife," he said, laughing foolishly.

"And what if they did?" replied Sarah.

"Nothing," answered the miller, "only I wish it were true."

Sarah walked on in silence ; but more and more firmly till she reached the homestead-door, and then she said with a calmness that was fearful to hear, "There is a rumor abroad that I am to be married the day after to-morrow—it was a silly jest of mine—if you please you may make it truth."

When she had received the miller's affirmative response, she coldly silenced his tender demonstrations, and forbidding him to see her again till the hour appointed to unite their fates, she retired to her chamber, and gave herself up to the awfullest of all tortures—the rack of unrequited love.

And the wedding day came, and the guests stood silent and wondering when they saw the bride, for her eyes had lost their lustre, and her cheek was hueless as death ; but in due form she was made the wife of Mr. Hilton, and in due time she accom-

panied him to the gloomy old stone house. From her marriage-
day she was never seen abroad, and her gay laughter was never
heard to ring out anywhere ; her bright saddle was hung up
in the dusty garret, and her bright cheeks faded and grew thin.
The gallant grey was tied to the mill-wheel, and trod his sober
round ; and Sarah trod her sober round, doing her duty, but
scolding the miller as loudly and sharply as her mother had
scolded Job. In the main, however, she was a good wife, and
if she scolded the miller, so the neighbors said, it was no more
than he deserved, for he was a hard, selfish, and tyrannical
master.

Many years they plodded on together ; but at length the
miller was gathered to his fathers ; and other years Sarah lived
on alone, wearing a mourning dress, and caring little to conceal
the silver streaks that were beginning to show above her tem-
ples. One winter night as she sat by the blazing fire, the
flinty snow rattling against the pane, there was a loud knock-
ing at the door, and the next moment a strange gentleman was
borne in, who had been thrown from his carriage at her gate,
and considerably hurt. He was carried immediately to bed,
and the village doctor called, who pronounced his patient
badly bruised, but in no wise seriously injured. He was par-
tially unconscious at first, but after his face for a few minutes
had been bathed, he recovered sufficiently to thank his hostess,
and to inquire whether his luggage were safe—one box he was
particularly solicitous about, and could not rest till Sarah had
brought it to his bedside. On seeing it he smiled, and shortly
afterwards fell asleep. That smile seemed to join itself to some
old memory, but Sarah could not tell what ; it might be with
Rodney perhaps, but if it were, it stirred no troubled thought.

The stranger was certainly handsome, and from his dress and belongings was evidently of no mean position in the world—a man of leisure and money, Sarah thought, travelling probably for his health, and while she mused and turned her eyes from the refined and expressive face to the little white hand that seemed reaching towards her, wondering who her guest was and when she should find out all about him, the clock struck twelve, more loudly than it had ever struck till then, it seemed to Sarah, and the sleeping gentleman unclosed his eyes, and fixed them earnestly and tenderly upon the watcher by his side, and as he gazed his pale cheek blushed, and his mouth lost the firm expression of manhood, and took the sweet sensitive look of the loving boy.

"Can I do anything for you?" asked Sarah, not well knowing what else to say.

"Yes," replied the stranger, "I fear a long cherished treasure is lost from this box. Will you please remove the lid that I may see?"

Sarah slipped the covering aside, and for a moment stood paralyzed, and then, as her eyes fell inquiringly upon the stranger, the blush of twenty years again colored her cheek.

The box contained a coarsely-braided rye-straw hat, trimmed with a faded blue ribbon!

Elijah! Sarah! was all they could say in the first joyous shock of surprise. What more they said ultimately, let us not care to inquire—enough that the day broke for them at midnight, and there was never any more darkness in all their lives.

HOUSE WITH TWO FRONT DOORS.

TWENTY-FIVE years ago there stood in a straggling village on
the banks of the Ohio, an old house, with two doors, and a
good many irregular windows in the front.   Two clumsy chimneys of stone showed squattily above the steep red gables—the
one for architectural effect, simply, the other the extension of a
veritable flue ; and from this last, a cloud of black smoke
worked itself out, and after a little vain effort to keep itself up,
sagged towards the ground, for the air was heavy—the orange
light rapidly blackening against the yellow moss on the tops of
the western hills, and the evening coming in with the promise
of a wet night.

The village was not at all picturesque ; a great hill that
extended as far as the eye could see, and the summit of which
seemed almost to touch the sky, formed its background, and
completely shut out the view in that direction.   It was not one
of those poetic hills that are beautified with pasture-fields, shady
trees, flowery thickets—on the contrary, its village-side was
bare of vegetation, except, indeed, a scanty growth of stunted
oaks, together with some thistles, and dwarf blackberry vines,
which, in some sort, relieved its monotony of baked clay,

151

cracked by the sunshine, and washed into deep gullies by the rain.

The village streets were still less attractive—unpaved for the most part—full of ruts, where refuse soaked and rotted, and obstructed at all points with idle carts, coopers' stuff, heaps of shavings and the like. They had their share, too, of stray cows and quarrelsome dogs, and were provided with mud-holes, at convenient distances, where swine, with patches of bristles scalded off by the ill-natured housewives, took such ease as their nature loveth, and by grunting and squealing further provoked the wrath of their oppressors, for the hearts of women are not always so gentle as poets say, and if the truth be fairly spoken, are, I am afraid, no less accessible to induration than the faces with which hard fortune plays such terrible havoc. But notwithstanding the facts recorded, the town was not without pretensions which no transient abider therein could gainsay without disadvantage.

The clergyman's house, with its close-shut windows, carved portico, and grey garden wall, set round with austere box—its gravelled walk, along which tall sunflowers baked their great cakes brown, together with the red brick meeting-house, with its solemn burial-ground, where a thousand low head-stones shrugged their shoulders beneath the two or three grand monuments, were perhaps, the distinguishing ornaments of the place—the centre about which clustered the more exclusive piety—the evangelical pride, so to speak, of the village folks.

The market-house, which was, in point of fact, a dismantled canal boat set upon dry land, was also an object, not only of general interest, but one which kindled local admiration almost to enthusiasm. Real estate in this vicinity was estimated to have doubled its value in consequence of this " improvement," and two or three owners of lots thereabouts retired from business, and were thereafter clothed and fed, simply by virtue of the market-house. No one will be disposed to doubt this statement who has observed what a number of idlers a single grocery store or turnpike-gate will maintain. I once knew two able-bodied men to support themselves and their families on the merits of a cross-road—but this, perhaps, was an extreme case.

Then there was the squire's office, a diminutive lean-to of the corner dry-goods store, in the official glory of which all ordinary considerations of right and morality sunk completely out of sight. The squire wore a weed on his white hat in memory of the lamented Mrs. Bigsham, and this drew after him more than a third part of the feminine sympathy of the town, and was perhaps the basis of his popularity—every unmarried woman felt as if that black band was an electric link between herself and the great squire, which might at any time be converted to a bond of perpetual union.

" The office," as it was called, was the habitual resort of the big academy boys—decayed pilots of river-boats, doctors' students, who jested about " subjects" and drew teeth for half-price —and, as may be inferred, the convocations of these learned disputants were not a little promotive of exclusive feeling in the neighborhood. True, the legal prestige was somewhat marred by the fact that a poor shoemaker plied his trade in the rear of the magisterial office, but aristocracy did all it could in self-defence by suspending a curtain formed of a mosquito-net between the bench of the obnoxious workmen and the arm-chair and the mottled spittoon of the squire. Inadequate as the screen would seem, it required not even that to separate the young shoemaker, who was lame and melancholy, from the rude and boisterous frequenters of the official department, so that a more impenetrable stuff was not in the least necessary. He had been in the village a year, or more, and nobody knew anything about him except that he was a faithful and honest worker, and put himself in nobody's way, for he moved about quietly as a ghost, and with as little interest in the earth apparently. He was known to the old woman with whom he boarded, as Peter Gilbraith, and to the other towns people, who knew him at all, as "Shoe Pete"—but whether called by one name or another elicited from him no indication of pleasure or displeasure. Nature had gifted him with eyes of wonderful beauty—hair that curled itself all the more gracefully for his careless management, and a smile of that strangely fascinating sort, that seems made up of mingled scorn and sweetness ; but accident had dishonored his fair proportions by curtailing one leg of its rightful dimensions, which obliged him to walk with a stick, and gave to his shoulders a perpetual stoop.

Whether it were poverty or lameness, or both, that made him shrink from the little observation he excited, or whether misanthropy were a part of his nature, nobody knew, and very soon nobody cared—for in what way could " Shoe Pete," they argued, enhance the value of town-lots, or contribute to social pleasure ? And true it is that his great sad eyes seemed to rebuke the spirit of mirth, and his smile made the beholder of it feel as if he were more than half despised. His dress was careless (with the exception of the high-heeled shoe, which was neat in the extreme) not slovenly, however, and it always bore evidence of refinement, as did also his pale face, in spite of neglected hair and beard.

From sunrise till sunset his hammer was never still, and sometimes late into the night, even, its whack, whack, sounded upon the soft leather, so that it is not strange that reports gradually went into circulation, that Shoe Pete was " laying up" money ; nor that overtures towards his acquaintance began to be warmly pressed. He remained inaccessible, however, and was observed to walk with less stoop, and to show a bright indignant spot on either cheek, after some customer had been unusually condescending with him.

But whether the season was a busy one or not, the young shoemaker was never idle—his candle made the small window above his work-bench shine till midnight, and his leather apron was in requisition late and early. There was always a book or a newspaper under his pillow, in the morning, his landlady reported, and this fact was accepted by her as presumptive evidence, that Peter Gilbraith was a great scholar, and though it may seem like a small basis on which to found a reputation for scholarship, it was sufficient, and puzzling questions in geography and grammar began to be propounded to him by the young villagers when they came to have their feet measured. Nevertheless, the sun threw his last rays from the yellow moss on the tops of the western hills and sunk completely out of sight on the evening upon which our story opens, and the shoemaker had never as yet received the slightest recognition from the great Squire Bigsham. Is it very singular if he started and let fall his hammer, as the great man pulled his chair about so that he faced the mosquito-net curtain, and said with easy familarity, and as if he were in the habit of addressing him every day—

"You are a happy dog, Gilbraith—I almost wish I was a shoemaker instead of the public functionary I am ?"

Gilbraith smiled, and took up his hammer.

"Let me see," continued the squire, "how long have we been acquainted ?"

"I have worked in your office about a year, sir."

"A year ! Zounds ! why it seems jest t'other day you come !" He knew the time very well, but he wanted to make believe that he was surprised so much time should have elasped without his having cultivated friendly relations with his excellent neighbor.

The shoemaker had resumed his hammer and his old expression of sad indifference.

The squire went on : "Bless my soul ! a *year !* I wouldn't a believed any feller, if he'd a tole me that, exceptin' you, yourself." He laid special stress on the *you*, as if he held the young man's veracity in high esteem.

The shoemaker smiled again at the implied compliment, but made no other acknowledgment.

The squire was not to be thwarted, however—the news had come to his ears that morning, that Shoe Pete had actually purchased a lot adjoining the market-house, and paid a *hundred* dollars *down*, for the same ! so he gathered up his feet and said —"Look-a-here now, did you ever see any man make a boot to fit a feller's foot like that ?"

Gilbraith clutched his hammer, or it must have fallen again —the squire had, of a verity, indicated that shoemakers were *men*, and at the same time had designated himself as a fellow ! He was too proud to disparage another man's work, and said something to the effect that the boots seemed to have done good service.

"Well, sir, I'll tell you, sir," continued the squire, bringing his courtesy to a climax, "I want for you to make me a pair of tip-top stogy boots, and you may jes put your own price onto 'em, too." The shoemaker said his time was fully engaged for a month or more, but that he would attend the order at his earliest convenience, and limping forward he took the requisite measure with the air of conferring, rather than of receiving a favor.

The customary loungers dropped in one after another, and each, after a little subdued talk with the squire—the upshot of which was, it is reasonable to infer, the prosperous fortunes of the shoemaker—dexterously dipped his conversation so as to include that hitherto ignoble person. But his replies were brief and cold, and on the entrance of the doctor's student, who was usually inflated with great news—the mosquito-net resumed its ancient effectiveness, and Gilbraith, the transitory man, was resolved once more into Shoe Pete.

"I say, Doc, what is it ?" said one of the idlers, smelling the news afar off, "anything new about that ere miss what was smuggled into the two-door house t'other night ?"

"A few particulars have transpired," replied the student whom they called Doc, and sliding his legs apart, he thrust his hands deep in his pockets and waited to be questioned further.

"What miss ?"—"Which two-door house ?"—"Yon one with so many winders ?" were a few of the twenty questions asked in a minute.

"He means the house with the two front doors into it, and the two stone chimbleys onto it—well one ov them chimbleys is false, and maybe there's someten else 'ats falser an what the chimbley is, about that ere house—my daughter posted me up as we went to meetin' last night."

Having thus brought himself to a level in point of importance, with the young doctor, the squire moved his hand graciously towards him, and abdicated in his favor. He, nevertheless, was slightly offended—slid his legs a little farther apart, and said haughtily " that he didn't know that he could enlighten the fellers so well as Squire Bigsham." This obliged the squire to make a humiliating confession—to say, in fact, that he " knew nothing except that a young woman, no better un what she ort to be, appeerently, had been lately smuggled into the two-door house, and that the feller what brought her, had shortly afterwards disappeared between two lights, leaving her with a limited amount of chink, and with no livin' soul to do for her, except the greenest kind of a greenhorn."

The shoemaker had lighted his tallow candle, and the squire his big lamp, for it had grown quite dark, and a sudden gust had just driven a dash of rain, mixed with yellow leaves, against the window. The door burst suddenly open, and a slender, freckled-faced girl, with blue eyes, staring wide, and red hair flying in wild disorder, stood fronting the wondering group, and with many catchings of breath and earnest gesticulations, made known the facts that she lived with a lady " that was took awful sick—that she had been after the ould dochther and the ould dochther wasn't in it, and she was afther the young dochther to come with her to the lady, who lived in the house beyant, wid the two doors—and the young dochther had a right to go wid her if he had any sowl."

" Hooraugh !" shouted some of the rude fellows, " Go *wid*

her, Doc! Why if the chap ain't a blushin' up to his eyes—thought he had more pluck."

And one of the most disreputable of the fellows seized his hat, and volunteered to accompany the frightened girl, asseverating that he himself was the young dochther.

All at once the shoemaker dashéd aside the frail curtain, and with his eyes flashing fire, stood in the midst of the vulgar crew, almost erect.

"Whoever dares to lie further to this poor child, or to insult her in any way," he cried, "does it at his peril." And leaving the dastards dumb with astonishment, he motioned the girl to follow him, and without another word went out into the rain. Ten minutes afterwards the old woman with whom he boarded, wrapt in shawls and bearing a lantern in her hand, was feeling her way through the wet weeds of an alley towards the old house with the two front doors.

Presently, through the windows of an upper room, the curtains of which were carefully drawn, the lights were seen to shine, and shadows to pass, as if there was hurrying to and fro within, but the most watchful gossips could discern nothing more. Rumor had not exaggerated the truth—that night, when the storm was loudest and the sky blackest, the poor young lady who had been a few days before cast helpless upon her own sad fortune, took in her trembling arms the unwelcome child that must bear witness to her frailty, through time as deathless as the years of God

The little window by which the shoemaker worked looked toward the house with the two front doors, and often as he drew out his long threads, his eyes wandered that way, his own isolated condition quickened his sympathies for the young mother, at whom so many even of her own sex were ready to cast stones. Sewing, and hammering, and pegging, he dreamed a thousand dreams of improbable ways in which he might serve her, and as he took his walk to his evening meals he now and then went round by the lonesome house, and the oftener he took that road the shorter it appeared, until it seemed to him at last, as he climbed the weedy hill and crossed the bare common, only to pass that house and hobble down the hill again that he was taking the shortest way home.

So far from losing anything in the estimation of the young fellows who frequented the "office," by the spirit he manifested in defence of the poor girl and her mistress, he was thereby promoted to a considerably higher degree of importance, and it soon became a matter of no unfrequent occurrence for them to address directly to him such narratives as involved the exhibition of what they esteemed the most admirable manly courage. But these polite attentions gained imperceptibly, if they gained at all, upon his kindly feeling, and a brief word, or a careless nod, was usually the only acknowledgment he made.

The squire's boots were a complete success, and served to give him at once the reputation of a "tip-top" shoemaker; but this was not enough to lift him out of the socket of obscurity in which he was sunken, and give him anything like a desirable social position. But what was termed genteel patronage began to be extended to him and by degrees he became known as *little* Gilbraith, and to be called Shoe Pete only behind his back.

One evening, when an importunate creditor presented himself to the squire, he suddenly turned round with the inquiry, "Mr. Gilbraith, could you make it convenient to lend me five dollars for a day or two?"

"Certainly, sir, with the greatest pleasure," replied the shoemaker, with a heartiness that he had never before been known to use, and opening a well-filled purse he presented the note.

As the squire went forward to receive it, the mosquito-net curtain intercepted his way and with one dash of his great hand he swept it to the ground, with the outraged exclamation: "What dingnation fool ever put this thing up here anyhow!"

As may be supposed, it was never hung up again, and thus the line of demarcation between the "office" and the "shop," became somewhat wavering.

The yellow leaves were coming down in the fall rain, when the shoemaker invested his first earnings in the lot adjoining the market-house, in consequence of which the squire acknowledged his humanity, and when the Christmas snow hung its white garlands on the box along the clergyman's grounds, heaped higher the mounds in the graveyard, and lay all unbroken before the house with the two front doors, a bright tin sign bearing the name of Peter Gilbraith, between two gilt boots, was nailed on the office door in close proximity to the squire's letter-box, and an apprentice had been taken into the shop, and with this assistance the young shoemaker found it difficult to fill his orders.

"I think I will not go to supper to-night," he said to his apprentice one evening, as the last sunlight glittered on the snow that hung over the eaves of the house with two doors.

There was a great deal of work to be finished that night, and he had just lifted his hand to draw the curtain across the little window, preparatory to lighting the candle when a new and joyous light came suddenly into his eyes, and leaving the curtain undrawn, he leaned his face against the window for some minutes, and said, at length, with a changed tone and manner : "I believe I will go, after all."

The next minute the apprentice looked out, and was surprised to see him going up the hill through the unbroken snow, directly away from the house of the old woman with whom he took his meals. He did not see the house with the two front doors—much less the young woman at the window, holding a little child in her arms, and trying to make it see the moon come up, and if he had he would have been just as much at a loss to know why Peter walked that way, and indeed that young man might have found it difficult to explain the puzzle himself.

"I never saw his lameness interfere so little with his walking, as it seems to now, in spite of the snow," mused the apprentice, and he drew the curtain, and lighted the candle.

The snow hung in a great roll over the top of the stone chimney, unstained and unmelted. "There is no fire below," thought Peter, and he sighed.

"Perhaps it is the woman's black hair that makes her face look so pale," he thought, as walking slowly he gazed upon her ; but suggestions of scanty fare would not be silenced, and he sighed again and walked more slowly than before. Just then the little child thrust its naked arms from out the ragged blanket in which it was wrapt, and began to cry bitterly.

Peter stopped and stood still. In spite of the tender coaxings and cooings of the woman, which Peter could hear from where he stood, the child cried more and more bitterly. Moved by a sudden impulse he walked directly to the door nearest to which the woman stood. She saw him and opened it at once, with an air of such modest sweetness, as caused him to take off his hat—a civility he had never shown to anybody since coming to the village until then.

There was no fire, sure enough, and the other evidences of comfort were all as meagre as imagination could have pictured them. He hesitated for a moment when the young woman paused as if expecting him to make known his errand, but charity is never long in suiting means to ends, and he replied to her silence that he was in need of a person to bind shoes, and not knowing where to seek with the hope of success, had ventured to inquire of whomever he chanced to see.

Before he had spoken half-a-dozen words the baby lifted its head from its mother's shoulder, and with tears in its bright wondering eyes remained looking at him, perfectly quiet—one dimpled shoulder peeping from the ragged blanket above and two little bare feet, blue with cold, dangling below.

Is it any wonder if Peter took both those little feet in his hand, and tried to warm them under the pretence of seeing whether he had ever made so small a shoe?

When he returned to his shop that night, he found two young women, one of them the squire's daughter, waiting to have measures for shoes taken.

They whispered and laughed with one another, not a little rudely the shoemaker thought, as he was getting ready his measure, and their orders were given in a manner that certainly bordered upon insolence—the squire's daughter was especially presumptuous and troublesome.

She doubted very much whether he would be able to suit her at all, she said, as she tossed her golden curls from her fire-red cheeks ; but she should not hesitate to send him back twenty pairs of shoes, if he failed so many times to please her —it was so hard to make *such* people understand what one wanted—and with this little indication of her superiority and willfulness, and with an indignant fling of her flounced skirt, she withdrew without so much as the slightest bend of her pretty neck.

But Mr. Gilbraith gave little attention to her saucy airs— his thoughts were too busy with the pale-faced mother, and her shivering baby.

When spring came, two more lots were added to the first one, and the prosperous shoemaker built himself a fine new shop with a great square show window, and a sign almost as big as the squire's front door. And as a finishing stroke of finery, there was an imported carpet on the floor, and three yellow windsor chairs for the accommodation of the ladies.

He was called Mr. Gilbraith almost altogether, and his store was the fashionable one of the place ; and when a brick pavement was laid down in front of the door and an awning stretched above it, that direction became the exclusive promenade; and every day, after sunset, some twenty or thirty young women were to be seen tripping over the pavement, and turning their faces away from the window, of course. And last, and first, and oftenest, the squire's daughter was sure to go by, and more than any one else she stopped to examine the slip-

pers in the window, at which times she took occasion to toss
her curls coquettishly, and smile in a most bewitching fashion.
But the shoemaker worked on at these times just as if her
pretty face was not at the window, and stimulated by his indifference she stepped into the shop one evening and inquired the
price of a pair of slippers which she said had taken her fancy.
He replied without so much as glancing towards her. " I should
like to have them fitted," she said, with a little more deference
in her tone than she had hitherto used, and sitting down in the
yellow windsor chair she extended her little foot. The young
man motioned his apprentice to wait upon the lady, but she
would not be thus defeated. " They don't please altogether,"
she said, " perhaps it is the fault of the fitting—will you be
kind enough to give me your opinion, Mr. Gilbraith." It was
the tone rather than the words that elicited the young man's
attention. He laid aside his work, and shaking back his curls
with a grace of artlessness surpassing art, came forward, the
faint color of his face heightened for the moment to a flush of
confusion that made him positively handsome. The young lady
thought so, and apologized for the trouble she was making.
He was not used to such deference, and as he fitted the slipper,
held the little foot in his hand longer than need were.
" There ! that is perfect," exclaimed the beauty, referring to
the slipper.

" It is the foot that makes the shoe look so well," he replied ;
" shall I send them home for you ?"

Oh no ! the beauty would not give him so much trouble, she
was already greatly obliged—and with a bright smile and a
low courtesy that seemed to say she was receiving a favor, took
the parcel in her white hand and was just stepping from the

door as a pale young woman, with a bundle of shoes in one arm and a child hanging over her shoulder, came in.

All women love babies—the squire's daughter was no exception; and with an ingenuous exclamation of delight she stopped, took the rosy face of the little one between her hands, and kissed eyes and mouth and cheeks, prattling the while, in such a pretty way as went straight to the heart of the mother, and made a softer impression on the shoemaker than all her coquettish arts could ever have done, for some strange affinity had drawn him towards that little helpless creature from the dawn of its unfortunate existence. It often happened thereafter that when the village beauty passed the shoemaker's shop, he was at the door or window, and gradually the exchange of the evening salutation began to be looked to by both as the event of the day.

All the summer long the pale face was seen at the window of the house with the two front doors, and late into the night the candle would shine on the tired fingers that were always busy binding shoes. The path up the hill from the shoe-shop to the door was worn quite distinctly along the sod, and the shoemaker was observed to walk along it very frequently —more frequently, the neighbors thought, than business required.

Meantime the baby grew more and more in the affection of the young shoemaker, and he would often take with him when he went to the house, a flower or an apple or some other trifle to please her baby eyes, and she would reach her hands up to be taken on his knee, and he would bend his head and allow her to make playthings of his curls, at will. No wonder she grew fond of him and learned to clap her hands and crow when she saw him, for is it not true that Providence "creates the love to reward the love?" And when this little child had found access to his heart it became gradually more accessible to others, for the humanizing influence of love, even for a flower or a dumb animal, is beyond calculation. Like the dew and the rain that help to mould the dust into the rose, it falls into the desert of life, and straightway a garden is produced.

Everybody said, "What a change has come over Gilbraith —he is not the Shoe Pete he used to be at all ;" but no one dreamed what had wrought the change.

And the summer went by and the bright leaves fell on the brighter head of the little girl as the shoemaker tugged her about among the hollyhocks and poppies of the door-yard.

The house with the two front doors had a smoke in its chimney all that winter, and the gossips said the mistress of it was binding the shoemaker's heart as well as his shoes, but the wisest gossips are at fault, sometimes.

It was the week before Christmas and the pale-faced shoebinder was at her work, paler and perhaps more melancholy than usual, for it was hard to get along at the best, and it was now mid-winter, and her health, less robust than it used to be, was scarcely equal to the demands upon it.

Little Orphie, for so the fatherless child had been named, had learnt to lisp, "mother," but she called that name less often than Gabriel as she persisted in designating Mr. Gilbraith. She had fallen asleep in his arms, and her upturned face seemed asking to be kissed as her bright little head rested against his bosom. He pulled down her coarse scanty dress, for her bare legs dangled out of it, and said speaking partly to himself and partly to the child, "Next birthday little Orphic shall have a new dress, bright as the poppies she likes so much."

Perhaps it was the allusion to her birthday that awoke in the mind of the mother unwelcome memories, for throwing down her work with angry haste, she laid the child in the cradle, and with a scornful flush on her cheek removed it from the warmth of the firelight into the darkest corner of the room.

"What did you do that for?" asked the shoemaker with both authority and displeasure in his tone.

"What right have you to dictate in reference to *my* child?" she replied, and resumed her work with an averted face.

"The right which my love for her gives me," he said, in a tone very gentle and winning.

The mother's heart was touched, and hiding her face in her hands she burst into tears—poverty, shame, pride, and sorrow, had produced a momentary feeling of harshness even for her child, but the next instant she was humbly and heartily repentant.

"I wish I was dead," she sobbed, at length, "or that I never had been born—that would be better; nobody cares for me in the world, and even you are stealing from me the heart of my child!"

The young man was making some tender apology, to the effect that it was through the child's heart that he had hoped ultimately to reach the mother's, when a loud knock on the door arrested the attention of both parties, and caused the baby to sit suddenly upright, and stare wonderingly about.

"You may bring her cradle back where it was," said the mother softly, and hastily brushing the tears away, she opened the door with a smile that changed to an expression of pleased surprise when she saw that the visitor was Squire Bigsham.

"You need not trouble yourself about the cradle," she said, almost coldly, and aside, as it were, to the shoemaker, and from that moment, gave her undivided attention to the more distinguished guest.

When Mr. Gilbraith returned home he found a dainty little note awaiting him—Miss Bigsham presented her compliments and begged the honor of Mr. Gilbraith's company on Christmas Eve.

"By George! but she's the prettiest girl what's in this town?" exclaimed the apprentice, as he presented the note, and he added, as he saw the smile on his employer's face, "I cut the best piece of ribbon in the store to make rosyetts to put onto her shoes!"

"Quite right," replied Mr. Gilbraith, and refolding the note, he placed it carefully in his vest pocket.

The following evening the mistress of the house with the two front doors failed to return her work, as usual—the next day the apprentice was sent for it, and received the answer that it was not yet completed. Among the rest were a pair of slippers for Miss Bigsham. They must be sent home before the Christmas Eve, and having waited as long as he could, Mr. Gilbraith went himself, and in a mood less amiable than common. Not a stitch had been set in the slippers, and the fingers that should have done that work were busy making a shirt for Squire Bigsham.

The shoemaker was angry, but his first expression of displeasure was arrested by little Orphie, who clung to his knees, saying, "Gabriel, Gabriel," in her almost wild delight. He stooped and kissed her, and without another word left the house.

Christmas Eve saw him at Squire Bigsham's, and no one of all the gay assembly so much honored by the squire's beautiful daughter as he. She was noted for her graceful dancing, but that night she preferred, strangely enough, her friends thought, more quiet amusements. Mr. Gilbraith, however, was not ignorant of the fact that his inability to dance influenced her preference, nor could he remain quite insensible to that preference, for Miss Bigsham was the admiration of the village, and he to whom she extended her lightest favor was deemed fortunate indeed. Pride has more authority in matters of love than we are apt to believe, and the shoemaker's heart had its share of vanity and weakness.

Many a night after that, when he had been passing the evening with the squire's daughter, he would go home by the way of the house with the two front doors, and sometimes linger a long time watching the lights as they moved about, sighing regretfully ; for the breach created between him and the pale-faced young woman on the occasion of the squire's first visit to her was destined never to close up, and be as it was before. Little Orphie, however, did not share in the alienation, and when her birthday came round, true to his promise, he gave her the new dress, red as it could be, and exceedingly beautiful in her eyes.

" You had better give it to the great beauty who has made you so blind to everybody else," said Orphie's mother ungraciously.

" Why do you decline to-say Miss Bigsham ?" answered the shoemaker, " for doubtless it is she to whom you allude—surely that name is not so obnoxious to you."

A conversation beginning thus was not likely to end in a more agreeable state of feeling than had previously existed, and from that day the old breach was visibly widened, and the intercourse between the lovers, for such they had really been, was restricted entirely to the shoe-binding.

Once, indeed, afterwards, he knocked on one of the two doors with the express design of humbling all his pride, and expressing fully the sentiment which needed not the warranty of expression, but when the door was opened by the hand of Squire Bigsham, his tenderness and courage received together a stroke from which they never recovered.

The springtime just beginning to bud in his nature was blighted—he withdrew into himself, and suffered the old hardness and indifference to divide him from men and women again.

The squire's daughter lost her brief power, and though she tried to cover her discomfiture with gaiety and flirtation, she steadily refused all offers of marriage, and the roses died out of her cheeks, one by one.

When five years were gone her curls were put plainly away, and she was grown as quiet and reserved almost as the shoemaker himself, with whom meantime the world had continued to prosper, and he was become one of the richest and most influential of the citizens among whom he lived, for the little town where he settled had grown to a city.

Little Orphie was big enough now to bring and carry work to and from her mother's house ; every day she was seen tripping down the hill with a bundle in her arms, and every day the shoemaker kissed her and called her his little sunbeam, and so she was in fact, for she lighted his lonesome life more than anything else.

The squire's daughter and he had been almost estranged for the last year. One day, to his surprise, she came to see him, her face pale and her eyes swollen from weeping ; her father was about to be married, she said, to the woman who lived in the house with the two front doors—she could never be reconciled to such a marriage, and was about to leave her native home to make room for the intruder, and could not go away without seeing Mr. Gilbraith once more, and feeling that they parted good friends. Her trembling voice and wet cheeks told how bitter, at best, that parting must be ; suffice it that it never came about, and that instead, she became in due course of time, the mistress of a fine house of her own, and the wife of Mr. Gilbraith.—Everybody envied the couple and thought them very happy, and so perhaps they were ; nevertheless the husband had his fits of melancholy, and had, it was reported, a room set apart in his fine house where he was accustomed to retire for hours together, during which times even his beautiful wife was excluded from his sympathy.

The house with the two front doors was deserted, and when Squire Bigsham's wife sat in the front pew of the church, or invited her friends to dine, it was no longer remembered that she had ever lived there in neglect and poverty.

When little Orphie was sick, Mrs. Gilbraith went home, and when she died Mrs. Bigsham shook hands with Mr. Gilbraith, and in the child's grave all unfriendly feeling was buried.

When Peter Gilbraith, junior, was christened, there was a great merry-making at Squire Bigsham's, and when he was six years old there was no boy to be found who had so fine a beauty and so manly a courage as he. It was the autumn of that year, a rainy night, and the yellow leaves were coming down with every gust. Mr. and Mrs. Gilbraith sat chatting before a little fire, very happily, and making plans for the celebration of their wedding day. Little Peter was playing in the room specially dedicated to his father—he was fond of being there because it was a liberty not often granted him. Suddenly he came staggering towards his parents—his eyes staring wide, and his face white as it could be. As soon as he could speak he said that while he was at play, a little girl wearing a red dress came to him and kissed him, and that when he spoke to her she turned into a shadow. The anniversary celebration was talked of no more that night.

UNCLE JOHN'S STORY.

"Halloo the house!"

"Halloo! Who is there?"

It was about eight o'clock of a March evening, a good many years ago, that I sat in the chimney corner at my grandfather's house, watching the smoldering logs, and listening to the rain, which had been pouring and pouring for three long days. The meadows were soaked, the creeks swollen, and pools of water standing everywhere.

I was lonesome and homesick, for I was away from home for the first time in my life ; and though it was at my grandfather's house, I received none of those privileges and petting attentions that children are now a-days accustomed to expect from grandparents.

The ancient homestead was one of the most retired and altogether unattractive that ever resisted the peltings of a March storm. Indeed, it would be difficult to imagine a less enjoyable situation for a young woman of twelve years old, or thereabouts, to be placed in. Too young to appreciate the sage and solemn doctrine that made up the discourse of the old people, and too thoughtless to press reason into my service, there was little for me to do, but suffer and be still.

If I looked through the small window-panes, down which the rain was pouring in streams, I could see nothing but a circle of woods, if my eyes wandered beyond the patch of cleared land that held the house and barn and mill, the main road being quite out of view. If I had been a few years older, I might have found the sunshiny face of Cyrus Hall, who was my grandfather's hired man, genial as the sunshine itself; but as it was, though I received alleviation, even comfort from his kindnesses, I was far from that state of beatitude which bringeth utter forgetfulness of clouds. He had told me over and over that it would stop raining in a day or two, and that the wet cornstalks which lay between the wood and the mill would in a single day get dry enough to burn; and then he would gather them up in heaps and burn them after nightfall, and have—oh, such fun! But he found it hard to make me believe, in my then state of mind, that the sun would ever shine again, or that the cornstalks would ever be dry enough to burn, and if they should be, grandfather would not allow us to burn them, I argued, for my mood of mind inclined me to augment my sorrows.

To the best of my knowledge and belief, my ancient grand-mother would continue to knit at the stocking she was busy with till the day of doom, and that my grandfather would ever close the big Bible from which he was reading, and speak or smile again, I had not the remotest idea. The very cat stretched across the hearth, seemed to me indicative of final repose. No wonder the tears would start now and then.

There was one candle burning, and besides a little glow from the fire there was no other light, except what Cyrus's eyes made, and they were as bright as they could be with hope and good humor. He was about twenty years old, red-cheeked, and beautiful as a young rose, and in exuberance of spirits contrasted strikingly with the severe gravity of my white-headed grandfather.

Now and then, the cattle in the sheds lowed uneasily, for they, too, were tired of the rain ; or one of the work-horses put his head out of the window of his stable and neighed, and except these, there was no sound but that of the rain on the roof, and the ticking of the clock ; for Cyrus talked in whispers as a single word spoken above the breath, while my grandfather was reading, would have been an awful breach of family discipline.   He had exhibited whatever he possessed that could amuse me—from the *picture*-book presented by his schoolmaster, with "Reward of merit" written on the fly-leaf in flourishing characters, to a late purchase of a silk pocket-handkerchief and razor ; and at the time our story opens, was telling me the history of his life—partly, perhaps, for the want of a better listener.   His father was a wood-chopper, who rented a cabin, and moved from one place to another, as opportunities of work offered inducements ; at nine years old, he himself had been compelled to earn his own living, and in his tossing about the pendant world, had gained all the knowledge he was possessed of.

There fell a shadow across his face towards the close of his story, such as I had never seen it wear before, and when I asked him what the matter was, he answered "nothing," and then said he was thinking of something I could not understand. I said I would try, and then he told me that he knew a young woman once, not much bigger than I, whom he liked better than he ever liked any one else, but that she was rich and himself poor, so he had come away from the neighborhood where she lived, and never expected to see her any more.

Suddenly he ceased his narrative—my grandmother let fall her knitting work, and my grandfather, closing the old Bible, walked straight out into the rain, and responded—

"Halloo! Who is there?" to the "Halloo the house!" recorded in the opening of this chapter. The wonder who could be coming at that time of night, and in so terrible a storm, held us all breathless.

"Cyrus, bring out the lantern—quick!" called my grandfather, and in a moment, without hat or coat, Cyrus was in the yard, the lantern glimmering before him.

How much I wished to ask my grandmother who she thought was coming, but to ask direct questions was not among my privileges, so I contented my curiosity as well as I could by listening towards the open door through which the rain was driving freely.   The door-yard gate creaked on its hinges, and then came a noise like a team drawing a wagon that cut its slow way heavily through the soaked earth.

"Whoa!" was heard next, and the team stood still right against the blue stones at the door.

"Take my hand, Uncle John, and step here!" I heard a voice that was all music and melody say, and presently a young woman, muffled in a shawl and hood, came into the house, leading by the hand a grey-haired man with a very pale face.

"Bring your lantern this way, Cyrus," called my grandfather, as he saw them feeling their way through the dark, but no Cyrus appeared, and presently, his white hair clinging to his head, and accompanied by a boy of some fourteen years, he entered and, closing the door, presented the strangers by saying, "Here are some travellers come to stay all night with us—the bridge is swept from Bear Creek, and they can get no further at present."

"We are very sorry it happened so," said the pale man, "but you must not allow us to make you more trouble than is necessary—myself and Thomas can lie on the floor before the fire, but Nanny here is sickly, poor child, and if you could give her a bed, why, we will do as much for somebody some time, if not for you."

He put his arm around the waist of the girl, as he spoke, and I saw that she was trembling—almost crying.

"You are wet, poor Nanny," he said, untying her hood, and passing his hand tenderly along her hair.

She evidently made a strong effort to recover herself, and answered in a tone of assumed cheerfulness—

"I shall do well enough, Uncle John, but you will be sick I am afraid ;" and she placed a chair for him, saying apologetically as he felt about awkwardly to find it—"My uncle is blind, and I bespeak the spare bed for him."

"I guess," said my grandmother, "we can give you all beds, and something a little comforting besides." And relieving Nanny of her wet shawl and hood, she hastened to put on the tea-kettle.

My grandfather, meantime, was brightening up the fire, and entertaining Thomas with an account of the damage done in the neighborhood by the rain.

Nanny was pretty, but her blue eyes had, I thought, a bewildered and frightened look, and she almost clung to the hand of Uncle John as it lay in her lap.

"There was another one who came out and assisted us in," said the blind man, directly, as he listened to the different voices—"where is he, Nanny?"

The girl's face flushed red as fire, and she answered nothing.

"That was Cyrus, my hired man," replied my grandfather, speaking very loud, as if a blind man was necessarily deaf too, "and he is feeding your horses."

"I wonder he don't come in," he added, speaking to himself. Nanny's face had grown white now, and she leaned against Uncle John's shoulder, saying, in answer to his inquiries, that the fire made her feel faint, she believed. My grandmother proposed all the cordials at her command, but Nanny steadily refused, saying she would be better directly. She gave no signs of being better, however, and when it was proposed that she should lie down till supper was ready, she acceded with an eager thankfulness, and was led away to the tiny bedroom where my grandmother kept her silver spoons, and extra china, in a corner cupboard.

My services were brought into requisition in the arrangement of the supper-table, and on going to the corner cupboard for the spoons, I perceived that Nanny had turned her face from the light and was evidently crying.

I forgot my own homesickness in my anxiety to do or say something that might comfort her, but I was bashful, and only dared to shade the light and walk on tiptoe by way of manifesting my interest. At last we had the supper prepared, toast and tea and honey, and I know not what all besides, and my grandmother set the tea to draw in the best china teapot, and the puffing tea-kettle close by it, and we ranged ourselves round the fire to wait for Cyrus to come in.

All eyes turned to the blind man—my grandmother sighed heavily, and there fell a sympathetic silence over the group.

"I see how it is," said Uncle John, smiling, "but there is no need that you should pity me ; and if you have any pity to spare I entreat that you will give it to my little niece, Nanny, for whose sake, in fact, we are on our travels, more than for anything else. We hoped it would divert her mind from an unhappy memory, but it seemed to-night as if the old feeling mastered her again—I knew it by her trembling voice and hand."

"Poor dear child !" said my grandmother, with a woman's quick sympathy—"I'll go straight and carry her a cup of tea —I hope she did not catch cold ;" and she had Nanny's little feet in her hands, almost while she spoke. She presently returned, saying with a cheerful manner, and addressing herself particularly to Thomas, that his sister seemed to be sleeping very sweetly.

I have suspected since that the sweet sleep was all an affectation.

"How did it happen that you lost your eyes ?" asked my grandfather, perhaps more to arouse the blind man from the revery into which he had fallen, than from curiosity.

"Tell them all about it, Uncle John," said Thomas, speaking for the first time, and blushing with embarrassment, "it's good as a sermon."

"Oh, it's no story at all," replied Uncle John ; but we all said, " tell us about it, at any rate ;" and having listened for a moment at the door to see whether Nanny were still asleep, he began :

"I may begin by saying, so as to prevent further waste of

sympathy, I am voluntarily blind. My earliest memory is connected with lamentations about my blindness. My parents were wealthy, and I, a fondly-expected son, so you can perhaps imagine the suffering occasioned by what they termed my misfortune ; it was the first great sorrow of their lives, and my own happiness was constantly diminished by the knowledge that I was a heavy burden to their hands. Sometimes hearing the merriment in the parlor, I would feel my way along the walls and by the furniture till I would touch my mother's knees ; but it seemed as if a great melancholy shadow fell over them all at my entrance, and the voices were subdued, and the laughter hushed ; so I learned by degrees to live much alone, and it is astonishing within how small a compass we can find enjoyment enough. I was naturally of a happy and contented disposition, and in sitting in the sunshine often experienced more delight than my playmates seemed to find in their greater privileges.

" I learned to read, and what with my books and my play made myself so happy that my parents felt their burden lighter, and finally, as they became used to my condition, I believe I really afforded them a good deal of comfort. I was always, however, called poor unfortunate little John, and to the end of their days they held frequent consultations concerning operations, which my mother could never quite consent to, and of famous opticians who had made the blind to see.

" I did not feel the loss they lamented so much, and could run up and down the stairs, from room to room, and about the door-yard as readily as any one. I could distinguish everybody I knew by their step—all the colors I had fixed in my mind, which was stored, too, with pictures of all my friends. My parents died, thank God, without my having ever seen either of them.   Not for the world would I have had the sweet impression I still retain of their faces, unsettled.

"I was forty years old when I went to live with my brother Moses, and then came a new torture in the shape of new sympathy. It was all 'poor Uncle John,' now, as it had been 'poor little John' when I was a boy. Only Nanny, dear little girl, never mourned over me—I wish I never had over her ; she used to climb on my knees and read stories by the hour, and sing songs for me, and tell me how everything looked that I could not see, and laugh and clap her hands at the odd fancies I had formed. She was full of frolic and fun, and made the house gay with her chattering from morning till night—poor Nanny !

"When they told me she was fifteen years old, I could not believe it, for to me she was a pet and plaything, and try as I would I could not make her a woman. About this time my brother Moses, who was beginning to grow feeble, hired a young man to assist in the farm-work, Thomas being then at school. He often talked of his poverty, and told us stories of the hard times he had seen ; but he was hopeful and genial, almost making a jest of his misfortunes—then, too, he was so industrious and obliging that we all learned to love him. As for myself I liked him none the less on account of his poverty—I could not feel any difference, and as I could not see any, why it made no difference to me whether he were poor or rich.

"One frosty evening Nanny was sitting on my knee, singing one of my favorite songs, when 'Cy,' as we always called him, came in from the field and sat down by the fire.

"'Dear me, Uncle John !' exclaimed Nanny, breaking off her

song, 'Cyrus has no stockings on!—mustn't he be cold?'
'Cold! No,' replied Cyrus, 'I have seen the time I had no
shoes—did I never tell you about my first pair?—I was ten
years old when I got them, and earned the money to buy them
myself.' 'Pray tell me all about it,' said Nanny, and she
was off my knee and sitting beside the young farmer, in a
twinkling. I don't remember what the particulars were, and
no matter—enough that Nanny found them interesting; and
not long after this when I missed a ring I had put on her
finger, and inquired what she had done with it, she replied
artlessly that she had given it to Cyrus!

"So it came about that I liked the young man less and less,
and Nanny liked him more and more—indeed she was never
weary of praising him.

"My brother, who was growing feebler all the time, seeing
that his end approached, became doubly anxious that my eyes
should be operated upon. If he could leave me guardian of his
children he would die happy, he said. How little we under
stand what we ask for.

"As if in answer to his wishes, there came into the neighborhood a great oculist, and partly to soothe my dying brother,
and partly to realize the heaven I had been taught to believe I
should find if I but had my sight, I submitted my blind organs
to his operative skill, and to the astonishment and joy of every
one, I was made to see!

"Bequeathing me the care of his children, Moses died happy,
and more than happy.

"But whatever pleasure my new sense gave to others, it was
only a source of discomfort to me. It was quite superfluous,
and I could do nothing with it. It clashed with all my previous

ideas of things, and I could not reconcile anything. Colors I
could not distinguish, except by the old method of passing my
hand over them ; of distances I could form no idea, and I fell
down continually if I undertook to walk, so when I desired to
go from one place to another I was obliged to close my eyes
and feel my way as I used to. In fact, I had no pleasure, so
continually was I running into the fire or the water, or against
the wall, except in bandaging my eyes and making believe I
was blind again.

"My friends I did not know, and strange to say, did not like
as my new sense revealed them. I became dissatisfied with
myself, and with everything ; irritable, and ultimately, I think,
not far from insane. Is it any wonder if Nanny became more
and more alienated from me, and more and more attached to
Cyrus ?

"Glad of any pretext, I argued if his motives were honorable it was necessary he should he more explicit, for with all his
demonstrations, he had never said he loved Nanny, as she
owned, and never asked her to marry him. Besides, I said it
was a scandal that she, who was an heiress, should marry her
father's hired man ! Poor Nanny could only hide her face and
cry ; and the end of it was the dismissal of Cyrus upon some
false pretext and the breaking of Nanny's heart.

"When he had been away six months you would not have
known her for the same girl—there was no singing, and no
story-telling any more, but only moping and sighing from morning till night. I settled all my fortune upon her, but she never
smiled half so brightly as I had seen her when Cyrus but gave
her his hand.

"I sent for the physicians whose skill recommended them,

but spite all they could do, she grew quietly and steadily thinner and paler, until she became the sickly and unstable creature you saw to-night. I was glad when I found the darkness spreading over my eyes again, and hiding from me her reproachful face.

"My friends besought me to have recourse to the oculist anew, but I steadily persevered in my refusal, and joyfully went back into blindness, and gradually my confused brain became clear and quiet again.

"We hoped the little journey we are taking might make Nanny better, but unless we hear tidings from Cyrus, I think we shall make her a bed by her father before long." He groaned and covered his face, as he finished the story.

"I wonder where *my* Cyrus lived before he came to work for me?" said my grandfather, rising and stirring the fire.

"He lived with Uncle John, and loved Nanny, though he never dared to tell her so," answered Cyrus, as he came forward and grasped the blind man by the hand.

He had come in in the middle of Uncle John's story, and seating himself quietly in the corner, had remained there till its conclusion, unobserved.

So much merry noise as there was in my grandfather's house had never been heard there till that night. I think only for a moment was there silence—when, having placed the teapot on the table, my grandmother went to bring Nanny out to supper.

And such rosy cheeks were never seen as she and Cyrus presented when they shook hands, just as if they had not seen and recognized each other when they met in the door-yard.

What a pleasant supper we had, and what a happy time we

had telling stories round the fire afterwards, and what laughing, when grandmother said she would give her spare bed to Thomas and Uncle John, for she was quite sure Nanny could sit up all night, well enough !

The following morning the sun was shining brightly, as Cyrus had predicted—the strangers remained at my grandfather's all day, Thomas assisting Cyrus to rake the cornstalks into heaps, and when night came, Nanny and I went out to the field and helped to burn them. Why should I linger ?— everybody who has ever loved, guesses the end of the story, and those who have not, will feel no interest in hearing.

MAKING THE CHILDREN SOMETHING.

———◆———

Five o'clock in the great city—a roar as of a mighty sea in the streets, for the multitude is heaving hither and thither in pursuit of interest or pleasure. "Dinner-time," said Mrs. William Hartly, looking up from the torn lace she was trying to stitch together, "and I have not seen Annie to-day—what can the girl be about?"

The door opens, and a feeble little man, with no more color in his face than is in his handkerchief, enters, and in querulous accents inquires, "What are you doing, my dear? and why are you not dressed?" and opening his watch, he continues— "five minutes past five," which in the lady's estimation seems equivalent to having said, "You outrage all propriety;" for she hastily puts down the torn lace, and disappears with an air not the most amiable in the world.

The white-faced feeble man walks nervously about the room for some ten minutes, more or less, when the lady returns, "made up" for the ceremony of dinner, which the bell has rung for twice during her preparation.

"You are looking very sweetly, my dear; and Mr. William Hartly slips the ringed fingers of his stout wife through his own tiny and wiry arm, and in pompous solemnity they descend together.

"Where is Pet?" he asks, placing a chair for the stout woman, and crooking his lips into what is meant to be a smile.

"If you mean Annie," answers the injured wife, "I don't know anything about her."

"Very strange, madam," says Mr. Hartly, unfolding his napkin with trembling hands, "that we can't even eat and drink like other folks—where is Albert?" The wife and mother simply shakes her head this time, and the sensor continues : "Have you resigned the government of your own household, madam ?"

And he goes on with some complaint about the soup, while the wife, with eyes bent intently on the name of "Hartly," graven on her silver spoon, answers, with no submission except in her words, that she will have nothing to do with children or servants any more, and that if her husband thinks it so easy a task to put his own notions into other people's heads, he is welcome to try—she has tried and tried till she is tired, and she can't make anything of either Albert or Annie, and she is quite willing to resign the task to abler hands.

Mr. Hartly bows in acknowledgment of the compliment, and says he will see what can be done, and his tone has in it something of the authoritative meaning of a schoolmaster ; for he was bred in early life to the profession of one. His iron-grey hair stands up with a more determinate expression, and his white face grows whiter in the calmness of settled resolve.

A lubberly, yellow-haired boy of twelve years old kicks open the door at this juncture, and with his fine and fashionably-made clothes soiled and torn, dashes his cap at one of the servants in waiting, by way of eliciting attention to his wants, and seats himself at table, without noticing father or mother. "Albert, my son," says the father, "what has detained you? have you no excuse?"

"Detained myself," replies the boy, "and that's the reason; and besides, I stole a piece of molasses cake at school, and did not get so hungry for dinner as common."

Mr. Hartly frowned and Mrs. Hartly sighed, the one looking the picture of indignation and the other of despair.

"Tell you what, old folks," said the boy, without noticing the troubled expression of his parents, "I'll run away from school if you make me go there, 'cause I hate books—there haint none of them got no sense in them—and I hate masters; there never was a schoolmaster that had sense: I'm a going to hire out to a livery-stable, and learn to nick and dock, that's what I'll do; and when I'm sixteen I'll be sot up in the trade, and I'll keep the fastest trotters in town. Old folks, do you hear that?"

Both father and mother looked as though they did hear; Mrs Hartly dropping knife and fork, and limberly falling together as if there were no more courage in her, and Mr. Hartly bracing himself up as though about to be swept over the Niagara Falls.

"What's matter? Anything in my composition surprise you?"

"I think there are some things in your composition that must be beaten down or wrenched out," said the father; "and now, sir," he continued, "don't open your mouth again till I give you liberty."

"How will I eat, old man," replied the boy, "if I am to keep my mouth shut?"

Mr. Hartly here arose, and having struck the broad shoulders of the lad with his little delicate hand, led him away by one ear, assuring him that for the next forty-eight hours he should have nothing but bread and water to eat.

Annie, ignorant of how matters stood, made her appearance at this moment, carrying a great platter of steaming pudding, her flushed face radiant with smiles, for she had made the pudding with her own hands, and evidently in the expectation of affording her parents a happy surprise.

No smile answered hers, however, as she placed the pudding dish on the table, timidly turning her eyes from father to mother.

"Doesn't it look nice?" she ventured to say at last; "Mr. Wentworth showed me how to make it—shan't I ask him to come and eat with us?"

"I think *you* look nice," said the mother, eyeing the flour on Annie's apron, and the rosy face indicative of the cookery she had been engaged in; "it's no use," she continued, as Annie stood still aghast, "I can't make anything of you, and I may just as well let you run wild—go and live with Mr. Wentworth, and learn to make butter and cheese; I expect that would suit you better than going to dancing-school and practising your piano, as you ought to do. Your father and I have used every means in our power to make something of you and your brother—you have had money enough spent on you, the dear knows, to make you as accomplished as anybody in the city; and then, to the neglect of your proper duties, you go in the kitchen and talk about pumpkins with Mr. Wentworth, if that is the man's name, and make puddings, and appear at the dinner-table with your hair in that frightfully plain fashion—it's enough to break a mother's heart."

Annie answered that she did not know it was wrong to make a pudding, nor to ask Mr. Wentworth to eat some of it when he was so good as to show her the way to make it—and it was such a cheap way.

"Economy is not the chief end and aim of *our* lives, my dear," said the father ; " there may be people to whom a pound of flour, more or less, makes a difference, but I humbly trust you will never be in their sphere of life ;" and for a moment Mr. Hartly subsided, and seemed to be saying, " Does the forty feet stone front of our house look like practising economy in the making of a pudding ? Do the stone steps and the stone baluster look like it ?   Does the man-servant who attends the door-bell look like it ? Do the lace curtains, ten in all, look like it ? Do my wife's brocades look like it ? Do the entertainments I give look like it, or anything in any way appertaining to us ? No, no ; nobody would suppose us to be people to economize." And having thus mentally soliloquized, he turned to Annie, who stood at the foot of the table like a culprit. " No, my dear, no ; *we* are not the people to count the eggs that go into a pudding ;" and having emphasized the fact by tapping his silver fork lightly against his plate, he added. " Whom have you in the kitchen, and what is his occupation ?"

" Why, father, it is Mr. Wentworth—you know him," said Annie, looking a little encouraged.

Mr. Hartly slowly moved his head from side to side, as though he said, " I wash my hands of it—I know nothing of him."

" One of these men, you know," said Mrs. Hartly, in an explanatory way, " who make pumpkins and milk, and cultivate butter, and manufacture corn and cattle, and such things—-a man that lives in an open place, you know, where there are trees, and where there are no streets, you know ; no houses, only wigwams, or bamboo huts, or something ; you know, William, it's the old person that brings us our butter and apples."

Mrs. Hartly said *person*, to indicate that she did not know exactly whether he were black or white, man or monkey. It was a sheer affectation on her part, for Mrs. Hartly was a woman of naturally good plain common sense, if she could have been satisfied to let plain common sense be plain common sense, but she could not ; she had a large amount of that " vaulting ambition which is apt to o'erleap itself and fall on t'other side."   She was the daughter of a retired horse-jockey, and could, in her youth, drive or ride the most unmanageable animal in her father's stable, and not unfrequently did ride without saddle from the suburbs of the village where she lived, to the city, half a dozen miles away, where she served apprenticeship as a milliner, and afterward herself kept shop. All these things were doubtless forgotten, for they were long ago, when stout Mrs. Hartly was gawky Debby Smith, and before her nature was smothered and lost in affectations. Somewhere about the same time, Mr. William Hartly, the present opulent merchant, was a country schoolmaster, near the village of the milliner, carrying his candle to the log school-house for the evening meeting, and paying board by working in the garden of nights and mornings.   In the course of time it came about that Debby Smith was employed by the schoolmaster, aforesaid, to make shirts—for plain needle-work entered into the young woman's accomplishments—and from these beginnings had come the present wealthy merchant, the stone-fronted house and all the appurtenances thereof, the pompous Mrs. Hartly, the young woman Annie, and the hopeful Master Albert.

There had been no sudden influx of wealth, such as often turns the heads of silly people—all had been the growth of years of steady industry and economy, attended with constant good luck. And with the wealth, affectations had grown, for Mr. and Mrs. Hartly were under the impression that their present position demanded it—it was a duty they owed to the world at large, in view of the stone front, the man-servant, the rosewood furniture, and the inheritors of their great fortune, Annie and Albert; the first a most active, good-tempered young woman, but plain, and "without hope of change;" the latter a coarse, vulgar lad, on whom no refinement could be ingrafted, and whose natural abhorrence of books and love of horses were not likely to be easily overcome.

So there they were together in their fine house, being supposed to be dining at five o'clock, easily and elegantly, having taken luncheon at twelve, and with tea and supper to be served in due and *proper* course of time—supposed to be, I say, for the luncheon, and the supper, and the tea, were all myths ; the luncheon, when traced to its reality, consisting chiefly of bread crusts, strong butter, scraps of meat, and the like, kept in the closet, and resorted to from time to time by such members of the family as were about the house, and felt the demands of appetite too importunate to be refused till the regular dinner hour. Mr. and Mrs. Hartly had done well for themselves, as they believed—all they could do ; they wore good clothes, and used what they thought good words ; they affected high breed-

ing, and believed in their hearts that the pretence was the possession—paste was not less genuine to them than diamonds·
Mr. Hartly had worn himself thin and pale ; had, in fact,
coined his life-blood into money and the effort to be genteel.
Mrs. Hartly had, as she supposed, expanded easily to a model
of dignity and deportment ; but she saw not herself as others
saw her—she was, in fact, in her best phases, a big woman
with fine clothes on.   Her misfortune was, that nothing would
fit her ; rings and ear-rings seemed hung on ; dresses seemed
pinned on and hooked on, but not to have been especially made
for her, or in the least becoming to her ; they might have belonged to Mrs. Lundy, or any other woman who had money
enough to buy them ; she was a personage on whom all these
things were hung, and when she wore a velvet train, she was
simply a big woman with a velvet train, and she was nothing
more.

Whether she improved her broad flat face in any very great
degree by the little curls she was at infinite pains to twist
along either temple was questionable to everybody but herself ;
and whether the powder which she deposited among the pimples of her face was not calculated to call attention to her
sorry complexion, was also questionable ; but these were Mrs.
Hartly's taste, and in some sort the necessities of her station,
she thought.   They had taught themselves divers little forms
and ceremonies, in the use of which they were most punctilions,
and a dozen times a day Mrs. Hartly sent her compliments to
Mr. Hartly, with some sweet and lady-like inquiry as to his
health, or wishes with reference to what dress she should appear in at dinner, and as often Mr. Hartly sent back his compliments, from the garret where he was putting in a pane of

glass, or the cellar where he was sawing wood, as the case might be, begging that Mrs. Hartly would oblige him by wearing the blue dress, or the green one, and he often topped these princely messages by a request that Mrs. Hartly, if she could make it consistent with her previous engagements, would do him the favor to accompany him on a visit to the house of general, or governor so-and-so. The Hartlies liked to hear themselves sending these messages ; it had a lofty look in their eyes to appear to know little about each other's affairs ; their house was so big, and the duties of their station so multifarious ; their suits of apartments so vast and separate, that they could not be expected to know much of each other's movements. These affectations were all that was left of them ; as the moss grows over a dead tree, so they were overgrown by them. Thus they stood, ornaments of their age and generation, in their own estimation—shams, to other people. If by any means the children could have been screwed up, or pinched down ; stretched or flattened to genteel proportions, it would have been done—but alack ! they had been put through the artistic mills in vain—they would not be made anything of.

This conviction, forced home upon Mrs. Hartly to-day, reduced her to the ill-natured and somewhat natural demeanor, of which she was grown mortally ashamed, and which she essayed to cancel by the double distilled affectation about cheese and butter. And to the close of this exquisite manifestation of ignorance we return.

"A decent sort of person, I suppose," said Mr. Hartly, in the benevolent supposition that it is barely possible, and he is inclined to hope for the best.

"Oh, he seems such a good old man, and he has got on

such a nice coat that he says his wife spun !" exclaimed Annie, in ecstasy at the kindly disposition of her father.

"How foolish you are, Petty !" said Mrs. Hartly, in a kind of softened and polite scorn ; and she added, in a sweet pouting style, "I would not have a big ugly wheel in my house, they make a noise like one of these great winnow things that countrymen have to put their chaff through. My grandfather told me about one once. I never saw one. I would not look at it."

All this time Mr. Hartly has been sitting with knitted brows, and twitching almost with the culmination of some most important matter. At length he says : " Annie, my daughter, I am resolved to send you to the wilderness with this old man as you call him, and keep you there too, till you will be glad to come back to civilized life." Annie bites her red lips together, trying to look demure ; but a smile breaks out in her face that is brighter than was ever there before.

Mrs. Hartly lifts up her hands and looks heavenward, as though incredulous of her mortal understanding. "I am determined," continues Mr. Hartly, "that in some way I will make something of my children. I have used bribes, and now I shall use punishments. I have spent thousands of dollars to accomplish my children, and what good has it done ?" He broke off abruptly, and sent his compliments to Master Albert, with a request that he would drink a glass of wine with him.

The lad sent no message in return ; but with cap pulled down over his red eyes, and lips puffed out with anger, thrust his sister aside, and commenced eating the pudding with a table spoon. "Don't, my dear, don't," said the mamma softly ; "I am afraid that odd-looking dish won't agree with you."

"If you think this kind of stuff is going to hurt *you*," replied the boy, "I am glad of it—cause I could eat a bushel."

"Mother, shan't I give you some?" asked Annie, looking proudly at her pudding.

"Petty, you speak so loud—it's vulgar," said the mamma ; and she sends a servant to the other end of the table with her compliments, and the reply that she will trouble her daughter to be so good as to send her part of a spoonful. And having received, she cuts it apart, and dips it up and down in order to see whether it is made of anything of which she has any knowledge, concluding, as it appears, that she has not —for she tastes not, and presently ceases to touch and to handle.

"My son," said Mr. Hartly, lifting his glass.

"I see you," answers the hopeful ; "and when I finish this pooden, I'll drink a bottle or two ; haint got my appetite squinched yet, and come to my drinkotite. I was at confession, you know."

For a while Mr. Hartly's head falls, as if a hammer struck him ; there is no doubt but that his suffering is sincere. At length he says, in subdued and sorrowful accents : "Albert, it has been the aim and the hope of my life to make something of you, and now the time has come that you must choose a profession, or rather begin one ; for I am resolved to make a painter of you. I shall send you to Florence at once, to study the old masters."

"I've studied you, haint I?" replies Albert ; "I saw you paint the kitchen floor, and I didn't learn nothing as I know of."

"I don't mean to paint houses, my son ; you misapprehend—
I intend you shall make great pictures."

"Well then, say what you mean, and don't go to sticking on
airs, and I'll tell you what trade I want to go to. I want to
be sot up in a stable—and you can fork out the cash as soon as
you like."

"Why, baby dear," says the mother, "you are just in fun—
a real live horse would scare you to death."

"Scare your granny !" replies the baby ; "just as if I didn't
run away from school every day, and curry horses and such
things, in the stables. You don't know me, do you ?" And
with such a saucy, impudent look, as can't be described, he goes
on with the pudding.

Mrs. Hartly sends her compliments to Mr. Hartly, with the
suggestion that they make a poet of the hopeful ; and Mr.
Hartly sends compliments in turn, though only the table
divides them, and begs that Mrs. Hartly will consider the
matter settled—the hopeful must be an artist, which is
responded to by a whisper of—"Just as you please, my
dear."

This, then, being concluded, the person whom Annie had
so audaciously called an old man, and who, whatever he may
be, is supposed to answer to the name of Wentworth, is summoned by his great patrons, and promptly answers the call ;
not humbly and deferentially, but with a firm step, and a manner of self-respect that commands respect.

Mr. Hartly waves him to a seat in a distant part of the
room, and proceeds to inform him that he desires the girl who
has just made his acquaintance in the kitchen, to be banished
to his residence, wherever that may be, and kept there on

bread and water, or whatever else the person may be in the habit of eating himself, till she shall be willing to return home, and appreciate her advantages. Annie sits down on a stool close by the old man, and rubs the flour from her apron by way of keeping down her disposition to laughter ; and *the person* replies that he hopes to give his visitor something better than bread and water, though the accommodations of his house will be far short of what she is used to.

Mr. Hartly replies that it is not as a *visitor* that he proposes to send his child, but as a boarder, or rather a prisoner.

Mr. Wentworth smiles, and says his folks have never taken boarders or prisoners, but he is sure they will not object to receive his little friend, for a time. She looks as if she might make bread or butter with the smartest young women he knows ; and he smiles and lays his toil-hardened hand on Annie's head as the finishing of his compliment.

Mrs. Hartly begins a little scream, which she concludes by whispering in the white ear of her white-faced husband, that she supposes *the* person don't know *our* child from any common child and so the affair is negotiated.

While Annie is being denuded of ear-rings and breast-pins, and all other ornaments, and having laces, and flounces, and furbelows packed away for the uses of the genteel time that is to come after her banishment—and such plain ginghams, calicoes, aprons, and the like, as are thought suited to the term of her imprisonment, made ready—Mr. Hartly, who is unwilling that even the person, old man, farmer, or whatever he may be, should remain ignorant of his great consideration, asks condescendingly, whether he has ever seen so fine a house before.

The old man, who seems in no way overcome with the grandeur about him, answers that it seems to be a good house ; but that, for his part, he prefers his own little farm and house. It may be very fine, he thinks, but he doesn't want it.

" Good heavens !" exclaims Mr. Hartly ; " you ain't in your right mind, are you ? have you seen what my house is ? have you seen the stone front, the balustrade ? Why sir, the window-curtains cost me five hundred dollars each—more than all you are worth in the world, I expect."

The old man says, it may be so ; still he seems disposed to regard his own possessions as preferable.

Mr. Hartly confronts him as he sits quietly contemplating the carving of the marble mantel—thrusts his thin white fingers through his iron-grey hair, sets his teeth together, and sucks in a long breath, and then as though the countryman were an idiot that he would make see if there were any eyes in him, he takes him by the hand, and leads him up the broad flights of stairs, and through all the rooms with their splendid appointments ; however, the old man sees nothing but things that have cost money. It is all very well, he says, for people that like it ; but, for his part, he would not have the trouble of taking care of so many things, even if they were given to him.

In the great easy-chair of the parlor Mr. Hartly sinks down exhausted, and locking his little white fingers together, repeats to himself : " Well, well, well !" each time a little louder, and as though nothing could be said of such stupidity. Meantime the farmer makes his way out into the sunshine, seeming to find that more genial than the heavy, damp air within the thick walls. The stout horses, having eaten their dinner of oats, are ready to go home, and the coverlet is spread over the straw that fills the wagon-bed, for the accommodation of Annie, who presently makes her appearance and tells her friend that her father wishes to speak to him.

"Old person," says Mr. Hartly, as though it were not likely the man had a name, "I consign my daughter to your charge for a certain time, and for reasons that to me are greater than you can comprehend ; and I wish you to receive an equivalent, that is pay, for the trouble she may give you—what sum shall you accept ? Not that it makes any difference to me—money is to me no object."

These are not precisely his words, to be sure ; but both manner and words indicate, or are meant to indicate, that he has had money till he is tired of money. However, it is finally arranged that Annie shall work for her board for her own punishment merely, and not to save a few sixpences, more or less. She is also required to keep a journal of her exile life, and once a week submit the same to her very loving parents, which letter-writing is supposed, on their part, to pave the way to making her a famous author. And she is informed, that when she shall find herself willing to come home, and wear silks and laces, and learn dancing and music, keep out of the kitchen, and, in short, be made something of, she shall return. She is furthermore bidden to take an affectionate leave of Master Albert, who, she is informed, is to be sent immediately to Florence to be made into a painter. Miss Annie essays an embrace, but the hopeful twists out of her arms, and with a rude push informs her that he means to run away and be a horse-jockey, for that the old folks can't make him over into anything that he aint.

" That has been my notion pretty much," said the old man ; "I have always thought it was best to let *natur'* have its way ; and Joshua, that's my eldest son, has made a preacher ; and Cliff, who is sturdy and stout, and full of fun, has staid on the farm with me. It seems to come *nat'ral* to him to work, somehow."

Mr. Hartly looks pityingly on the old person's ignorance ; and abruptly turning away, offers his arm to dear Mrs. Hartly, and with one or two affected little sobs, she is led off.

I will pass over all the preparation made for the departure of Master Albert, nor trouble the reader with an account of Mrs Hartly's protracted darnings of lace, and hemming, scalloping and fringing, crimping and curling—all the hanging on, and the taking off of fine things—all the powdering, and the combing of her poodle—and likewise pass by all Mr. Hartly's examinations into the quantities of meat cooked for dinner, all his parcellings out of beans and potatoes, all his contemplative pacings up and down before his own house, in happy admiration of the extent thereof—all compliments sent back and forth for the space of eight days, when I must beg the reader to imagine him in his great chair—spectacles shoved up over his hair—a sealed paper lying before him on the table ; and also to imagine the transport with unusual form and dignity, to Master Hartly of his compliments, begging that he will oblige his father by his immediate presence—also of a similar message to Mrs. Hartly, with fear that she may be detained by the general pressure of her position.

The simple fact is, a letter has been received from Annie, which is about to be read. That it is a sort of humiliation and prayer to be permitted to return home, is expected ; and

that the effect on the hopeful may be salutary, is believed—
but he, failing to make his appearance, the reading goes on.
The letter was as follows :

"DEAR FATHER AND MOTHER :

"I have so many things to say, and am so little used to
writing, that I don't know how to begin ; but as I promised to
keep a sort of journal of every day's experience, I suppose I
may as well begin now, for this is the second night of my being
here. You can't imagine what a nice ride we had in the open
wagon, so much pleasanter than being shut up in a coach—it
was such a pleasure to see the stout horses pull us along, and
trotting or walking just as Uncle Wentworth directed : I say
uncle, because I like Mr. Wentworth, and wish all the time he
was some true relation. The straw in the wagon smelled so
sweet, sweeter than flowers, it seemed to me ; and when we got
into the real country everything looked so beautiful, that I
laughed all the time, and Uncle Wentworth said folks would
think he had a crazy girl. I was very much ashamed of my
ignorance, for I thought all country people lived in holes in the
ground, or little huts made of sticks, and that cows and horses
and all lived together ; but we saw all along the road such
pretty cottages and gardens, and some houses indeed as fine as
ours. I kept asking Uncle Wentworth what sort of place we
were going to, for I could not help fearing it was a very bad
place ; but he only laughed, and told me to wait and see. A
good many men were at work in fields of hay—some cutting
and some tossing it about—and I kept wishing I was among
them, they seemed so merry, and the hay was so sweet. In
some places were great fields of corn, high as my head, with

grey tassels on the tops of it. I thought men were at work there too, it shook so; but Uncle Wentworth said it was only the wind. And back of the fields, and seeming like a great green wall between the earth and the sky, stood the woods. I mean to go into them before long, but I am a little afraid of wild beasts yet; though uncle says I will find no worse thing than myself there. We met a good many carriages, full of gayly dressed people coming into town; and saw a number of young ladies dressed in bright ginghams, tending the flowers in front of the cottages, sometimes at work in the gardens, indeed, so my dresses will be right in the fashion. In one place we passed a white school-house, set right in the edge of the woods; and when we were a little by, out came near forty children, some girls as big as I, and a whole troop of little boys, all laughing, and jumping, and frolicking, as I never heard children laugh. I asked Uncle Wentworth if it were *proper?* and he said it was their nature, and he supposed our wise Father had made them right. Some of the boys ran and caught hold of the tail of our wagon and held there, half swinging and half riding, ever so long. Pretty soon uncle stopped the horses, and asked a slim, pale-faced. girl, who was studying her book as she walked to ride; and thanking him as politely as anybody could do, she climbed up, right behind the horses, and sat down by me, and spoke the same as though she had been presented. She had a sweet face under a blue bonnet, but was as white, and looked as frail, as a lily. After she was seated, she looked back so earnestly, that I looked too, and saw the schoolmaster come out of the house and lock the door, and cross his hands behind him as he turned into a lane that ran by, which seemed to go up and up, green and shady as far as I could see. I could only see that his cheeks were red, and that he had curls under his straw hat. The girl kept looking the way he went; but if it were he she thought of, he didn't turn to look at her. Close by a stone-arched bridge, from under which a dozen birds flew as we rattled over it, Uncle Wentworth stopped the horses, and the young lady got out, and went through a gate at the roadside; and I watched her walking in a narrow and deep-worn path that was close by the bank of a run, till she turned round a hill, and I could not see her any more; but I saw a lively blue smoke, curling up over the hill-top, and in the hollow behind, Uncle Wentworth said she lived.

"We were now eight miles from the city—the sun was almost down; we saw great droves of cows coming towards the milk-yards—not driven as they are in the streets, but coming of themselves, and flocks of geese waddling out of ponds, and going towards home; I began to feel a little tired, and sleepy, with the motion of the wagon, when all at once the horses began to neigh and trot fast, and Uncle Wentworth said, 'Here's your prison, Annie; how do you like the looks of it?' We were right before a white gate that was being opened by a black man, who was smiling so as to show all his teeth, and who bowed twice to us as we drove through and along a gravelly narrow lane towards a barn as large as our house. I could hardly think it the place where I was to stay, at first— all was so beautiful. The house itself is really as good as our house, built of stone—blue hard stone—better than is in ours; and on every side of it is a white porch, curtained with green vines, some bearing red, and others blue flowers. About the house is a large yard inclosed by white pickets, against which is a perfect thicket of currant-bushes, raspberries and roses. It

is like an orchard, all about, with cherry, and apple, and
quince, and peach-trees—the latter sticking full of little green
peaches, and some of the apples turning red and yellow.
There were flowers of all colors growing here and there ; and
while I sat in mute surprise, a huge dog lifted himself up on the
wheel of the wagon, and frightened me so, that I almost cried,
though he neither barked nor growled. Uncle Wentworth
said he was only saying 'How do you do?'   And, indeed, it
seemed as if that was what he meant ; for as I went towards the
house, he walked along by me very quietly.   A middle-aged
woman came to the door to meet us ; she was wiping her hands
on a towel, and by her heightened color and the speck of flour
on her apron, I saw she had been at work in the kitchen. She
shook hands with me as though I were some friend, when
Uncle Wentworth said who I was, and went with me herself
to the tidiest little bedroom you ever saw, telling me, just as
though she had been my mother, to put all my things away
neatly, showing me where ; and when I had done so, to come to
her in the kitchen.   There was no carpet on the floor, which
was very white, and the bed-spread and the curtains were
white too.   I had my dresses hung up and my other things in
the bureau very soon, and hearing some one speaking in the
yard, I raised the window, and saw coming down the straight
walk, which was carpeted with tan-bark, Uncle Wentworth,
and a young man with a scythe swung over his shoulder   He
had on a broad-brimmed straw hat, grey trowsers, and a
shirt of white and blue calico fastened about the waist with a
leather strap.   I drew my head in a little when I saw him, but
not till Uncle Wentworth had spied me, and calling out aloud,
(for I was up stairs), he said, 'Annie, this is my boy, Cliff—

you must go out and help him mow to-morrow.'　It was such
a funny introduction, that I felt my face all burning red as I
tried to answer the polite salutation of the young man, for he
took the straw hat quite off, and bowed so low, that his brown
curls fell along his forehead, and made him look just like a picture.

"I now began to consider my dress, for it was full of
wrinkles with sitting on the straw, and riding so far, and looking in the glass that hung over the bureau, I found my face
was white with dust.　There was no water in the room ; so I
went down, and finding Mrs. Wentworth, whom I call Aunt
Margaret now, taking biscuits out of the stove, I asked her for
water, and she directed me to a shed outside the door, where
there was a cistern, and all conveniences for washing.　I
was quick, you may be sure ; for I feared Cliff, whom I
heard talking to his dog on the other side of the house, might
come round and see me ; and as I went towards my room tc
put on a smooth dress, Aunt Margaret patted my cheek and
told me I must be very smart, for that supper was all ready.
I told her not to wait—that I would come presently ; and I
did try to, but everything went wrong—the hooks were off
from one dress, and another fitted so ill, and then my hair
never looked so badly ; it was nearly dark in my room, and I
had no light, so that altogether I was vexed and flurried a
good deal when I went down.　Aunt Margaret had taken me
at my word, and Uncle Wentworth and Cliff were already gone
away from the table ; they had their evening work to do, she
said, and would not stand upon ceremony.　She had kept some
tea and biscuits warm for me, and I ate heartily, for the ride
had made me hungry.　While we were yet at the table, the
black man who opened the gate, and whose name is Peter, and

a yellow woman, called Maria, who is his wife, passed along the porch, carrying four tin pails full of milk, and Aunt Margaret said I might have a bowl of it, which I accepted, and found sweeter than any milk I ever drank.   I found Peter and Maria very nice and kind, and while they took their supper I staid by and talked with them, which seemed to please them very much.   Peter offered to make a swing for me, to show me about the barn, to teach me to milk, and many other things ; and Maria said she would make me as good a cook as herself, when I told her about the pudding I had made.   Aunt Margaret came into the kitchen, and as Maria washed the dishes, dried them on a towel, and helped about almost everything. Coffee was ground for breakfast, and short-cakes made, and all the parcels which Uncle Wentworth had brought from town were put each in its place, sugar and spice and dried beef, and I don't know what all.   Among the rest, or rather above the rest, was one paper carefully pinned up, at which Maria and Aunt Margaret wondered not a little, and opening it they found it to contain the neatest little cap that ever was —it had no flowers on it nor ribbon, except the strings, but it was real lace, and prettier, I thought, than ma's gay caps. Maria lighted another candle to look at it, and doubled her-self together with laughter, she was so pleased, and Aunt Margaret said it was just like Uncle Wentworth, he was always buying things she didn't send for, and that she would rather he had bought a new hat for himself.   She is a good woman, and I loved her the more when she said so.   Maria would make her try it on, and she and I thought it becoming ; but Aunt Margaret says she thinks it a little too small—though she would not say so to Uncle Wentworth for anything.

" He and Cliff had taken some chairs out beneath a cherry tree, and staid there talking together in the moonlight ; the great dog, whose name is Guard, lying by them on the grass. The moonlight fell about them pleasantly, and if Cliff had not been there I would have gone out ; but I thought he would think me bold, or perhaps not want me there. The big-clock which stood at the foot of the stairs where I came down, struck nine directly, and Aunt Margaret said I must be tired and had best go to bed, for that they eat breakfast at six o'clock in the morning. She gave me a candle and told me to find my way, which I did, and on opening the door I saw a whole handful of flowers—some lying about the floor, and others on the pillow—looking as if they had been thrown in at the window and lodged just as they were. I don't know who could have done it ; perhaps Peter—but I don't care who did it, they made the room very sweet, and I left them scattered just as they were, on bed and floor. I was not sleepy, I suppose, because of the strange place, and sitting down by the table at the window, I found a book lying upon it, which proved to be a volume of bound newspapers. On the blank leaf was written, ' The property of Clifton Wentworth,' in the roundest, best hand I ever saw ; I could read it as well as print ; so the young man knows something if he does live in the country. I read a good while in the papers, selecting the pieces which seemed to have been most read, for I supposed they were the best ; and, indeed, I found some excellent articles, better than I remember to have read before. I went to bed under the roses, at last, and listened to the strange sounds in the air, of birds and insects. Nothing else could be heard, except now and then a team rattling along the turnpike road.

"The sun was shining bright across my bed when I woke, and afraid I had slept too long, I hastened down, and sure enough, breakfast was over, and Uncle Wentworth and Cliff gone out to the fields, and milking done, and Aunt Margaret making bread, for it was after eight o'clock.

"I asked why she didn't call me; and she said she knew I was tired and sleepy, and that I would soon learn their way, and she complimented me by saying I seemed very smart and clever. I tried to atone for my sloth, and be as good as she had thought me; so I told her she must not let me sleep so late again—that I was to work for my board, and would begin then. I hope Uncle Wentworth did not know I was sleeping so late—he might think badly of me; Cliff, of course, would not think of me at all.   I breakfasted on milk-toast, and then having put my room in order, went with Maria to the garden, where we picked a basin of currants, and another of green beans; and afterwards, sitting in the shade of a tree, prepared them to cook.   It is not lonesome here as I thought it would be; everything seems happy and busy; bees, and birds, and butterflies, and chickens, and men and women the busiest of all.   It was noon before I dreamed of it, and Aunt Margaret said it was time to 'set the table,' which she showed me how to do, telling me I was 'handy,' and that work seemed to come natural to me. I like her more and more, she is so kind to everybody, and working seems to her like play; her bread bakes just right, and everything is just where she wants it. She says we must like work in the first place, and then have a place for everything and everything in its place, and all will go well; and she says if I keep on for a week as well as I have begun, I will more than earn my board, and she will give me a dollar. I mean to be up to-morrow morning in time to help get the breakfast. We had for dinner to-day beans and pork and potatoes, and baked apples, and custard pies, and milk ; I blew the dinner horn myself, as well as anybody, Aunt Marga-ret said.

"Cliff was gone to get his scythe mended, and he did not come home to dinner, which I was sorry for, though no more for him than I would have been for Uncle Wentworth. He said the dinner was very nice, and he supposed it was because I helped to prepare it.

"When the dishes were put away, Aunt Margaret put on a clean dress and cap, and sat in the porch with some sewing, and having given the required attention to my own wardrobe, I sat with and assisted her for the rest of the afternoon. We had a pleasant time together, and though we talked all the while, I made two shirt-sleeves for Cliff, stitching the wrist-bands, which was more than Aunt Margaret did.

"At sunset I assisted to set the table again—this time on the porch ; and just as the light became a little dim, we sat down, altogether. Aunt Margaret told Cliff I had made a pair of sleeves for him, and said a good deal more about how smart I was, which made me ashamed—he did not share my embarrassment, but laughing, said, as he shook his curls away, that was very well for me, but that he knew a young lady who could make an entire shirt in an afternoon. His mother said that was one of his stories, and I believe it is—I am sure he doesn't know any such young woman. After supper I went out with Peter to learn to milk, and Uncle Wentworth told Cliff to go and show me ; but though he came along, he only laugh-ed at my awkwardness a little while, and went away—he is most provoking, but as handsome a young man as ever I saw—the dress he wears is so becoming. I have not yet seen him wear a coat, but am sure he looks better without than he would with one, and I don't believe he has studied dress as an art at all. I found him examining the new sleeves when I came in, and he politely offered me his chair, providing another for himself—for all were sitting together on the porch. I don't know why, but I declined, and went straight to my room, where I found on the table a small leaf basket full of ripe blackberries. I don't know who put them there; it could not have been Cliff, for he don't think anything about me. The book was open too, and a rose laid on this verse :

"'To please my pretty one, I thought;
Alas, unhappy I,
The simple gift of flowers I brought
Has won me no reply.'

"I wonder if Cliff had anything to do with all this ? More likely it was the work of Peter or Maria.

"THIRD EVENING.

"Two days have gone since I came here, and two days so short I never saw, and yet they are not broken in upon by calls, by dressing, or by going out, though Aunt Margaret says we shall go, visiting a little and see some visitors, she hopes, when the harvest is past. I do not feel the need of any change yet; it will keep me busy for a month more to see all the things on the farm, and it will require longer than that to learn to keep house well, Aunt Margaret says. While it was yet dark in my room I heard such a crowing of roosters as I never heard before—it was like a band of music, almost, and especially when, as it grew lighter, a thousand birds in the trees and bushes about the yard began to shake their wings and sing as if it did their hearts good. I cannot make you understand how sweet it was—I could not bear to lie in bed, and as soon as I could see to dress, arose, and throwing the window open wide, looked out: there was no dew on the grass, though yesterday morning it was all wet, and streaked with green paths where footsteps had been. One great white star stood away in the south, as it were right in the tree-tops ; and where the sun was coming up lay a long bank of clouds, red as fire. No wind stirred the leaves, or the curtain of my window, and I could not smell the hayfields as I did yesterday. I heard dogs barking across the hills, and boys calling the cows, but mostly it was very still. While I staid at the window I saw a young man walk along the turnpike road, with a brisk lively step, and an energetic swing of the arms, as though he had something important to do, and was thus early astir to do it ; as he passed by I knew it was the schoolmaster, and on telling Aunt Margaret about it, she said he walked so every morning— sometimes two or three miles—for his health's sake, and that he is thought a young man of great promise, and is educating himself to go as a missionary to some distant country. I thought about the young schoolgirl, and wondered if she would go with him.

" I put my room in nice order before I left it to-day, which Aunt Margaret said was greatly better than coming down an hour after breakfast. I thought to be the first one up ; but Maria and Peter were already gone to milk, the tea-kettle was steaming, and Aunt Margaret was spreading the table.

" Seeing nothing I could do, Aunt Margaret told me I

might go out and feed the chickens, and she showed me how to make food for them by mixing corn-meal and water together. I had two quarts or more of it, which I scattered about the ground, calling the chickens to come ; and I do believe two hundred of them came running from every direction : roosters, red and black and speckled, with tails shining like a peacock's ; and hens of all colors—some old and having feathers hanging loose ; others with cunning brown eyes, and combs as red as roses, and looking plump and sleek, and well to do—these I take to be the young lady hens ; and then there were faded prim-looking ones that kept apart and made no noise, and these I supposed to be the old maids : the lean ruffled ones, seeming cross and picking at other hens, I thought were the worn mothers of hungry broods, themselves giving all to their little ones.   But the dear little chickens were prettiest of all—some yellow as gold, and some black as a crow, and others speckled—I could not tell which was the most cunning, all were so pretty.   I caught one or two of them in my hands ; but the mother hens, seeing me, flew right at my face, and I was glad to let them go.   While I was feeding, Uncle Wentworth came along from his morning work at the barn, and I said to him I wished Albert was there to see the chickens and ride the horses, but that I supposed he was gone to Florence before that time to learn to paint.   He asked me if Albert had any genius for painting ; I told him I did not know, but that I was sure he liked horses better than pictures ; and he then said money would not put genius into anybody—it must be born in them, and that a great thing couldn't be got out of a man unless it was first in him.   The minds of people, he said, were just as various as their bodies, and we could not greatly change the form of the face, nor could we any more the mind. It seemed to me worth thinking about, but perhaps you will not agree with me.

" While we were talking, Cliff joined us, having in his hand a small basket full of eggs—all fresh and white : he said he would show me where the nests are, that I may gather them to-morrow myself. He is very handsome, but I don't believe he gave me the berries. I went this afternoon to the meadow where he was at work to see if I could find any—I thought, perhaps, he would think I came to see him, and so I kept on the other side of the field. Uncle Wentworth came and showed me where there were plenty of berries, and I soon filled the little basin I had quite full. I then thought I would sit a little while in the shade of a walnut tree that grew in the meadow, and see them make hay, for there were a dozen men in the field, some mowing, some pitching, some raking, and others loading and hauling it into the barn. All worked as fast as they could, for uncle said it would rain—black clouds were flying about the sky, and now and then a gust of wind swept through the corn-field, making a solemn sort of noise, and away in the orchard I could hear the apples falling from the *early trees*, as they call the harvest-apple trees. The horses were almost covered up with the great load of hay, as they drew it towards the barn—two or three men followed, the others remaining to work in the field, for the clouds grew blacker and began to close together. I was not near the house, yet I thought I could run home when the sprinkling began, and sat still. I could see the schoolhouse across the field, and see the children when they came out to play—up and down the woods they ran, talking and laughing so loud that I could sometimes hear what they said. I noticed the young girl that rode with us—I knew her by the blue bonnet, and the quiet, melancholy way she had ; for she did not join in the playing nor the talking, but went apart, picking flowers. I left my berries, crossed the meadow, and joined her in the woods, intending to ask her to come and see me at Uncle Wentworth's ; but we were scarcely seated on a mossy log together when the rain came dashing down in a perfect torrent, so that I was forced to go with her into the schoolhouse for shelter. The master made me welcome very politely, saying many pleasant things which I do not remember. The name of the young girl is Mary Bell, and the master's name is Hillburn. I noticed that Mary kept the flowers she had gathered in her hand, and I could not help thinking she would gladly have given them to the master, but she did not, and presently seeing that she was picking them to pieces I took them out of her hands, and the master coming that way shortly after admired one of them very much, and on my giving it to him he set it in his button-hole and wore it while I staid, which was not long, for the storm was soon past, the heavy wind seeming to drive away the clouds. The trees swung their tops together, and we heard the fall of some dead limbs in the woods, which made me a little afraid. The master told me there was no danger—that the trees near the schoolhouse were too sound to break, and that the wind was not strong enough to uproot them. Mary, who sat by me, was trembling with fright, and her pale cheek was paler than ever, but he spoke never a word to her about her fear or anything else. She is a sweet, modest girl, and I could not help putting my arm around her and kissing her when I came away. The schoolmaster is handsome, having black curls along his smooth forehead and large black eyes. His smile is sweet, and his manner for the most part that of one whose thoughts are upon himself. He is quiet, but I should think not easily turned aside from a purpose when once fixed. As I said, he spoke most politely to me ; nevertheless I could not feel as though he thought of me even while he was speaking—I wish I had not seen him—I can't get the picture of his sad sweet face out of my mind—if he is happy it is happiness so subdued that I cannot understand it.

"Whether my going into the schoolhouse was a fortunate thing for the master or not, it certainly was to the children, for I was never so much looked at in my life—not one of them could see a book while I staid ; some of them, indeed, held their books before their faces, but their eyes were fixed on me —and so many bright eyes I never saw—I think they would light the house at night without any candle. The little schoolhouse stands on the edge of a green maple woods, and as I walked through them on my return home, I could not help building a little cottage there in my mind, and of putting Mary and the schoolmaster in it. Why I should have joined them together from the first I don't know ; but I did.

"Half an hour after the rain began the clouds broke apart and the sun shone again, hot as ever. Crossing on the green swaths of hay to the tree where I had left my berries, I found the basin heaped full with finer ones than I had gathered. I asked Uncle Wentworth if he did it, but he said no, and told me to inquire if Cliff knew anything about it. Just then I saw him drop his scythe and lift up one hand, from which the blood was streaming ; and putting down my berries, I ran to him and found that he had cut two of his fingers badly ; he

said it was nothing, and would have gone to work again, but I
bound up the hand with my handkerchief (it was not a lace
one), and ran and told Uncle Wentworth how bad it was ; he
laughed, and said it was a trick of Cliff's, done for the sake of
being allowed to go to the house to stay with me ; Cliff grew
angry at this and threw himself down in the shade of the tree
where my berries were. He had been out in all the rain, and
his clothes were wringing wet ; I thought he might get his
death-cold—so I coaxed him to go to the house with me, for I
would not have left anybody lying alone on the wet grass if I
could have helped it. The mowers laughed when they saw us,
and one of them said he thought Cliff more of a man. I told
Cliff I did not hear what he said, and I did not care either,
and that I supposed if one of his hands was cut off he would
be glad to leave working. Cliff turned his head away, and I
am sure there were tears in his eyes ; poor Cliff !—it was
heathenish in the mowers to laugh ; I hope Uncle Wentworth
did not give them one drop of whisky the whole afternoon. I
think it strange if one person cuts off a hand, and another
person ties it up, that other persons must laugh. Aunt Margaret said Cliff must not go to the field any more that day—
and she called him an unfortunate boy ; but he is not a boy—
he is, he will be twenty-one years old next year, and I am sure
that is old enough. She gave him the new shirt that I helped
to make ; I dressed the hand myself; I knew just how it was,
and could do it best ; Maria, who stood by, had to say that
Master Cliff's hand didn't look much like Miss Annie's ; I told
her I wished she would go back to her work, and mind her
work ; but she did not, and Cliff said, ' No, Maria, my hands
look more like yours ;' and he put his head down on his arm

and kept it there a good while. If he thought I hated him because the sun had made his hands a little brown, he thought what was not the truth, and I wanted to tell him so, but I could not say it—and so I turned back my sleeves and began to scour knives to show him that I was not afraid of my hands, and tried to make him forget the mowers and Maria too, by telling him about my visit to the schoolhouse. He smiled directly, and asked me if I thought Mr. Hillburn was handsome? I said yes; upon which he told me that he and Mary Bell were thought to like each other very much. I told him the master had worn my flower, at any rate; but still he would not give up that he liked Mary better than any one else.

"When I came back, after a short absence from the room, I found Cliff looking at the stitching in the wristbands of his new shirt. I asked him if he liked it, for the sake of saying something, and he replied that he liked anything I did—he is so kind you would like him, I know. I read for him some amusing stories I found in the paper; but the night seemed to come in a minute; so I left the reading to assist about the supper, for I don't want Cliff, nor any of them, to think me lazy. Maria could not get water enough to fill the tea-kettle out of the well to-night, and Peter took a bucket, and I went with him to a spring at the foot of the orchard hill, which, he said, was never known to be dry in his time. The water breaks right out of a bank in a clear, cold stream as big as my arm, and falls into a shallow well, about which is a pavement of flat stones, and running over this, it flows along the hollow in a stream half a foot deep in places. If the drought continues, Peter said, the cattle will all have to be brought there to drink, for there is no other such spring on the farm. Flags and broad-leaved grass grow along the sides of the run, and two or three brown birds, having very long legs, flew up before us, and one rabbit started from its hiding-place, and ran so fast I could not see what it looked like. Uncle said at supper-time, the rain had not done any good at all ; that the ground was not wet to the depth of an inch, and that the corn-leaves are all curling together for the want of it. Cliff looked pale and did not eat much, nor say much. I am afraid the wound is going to make him sick ; even Aunt Margaret, who is so good and kind, does not seem so much alarmed as I should think she would be. When the meal was concluded, Uncle Wentworth sent Cliff about the farm to see if there was water enough for the cattle ; I wanted to go with him—I thought it would be a good oppor-tunity for me to see all the farm ; but no one asked me to go, so I left Maria to do her own work, and came to my room to write to my dear parents. The sun is gone down behind the trees, and all the western sky is golden and orange, shaded with black—one star stands out, clear and beautiful, but I can see to write by the daylight yet. Aunt Margaret says I must be up at four o'clock in the morning and help to churn, and if the day bids fair she will have something to tell me. I wonder what it can be. There is Cliff, standing under my window, with his hands full of scarlet and blue flowers—he says I may have them, but he can't throw them up to the window, so I must go down.

"FIFTH EVENING.

"When I dropped my pen the third evening, it was with the intention of taking it up in a few minutes ; but Cliff seemed so lonesome, I thought it my duty to stay with him.

I told him I would walk with him another time, upon which he said it was not then too late ; so we strolled together into the high road, and turned down the way I had come from the city. We could hear voices across the hills at the houses of the neighbors ; some, indeed, were just calling the cows home— could hear the tinkling of bells, and sometimes the chirp of a bird, and that was all.   Cliff told me about his college days, and how much he had tried to like study as well as did his older brother, but that he would always rather plough an acre than commit a Latin lesson, and that after he had obtained a certain amount of knowledge, it seemed to him that he was losing time, and that for the future he could better learn by experience as he went along than by books alone.   His idea of happiness, he says, is fifty acres of ground, containing woods, and orchards, and springs of water, and being nicely stocked with cattle, and horses, and sheep ; having on it all the best implements of husbandry, a good little house full of everything to make comfort.   But what that everything would be, Cliff didn't say.   I cannot repeat half so well as he said it ; but if you heard him, you would be convinced that a farmer's life is the happiest one in the world.

"We were standing on the stone bridge and talking, when we heard some one singing the sweetest and saddest song I ever heard ; and looking about, we saw Mary Bell sitting beneath a walnut tree, a little distance down the hollow.   She did not see us—and with one hand pushed partly under her hair, and her blue bonnet on her knees, was singing to herself. The water from the spring at Uncle Wentworth's made a pleasant sound, as it ran a little way from her, and blue and white violets were thick all along the bank ; but she had not gath ered any of them, and did not seem to see them. A strip of bark was peeled from the top to the very bottom of the tree against which she leaned, and the wood was cracked apart, in some places wide enough for me to have slipped my hand in the body of the tree. It is very tall, and has been struck with lightning, Cliff says, two or three times. We called Mary—and tying on her hood, she presently joined us ; and turning into the long green shady lane, which I noticed when I first passed by, we walked up and up ; Cliff quite forgetting his hand, and talking and laughing gaily all the time. But no matter what Cliff does, it seems the properest and most becoming thing in the world, and I wish he would keep on ; but when he turns to something else, it seems better still. I never saw anybody like him—he could not do anything that he would not make graceful.

" Mary smiled now and then, for no one could help sharing somewhat in the merriment of Cliff; but she did not once laugh outright, and often seemed not to hear what we said. We had gone a mile, perhaps, without passing a house, or seeing anybody ; now and then we met some cows feeding along the roadside ; but it was quite dark, the working was done, and only we seemed out for pleasure, when we came in view of a large red house standing near the roadside. All was still about it, for the country people go to bed very early ; but in one of the chambers next the road a light was burning, and seated by the open window, with his book before him, was the schoolmaster. Cliff called him to come out ; and putting down his book as quietly as though our visit were just what he expected, he came out ; but when we asked him to walk with us, excused himself by saying his studies would not permit. Cliff would not hear of it, and told him, laughingly, that he might never have another opportunity of walking with us all ; and after some further pleasant urging, he finally came along ; and, don't you think, most provokingly offered his arm to me. I was so vexed I didn't hear what he said ; but try all I could, I could not invent any way by which I could amend matters. Coming to a mossy log, Cliff said we would sit down,' and came to me to get the bandage tightened on his hand, and when that was done he sat by me ; and when we went forward again, he slipped my arm through his, leaving Mr. Hillburn to walk with Mary. I heard him tell her that he had fixed the day of his departure from the neighborhood, and that that walk would probably be the last they should ever take together. I did not hear what Mary said, her tones were so low ; and presently we fell further apart, and soon lost sight of them altogether.

"When we gained the stone bridge again we met the schoolmaster, returning home with a brisk step. He had taken Mary home, and was thus soon returning, so it cannot be he loves her. The moon was coming up when we reached the house, and so bright and beautiful it looked, that we sat on the porch a little while to watch it ; but Aunt Margaret came to the door pretty soon, and told me it was ten o'clock, and she feared I would not be up in time for the churning in the morning.

"I was not sleepy, nevertheless I went to bed, though for hours I lay wide awake, thinking of a great many things that would not interest you, if I should write them. The clock struck twelve, and I was listening to hear it strike one, the last I remember.

"It was not quite light when I awoke. I heard Maria singing a hymn at the kitchen door, and hastened to dress and join her. The cream was in the churn, and with right good will I set to work ; and when Aunt Margaret came, I had taken up six pounds of hard yellow butter. After breakfast, which Maria had ready in a twinkling, Aunt Margaret asked me if I could ride on horseback, and said inasmuch as Cliff could not work that day, she had fixed in her mind a little visit for us to her brother's house, six miles away. I was pleased with the thought of riding, and Cliff said he knew I could manage a horse without trouble ; so it was soon arranged that we should go. Aunt Margaret's side-saddle was brought from the garret, looking as bright and nice as new ; and a beautiful little black mare, that uncle said was gentle as a lamb, was bridled and saddled ; and a dark grey, with fine limbs and little sharp ears, was placed beside her for Cliff.

" ' Oh, what shall I wear ?' I said, when I thought of it, for I had no riding-dress nor hat. But Aunt Margaret, who has always some provision, found for me au old black skirt of hers, and Uncle Wentworth said I might have his hat, if I wanted it. I said I would take Cliff's cap—at which they all laughed very much ; but when I had tied my green veil on it, they agreed that it became me charmingly ; and having taken charge of many messages, we mounted and rode away. I felt strange, a little afraid at first, but we went slow till I got more courage. I managed my mare admirably, Cliff said, and he ought to be a judge, having been used to horses all his life.

" We soon left the turnpike-road, and turned aside into a road much less travelled, narrow and crooked, and running for the most part through the woods. The day was hot, not a leaf

stirring nor a bird singing in the trees—we could see no clouds,
and the parched and dusty grass made us look for them often.
We rode slowly, partly for the sake of talking, and partly because I was not used to riding ; so it was not far from noon
when we turned the heads of our horses into a lane almost
overgrown with grass, and having thistles and briers along the
fences. It seemed a lonesome place, and I should have felt
homesick but for Cliff, who had never been more merry. I
asked whether the aunt we were going to visit was like his
mother ; and then it was that I first learned, the aunt, whose
house we were going to, had been dead many years, and that
his uncle was a man over fifty years old, with whom two
grandchildren lived, and that the woman who kept house for
him was a widow, named Mickmick ; 'and I think,' said Cliff,
'she would not be averse to becoming my aunt.' As we talked,
we came to the barn, which stood on the side of the lane opposite the house, and a hundred yards from it perhaps. The
doors were open wide, and looking in, we saw two young girls
there spinning wool—they stopped their wheels when they saw
us, and stood still bashfully, for it is not often, I suspect, they
see visitors. We dismounted by a great block near the gate,
and took our way down a narrow path towards the house.
Stepping-stones were laid along, but the path was not regular-
ly paved. The dwelling stood on a little eminence slopoing
either way, and on one side was the garden where we saw
bean-vines in abundance, with hollyhocks and sunflowers growing among them. Quite a hedge of herbs grew along the pal-
ing fence, and underneath them a great many hens and chickens were wallowing in the dust. I think they knew we were
strangers, for they cackled and ran fluttering away like wild-

10*

fire. The house is built partly of brick and partly of hewn logs, and is quite overgrown with moss and creepers.

"In the hollow opposite the garden, and beyond the house, stands an old mill, moss-grown too, and the day of our visit it was making a lively click. We rapped again and again, but our summons was not answered: so we went in; the door stood open, and Cliff said I might sit down, and he would see if he could not find Uncle John—that he was somewhere about, he knew, inasmuch as the mill was going. Mrs. Mickmick was seated on the porch next the mill, and hearing our voices, came in with no very amiable manner. Thieves might break in and steal the silver spoons, she said, for anything she knew—not a man about the house to tend to things—she didn't know as she need to care if everything was burnt up; and yet she was such a fool, she could not help but care. She told Cliff he could put his horses in the stable, if he had not got too big to wait on himself in consequence of keeping tip-top company, and she glanced at me as though she could not determine what I was. Finally, she said she would ask me to take off my bonnet, if I had one on; but as I had not, I might do as I pleased.

"Having inquired of Cliff if his mother was well, she said she should think she had enough to do without waiting on townfolks; and on being told that I was come to learn to work, she replied that the room of some folks was as good as their company. I did not like Mrs. Mickmick; she is tall and dark, and I should think had not smiled for many years. Her frock and cap were in the fashion of half a century ago, and she seemed vexed that I was not so too. She wore no stockings, her shoes were very coarse, and her bony hands were the color of Maria's, from having been dyeing wool.

"'Where is Uncle John?' asked Cliff. 'How should I know?' she replied; 'but if he is not deaf and dumb, I'll make him hear;' and taking down a tin horn that hung beside the door, she puffed her withered cheeks quite round in blowing on it. 'There!' she said, after tooting for five minutes; 'if John Gilbraeth don't hear that, it's because of the gabble of old widow Wakely.'

"Uncle John did hear it, however, and stepping out to the door of the mill, asked what was wanting; but Mrs. Mickmick told him sourly to come and see; upou which he came slowly forward, looking both ashamed and afraid, I thought, and more like a boy about to be whipped, than a man in the midst of his own possessions. 'There's your nephew in the house,' she said, when he came near, 'and a girl from town—it's them that want to see you, and not me, I'm sure—little do I care how long you stay in the mill talking to old widow Wakely.' Uncle John shied as though fearful she would scratch his eyes out, and coming in, shook hands with us very cordially, and sitting down, asked Mrs. Mickmick why she had not called the girls. 'Because,' she said, 'the girls had no time to entertain visitors—if we had come to see the girls we could go where the girls were—as long as she had any authority about that house she was not going to have the spinning stop for every town flirt that didn't know how to wash her own hands.'

"Cliff said, very provokingly, that he would go to the mill and find Mrs. Wakely—that she was a good-natured and lovable woman; and without more ado he left us and went to the mill, sure enough. Uncle John and I now went to the barn together, where the young ladies were still at their spinning. Sweet, modest girls they are, and as pretty as I have seen in a long time. Uncle told them to put by their wheels, and employ the day as they chose, and with radiant faces they hastened to obey, and having reeled up their yarn, we all went to the house together. The grand-daughters were soon clad in holiday dresses, and with slippers which they had probably not worn till then, except to church. Mrs. Mickmick lifted up her hands in horror, and ordered the girls to go straight to the chamber and strip off their Sunday frocks, and go back to their spinning again. At this instant Mrs. Wakely, a tidy, nice-looking little woman, who it seemed had ridden to the mill to buy a sack of flour that morning, appeared at the door, having come as she said to see me ; and Mrs. Mickmick, thinking it a good time, doubtless, to show her authority, repeated her order, and said, 'if John Gilbraeth didn't see fit to make them girls mind her, he might find another housekeeper as soon as he chose, that was all.' The youngest grandchild, whose name is Dolly, with the tears in her blue eyes, went close to Mrs. Wakely, and putting one arm around her neck, said, ' Won't you come and be housekeeper ?'

" ' Well,' said Mrs. Wakely, looking at Uncle John, ' that depends on what your grandfather says.'

" ' Well, then,' says he, shying away from Mrs. Mickmick, ' I say, Come.'

" Cliff threw up his hands and shouted. I felt delighted ; the girls laughed and cried together ; and Mrs. Mickmick, slinging a sun-bonnet on her head, flew across the fields like a mad woman, to tell the scandal to the nearest gossip she could find.

" Just then Squire Wedmam rode past the house towards the mill ; Cliff called him in, and by virtue of his authority, Uncle

John and the widow Wakely were made one and inseparable. I rejoiced that so speedy a termination was made, for I knew if Mrs. Mickmick once got her bony hands on Uncle John, he would never be free again.

" A happy day we had, though the beginning was inauspicious enough. The widow said she was not dressed just as she would like to have been, but it did not make much difference, and turning back her sleeves, she fell to work as readily as though it had always been her own house. We—girls and Cliff—went to the woods, and brought home green boughs and flowering twigs, with which we filled the fireplace and ornamented the wall ; and when the table was spread with the extra china and plate, the girls said they had never seen the house half so cheerful and pretty in their lives. Mrs. Wakely seems a famous cook, and as fond of her children, as she calls them, as if they were her own. She cut the pattern of my sleeve, and says she will go to town and buy them dresses like mine with her own money, and that they shall not be tied to the spinning-wheel in the barn all the time—it must not be all work nor all play, she said, but a wholesome mixture of the two.

" The ride home seemed very short, so engaged were we in talking of the new turn affairs had taken. The widow Mickmick, Cliff told me, had been his Uncle John's housekeeper for seven years, and that she had appeared to him to be mad all the time because his uncle did not marry her—' and I believe in my heart,' he said, ' uncle would have done so some time or other, but for the accidental combination of circumstances to-day.' Uncle John had seemed to me to grow taller and larger, and more of a man, the moment Mrs. Mickmick was out of the house ; and Mrs. Wakely was so sweet and motherly to the girls, that I loved her from the first : it is a happy change for them, I am sure ; two or three visits were planned, and one day was set apart to go to town, before we came away ; so they will not be left to spin barefoot in the barn, all the time, I am sure. They walked to the end of the lane with us to drive the cows home from the meadow; as we rode away, and after we were out of sight of them, we could hear them laughing. They are to visit us in a week or two, and their new grandma with them.

" It was after sunset, but not yet dark, when we got home. Aunt Margaret sat on the porch looking for us, and beside her a grave, handsome young man, whom she introduced as her son Joshua. He has the manner and look of a city-bred man, is taller than Cliff—whom he does not much resemble in any way I suppose most folks would think him finer-looking, but I don't. Cliff seemed to lose all his merriment when he saw his handsome and finely-dressed brother, and said to me, aside, that if Joshua had anything to do in town, he might as well stay there and do it.

"Aunt Margaret told us that we were all invited to drink tea at Mrs. Bell's the next afternoon.

" While we were talking, Cliff complained of his hand, which he said had not been so painful all the day past, and asked if he dare trouble me to make another application of the balsam with which it had been dressed.

" I told him it was not any trouble, and I am sure it was not. I would be very hard-hearted if I could refuse to do so small a favor as that. I found it so neatly bandaged that I thought it were best not disturbed till morning ; but when I said so Cliff replied pettishly, that he would do it himself, and not any longer keep me away from the very profitable conversation of the great Joshua. I can't think what makes him so pouty. I never saw him so before.

"I was tired and went early to my room, with the intention of writing on my journal, but I kept thinking of Cliff, and of what he said to me, and could not write at all.

"This morning I was up and milked a cow before breakfast; to be sure Maria milked three while I was milking one, but I shall keep trying till I learn to work as well as she. Cliff says the most useful and active life is the happiest, and I think so too. Good words, he says, are good as far as they go, but they are less than good works. He could not go to the field to work, and so he and I weeded the garden beds. Joshua came into the garden, and picked and ate some currants, but he did not offer to help us work. Cliff told him the sun was burning his face as red as fire, which seemed to alarm him, for he presently returned to the shade of the porch, at which Cliff made himself merry. Aunt Margaret called me directly, upon which Cliff said he expected she wanted me to listen to the edifying conversation of his wonderful brother, and that he could not pretend to outweigh such an attraction; but when I told him I would rather weed the garden all day with him to help me, than do nothing with Joshua to help me, he gathered and gave me a cluster of ripe red currants, and said he was not worth my thinking of, and that his brother Joshua was a great deal wiser and better than he was. Poor dear Cliff! I don't believe any. body is better than he is. Aunt Margaret wanted me to find her some fresh eggs, so I must needs ask Cliff to show me the nests; it seems to happen so that we are together a great deal.

We had no sooner opened the barn door, than away ran a hen from a pile of fresh straw, cackling so loud that she got one or two roosters to cackling with her, and peeping into the straw-heap, there was a nest full of white, warm eggs ; we took out nine, leaving one, which Cliff called the nest egg, and returned, to the surprise of Aunt Margaret, who had not expected us so soon. She gave me a bowl and told me to break six of the eggs and beat them well ; and when I seated myself on the porch with the bowl in my lap, Joshua brought his chair near me and began to talk ; and seeing him, Cliff said, a little spite-fully, I thought, that he would go to the field, and rake hay— he guessed he could do a little good with one hand.

"I had the eggs soon ready, and Aunt Margaret, measuring some sugar and flour, baked the nicest pound-cake you ever saw—it was not like those we buy at home at all. We had spring chickens and an apple-pudding for dinner, the latter eaten with a sauce of cream. I wish you were both here for a week—I think you would feel like new-made butterflies—I do ; I have thrown away my corsets, and for two days have not tried to make my hair curl. Uncle Wentworth says, if it is not the nature of it, it will only make it dry and harsh to twist it into curl. At three o'clock Aunt Margaret and I were ready —that is the fashionable hour of visiting in the country—and Aunt Margaret wrapped the cake in a napkin and carried it with her : not but that Mrs. Bell would have enough and to spare, she said ; but that her pound-cakes were a little better than most folks made, if she did say it herself. I forgot to tell you in its proper place, that I carried home from Uncle John's a half peck of apples, tied in a handkerchief, and hung on the horn of my saddle, and that Cliff carried as many potatoes—enough

for us to taste, Uncle John said.   Aunt Margaret wore her new
cap and a nicely washed and ironed dress of small brown and
white checks, a white silk shawl on her neck, and a close fitting
grey bonnet.   I wore the pink gingham with the plain skirt ;
I did not like to wear ruffles, because I knew Mary Bell would
not have them.   I was careful to be tidy ; but with a rose in
my plain hair I looked quite stylish enough, Aunt Margaret
said.

"We went through the gate by the stone bridge, and along
the path by the run, round the base of the hill, and were there.
Mrs. Bell and Mary were at the door looking for us.   The house
where they live is very small, having only two rooms, made of
logs—but whitewashed within and without, and looking very
comfortable.   Green boughs ornamented the wall and filled the
fire-place ; some pots of pretty flowers were in the windows, and
on the bed was a red and white patch-work quilt.   Over the
door was a porch roofed with green boughs, and a dozen yards
or more from the house was a baking oven, over which a shed
was built, and against which a fire was burning—for it is here
that Mrs. Bell does her cooking in the summer.

"We took sewing-work with us, and all sat on the shady
porch together, and worked till sunset, when our hostess set
about preparing the tea-table.   Mary was joyous and full of life
during the afternoon, but her spirits flagged when it was time
for the schoolmaster, who did not come.   I too was disappointed,
seeing that Joshua came alone.

"The table was kept waiting till nearly dark, and Mary and I
walked out to the bridge, and looked down the lane—in vain—
we saw no Mr. Hillburn.   We saw Cliff bringing the cattle to
the spring ; he waved his straw hat to us, but shook his head

to indicate that he was not coming : so we went sorrowfully back. I had little appetite for all the excellences spread before us ; and Mary could not eat at all, even of Aunt Margaret's cake. Joshua tried to entertain us, but we could not make right answers to what he said.

"Mary walked with us to the gate on our return home ; and when she turned back alone, I could not keep the tears from my eyes. She is melancholy, and most of the time muses silently, and I think it is the master she is thinking about. Everywhere the talk is that he is to go away shortly, and whenever Mary hears it I can see that it gives her pain. The grass is withered and the cornblades have lost much of the brightness which they had a few days ago ; the blue bells of the morning glories scarcely come out at all ; everything is suffering for the want of rain. It is so close in my room I can scarcely breathe. The dust is settled all over the rose-bushes, and uncle is afraid his good spring will dry pretty soon. I did not see Cliff when we came home. I can't think where he is. It grows late, and I will stop writing for this time. The lightning runs along the sky all the time, yet there are no clouds.

"SEVENTH EVENING.

"When I laid down my pen the fifth evening, I expected to resume it on the sixth ; but how short-sighted we are at the best. The day following our visit to Mrs. Bell's was still and sultry ; one black cloud lay low in the west, and that was all —we sat on the porch with fans nearly all the day, wishing and wishing for rain. I have no recollection of the day except a sense of suffering and a looking for clouds. We could see the men in the field wiping their faces often and looking at the sky, and great clouds of dust going after the teams, as one after another went along.   About four o'clock a sudden breeze sprung up, turning the leaves of all the trees wrongside up, and filling all the air with dust ; then came a distant growl of thunder, then another louder and rattling up the sky, with clouds, black as midnight, behind it.   The shutters blew round, striking violently together, troops of swallows came hurrying home to the barn, and shortly after, the cattle, running one after another, some of them bellowing, others pawing the dust, or turning their foreheads up to the fast-blackening sky.   I was afraid, as the wind tore down the vines from the porch, and a flash of lightning, that almost struck us blind, was followed by such a clap of thunder as I never heard.   The rain now came plashing down, sending the smoking dust up at first, and in a moment driving furiously against us, and forcing us into the house.   We heard the limbs of the trees cracking and falling, and then the men from the field came running in.   I hurried to Cliff, and held fast his hand, and would not let him go away, I was so much afraid he would be killed.   He told me not to fear—that the greatest danger was passed—but that he believed the lightning had struck somewhere near by.   He had no more than said this, when Mr. Peters, the neighbor who lives nearest to Uncle Wentworth, came to the door, the water dripping from his hair, his clothes completely drenched, and his lip trembling : 'Mrs. Wentworth,' he said, 'I want you to get ready as quick as you can and go with me to Mrs. Bell's—poor Mary has been killed with lightning ;' and when he had said so, he hid his face in his good honest hands for a minute before he could say any more.   Presently he told us that as he was cross ing the stone bridge, on his way home from town, he heard his dog, that always went with him, howl, and turning his head, saw him with his fore paws lifted on the gate, and saw at the same time a woman lying beneath the tall walnut tree. He hurried to her, and found it to be Mary. 'I carried her in my arms,' he said, 'to her mother's house, and she lies there on the bed—poor Mary!' And through the driving rain Aunt Margaret and Joshua went together to the house of death. We were stunned speechless, almost ; and sat all together—Maria and Peter and all—till late at night. Cliff held close my trembling hand, and I am sure we felt the worthlessness of everything in comparison with love.

"To-day was the funeral. Joshua, who had known Mary from a baby, spoke an hour in such a sweet, comforting way, that even Mary's mother was still to hear him. I felt, as I heard him, that he was a good man, and that his hopes were, indeed, anchored beyond this life. I determined then more than I ever had to live a good life, and to grow in grace as much as I can. Mr. Hillburn sat close by the coffin with Mrs. Bell, and his suffering seemed greater than he could bear. Over Mary's bosom lay beautiful flowers, and when he had looked at her and kissed her, he took up one of them and kissed that too ; he would not have done it if she had been alive. All the school-children walked behind their mate, holding each other's hands tightly, and seeming to be afraid.

" When the grave-mound was heaped smooth, Mr. Hillburn, who had all the time been with Mary's mother, walked with her to her lonesome home. An hour ago Joshua was sent for, and he has not yet come home. I cannot make it seem that sweet Mary Bell is dead ! Where is her home, and what are her thoughts now ? Surely she needed but little change to become an angel. Life is a great, a solemn thing.

"Cliff has just come to my door, and asked me to come down stairs—he is so lonesome, he says. So for to-night, good bye.

"EIGHTH EVENING.

"I asked Cliff what he would do when I was gone, and he replied I must never go away—the house was big enough for us all, and I would never find any one to love me. better than he did.

"The sun is not yet set ; I came early to write you, that I might have the twilight to walk in the yard with Cliff, who is impatient at a minute's absence—he is the best young man in the world.

"Aunt Margaret told me to-day that Mr. Hillburn told Joshua last night the story of his life, and that it is indeed true he loved Mary Bell, but that he was pre-determined to become a missionary, and to leave behind him all he loved. It appears, she says, he designed it as some atonement for what he considers a sin of early life. He loved books, and was of a serious and thoughtful turn of mind always ; but his father, contrary to his wishes, apprenticed him to a blacksmith, from whom he ran away, and by dint of industry and perseverance, succeeded in finally educating himself. But when he thought to return home in triumph, he found his bright anticipations turned into the bitterest sorrow—his parents had died in extreme poverty, crushed to the earth by what they esteemed the ingratitude and worthlessness of their son. Penitent, and broken-hearted almost, he resolved to consecrate his life to some good work ; and with the view of enabling himself to prosecute his studies for the ministry, undertook the school in the neighborhood of Uncle Wentworth's, where the sweetness and gentleness of Mary Bell quite won his heart ; but he guarded his foregone resolve, and never spoke that sentiment which she, nevertheless, silently received and responded to. Aunt Margaret thinks it likely he will remain with Mary's mother, and continue the school for a year at least ; but he scarcely seems to have plans or purposes left. She says I am sure he meant for the best, and how sadly has it all ended !

"When Uncle Wentworth came home from the near village to-day, he brought me a letter from the post-office there, and on opening it I found it was from Albert, telling me that he had run away from home, and engaged to ride the horses of a canal-boat. I therefore hasten to let you know, that you may not be so much alarmed about him.

" MIDNIGHT.

"Here I am in my pretty, quiet room again. The moon is smiling out of the sky as gently and lovingly as though she looked not on fallen harvests and broken boughs, where the storm went yesterday. The stars are as thick as the dew in the grass almost, and I never saw them so bright. I have been sitting at the open window, and as I looked out upon the beautiful world, I felt more humbly grateful, more truly and reverently prayerful, than I ever felt till to-night. Heaven has been very good to me always : but especially so, I think, in bringing me to this pleasant home, and making me loved and useful here.

"As I promised, I joined Cliff at twilight, and we walked

among the flowers, cutting off the broken limbs and picking off the blossoms which the storm had broken to pieces. It was a sweet silent evening, and we were very happy, and yet sad too, thinking and talking of Mary and Mr. Hillburn.

"We sat together on the stone door-step, and made pictures of the happy home they might have had—a cottage in the woods, where Mary might have milked the cow and tended the flowers, while the schoolmaster might have continued to be a schoolmaster year after year, teaching the children, and then the children's children, and so going on happily and usefully to the end.

"'But,' said Cliff, looking very close in my face, 'if the master had left teaching, which is wearisome, and had become a farmer, having some land of his own, and fine cattle; and if Mary had been a little more like Annie; what a heaven they might have made?' And when I said, 'Yes,' he asked me why we could not make just so sweet a home as we had pictured? For the life of me, I could see nothing in the way; so do not be troubled any more about making something of me; for before you hear from me again, I shall have made a farmer's wife of myself."

THE APPLE CUTTING.

Surely they need our pity who are so intent on ambitious projects—on what are falsely termed the great aims of life— that they cannot stop to plant by the way some little flowers of affection.

For myself, though I had power to make the wisdom of the past and the unrevealed truths of God my own, I should feel life to be an incompleteness, a failure, if there were no eyes to gather new light "when I looked down upon them, and when they looked up to me."

Whether blind contact and the strong necessity of loving something are usually chiefly instrumental in drawing heart to heart, I know not, but in the little story I have to tell they may take some credit, I think.

Years ago, no matter how many, there came to live in our neighborhood a widow lady of the name of Goodhue. Her husband, shortly after purchasing the farm to which she and her daughter, Louisa, came to live, was attacked with cholera, and died ; so the two ladies, and the three servants whom they brought with them, made up the family. I well remember the much notice they excited at church the first Sunday their heavy and elaborate mourning filled one of the homely slips.

240

Even the young clergyman, it was thought by one or two of our gossips (and what village has not its gossips?) directed his consolatory remarks almost entirely towards the new comers, only once or twice remembering the three poor orphans who sat in the rear of the church, thinking of the lonesome grave of their poor drunken father, whom nobody had wept for but them. "We suppose," said the aforesaid gossips, "he couldn't see through the thick black veils of the *great* Mrs. Goodhue and daughter, to the scantily trimmed straw hat of Sally Armstrong." Others there were, however, who said that brother Long had preached a good *feeling* sermon for the drunkard, and that he had told the children the sins of their father would be visited upon them to the third and fourth generations, and they were sure the children and everybody else ought to be satisfied.

They looked almost like sisters, mother and daughter, people said, and indeed it was hard to believe there were twenty years difference in their ages, for the elder lady was the younger in behavior, and altogether the most stylish in appearance. Her manner was set down against her for pride; but I suspect she had not more than most other persons, though its manifestations were more showy.

"I wonder which one the preacher is trying to comfort," said the neighbors, "Louisa or her mother;" for whether or not their veils had blinded him on the occasion of their first appearing at church, it was certain that he availed himself of the earliest opportunity of making their personal acquaintance, and Aunt Caty Martin, who nursed all the sick, helped to make all the shrouds, and cook all the wedding dinners in our neighborhood, remarked laughingly one day, as she was visiting at our house, the while she hemmed a checked apron, that she expected to need it, before long, in the preparation of the biggest dinner she had ever cooked. It was not worth while to call names, she said, but it was generally thought that a certain young preacher and a certain young lady, whose name began with L., would make a match before long.

Wiser folks than Aunt Caty have been mistaken—but let me not anticipate.

It was March when the Goodhues came to our neighborhood, and as rough and unpromising a March as I remember ever to have seen. The old house to which they came looked especially desolate, for it had been vacant for a year, and the long un-pruned cherry trees and late-budding elms creaked against the broken windows, and dragged along the mossy roof, dismally enough. The wind had not whistled up a violet, and no wood-flower, between the layers of frosty leaves, had pushed its way into the light. Mr. Goodhue had proposed to build a fine new house directly in front of the old one. The digging of the cellar had been accomplished, but the work was interrupted by his death, and the great clay pit stood there, partly filled with water, out of which the black snakes lifted their ugly heads, and into which the frogs dashed themselves when a step drew near.

It looked unpromising when they came, as I said, and during the summer the appearance of things was but little bettered.

The widow and her daughter had never lived in the country, and knew nothing, of course, about managing a farm, but like many city bred people supposed rural life to be a holiday. They began energetically, to be sure ; in addition to the three servants they brought, they hired workmen enough to cultivate the grounds, and put the fences, barns, and orchards, all in complete order ; but there was no directing hand among them, and the consequence was, nothing was done properly, nor in season, and after a large expenditure, with small gain, the lady dismissed her workmen aud offered the farm for sale.

She had come to the conclusion that her good husband had for once erred in jndgment, and bought the poorest land that could have been found in the whole county.

In the time of garden-making, a garden was made ; but the weeds grew faster than the vegetables, and the inexperienced servants pulled them up together ; so the ground was ploughed and sowed anew, but the second gardening was worse than the first—the dry season came on, and the work was all lost.

"Really, Louisa," said the widow, one morning, as she held up her mourning dress, heavy at the bottom with dew and dust, "I wish I could get rid of the old place, on any terms. I would willingly sacrifice two or three thousand to be rid of it."

"O mother, I do wish you could sell or give it away," replied Louisa—"it is the dreariest place I was ever in in my life. If it wasn't for Parson Long I don't know what we should do, for I believe he is about the only civilized man in the neighborhood. And, by the way," she continued, "he has asked me to ride to the city with him to-morrow, and come home by moonlight. Won't it be sentimental ?" And the young girl laughed heartily at the idea of a sentimental ride by moonlight with the parson, who was really a person of fine education and cultivated tastes. In all our neighborhood there was no other gentleman with whom she for a moment thought of associating on terms of equality, and as for marrying one of the "rustic bumpkins," as she called the young men, why, she scorned the suggestion.

The summer was gone at the time of this little conversation between Louisa and her mother, and the warm September sun pierced not between the thick boughs of the cherry trees which still remained unpruned, for though Parson Long, in kid gloves, had been seen cutting the dead limbs from among the roses and lilacs, he had not ventured to touch the trees ; and in shady and damp isolation the old house stood, and there, in discontented and thriftless seclusion, the two ladies lived.

They were in the midst of rather an uncharitable conversation about the neighborhood, which they termed "horrid"—the simple-hearted people were "good enough in *their* way," as they said, but persons in whom they could by no possibility have any interest—when they were interrupted by a loud and confident rap on the front door—an unusual thing—for most of the country people, who ventured there at all, made their entrance at the side door, as the family were not supposed to be in the parlor of week days—or, at least, other families were not.

The servant who opened the door came presently and, with a smile of peculiar significance, announced Mr. Warren Armstrong.

"And pray, Louisa, who is he ?" asked the mother, her face reddening as she went on to say, "not the son of the Widow Armstrong, who lives in the cabin across the field ?"

"Even so, mother," answered the proud girl, arranging her curls and straightening her lace kerchief in mockery, and as if she feared to enter the presence of so distinguished a person-age ; "you see our kind neighbors are determined to overcome our timidity. Well, I am sorry they give themselves such useless trouble"—and turning to the servant she said, "Did his honor ask for mother, or me, or you?"

"You, miss," replied the maid, her smile this time widening into a grin.

"Perhaps he wants me to help his sister Sally spin," continued Louisa, talking partly to herself and partly to her mother; "I heard the thunder of her wheel, the other day, when Parson Long and I were walking in the woods."

"And what did he say of them?" inquired Mrs. Goodhue, looking up from her embroidery.

"Oh," he said "they were goodish people—poor, but respectable, in short, and that, since the old man went the way of all the living—which he did last spring, having been a drunkard for twenty years—they seem to be increasing in worldly goods."

"Well, dear, don't detain the young man any longer," said Mrs. Goodhue.

"You are considerate, but no doubt his time is precious. I should have remembered that—is it the time of sheep-shearing, or potato planting, or what season is it with farmers? and she ran laughingly towards the parlor, waiting only to say, "I wish you could see *mother* Armstrong—her face is browner than our cook's, and she dresses so queer."

Her face, as pretty and genial a one as you would wish to see, in its usual expression, grew severe and haughty as she opened the door and appeared before Mr. Armstrong with her stateliest step.

He was leaning carelessly over the rosewood table, and looking into a volume which adorned it. One hand pushing

back the brown curls from his brown eyes, and the other resting on the brim of his straw hat which hung over his knee, as
indolently graceful as though he had been used to fine books
and fine furniture all his life.

"Did you inquire for me, sir?" asked the lady, in a business-
like way, but as though she could hardly think it possible that
he had inquired for her. "Pardon me," said the young man,
as he bowed with natural gracefulness, "though we have had
no formal introduction, I could not fail of knowing Miss Goodhue. My name is Armstrong—Warren Armstrong."

Miss Goodhue said she was happy, and sinking to a sofa,
motioned him to be seated again. He declined, however, and
did his errand so simply and politely that she found herself saying, "Pray, accept a seat, Mr. Armstrong," before he had
concluded.

In a minute, and without having made any remarks about
the weather, or asked her how many cows they milked, he was
gone; and slily pulling the curtain back, Miss Louisa Good
hue was watching him down the path.

"Well, daughter, what did the clodhopper want?" asked the
mother directly.

"It seems to me you might call him by his name."

"Indeed!"

Louisa laughed gaily, partly to cover her confusion and partly at the unintentional earnestness with which she had spoken;
and saying he seemed a civil young person, explained that he
had called to ask her to come to an "apple cutting," at his
mother's house, on the evening of the day after the next.

"And are you going, my dear?" asked the mother deferentially.

"Pshaw! What do you suppose I want to mix with such a set of people for?" And going to the window, Louisa watched the clouds with great interest, apparently.

There was a brief silence, broken by the mother's asking if Mr. Armstrong wore cowhide boots and homespun, or in what sort of costume he appeared.

"Really, mother, I don't know what he wore, replied the girl, ingenuously—I saw nothing but his smile and his eyes."

Mrs. Goodhue laughed, and said she would buy a spinning-wheel for her child.

"Why, mother, you grow facetious," and tying on her sun-bonnet, Louisa took up a volume and set off towards the woods, either by choice or accident turning towards the one which lay nearest Mrs. Armstrong's.

The following morning the sun came up large and red, disappearing shortly behind a great bank of black clouds; the leaves dropped off silently, the air was close and oppressive, and the water dried fast in the big clay pit.

Louisa asked everybody if they thought it would rain, and everybody said they thought it would. Still she could not see any signs of rain herself, she said; if Parson Long called for her, she believed she would go to town; and by way of testing her mother's views, she added that she wanted to buy a yard of gingham to make an apron to wear to the "apple-cutting."

"Do, dear, go if you want to," replied the mother; "it will be a harmless pastime enough, and no doubt gratifying to our simple neighbors."

Louisa said she was only jesting about the apron but that, in truth, Warren Armstrong had quite a little manner of his own, and the prettiest brown curls and eyes!

In due season the clergyman called, mingling, a little more than was his wont, a worldly interest with his soberly-gracious manner.

His well-fed black horse pricked up his ears and stamped impatiently, but he was not in gayer mood than Louisa. She didn't know why, she said, but her spirits had not been so buoyant since they came to the old farm.

The lane leading down past Mrs. Armstrong's house looked quiet and cool between its border of oaks and elms, and she wondered she had never gone in that direction for a walk—she would the very first time she went out again.

This purpose she expressed to Mr. Long, by way of assuring herself that she could walk by the house of Warren Armstrong, or talk of it as freely as of anything else, if she chose.

"You seem intent on the landscape, Miss Goodhue," he remarked, in a tone of dissatisfaction, for she had kept her face turned away longer than was flattering to his vanity.

"What did you say?" she replied, abstractedly, after a minute or two, during which she had been interesting herself in the five cows that stood about the spring under the oak before Mrs. Armstrong's house—and perhaps, too, in the light cart that, with its white linen cover and smart grey horse, was standing by the door, and about which Sally and her mother, and a little boy, were busy handing in pails and· baskets, etc., etc. Warren was nowhere to be seen.

"What were you saying?" she asked, having completed her survey.

"Nothing—at least, nothing that could interest you," and the clergyman suddenly discovered that the management of his horse required both hands, though one had previously rested on that part of the carriage seat against which Miss Goodhue leaned.

But little cared the lady whether he drove with one hand or two, and, with the exception of one or two common-place remarks, five or six miles were driven over in silence.

At length Mr. Long fell back upon his clerical prerogative, and asked Louisa, in a fatherly sort of way, if she didn't think the flowers in her bonnet unbecoming—especially with mourning habiliments.

"No," she replied, tossing her willful head ; "I think they are pretty."

"Vanity and vexation of spirit," he answered.

He next inquired if she found prayer the greatest consolation for earthly afflictions, saying that was the true test of a Christian spirit.

"Sometimes I do, and sometimes I don't," replied the saucy girl, "I make no pretensions to perfection." And abruptly changing the subject, she said she fancied she could drive as well as he, and playfully taking the reins from his hand, the gay black horse passed over the remaining distance so fast as to preclude conversation.

"Call as early as six o'clock, if possible; I am fearful of the night air," was the request of Louisa, as Mr. Long set her down at the door of her friend, Mrs. Jackson.

The clergyman replied civilly, and yet in a way that indicated he had some interests of his own which might conflict with hers, and which he should be at no pains to set aside.

Truth is, Louisa was in no haste to be at home, neither was she afraid of the night air—nor had the young man interests which he preferred to hers. Both were pettish, and willing to tyrannize in a small way.

So they parted—the one saying, "Pray don't give yourself trouble," and the other replying, "to serve you at any sacrifice would be a pleasure."

Mrs. Jackson was one of those sweet, loving women who find sermons in stones and good in everything. Instinctively a lady as well as by birth and education, she recognized the natural excellence and refinement in others, nor did she ever fear of compromising herself by associating with persons whose hands were less white, or whose purses were less heavy than her own.

"Let me see," she said, pausing with puzzled expression, as if she were settling some matter of great moment in her mind, after asking all about the neighborhood. "My paragon, Mr. Armstrong must live somewhere near you. Do you know a family of that name ?"

A family of that name lived very near them, Louisa said— poor, but good people, she believed.

"You may well say good people," replied Mrs. Jackson, "there is no family of my acquaintance I like better. Warren and Sally, and the old lady, and timid little Moses—I like them all."

Here she proceeded to relate how she had first found them out by the excellence of the butter they brought to market ; how she had engaged a regular supply, and so had made friends of the entire family.

"Almost every week they send me," she said, "some fresh eggs, or vegetables, or some other nice things they have, and I acknowledge the favor by filling the basket with something which they have not. When they come to town, they eat dinner with me, and I am going to the country to stay a week, and eat bread and milk, and apples fresh from the trees. Oh, they are dear, delightful people—how much you have lost in not knowing them."

Mrs. Jackson's great wealth and high social position embold-ened Louisa to say she had actually seen Warren Armstrong, and spoken with him ; that, in fact, he had asked her to a little party, at his mother's house. She did not say " apple cutting," lest Mrs. Jackson might be shocked ; but that lady knew all about it, and, opening the cupboard, showed her a huge fresh pound-cake which she designed sending for the occasion, by Warren, whom she was every moment expecting to bring her the week's butter.

" Go to-morrow night, by all means," she continued ; " they have shown a disposition to give you pleasure, and you would not pain them, I am sure, even though it afford you no special gratification to go ;" and putting her arms about the plump shoulders of Louisa, she repeated, " you will go, I am sure."

" Would you, now, really ?" said the girl, looking up ; " it will be so queer, and with such a set of people."

" Why, the Armstrongs are not queer, but here comes War-ren"—and Mrs. Jackson left her guest to meet and welcome him. Louisa could hear their voices distinctly, and much jesting and good-natured talk about trifles there seemed between them, as baskets were unpacked, jars were untied, and jugs of milk were emptied. She would gladly have joined them, but timidity, for almost the first time in her life, kept her in her seat ; and, before she could overcome it, she heard the firm step sound along the paved walk, as the young man went away.

When Mrs. Jackson returned, she wore a disappointed ex pression. Warren Armstrong could not dine with her, he would only call for a minute in the evening, for the cake and the bottle of yeast which she would have ready for him.

Louisa wondered what time he would return, though she didn't know as she cared about seeing him; but she had told Mr. Long to call at six o'clock. Possibly she might go to the "apple-cutting." She didn't think she should; nevertheless, amongst her purchases that day was a yard of black and white gingham, suitable for an apron.

The clouds, which had been slowly sailing about all day, intermingled at sunset, and the sky was presently a dull leaden mass. Louisa looked out anxiously—six o'clock went by; seven came, and with it a slow, drizzling rain, which promised to continue through the night.

"If Mr. Long had come at six, as I requested," she said, "we might have been at home. He wants to take his own time, that is all," and she pressed her flushed face to the pane, tapping violently with her little foot on the carpet.

Suddenly the flush deepened, as a hearty, good-humored voice, not altogether unfamiliar, gave the salutation of the evening.

Louisa said she was not expecting him (for it was Warren); she was watching for Mr. Long, who had brought her to town, and whom she had expected an hour ago.

Mr. Armstrong manifested no confusion; but, taking off his hat, turned his face skyward, and, shaking the rain-drops from his curls, with a pretty carelessness, said he was sorry for her disappointment; that her friend would certainly not detain her much longer and that his carriage was doubtless a sure protec-

tion from the storm, which he trusted would not be very violent ; and with a bow which seemed to indicate a leave-taking
of *her*, he passed to the rear portion of the house, where Mrs.
Jackson's kindly preparations awaited him.

"I wish he had only asked me to ride home with him,"
thought Louisa. "I am under no obligations to Mr. Long,
that I should wait here all night ;" and, moving restlessly to
and fro, she saw the young man passing from the kitchen to the
street, and placing in the wagon, jugs, baskets, and boxes
again, as regardless of her as of the Newfoundland that lay at
the doorway.

"I could go with him just as well as not," she thought ;
"his wagon-cover would protect me from the rain, and if it
didn't, why, a little rain wouldn't hurt me—and then I should
be revenged upon Mr. Long."

But while she thus thought, the preparations were completed ;
and, with the rain-drops standing bright in his hair, and his
ungloved hands wet and red, Mr. Armstrong was climbing into
the wagon.

"Would it inconvenience you much to take me ?" called an
unsteady voice, and throwing up the sash, Louisa leaned anxiously from the window. The youth, for he was scarcely more
—something past twenty-one, perhaps—was on the ground in a
moment. His poor accommodation was quite at her service ;
he only regretted it was not better. The storm looked threat-
ening ; had she not better consider ?

"I will pay you whatever you ask," said Louisa, coldly,
piqued at the young man's indifference, for he stood with one
hand resting on his stout grey and the other held discouraging
out into the rain.

"I think we shall be able to settle terms, Miss Goodhue," he said, laughingly, "if not, we will 'leave it to men,' as farmers do sometimes, when they make a trade."

Louisa joined in the laugh, for his good humor quite disarmed her, and, wrapped in Mrs. Jackson's great blanket shawl, she was presently assisted into the wagon.

Before they reached the suburbs it was quite dark, and the rain, which had been only a drizzle, fell in larger and colder drops. The road was muddy and broken, and a slow drive unavoidable.

But, strange to say, Miss Goodhue was not afraid of the night, nor the rain, nor the rough roads. Was it because she had retaliated upon Mr. Long? or because she felt a greater assurance of safety and protection than she had ever felt before?

I know of nothing more favorable to familiar intercourse than a rainy night and a lonesome old house, or a lonesome road. Almost any two young persons, who find each other likeable, will, travelling slowly through the storm, or sitting by the ember'fire, open their hearts as they would not in the inquisitive noonday, But whether or not this be generally true, it was in this particular instance.

A mile was not gone over when the rain plashed through the cover of the wagon. Mr. Armstrong feared for the lady, and she in turn feared for him—he would really be quite drenched; her shawl was ample enough for both. Of course, the young man's fears were all for her, not for himself; he had been used to hardship and exposure, and she was so delicate, so frail.

I can't tell all they said, for I don't know. I wish I did, believing it would interest us, as it always does, to read the human heart; but I do know the drive seemed very short to both, notwithstanding the ugly night; and that Louisa declared, when Mr. Armstrong set her down at home, that she was just as dry as if she had been all the time by the hearthside. She would not suffer, she knew; and Mr. Armstrong would find her the gayest of all on the following evening.

"I hope so," he replied; "I had feared you would not honor our little merry-making, but our humble life and homely pleasures might at least amuse you."

"True honest manhood and womanhood," replied Louisa, with dignity, "are the best and noblest attainments; and I hope I have at least enough of the one to recognize the other, though it be beneath a roof a little lower than mine."

For the first time in his life the young man had spoken depreciatingly of his station and its pleasures; and for almost the first time in her life Louisa had uttered a sentiment worthy of her real nature.

The morning looked unpromising, but about noon the clouds broke up, and at one o'clock the sun shone bright and clear.

Mrs. Goodhue made herself merry, when she saw her daughter sewing the gingham apron; but her estimate of the Armstrongs was modified somewhat when she learned that Mrs. Jackson had spoken well of them; and at last she concluded that girls would be girls, and if Louisa had a fancy for going to the "apple cutting," why, she would allow her to go.

Active preparations had been going forward, at Mrs. Armstrong's, all day. Moses, who was a pale, thoughtful boy, had been unusually lively. Sally had sung, "When I can read my title clear," in a key louder than common, and the mother had seemed quite rejuvenated, as she beat eggs, and rolled sugar, and assorted spices and plums. Only Warren had been silent, seeming scarcely soberly glad. Sally, who was not much given to sighing, rallied him repeatedly; but though he said nothing was the matter, and he was sure he didn't see what they found about him to laugh at, it was evident his thoughts were not on his work, as he brought in basket after basket of fine apples, and arranged the boards on which they were to dry.

Shortly after sunset all was in readiness. Moses, in his new boots, and wearing a broad linen shirt collar—the first one he ever had—stood at the little white-curtained window, watching down the lane for the first arrivals. Sally, wearing a pink dress and white apron, was trying the effect of some red brier buds in her hair; and the mother in her plain black gown, sat in the big rocking-chair, with a fan of turkey feathers in her lap, placidly contemplating the appearance and prospects of things in general. As for Warren, he was yet lingering about the fields, half wishing the "apple cutting" had never been thought of.

"Oh, Sally! there is a lady, somebody I don't know," called out Moses from his station at the window.

"Well, well, child, come and sit down," said the mother; but Sally ran to see, and in a moment reported in a whisper that she believed in her heart it was Miss Goodhue, for she wore a white dress, and a black apron.

A minute more, the old gate creaked, a light step sounded on the blue stones at the door, and Miss Goodhue was come.

She advanced at once to Mrs. Armstrong, and extending her little white hand, said she had taken the liberty of coming early, that she might learn to feel at home by the time the others should arrive.

Truth is, she had come thus early in order to make excuses and return home before dark, if on taking an observation, she should feel so inclined.

"How kind of you, darling," said Mrs. Armstrong, in her sweet motherly way ; and, seating her in the rocking-chair, she untied her veil, offered her big fan, and, in various ways strove so cordially to entertain her, that she quite forgot her intention of making excuses and returning home. Moses brought her a bright red apple, and Sally showed her the garden, though there was nothing in it to see, she said—and, sure enough there were but a few faded hollyhocks and marigolds ; but the kindly spirit was the same as if there had been ever so many flowers ; and, recognizing this, Louisa's heart softened more and more, till before an hour had gone, she laid aside all restraint and affectation, and even outvied Sally in merry laughter and talk. Everything was so new and strange, and made so welcome and so at home, she ran about the house like a pleased child. A humble dwelling it was, consisting of but three rooms—all perfectly neat and clean, and even displaying some little attempts at taste and ornament. The low ceilings and rough walls were white-washed ; the window curtains were snowy white, and a plaided home-made carpet covered the floor of the best room ; and maple boughs, now bright crimson and yellow, filled the fire-place. But that which made the room chiefly attractive, on the night I speak of, was the table. How pretty the pink china (which Mrs. Armstrong had had ever since she was married) showed in the candle-light !

There were cups of flowers, and there was Mrs. Jackson's beautiful cake, with many excellent confections of Mrs. Armstrong's own making. In the kitchen, the tea-kettle was already steaming, the chickens were roasting, and the cream biscuit were moulded and ready to bake.

At eight o'clock, the guests were assembled—eight or ten in all—young men and women, neighbors and friends.

With right good will they set to work, and very fast, despite the mirth and jesting, the streaked, and red, and golden apples, were peeled and sliced ready for the drying.

It happened to Louisa and Warren to sit together, and it also happened the rest of the company were not much edified by what they said.

At half-past nine, came Parson Long. The work was so nearly done, it was not thought worth while for him to join in it; and so, seated in the best chair, and slowly waving a turkey-feather fan before his face, he looked graciously on the volatile people before him. At supper, it chanced that he and Sally were seated together, and whether it was the red buds in her hair, and the pink dress, or whether it was that he learned the cream biscuit, and the crisp pickles, and the plum preserves, were all of her making, I know not, but certainly he manifested a new and surprising interest in her; and Louisa, so far from feeling any pique, appeared delighted with his preference—that is, whenever she sufficiently disengaged her attention from Warren Armstrong to notice him at all.

But I cannot linger over that supper, which Louisa said was the best ever prepared; nor over the merry-making afterward, which lasted till twelve o'clock; nor can I describe the pleasant walks homeward, which, in separate pairs, the young people enjoyed—Warren and Louisa most of all.

In a day or two, that young lady tied on her black apron again, and went over to Mrs. Armstrong's to learn how to make the cream biscuit ; and at twilight, Warren walked with her down the lane to her own home—and that was the beginning of many such visits and walks.

Before the apples were half dry, Parson Long paid a pastorly visit to Mrs. Armstrong's. He had been intending to do so for a long time, he said, but there were always many things to come between him and his wishes ; and shortly after this, Sally stopped at Mrs. Goodhue's gate, one Sunday morning, to speak to Louisa. She was going to teach in the Sunday school, she thought she ought to do some good as she went along. But Miss Goodhue did not join her ; she went to church in the morning, and in the afternoon she liked to walk in the fields and woods, and worship through nature. Need I say Mr. Armstrong accompanied her in these walks ?

I do believe the course of true love sometimes does run smooth, the poet's declaration to the contrary, notwithstanding. I do believe there are kindred spirits, and happy homes, few and far between though they be.

Stop, O wayfarer, when you see eyes smiling back to eyes that smile, for you are very near to heaven.

Months the apples had been dried and hung in a bag, in the cabin kitchen ; the lane leading from Mrs. Armstrong's to the main road was white with the level snow ; the wind whistled up and down the hills, and night hung dreary over the world. But within doors, it was cheerful and warm. True, the genial face of Warren was wanting—but then, there was an honored guest seated by the hickory fire talking mostly to Sally (who wore a lace collar which Mrs. Goodhue gave her) but sometimes to quiet Moses, and sometimes to Mrs. Armstrong, whom he calls mother. Is it Mr. Long ?

Across the fields, and almost meeting their own, fall the window lights of Mrs. Goodhue, who has become reconciled to the
country, and thinks it less dreary in the winter than it was in
the summer. The fire is no less bright than Mrs. Armstroug's,
and beside it sit Warren and Louisa—lovers, now.

"By the way," said the young man, with an arch expression,
and passing his arm around the waist of the girl, " there is one
little matter which has not been adjusted—you have never paid
me, as you proposed, for that first bringing you from the city.
You know, at the time, I suggested leaving the settlement to a
third party ; I have selected Parson Long, and if you don't
object to him, pray fix the time as early as possible " The
reply she made was smothered by the sweetest of all impedi-
ments ; but it is certain she did not object to the parson, as
arbiter, and that the time was fixed, for she has been, for many
a day, one of the most painstaking and exemplary wives in all
our neighborhood—scarcely rivalled, indeed, by Mrs. Sally Long.

ELIZA ANDERSON.

———◆———

CHAPTER I

THE firelight was beginning to shine brightly through the one small window that looked towards the street—the one small window of a barely comfortable house that once stood in the suburb of a busy little town—busy in a little way. The one blacksmith was exceedingly busy : the clinking of his hammer was heard far into the night often, and on the beaten and baked ground before his door horses were waiting for new shoes from year's end to year's end. The storekeeper was busy too, for he was showman and salesman, and clerk and all ; the schoolmaster was busy with his many children in the day, and his debating schools and spelling schools at night ; the tailor was busy of course—and one man among them, who might be seen talking with the blacksmith or the storekeeper, or lounging on the bench in front of the tavern some time during every day, was busiest of all ; this man lived in the house where the light was shining at the window, and his name was George Anderson. He was always better dressed, and could talk more smartly than most of his neighbors—it was his boast that he could do anything as well as anybody else, and a little better, and he sometimes exemplified to his audience that his boast was not without truth—he could take the blacksmith's hammer and nail on a horseshoe as readily as the smith himself, and, moreover, he could make the nails and beat out the shoe, if he chose, but it was not often he chose so hard a task —he could wrestle with the bar-keeper and get the better of him, drink whisky with him, and in that too get the better, for George Anderson was never seen to walk crooked or catch at posts, as he went along. Now he would step behind the counter, and relieve the storekeeper for an hour, and whatever trades he assumed were sure to be to the satisfaction of everybody—he was good-natured and welcome everywhere, for he always brought good news. It was quite an event at the school-house to have him come and *give out* the spelling lesson, or hear the big girls parse some intricate sentence from Paradise Lost.

The scholars were not afraid of him, and knew they could catch flies and talk as much as they pleased if he were their teacher, and then they felt sure he knew more than the schoolmaster himself.

The firelight was beginning to shine so bright that you might have seen through the naked window all that was in the room—a bare floor, a bed, some chairs and a table were there —a pot and a kettle steaming over the fire—a little girl sitting in a little chair, before it, and a woman leaning on the foot of the bed. The table-cloth was laid, but nothing to eat was on the table.

Presently the schoolmaster was seen going that way, walking leisurely, and with a book beneath his arm—he boards . with Mrs. Anderson, and is going home. He entered the house, and in less than a minute was seen to come out without the book, looking hurried and flurried, and to walk towards the more crowded part of the town very fast, stopping once at the door of a small house much resembling Mrs. Anderson's own.

He finds the redoubtable George telling a story in the bar-room to a group of admiring listeners, and touching his arm, whispers something, but the story-telling goes on all the same. The schoolmaster repeats the touch, and whispers more emphatically. "Yes, directly," says George. "Now, this moment!" says the schoolmaster, aloud, and he tries to pull the talker away, but not till the story is finished does he start toward home, and then leisurely and smoking a cigar as he goes. The schoolmaster does not return home, but solemnly makes his way to a common not far from it, and crossing his hands behind him, appears lost in contemplating a flock of geese swimming in a shallow pond and squalling when he comes near. Meantime the mistress of the little house, at the door of which he stopped for a moment, has thrown a shawl about her shoulders and runs without bonnet to Mrs. Anderson's house. Another woman, spectacles in hand, and cap border flying, follows directly, and then another, summoned by some secret and mysterious agent, it would seem, for no messenger has been visible.

The window that looks into the street is temporarily curtained now with a woman's shawl—sparks are seen to fly out of the chimney rapidly, and there is much going out and in and whispering of neighbors about their doors and over their garden fences—and it is not long till one of the women comes away from Mrs. Anderson's, leading the little girl who sat by the fire an hour ago. Her black eyes are wide open as if she were afraid, or in doubt what would become of her, and she looks back towards her home wistfully and often, though the woman seems to talk cheerfully as they go, and lifts her with a playful jump over the rough places. Suddenly they turn aside from the path they are in—they notice the schoolmaster pacing up and down beside the pond, and join him, and after some embarrassed blushes and foolish laughter on his part, they go away together. He leads the little girl by the hand, and her thin, white face looks up to him more confidently than to the strange woman. They turn into a little yard, cross a dark porch and open a side door—a glimpse is revealed of a room full of light and children, and all is dark again.

A very good supper the strange woman prepared, of which the little girl and the schoolmaster partook, and afterward he lifts her on his knee, and with the other children gathered about him, tells stories of bears and pirates and Indians till she at last falls asleep, and then the strange woman opens a little bed and softly covers her, and the schoolmaster is shown to a bed in another part of the house. The morning comes, and she goes to school with the master without having gone home, and the day goes by as other days have gone at school —lessons are badly recited and spelling badly spelled; and the schoolmaster takes her hand and helps her down stairs, and walks on the rough ground, leaving the smooth path for her, and they pass the pond where the geese are swimming, and the strange woman's house, and go in at home, the child still holding the master's hand.

"Well, Lidy," says the woman, who is there preparing the supper, "what do you think happened when you were asleep last night?" Lidy can't guess, and the master says he can't guess, though older eyes than Lidy's would have seen that he suspected shrewdly. "Why," says the strange woman, "the prettiest little brother you ever saw in your life was brought here, for you!" Lidy's black eyes open wide with wonder, and she holds fast the master's hand, and looks at him inquiringly as if she wished he would tell her whether to be glad or sorry. He puts his arm around her and draws her close to his side, and says something about how happy she will be, but he says it in a misgiving tone, and smooths her hair as if it were a piteous case. The strange woman leaves her bustling for a moment, and whispers at the bedside there is no tea. A pale hand puts by the curtain, and a low voice says something about having told George, three hours past, to go to the tailor who owes her for sewing, get the money and bring home tea and sugar, and some other things, and she wonders he does not come. The strange woman says she wonders too, but she whispers to the schoolmaster that it is enough like *somebody* to stay away at such a time, and she lifts the tea-kettle from the coals, and lights the candle.

Lidy is told to sit down in her little chair, and make a good, nice lap, which she does as well as she knows how—and the dear little brother, about whom she is still half incredulous, is brought, and in long flannel wrappings laid across her knees. "Now ain't he a pretty baby though!" exclaims the strange woman, "with his itty bitty boo eyes, and his hair des as nice as any of 'em and chrysing." The latter part of the speech was made to the wonderful baby, whom Lidy was told she must kiss, and which she did kiss as in duty bound. The wonderful baby scowled his forehead, clenched his fists and began to cry. "Jolt your chair a little, sissy," says the strange woman.

and then to the wonderful brother, " Do they booze itty boy !
Well, 'em sant do no such a sing ! no, 'en sant !"   Then to the
schoolmaster, who is bending over his Latin grammar, she exhibits one of the feet of the remarkable boy, and says she
believes in her heart, he could hardly wear the moccasin of her
little Mary who is nine months old—then she falls to kissing
one of the hands of the wonderful baby, and calls him in her
loving fondness, " a great big, good-for-nossen sugar-plum."
Then she exhibits one of the wonderful hands, that clenches and
claws most unamiably as she does so, and informs the schoolmaster that she believes in her heart, the hands of the wonderful boy are as large, that very minute, as her Tommy's, and he
will be two years old the seventeenth day of next month—
then she addresses herself to the baby again, and calls his
feet " ittle footens," and makes a feint of eating both at once.

And all this while the remarkable boy has been fretting and
frowning on the lap of his little sister, who is told she is very
much blest in having a little brother, and who supposes she *is*
blest, and trots him, and kisses him, and holds him up and lays
him down again, but in spite of all her little efforts he frowns
and fidgets as if she did not, and could not do half enough for
him.

By and by a slow footstep is heard, and a whistle, and directly afterward Mr. Anderson comes in and gives the strange
woman a little parcel—briskly she measures the tea, and
briskly she fills up the teapot and rattles the cups into the
saucers ; the baby is smothered in his long flannels and tucked
under the coverlet.

" Come, Casper," says Mr. Anderson, " if you had been at
work as hard as I have, you would not want to be called twice."

The schoolmaster lays down his grammar and asks Mr. Anderson what he has been doing—the pale hand puts by the curtain again, and a pale face turns eagerly to hear.

"Why, I could not begin to tell," he says, helping himself freely to everything that is on the table, and he proceeds to mention some of the work. He has broken a colt, he says, which nobody else could manage, and made him kindly, both under the saddle and in harness—he has drawn a tooth which the dentist could not draw, he has turned off two flour barrels for the cooper, and driven the stage-coach seven miles and back, besides a dozen other things, none of which was the least profit to his family.. The light goes out of the pale face that turned so eagerly towards him, and a low voice says, " Did you see the tailor, George ?"

" Why, to be sure," he answers, "I sewed a seam for him as long as from here to the gate and back again." He has not answered her question as she expected, the hand that holds the curtain shakes nervously, and the low voice says,

" Did he—did—did you get the tea, George ?"

" Why, to be sure, and most excellent tea it is," and as the strange woman drains the last drop into his sixth cup, he adds, " won't you have a cup, mother ?"

He turns partly towards her as he confers upon her the honor of this inquiry, and the low voice trembles as it says, " No," and the pale hand lets the curtain drop. Poor woman ! perhaps she saw the bright new waistcoat that George wore, with its double rows of shining buttons, perhaps she saw this and knew the way her hard earnings had gone. The schoolmaster thinks he hears a stifled groan behind the curtain, sets his cup of tea aside, and will not eat any more, and directly returns to his grammar. Mr. Anderson sits in the corner and smokes for half an hour, and then recollecting that some business requires his attention up town, pulls on his gloves, and goes out. The schoolmaster follows shortly, and in a few minutes returns, and gives the strange woman two small parcels, one containing crackers and the other raisins—poor Mrs. Anderson thinks it was George brought them, reproaches herself for having wronged him, smiles and is blest again.

The remarkable baby cries and cries, and while the strange woman washes the dishes and makes the house tidy, little Lidy carries him up and down the room, and across and across the room till her arms ache, and she sits down

"Bless me ! you are not tired of your dear little brother already ?" exclaims the strange woman, and Lidy says she is not tired—she is very glad to carry him—only her arms won't hold him any longer.

When the house was set in order, the strange woman took the remarkable boy, and with some talk to his "ittle boo, scepy eyes," managed to quiet him, and tucking him away as before, she went home to attend her own house and little ones.

At ten o'clock Lidy had crossed the floor with her blessed brother in her arms hundreds of times, and in a temporary lull was fallen asleep in her chair. A rough pull at her hair caused her to open her eyes suddenly—the baby was crying again, and her father was come and scolding her angrily. "She had not a bit of feeling," he said, "and did not deserve to have such a beautiful brother—somebody would come and take him away if she did not take better care of him." Directly Lidy was pacing the floor again, and the baby crying with all his might.

"Seems to me you don't try to keep your poor little brother

still," says the father, for a moment taking the cigar from his mouth, and then puffing away again. He never thought of relieving the little girl, or even of speaking any words of pity and comfort to her—she was not born to pity or comfort from her father—she had committed the offence of inheriting the light of life some years prior to her brother, and from the moment of his birth she had no consideration except with reference to him. Even her mother, though she loved her, gave the baby the preference—Lidy's petticoats were appropriated for his use, and Lidy could not go to school because her shawl must be turned into a baby blanket. Everybody came to see the baby, and everybody said how much prettier than his sister he was, but that she seemed to be a good little girl, and of course she was very much delighted with her new brother—he would be big enough one of these days to play with her, and then she would have fine times.

Mr. Anderson was congratulated, and proud to be congratulated—he could afford to do almost anything since a fine son was born to him, and in higher good-humor than usual he made barrels for the cooper and nails for the blacksmith—treated all the town to brandy instead of whisky, and to the storekeeper traded a very good new hat for a very bad old one !

And patiently Lidy gave up her petticoats, and patiently she stayed away from school and worked all the day—and while her mother sat up in bed to sew for the tailor again, she climbed into her little chair and washed the dishes—it was all for her pretty little brother, her mother said, and by and by he would be big enough to work for them, and then he would buy a new cap for mother, and new slippers for Lidy, and oh, ever so many things.

Lidy quite forgot the sweeping and the dish washing, in the pictures of the new things her little brother was going to buy for her some time.

Now and then of evenings, when the baby was asleep, the schoolmaster would take Lidy on his knee and teach her to read, and she scarcely fell behind the children that were in school every day, he said. Once when he was praising her, her father said her little brother George would soon get before her when he was big enough to go to school. "George will never have her eyes, though," said the schoolmaster, proudly looking into their black, lustrous depths.

Mr. Anderson said the girl's eyes were well enough, he supposed, for a girl's eyes, but George would never suffer in comparison with her, and from that time the schoolmaster, whose name was Casper Rodwick, was designated as "Old Casper," by the father of the remarkable boy.

CHAPTER II.

Years went away,.and one frosty moonlight night, the same neighbor who led little Lidy away and kept her before, was seen hurrying across the common, again, and the schoolmaster to come forth and go searching about the town—the store-keeper laid down his measure, saying, "Is there any bad news, Mr. Rodwick?" for he knew by the manner of his inquiry for George, that poor Mrs. Anderson was dead.

The husband wore a new hat deeply shrouded with crape at her funeral, and new gloves, and George, who was grown to be a big, saucy boy, wore gloves too, while Eliza wore an ill-fitting bonnet that was not her own, and no gloves at all.

From that time Mr. Anderson did not look, nor seem like himself, people said, and it was believed he was grieving himself to death. They did not know, and he did not know, that he had drawn all his life from his wife—she had bought his food and his clothes, she had held him up and kept him up, and when the crape he wore at her funeral grew dusty and fell to pieces, he fell to pieces with it. He called Lidy to his bedside, one day, and told her that her brother would soon have a fine education—she must be content to suffer some privations till that was accomplished, and then he would repay her handsomely—he was a noble-hearted lad, and wonderfully gifted. Lidy must look to him for advice now, and in all things subserve his wishes.

" Dear, dear father," cried Lidy, " you must not die—I can not live without you," and with all the power that was in her, she strove to make pleasant the sick-room. She placed her geranium pots and myrtles where he could see them, and let the sunshine in at the windows that he might feel how bright the world was without—but his eyes could not see the brightness anywhere, and at length one night Casper was called to write his will—he had nothing to bequeath, and his will was a record of his wishes only. Little more was written than he had spoken to Lidy, and all was to the effect that George was her natural and proper guardian, that he was superior to her in wisdom, and should be so in authority, and that if ever his daughter forgot it, he wished her to read this testimonial of her father's will.

So they were left alone in the world, the two orphans, with no friend but the schoolmaster. Eliza Anderson had all her mother's energy and aptitude. She could not only sew for the tailor, but she could make caps and collars for the ladies of the town, and dresses too, and as she was not ashamed to work she got along with her poverty very well. George inherited all his father's smartness, and more than all his irresolution, but as he grew older he grew better tempered, and whatever he was to others, was seldom unamiable to Lidy. How could he be, indeed, unless he had been a demon?

Often when she sat with her sewing at night, she would tell the schoolmaster what great hopes she had of George, and how ingeniously he could turn his hand to anything. Sometimes he would smile and sometimes he would sigh, but whatever he said it was evident he shared none of her enthusiasm. This rather offended Lidy, for she received any slight to George as a personal insult, and she would sit all the evening after some hopeful allusion to him, silent, often sullen, saying to all the master's little efforts to please her, that she had not a friend in the world, and it was no use ever to hope for sympathy. It was true that from the first the master had not loved George much—first he had taken the petticoats from his little favorite, then her playthings, and then she began to be big enough to work for him, and from that time it was nothing else but work for him, and for the master's part he could see no prospect of anything else.

One night she appeared unusually happy, and to find her own heart company enough. Once or twice she seemed on the point of telling something to the master, but she checked herself, and if she said anything it was evidently not what she at first thought. "Well, Lidy," he said, at length, "what is it?" and at last it came out—about George, of course. He was going to stay away from school and work in the garden the half of every day ! and Eliza thought it not unlikely that he would learn more in half the day, after such healthful exercise, than he had done in the whole day. She had spent more money for the hoe, and the spade, and garden seeds, to be sure, than she could well afford, but then it was all going to be such an improvement to George, to say nothing of the great advautage it would be to her ?

"Don't you think it will be a good thing for us both ?" aud she went on to say it was a wonderful idea, aud all his own— she had never suggested anything like it to George. Did it not look like beginning to do in earnest ? and she concluded, " maybe, after all, you will find you were mistaken about him !"

" And maybe not," said the schoolmaster, cooly—" where is the boy ?"

Eliza did not know where he was, and to be avenged upon him for the hnmiliating confession he obliged her to make, she said she did not know as it was any of his business.

" Of course it is not my business, but I can't bear to see you so imposed upon," and he very gently took her hand as he spoke. She withdrew it blushing ; covered her face, and burst into tears. She was not a child, and he was her friend and schoolmaster no more. She was become a woman, and he her interested lover.

He had been gone an hour to the little chamber adjoining his schoolroom, where he had slept since her mother's death, when George came.

Lidy kept her face in the dark that he might not see how red her eyes were, for she could not explain why she had been crying. She hardly knew herself—and in a tone of affected cheerfulness told him of the garden tools she had bought, and produced her package of seeds.

"Call me early," he said, "I am going to work in earnest. I am twelve years old now, and can do as much as a man !"

Lidy promised to call him, and never once thought necessity ought to wake him, as it did her.

She was astir an hour earlier than common the next day— and having called George, set to digging in the garden beds with good-will. She was determined the schoolmaster should find the work begun when he came to breakfast. Two or three times she left her work to call George again, and at last, yawning and complaining, he came. "He thought he would feel more like working after breakfast," he said, "rising so early made his head dizzy," and sitting down on a bank of grass, he buried his forehead in his handkerchief, and with one hand pulled the rake across the loose earth which his sister had been digging. Poor boy, she thought, a cup of coffee will do him good, and away she flew to make it.

"Really, George," said the schoolmaster, when he sat down to breakfast, "you have made a fine beginning—if you keep on this way we shall be proud of you."

Lidy noticed that he said, *we* shall be proud of you, and in her confusion she twice put sugar in his coffee, and forgot to give sugar to George at all. He sulked and sat back from the table, affecting to believe that his sister had deprived him of sugar in his coffee for the sake of giving the master a double portion. And he concluded with saying, "It's pretty treatment after my getting up at daybreak to work for you."

"You ought to be ashamed of yourself," said the master, provoked by his insolent words and sulky manner beyond silent endurance, "as if you ought not to work for your sister, and moreover it is for yourself you are working." And he added between his teeth, "if I had the management of you, I'd teach you what pretty treatment was !"

"But you haven't the management of him, Mr. Rodwick," said Eliza, moving her chair further from him and nearer to George.

"I am aware of it, Miss Anderson," he replied, "and if you will uphold him in his ugliness after this fashion, I must say I should be sorry to be connected with him in any way !"

A look that was half defiance and half sneer, passed over the face of Lidy, but she said nothing. At this moment the blacksmith stopped at the door, to offer some seeds of an excellent kind of cucumbers to his neighbor, whom in common with all the village he greatly esteemed.

"You look pale, ma'am," he said, as he laid the seeds on the table beside her, "I'm afeard you have been working beyond your strength ;" and turning to the master, he explained how he had seen her digging in the garden since daybreak. Her face grew crimson, for she had not only suffered the master to attribute the work to George, but had herself helped to deceive him.

One glance he gave her, which to her appeared made up of pity and contempt, and without one word went away from the house. If her little deception had not been discovered, she could have borne herself very proudly towards the master, but now she was humiliated, not only in his estimation, but her own. She was angry with him, with the blacksmith, with George, and with herself. Yet for a good while she would not give up even to herself, but sat sipping coffee and eating dry bread, as if nothing disturbed her in the least, but all the while the bitter tears kept rising and filling her eyes, for she would not wipe them away. One moment she thought she did not care for what had happened, and that she had a right to work in the garden, and was not obliged to tell the master of it either, as she knew of, and that if he had ever given George credit for anything, she would not have tried to deceive him, and at any rate, what she did was nothing to him ; he had no authority over either of them, she was glad of that. But under all this bolstering, which she heaped up under her failing heart, she felt sorry and ashamed, and knew that the master was in the right, that he was a strict disciplinarian, and that in some sort he was entitled to some authority over George, at least. He had lived in the house with them always, had been their teacher, and since their father's death their friend and guardian. George was a bad, idle boy, she knew, and ran away from school when he chose, and she knew too that he required a severe master, and if Mr. Rodwick had softened matters a little she would not have cared ; but he was not the man to disguise plain truth—as far as he saw he saw clearly, and made others see clearly too.

But when it was all turned over and over, Eliza was angry with him more than with George, angry, because he knew the truth, and angry because the truth was the truth—in some way, his knowledge of facts made the facts, she thought.

And all the while she was turning things about, and yet not reconciled to herself, nor to the master, nor to George, he sat sullenly away from the table biting his finger-nails, and waiting to be coaxed to eat.

For once there was no coaxing for him, and the breakfast was removed without his having tasted it. Pulling his hat over his eyes, he was about leaving the house, when Eliza drew him back and demanded authoritatively where he was going. "To the tavern, to buy my breakfast."

"No, you shall not," she said, and forcing him to sit down she sat by him and repeated to him the sacrifices she had all her life made for him, "and what, after all, is the result?" she said, "why, the more I do the more I may, and the less you care for me?" and seeing that he was grinning in his hat, she told him that she knew somebody who *could* make him mind, thus owning to his face, like a weak, foolish, loving woman, that she had no power over him.

"Well, Madam Rodwick," he said, coolly, when she had exhausted all epithets of threat and entreaty, and tenderness and reproach, "if you have concluded your sermon I'll go and get my breakfast."

"You will go to work in the garden!" said the sister, "that is what you will do!" and straight way she fell down to entreaty, and with tears counted the money she had paid for spade and hoe and seeds, and how illy she could afford it, and how she had hoped, and how she still hoped that he was going to be a good boy, a help and comfort to her.

"Well, I shan't mind old Casper, anyhow," said the boy, at length ; and it was finally settled that he would go to work in the garden, and that she would prepare him a nice, warm breakfast. A few shovels of earth he moved from one place to another, but there was really no work done, and Eliza saw there was none done when she called him to the second breakfast. She was completely discouraged and broken down now, and told George so, and seeing that he heeded nothing, she buried her face in her hands and fell to crying. She did not know as she would ever do anything again, she said, and indeed she felt little courage to go to work. George would not help her, and she was tired of working alone.

"It was too hot now, to work in the garden," he replied, "and too late to go to school," and so he sauntered away, his sister saying, as he went, "She did not know as she cared where he went, nor what became of him."

It was noon before she knew it, and the master came home, and there was no dinner prepared; and the tailor called for some promised work, and Eliza had been crying all day, and it was not ready. He was disappointed, vexed, and said if she could not keep her engagements he would find somebody that would.

The master saw how it all was—that George was the beginning of trouble, and that Eliza herself was not a little to blame, and if he had said anything, he would have said what he thought, but she asked for neither advice nor sympathy; and having told her she need prepare no dinner for him, he returned to the schoolhouse and its duties, and as usual maintained a calm and quiet demeanor, however much he might have been troubled at heart.

When the school was done with, he did not return home at once as was his custom, but opening his grammar, remained at the window as long as he could see, and till after that.

All day George had not been seen nor heard of—and all day Eliza had done nothing but cry and fret; but when night came, and a messenger with it to say he was lying on the ground, a little way out of town, drunken as he could be, she began to see how much less to blame the schoolmaster had been than she had tried to believe.

From her heart she wished he would come, but though suffering most intensely she would not seek him, nor would she allow him to know her wretchedness when he should come, so she resolved. But all her proud resolves would not do. He came at last in the same calm, confident way he always came, and with some common words, meant to show that all was right, and that he felt as usual, opened his book to await his supper, which he saw no indication of.

"Mr. Rodwick," she said, directly, in a voice that trembled in spite of herself.

"Yes, what is it?" he answered, without looking from his book.

It was very hard and very humiliating to tell him what it was, but her love for George, and the fear that he might be run over where he lay, overcame the last remnant of her pride, and hiding her face, she sobbed out her sad confession and appeal.

He did not say, "I knew it would be so," nor "You are to blame:" he only said, "Don't cry, Lidy—don't cry," and putting down his book, hurried away. In half an hour he came back, and George with him, staggering and swearing, his clothes soiled and his face dirty—bleeding at one side where he had fallen against the rough ground. He would not be persuaded to have his face washed, and his clothes brushed, nor would he sit down or go to bed, nor do anything else, but swear that in spite of old Casper or his old sister he would go back to the tavern, he had enough good friends there.

Casper had returned to his book, and not till Eliza begged him to interfere, did he speak one word, or seem to notice what was passing, but he no sooner laid his hand on the boy, and spoke a few words in his quiet, determined manner, than he ceased to offer resistance, and was led away to bed without more ado.

When the supper was eaten, Casper would have gone, but Eliza said, " No, I want to talk about George."

" Very well," he said, seating himself, " what have you to say ?"

Eliza knew not what to say—she knew that she was troubled and tormented, that George was idle enough and unpromising enough, but that she loved him after all, and could not bear that he should be compelled to right ways by any one but herself. This was the amount of all she could say.

A clear, practical, common sense view of things the schoolmaster took. He loved Eliza, and he said so, he admired all that was good and discreet and womanly in her, and he said so : he did not love George, and he disliked and disapproved of her wavering and compromising course with him. He had no great hopes of him at the best, nevertheless he could bring him under subjection in some way, if Eliza would give him the right to do so.

He told her what his fortunes and prospects were, without exaggeration or depreciation ; he numbered his years, every one of them up before her, and her own, which were not half so many, and then he said that all he was, and all he had, and all he could do, which was not much, were hers to accept if she would, but with the understanding that George should be subject to his authority.

Eliza reminded him of her promise to her dead father : how could she break that and be at peace with herself? and, moreover, he admitted that he did not love George, and how could she hope the boy would be made any better by him? The schoolmaster argued that if she were willing to trust herself with him, it was natural that she should be willing to trust the management of her brother : and as for the sacred promise she laid so much stress on, it was a bad promise exacted by a bad father, and better broken than kept. And now, he concluded, with the calmness of a third party summing up evidence, "You have all the facts before you—look at them and decide as your conscience dictates."

The facts were unpleasant ones, some of them, and Eliza did not like to look them in the face—she did not like to say definitely what she would do nor when she would do it. When George was older and provided for, or capable of providing for himself, their lives should be joined and flow through all fortune in a sentimental sunshine. All of which to the schoolmaster was nothing but moonshine. With it he was not contented —he wished to see the ground he stood upon, whatever it was, and finally, when they separated, it had been agreed that whenever George should be provided for they should be married ; and that during school hours he should be under the master's control, and at other times Eliza's will should be his law.

Neither was satisfied with this arrangement, for both foresaw it would result badly, in the beginning.

CHAPTER III.

The breakfast was a pleasant one. George had been working in the garden for two hours, he said, and should have half the seeds in the ground before dinner.

Eliza was greatly elated, and saw the fulfillment of her best hopes speedily coming. She could not praise him enough, and she could not help thinking the schoolmaster a little ungenerous in accepting what seemed to her a wonderful performance, as a matter of course.

"Don't you think, Casper," she said, at last, determined to force some praise from him, "that George is a pretty good boy, after all ?"

She had better not have asked it. He had simply done his duty, Casper said, but the motive seemed to him questionable. It was partly the result of shame, and partly an effort to buy off punishment. As soon as George betrayed indications of any thorough reformation, he should be glad to acknowledge it.

Pretty industriously for half a day George kept at work, and with the assistance of Eliza, part of the seeds were got into the ground, and when at noon he related his achievement to Casper, she made no mention of the hand she had lent.

"Now you are to go to school," she said, when the dinner was past ; but George replied that he was too tired, and could not learn if he did. With much coaxing and many promises, he was induced to set out at last : but one excuse for loitering offered itself after another, and finally at the pond he stopped, and having pelted the geese for an hour, he stretched himself in the shavings before the cooper's shop, and slept away another hour ; another was passed in shaving hoop-poles and piling staves, and then the school was dismissed, and joining the other boys the truant went home.

With a good deal of coaxing, and hiring, and scolding, and some wholesome fear of the master, the garden was at last planted ; but Eliza, though she tried to conceal it, had done most of the work, and all the while George had only gone to school when he chose.

One day he told his sister he knew a little boy who had made dollars the last year by selling eggs, and if she would buy a hen and a dozen chickens, oh he would be the best boy in the world, and do everything she desired. He knew where he could get them if he only had two dollars.

Of course Eliza gave the money. She would work a little later every night and soon earn it, and of course she told Casper about it, and insisted that he should see in it great speculative ability on the part of George, but he could only see that she had thrown away her money, and said so, which displeased her, of course, and there was an interval of estrangement.

The seeds were soon mostly picked out of the garden beds, and the beds scratched level with the paths, and then the mother hen came daily home from travelling through the weeds, or from some neighbor's garden with a broken legged chicken, or with a diminished number, till finally she drowned herself in trying to rescue the last one from a pail of milk, and so ended the garden and the chicken speculation.

George now professed himself inclined to return to school. He believed he would be a teacher after all—Eliza concluded his strongest bent was towards learning, and he went to school.

But his zeal soon abated—he liked work better—the cooper would pay him four shillings per day ; and packing his books he went to work with the cooper. Eliza was telling the master how well he was doing, when he came in with one hand bandaged and bleeding—he had cut off two fingers !

In the course of a few months the wound was healed, but he should never be able to work, and one day, about the middle of the afternoon, found him in school. He soon told his sister

—"old Casper" could not teach him anything. Perhaps it would be the very making of him to send him to the academy three miles away. George would walk the distance, the exercise would be beneficial, and she must manage some way, she hardly knew how, to pay for it. His old hat would not do to wear to the academy, he must have a new one—his old coat would not do, the tailor would furnish one, and Eliza would sew for it. At last arrangements were concluded, and he went to the academy. He soon discovered the walk to be too long, it so overcame him that he could not study. He knew of a horse he could hire to ride for a trifle, and the horse was hired and George rode to school, and Eliza worked later into the night and earlier in the morning. She had never been so hopeful—he would be able to teach in the academy after a while, and all her troubles past. If he had the time for books, he said, that was consumed in riding to and from school, and then if he could have a room and study as the other boys did, of evenings, he should get on twice as well. So the horse was given up. It took almost as much to pay for riding as to hire board, Eliza said, and George was provided with board and lodging at the academy, and patiently she toiled on.

The days were the happiest now she had ever seen, Casper was all kindness when the boy was out of his sight ; they would be so happy, and her toils would all be over before long —she was telling him so, and he listening in half credulous delight, for what lover has not some faith in his mistress, when George, books and bundles and all, strode into the house, and a great chilly, black shadow came in with him.

He did not like the boys at the academy, nor the teachers, nor anything. He could not eat at his boarding-house—he was sick with all, and believed he was going to die : and Eliza believed he was sick, and feared he would die ; but the master neither believed the one nor feared the other, and so the old estrangement came again.

When the youth professed himself well he went to work with the tailor, but did not like it, and so was home for awhile ; then he went with the blacksmith, but that was too hard.: then he was home for awhile, helping her, Eliza said ; then he went into the store, grew tired and was home for awhile, helping Eliza again.

She was discouraged now, and a good deal in debt. She was growing old faster than years made her grow old ; the rose died in her cheek, and her eyes lost their lustre—even the master did not praise them any more, and this made her sadder than all.

Suddenly George formed the resolution of going to school again. He believed " old Casper " was a pretty good teacher, after all.

Eliza began to think she would allow Casper the right to control him now, by becoming his wife, but he did not urge the marriage any more. She was almost resolved to approach the matter herself. George should be kept at school whether he would or not—she would tell Casper so that night. She arose with the resolution and looked towards the school-house, and there came George, running crookedly home, his eyes blind with tears, and holding up the crippled hand as if it had been mutilated anew.

" The master had struck his poor hand with a rule," he said, " and all for laughing because he saw him kiss Sophie Swain, and not because he did anything wrong."

There was a quick revulsion of sympathies and resolves on the part of Eliza. Sophie Swain was a pretty girl of sixteen, the daughter of the richest man in town. She saw plainly enough now why Casper said nothing about marriage, and she thought it was too bad that he should take to abusing her poor brother as well as herself on account of his charmer. As long as she lived, George should not be maltreated in that way, that he shouldn't.

All this and more, Eliza resolved she would say, and all this and more she did say in tones of no measured mildness. Of course she did not care how often the master kissed Sophie Swain, nor how soon he married her, if he wanted to. She was sure she would not stand in his way if she could, and she knew very well that she could not ; he had ceased to feel even the commonest interest in her. But one thing she would and could do —she would prevent him from beating poor George to death.

When she had exhausted all epithets of reproach and denunciation, and was still from sheer prostration, the master replied in his perfectly quiet and self-possessed way, which to Eliza was especially provoking, that it was true as George said. He had kissed Sophie Swain, that he could not be blind to her beauty, and she seemed not averse to his acknowledgment of it. He had made no love to her, and did not propose to if Eliza would grant him the happiness of continuing his suit, or rather if she would be reasonable and terminate it in marriage, this he professed himself willing, nay, anxious to conclude at once. Not only his heart but his judgment, he said, sanctioned the proposal he had made her.

"It was true he had struck George," he said, "but not injuriously, and Eliza should have sense enough to know it.

And besides, the youth merited twice as much as he had received. It was the first time he ever used the liberty herself bestowed on him, and he insisted that then and there their relations should be definitely settled."

In all he said he neither elevated nor lowered his voice in the least. If he saw Eliza's tears, he did not seem to see them, nor did he once touch her hand, nor move one inch towards her, but having concluded what he had to say awaited her answer, snapping the blade of his pen-knife backward and forward, and not even lifting his eyes towards her.

This conduct was certainly badly calculated to make a passionate woman reasonable.

Checking her tears in very anger, she told him he was a strange lover. He replied that he had a strange mistress, and besides she must remember he was not a passionate boy. Eliza begged his pardon. She had, for the moment, forgotten that only his judgment sanctioned his proposal to her, and that his heart was averse to it—interested, doubtless, in a much younger and handsomer woman.

"If you will make gratuitous interpretations, you must make them," said the master, his lip curling slightly; "but I have no replies for them."

Eliza insisted that she had interpreted his words legitimately, and that for her part she saw no reason why he should drag his judgment in at all. To which he replied most provokingly, that he feared his judgment had been dragged forward less than it should have been!

There were some more words, as angry and unreasonable as they could be on one side, and most severely reasonable and concise on the other. When they parted, it was with the declaration, on the part of Eliza, that Mr. Rodwick was free to use his judgment as he liked, for the future, it was nothing to her. And when he asked if he might not hope for leniency, she said, " No !"

CHAPTER IV.

Years ago all this happened, and what either party, or both have suffered, only themselves know. The same house, shabbier than it used to be, with the one uncurtained window towards the street, is standing yet. Sometimes in the evening twilight you will see there a plain, pale woman, with grey hair, sewing by the last light. She does not smile, nor look as if she had smiled for many years, or ever would again. Often three bright, laughing children go in at the gate with parcels of sewing, and they climb over her chair and kiss her, and wonder why she is not gay and laughing like their mother ; and when they go away, they are sure to leave more money than she has earned, behind them ; they are Casper's children, and the woman is Eliza Anderson.

Sometimes you will see there a ragged, wretched man, lame in the right leg, and with one arm off at the elbow—his face has in it a look of habitual suffering, of baffled and purposeless suffering, as if all the world was set against him, and he could not help it ; and that is George.

Sometimes in the night, when all is dark and still, a white-haired man leans over the broken gate, forgetting the white wall of his own garden, and all the roses that are in it, and the pretty children that are smiling in their dreaming : and even the wife, gone to sleep too, in the calm, not to say indifferent confidence, that he will take care of himself, and come home when he gets ready. He leans there a long while thinking, not of what is, but of what might have been, and wondering whether eternity will make whole the broken blessings of time. That is Casper, to be sure—who else should it be?

13

MRS. WALDEN'S CONFIDANT.

Fourth of July ! The beating of a drum and the scream-
ing of a fife were heard in the distance—some few thin clouds
moved about the sky, as if to keep the light from dazzling—
the air was soft and refreshing, not over warm, just sufficiently
in motion so stir the young thrifty corn, and bring the scent
from the tomato and potato vines—the orchards looked well,
and the harvests generally had fulfilled a good promise. The
people all through the neighborhood were glad, and thought
their village was about as thriving a village as was to be found
in that part of the country—and so they well might think ;
the best farms commanded fifty dollars per acre—the soil was
productive, and there was abundance of wood, water and
stone ; fine clay for making bricks ; besides other advantages
which made the farmers about naturally a little proud—and
this pride extended from their own possessions to the property
of their neighbors, and took in the fifty lots and thirty dwellings,
the meeting-house, two grocery stores and tavern, which were
the pride of the Clovernook neighborhood. There was talk of a
seminary, and some prospect of the erection of half a dozen new
dwellings, besides the certain addition of a third story to the

290

tavern. The execution of a new sign was already in commission, and it was whispered the device was to be an eagle soaring towards the sun, with the motto beneath, " upward and onward." The commission had been intrusted to the wagonmaker, whose ability for the task nobody doubted. There was some regret that the sign could not have been completed and swinging before the " North American Hotel " on the glorious Fourth, but the regret was not enough to mar the general joyousness, and as for the landlord, the excellent Peter Holt, he had a secret project of his own that the completion of the third story, and the putting forth of the new sign, should give eclat to the general training in the fall. Therefore he compressed his lips and put his face under a dubious cloud when inquired of concerning the sign, saying simply, " we shall see what we shall see."

The people about the neighborhood had been astir before the cock on the day I write of, for a general celebration was to be held in the village, and in addition to the usual ceremonies, two of the oldest men in the neighborhood—real Revolutionary soldiers ; were to head the procession, which was to form at the North American Hotel precisely at ten o'clock, who were to bear between them the American flag ; and on each side of them little girls were to walk with baskets of flowers, garlands for the conquering heroes.

The village, which stood on a rising ground, could be seen two or three miles away, from positions where no woodland intervened, and now, even higher than the steeple of the church, shone the bright colors at the top of the " liberty pole."

Not more than a mile away, and plainly in view, not only of the steeple and the liberty pole, but also of the people gathering in front of the hotel, and in hearing of the music, lived the family of Timothy Walden, consisting in all of husband and wife, Matilda—a young woman of eighteen—and two boys, of fourteen and sixteen-years.

They had been early astir in common with their neighbors, but not joyously astir—they were not people who joined in celebrations—why, nobody knew ; they did not know themselves—but they honestly believed themselves too poor to be justified in spending so much time and money.

There had been some hope on the part of the young people, up to the last moment, that they might be permitted to join in the festivities of the occasion. Even to drive the geese from the common, and assist in the removal of hoop-poles and staves preparatory to the grand march, would have been esteemed a privilege by the boys, and to be allowed the most obscure position where she might see the procession and the green arbor over the dinner-table, would have made holiday enough to Matilda, and she would have been quite willing to forego the white dress and pink ribbons which the young ladies generally had.

When the breakfast was concluded, Mr. Walden went out to the harvest-field as usual, and apparently did not once think of a suspension of labors. Sullenly the two boys followed, half wishing it might rain and spoil all the fun for other people, for nothing so embitters the heart as the constant denial of innocent pleasures. And here let me say that Mr. Walden was the owner of sixty acres of as good land as was to be found in the neighborhood, besides all necessary horses, carts, and implements of labor generally. His fences were in repair, and a thrifty orchard and commodious barn had rewarded his industry. A house, too, he owned, or rather the foundation of a house, for it was unplastered, unpainted, and altogether unfurnished except the actual necessities about the kitchen and sleeping-rooms. The sun streamed across the bare floors through the uncurtained windows, and great piles of bedding and heaps of rags and wool filled the empty rooms—there were no flowers about the yard, and the garden in the rear was quite overgrown with weeds.

A patient, hard-working woman was Mrs. Walden—but she was not hopeful any more—she said she was tired of hoping. She had tried long and hard to get a little beforehand in the world, and what had it amounted to? Thoughts of this sort were busy in her mind on the beautiful Fourth of July aforementioned. It had never been her habit to indulge in hard thoughts, but some how that day she could not help it —the house had never looked so naked and comfortless ; she had never seen so little prospect of ever having anything, and in her absence of mind she let fall the coffee-pot and broke it in pieces as she cleared the table ; true, it had leaked a long time, but then it was better than none—dear me, what would become of them ! She had done her part—nobody could say she had not—who then was to blame? if it was not Timothy she did not know who was. This suspicion once allowed to come into her mind, made room for many accusations, and she put together all the Fourth of Julys and other holidays she had spent at home working hard, and no thanks from nobody, which meant from Timothy. They had never had a Christmas dinner nor a New-Year's dinner so long as they had kept house—and who was to blame ?—why somebody must be ; but no matter for that, she must try to do her duty at any rate—so she worked on, thinking harder and harder things. Happening to look towards the field, she saw the two boys turning somersets in the shadow of a tree, for they felt it to be their right to be idle on the Fourth of July, and for the moment she felt as if she was all the one that did anything to any profit, and this the more, perhaps, that as she looked she saw Timothy making his way to the fence, where young Dr. Meredith, who was just come home from prosecuting his professional studies in a distant city, was waiting to shake hands.

"Dr. Meredith, indeed !" exclaimed the unamiable woman, " a great doctor I guess he is."   And if her supposition that it was impossible for John Meredith to be a doctor could have been analyzed, it would have been found to consist chiefly of the facts that she had known John Meredith when he had but two shirts, she had known the colors of all his boyhood coats, and how hard his mother worked and how much she denied herself for the sake of educating him ; and more than this, she knew his mother before him, and all her family.   That she had ever known John to be other than a good and obedient boy she would not say—but what of that ?—there he was, dressed finely and going to pass the day in idleness—perhaps he would read the " Declaration " and be called " doctor " by some silly young girls at any rate.

Then her thoughts naturally reverted to her own daughter, and she became aware that her wheel was still, which added to her irritation, and in no mild terms she enjoined her to go forward with her work.

Still, ever and again there was silence in the room where Matty should have been spinning—how could she keep her eyes from the public road filled with wagons and carriages, and

young men and women on horseback and on foot, all with
happy faces and dressed gaily, going to the Fourth of July.
Among the rest there is one who looks earnestly towards her
and bows very low, and close against the pane she presses her face
before she sees it is Dr. Meredith ; but her sweetest smile and
a double recognition are given, for though she has played
" hide and seek " with him many a time—aye, and even beaten
him in the spelling class at school, she is pleased to see that
he has come home, and never once thinks it is not possible for
him to be a doctor. "Dear me !" says Mrs. Walden as the
wheel stops again, " well, I must work all the harder for the
idleness of the rest, I suppose," and with a shining tin pan in
her hand she makes her way to the garden. She don't know
what she will find, she don't suppose she will find anything,
and sure enough she does not ; the cucumber-vines are yellow,
and seem to be dying ; there is not a cucumber to be found
larger than her little finger, and as for the tomatoes, they might
just as well never have been planted ; there are a few
onions run up to seed among the weeds ; the cabbages are not
heading at all, and she can't tell where the beet bed was made.
So, through nettles and burs she makes her way out again,
stopping for a moment at the currant-bushes, as a forlorn hope
—she finds a few poor little berries, but if she picks them now
there won't be any left, so she leaves them for a greater emer- ·
gency, and with an empty basin returns to the house. The
flies are buzzing thick along the ceiling, and one or two old
hens are picking the crumbs from off the floor—they ought to
have plenty, but they have not—there are not more than half
a dozen chickens in all, about the farm ; the hens don't do
well—she don't know why ; possibly there is some fruit in the

orchard large enough to cook, but she don't know as she will traipse there after it, if there is ; there is part of an old ham left, she will cook some of that for dinner, and when that is gone she don't know what they will do. She is mending the fire when Timothy comes to the well for water, and seeing pieces of the broken coffee-pot says :

"How did this happen, Sally ?"

"I let it fall," she answers, " and I don't care if I did."

" Why, Sally, what put you in such a humor? I am sorry the coffee-pot is broken, but I did not mean to blame you ;" and he adds by way of lessening the disaster, " see here, I have been doing mischief, too," and he exhibits a hole in his shirt sleeve which he had caught in a brier and torn.

Sally does not speak, for she secretly believes that her husband does blame her, perhaps from the fact that she is blaming him.

"I am afraid our Fourth of July friends will get wet," says Timothy, looking up at the sky, and making a last effort to elicit some notice from Sally before he goes back to the field.

But for the first time in her life she refuses to speak, and with tears brimming up in her eyes, goes to the closet and takes from the shelf a bundle of old patched and darned shirts, and sitting down, adds patches to patches, and darns to darns—there are a dozen good new ones on the shelf, to be sure, but if they were worn out they would not be new—so with the tears falling fast, she works on. There is a rap on the open door, and looking up she sees Mrs. Eliza Bates—a neighbor whom she has known well ever since her marriage, and before, in fact. Indeed, they were quite confidants at one time. But their intimacy has not been very great for a long time—Mrs. Walden has never felt that it was right to have any confidant but her husband—and it is the fault of Mrs. Bates that she is given to talking over much, and Mrs. Walden knows it. She has had, too, great worldly prosperity, and this has cooled the friendship formerly existing between them, perhaps. But sympathy is sweet, and when Mrs. Bates says in tones of real kindness, "Why, my dear Sally, what can be the matter with you?" at the same time putting her arm kindly about her neck, she answered, crying all the time, "I am glad you have come, Eliza, for I felt lonesome and bad, sitting here alone."

"I knew I should find *you* at home, and so while all our folks were gone to the Fourth of July, I thought I would come and see you, though you don't never come to see me."

"How good you are," replies Mrs. Walden. "I suppose everybody knows they can find me at home of holidays, by this time," and she hides her eyes in her apron.

Mrs. Bates holds her hand saying, "really, Sally, it's too bad;" after which she makes moan without the use of words, for a few minutes.

"Don't, Sally, don't cry," she says, at length, "but tell me all about it; a body must have some confidant—now, I tell my daughter Kate all my troubles—but some mothers don't say to their children all they feel." And in thus drawing out her friend, Mrs. Bates was actuated by the kindest feelings.

"I suppose we all have our troubles," sobbed Sally Walden, for Mrs. Bates had spoken of hers, and therefore *she* could admit her private griefs more freely, and Mrs. Bates rejoined quickly, "to be sure, Sally, I know I have mine. Now, if you had seen what a fuss there was at our house this morning about going to the Fourth of July, you would think you were not the only person in the world that need cry; I got so worried out

that I just gave up, and said I wouldn't go at all. I tell you
Sally, my life is nearly tired out of me in one way and another.
Now Peter Bates is just the hardest man in the world to get
along with, and if I did not manage and twist and economize
every way, I could not get along ; but I am determined that
my family shan't be a whit behind anybody else." And here
she went on to explain how she had taken her own dresses and
made them over for Kate ; how she had managed to make old
things about the house look almost as well as new, and when at
length she stopped to take breath, Mrs. Walden could not help
giving some of her own grievances utterance ; she did not want
to say anything against Timothy, she did not intend it, but
she did. "It's too bad," said Eliza Bates, "and though
Timothy Walden is as good a man as ever was, and I believe
means to do what is right, he don't do his part by you, and I
don't know as it's any more harm to say it than think it, and I
have thought it a good while, and I am not the only one.
Everybody knows," she continued, "that you never spend
money—that you are always at home and always at work, and
can't help saying how does it happen that the house is never
finished, and that Matty is not dressed as fashionably as other
girls ? Somebody must be at fault, and every one knows it is
not you."

Now Mrs. Bates had thought many a time, and said it, too,
that Sally Walden was more to blame than her husband—that
she seemed to have no ambition and no pride since her marriage,
but suffered all things to go at loose ends. But now that she
sat beside her, and saw her thin cheek and old faded dress, and
saw, too, the bundle of coarse patched shirts she was mending,
her heart was softened towards her and hardened proportionably

against her husband, and for the sake of being agreeable, and as is human nature, under the circumstances, she could not forbear speaking more than she really thought, or more than at another time she would have thought. She even proposed, in the heat of her zeal for her friend, " to give Timothy a talking to."

Many things about her own private affairs she put into the keeping of her friend, Sally Walden, such as that Peter Bates did not always give her money for the asking—that herself did a good deal of the managing that he had credit for, and that her daughter Kate would not now be, as she was, one of the very leaders of society, but for her special exertion. And here she whispered very confidentially that Dr. Meredith had been two or three times to see Kate, and that she had reason to believe it would be a match. When Mrs. Walden arose to make some preparation about dinner, " Don't, dear Sally," said the confidant, " I can eat anything that you can, so don't give yourself any trouble."

" I could not give you anything if I were disposed," answered Mrs. Walden ; " there is nothing but ham and potatoes about the house."

" No matter, I had rather talk than eat," replied the confidant; and to ham and potatoes the neighbors sat down. Matty came from her spinning, and the boys from the field, but Mr. Walden did not come in to eat, he could not take time, as he was working hard to get some grain in the barn before it should rain. The neighbors had not noticed till then how cloudy it was, and Mrs. Bates cut her visit short as soon as the meal was concluded, assuring Sally, by way of parting consolation, that she would come again soon, and that she would not fail to give

Timothy "a piece of her mind." Tears came to the eyes of Mrs. Walden, for vexation with herself was struggling with gratitude to her confidant, and the annoyance was not lessened, when Mrs. Bates said, pointing to the worn-out shirts, "I'll declare, I would not try to mend such things, you lose more time than you gain, and if Timothy Walden would not buy better shirts, he might go without any for all of me."

Mrs. Walden did not say, "Timothy has a dozen better shirts," but she thought it, for her heart was beginning to turn to its true allegiance. And the two boys returned back to the field, and Matty to her spinning work, and Mrs. Walden put away the dinner things with a heavy heart, and sat down alone, trying in vain to reconcile herself to herself—she could not do that, nor see a clear way before her ; a feeling of bitterness and blindness, of inability and impossibility, kept her hands idle and drew her face into a frown. She did not see as she could do anything, and she did not know as she would if she could.

As she sat so, she failed to see or hear the flies that came humming thick and black along the ceiling, and the shadows that deepened and deepened where the sunshine had been ; she did not see the leaves turning their grey linings out, nor the clouds of dust that blew up along the road ; the tempest in her heart did not allow her to see the one along the sky. Suddenly a bright flash opened, and at the same time blinded her eyes, and the crash that came after it deafened her ears, and at the same moment made them sensible of voices, reproachful voices, that she had never heard so distinctly before. Quick she hurried to the door, and strained her eyes towards the meadow, that was divided from her now by the blackness of the storm ; a strong wind was bending the tops of the trees—she could hear branches breaking, and the frightened cattle lowing as they ran hither and thither ; the rain dashed heavily on roof and grass and dry dust ; and the eave-ducts ran over, and the wind as it came, bent in the very walls of the house. Matty left her spinning and clung to her mother as the lightning flashed again and again, and the thunder rolled as though breaking its way along the heavens. Awe-struck and trembling stood the mother, her eyes still bent on the meadow.

"Oh, they are coming," cried Matty, "I am so glad ;" but scarcely had she spoken the words when it was discovered that the children came alone ; to the frantic inquiries, for they came crying as they ran, they replied that a tree under which they had taken shelter was struck, and that their father was killed.

"Heaven have mercy on us !" cried Mrs. Walden, her face growing white, and her limbs sinking beneath her, and her daughter and sons answered by sobs and cries.

"What is the matter, my good friends ?" said a voice, kindly and earnestly, and a young man, that Matilda recognized as Dr. Meredith, stood in their midst. The awful calamity was explained, and the young man hastened to call the assistance of another neighbor, who was returning like himself from the celebration, and with a brief word of comfort and hope hurried to the field, accompanied by the oldest son.

Ages seemed to pass in the minutes till their return, and when they came, the pain and weight of ages seemed to crush down the hearts of the mother and her children.

Dead—they were bearing him home dead !

"Let me die, too," exclaimed the almost distracted wife, throwing herself on his bosom; but when the doctor said there was yet hope—he might be only stunned and senseless—the struggle between hope and despair became almost frenzy! never till now had she known how good Timothy was, and how much she loved him. With almost superhuman faith and energy the young doctor strove to subdue the last enemy, for he was not yet quite triumphant. "Oh! if he were only well—if he could only speak to me once more, and say I was forgiven," cried the poor wife, as she rocked herself to and fro and moaned for her own wicked accusations, as she now thought them, almost as much as for the lost; for there is no thought so bitter as the memory of a wrong to the dead. In her heart she accused herself of being his murderer; it was as if heaven had taken him away to show her how good he was. One who went to see how the tree was divided by the lightning, returned carrying a pitcher of blackberries, seeing which the youngest boy began to cry all the more; "he was picking them for you, mother," he said, "it was the last thing he did." Mrs. Walden could not speak; everything seemed to show her that herself was more and more to blame. Suddenly there was a cry of joy—the dead man was alive! No enemy, even death itself, it seemed, could stand before the love that fought him back. Words would fail to describe the joy of that household when the husband and father was able to sit up and speak.

The storm swept by—the breeze came fresh and cool from the meadow—the clouds broke to pieces and scattered from the heavens, and the sun came out broad and bright for the setting. Dr. Meredith's reputation was established, for all the people said "If he can bring Timothy Walden to life, what is there he can't do?" and so came one and another for his medical advice and assistance. Perhaps, the faith of his patients had something to do with it, but certain it is that great success attended him.

As may be supposed, Mrs. Walden found it the easiest and most natural thing in the world to say, " Dr. Meredith"—indeed, she quite forgot whether the coat he used to wear was black or brown, and as for the two shirts, she would not be positive but that he had had three ; and she was quite sure she had seen him at work in his mother's garden a thousand times when other boys were playing. There was new light come into her world, and as the work and bustle of her life stood still while she waited at Timothy's sick bed, she found time to see how many blessings she had, and how many she had neglected.

She made no complaint of the time she was losing—on the contrary, she had never talked so cheerfully and hopefully in her life, and it was perhaps as much owing to her good nursing, as to Dr. Meredith, that Timothy was so soon able to be about his work again.

" Now be careful, Timothy, and don't try to do much," said Mrs. Walden, as after a fortnight's illness he went forth from the house. He looked up in astonishment—came back a step or two—asked her what she said—perhaps for the pleasure of hearing it over, and when in substance it was repeated, he said he felt stronger and could walk better than he supposed he could. So grateful and so loving was the look he bestowed on her that Sally could not help saying, " Eliza Bates give him a piece of her mind, indeed—she had better attend her own affairs, and I will tell her so if she comes here meddling." And as she went from room to room to see what could be done with their contents, she kept communing with herself something in this wise. Here are rags enough to make a carpet, if they were sewed, and here are heaps and heaps of bed clothing—enough to last all my life, and Matty, poor girl, has been spinning all the summer to make more. I'll take the yarn I proposed to have made into coverlids, and have it colored and woven into carpets—I will see if I can't have carpets as well as Eliza Bates, and though we have not money to buy new furniture just now, we can make what we have appear better. So she worked on and on, and at the bottom of all her work was the thought that she would show Mrs. Bates that she had the best husband in the world.

Matty clapped her hands in glee when her mother told her she had concluded to make carpets and not coverlids of the wool she was spinning. "Oh, it will look so much better," she said, "when anybody comes," but she thought when Dr. Meredith comes. It was easy work spinning after that, and very soon the wool was made into yarn, and sent away to be colored and woven. Then the rags which had cumbered the house so long were cut and sewed and sent to the weaver's. Barrels and boxes were removed to the barn, and some curtains for the windows were made of chintz, and Matty and her mother thought they would look almost as well as *bought* curtains, when they were washed and ironed smoothly. At any rate, they were better than Mrs. Bates'—both were sure of that. And all the while the work was going forward, there was cheerfulness in the house that had never been there before.

They had so much more time than formerly, they could not understand how it was, for though they were getting so much done they were not all the time working—for now and then they stopped to plan and sometimes to admire what was completed, and yet they had never accomplished so much when they had not taken time to speak in all the day. "If Mrs. Bates can make dresses for Kate out of hers, perhaps I can make some for you out of mine," said Mrs. Walden to Matty, one day, "there is my wedding dress, and my old black silk and my white dress, and one or two ginghams and calicoes, I believe, in the old chest up stairs, and I shall never wear them again." The chest was accordingly opened and the dresses examined—the white one was bleached, and with the addition of a yard or two of new cloth made. Matty the prettiest dress she had ever worn—the silk, which had been an ample pattern in its time, proved all sufficient ; the calicoes were made to assume new fashions, and Matty was dressed like other girls.

"There, Sally, you have been doing so much lately you deserve some pay for it," said Timothy, as he threw a neat parcel into the lap of his wife one evening. It was a new dress, the first one she had had for a long time, and when she laid it in the closet she stopped to wipe her eyes, and having done so, she removed the old coarse shirts—they were just fit to wash windows with, she said, and she guessed her husband could afford to wear as good a shirt as Mr. Bates.

"No, Sally," said Mr. Walden, "I must wear the old ones a little while longer till we get the doctor's bill paid." And he untied his purse and began counting the money he had already saved for the purpose mentioned.

"If it were not for that debt," said Matty, archly, "we might have got the house plastered, might we not, father?" She blushed and lowered her voice, for the doctor was already at the door.

"We were just talking of you," said Mr. Walden, "and

perhaps I may as well ask now as any time what am I to give you for your services to me ?"

" Not a cent," said Dr. Meredith, " my little service was nothing compared to the great service you have done me, for it was through you that I obtained the confidence of all the village people."

" What a nice man he is," whispered Mrs. Walden to her husband, when the young people had walked apart ; and she added, " if he is in love with Katy Bates I don't see what he comes here for."

Mr. Walden smiled, and said he would see about the plastering the next day.

" Now, boys," he continued, " if you are a mind to help, I'll pay you the same that I do my other hands." Of course they were delighted, and when the house was plastered, half the money had still been saved, for to give it to the children seemed the same thing.

" Is it not beautiful !" exclaimed Matty, when the walls were finished and the curtains hung up and the carpets laid down— " why I never saw such a change with so little money."

" I wonder if Mrs. Bates' house looks any better ?" replied Mrs. Walden, as she walked from one room to the other, not knowing which to admire most.

" Mother and Matty have made the house so nice," said the boys, " we must see if we can't improve the yard a little." So they trimmed up the rose-bushes and swept off the grass and white-washed the fence, and the more they did the more they found they were capable of doing, and that a little *will* was better than a good deal of money. . They even began to believe they could, the next year, make as good a garden as anybody.

" To be sure you can," said their mother ; " but, somehow or other we get along with the table much better than we used to "——

But the " somehow or other " was that she herself made the most of what she had ; and when she had flour and lard, and sugar and fruit, it was easy to make short-cakes and pies. She had, too, butter and milk, and eggs—not so many as she would like—another year she must try to raise more poultry—she did not complain, however—the potatoes were excellent—the apples had never been finer, and she could exchange her extra butter for such articles at the grocery as they had not at home ; and she always finished her congratulations by saying, while they were all alive and well they must not complain, for she never forgot the terrible day that Timothy was brought home dead. Neither could she quite forgive Mrs. Bates, she often said she was sure she wished her well, and that she would not lay a straw in her way. Three months were gone since Mrs. Bates had made the proposal of giving Timothy a piece of her mind, and still that malicious work had not been performed.

" Suppose we give her an opportunity by inviting her here to supper," said Mr. Walden.

Matty warmly seconded the plan, and a day was at once fixed. Such a busy time there had never been seen at Mrs. Walden's as the supper induced. The house was set in complete order—the nicest coverlids were spread on the beds, and the frilled pillow-cases brought from the closets—a half dozen new chairs were bought—the silver was polished, and the china set in the nicest order. Mr. Walden was to wear his new clothes, and Mrs. Walden the new dress ; the boys were to make special preparation, and Matty was to wear her white dress.

Cakes were made, and custards, and a variety of delicacies I need not enumerate prepared for Katy Bates and her mother, in the most excellent style; and as a crowning triumph, Dr. Meredith was invited.

"It is all admirable," he said, when he was told why the supper was made, for since the Fourth of July he had been very intimate at Mrs. Walden's, "but I have an amendment to suggest, which is, that my mother and the parson shall be invited."

I need scarcely say that Mrs. Bates, notwithstanding the charming occasion offered her, never gave Timothy a piece of her mind. Training day saw the completion of the third story of the North American Hotel, and brighter even than the new sign, shone, upon that occasion, the faces of Dr. Meredith and his bride.

THE COUNTRY COUSIN.

"Oh, mother, mother! father has sold old Brindle and her calf, don't you think!—sold her for twenty-five dollars—a good deal of money, ain't it? There she goes, now; just look up the lane and see her; how she shakes her head and bawls. She don't wish to go, but her calf runs like everything—it don't care—look quick, Hannah; look Nancy, or you won't see her, she is just going out of sight, now;" and little Willie Davidson ran out of the house as he finished telling the news, and climbed to the top of the gatepost for a last glimpse of old Brindle. Nancy ran to the gate too, asking Willie if he was quite sure of what he said, straining her eyes to catch one more look of the cow she had milked so often, and that seemed to her almost like a friend. She did not return to the house at once, but fell to digging about some pink roots—perhaps to divert her thoughts.

Mrs. Davidson stitched faster on the work she was sewing, and the moisture gathered in her soft blue eyes as she did so, for she was a kind-hearted woman, and could not have even a dumb creature about her that she did not love.

"Oh, mother!" shouted Willie, "all the cows have seen

that Brindle is going, and they are scampering across the field towards her, as fast as they can ; Spot is tearing up the ground with all her might. Do you suppose cows can feel bad, mother ? If they can't, what makes them act so ?"

"Oh, I don't know, my child, never mind," replied the mother, her voice choked and her eyes running over by this time.   Hannah called Willie in presently, and asked him if he was sure Brindle was sold, and if he really knew what money she had brought ; and when he said that he saw the man count twenty-five dollars into father's hand, she smiled and burst into a merry song, as she skipped about the work, for the sun was going down, and it was time for the evening chores.

Nancy remained digging about the pink roots, and thinking of Brindle a long time, and of the pretty little calf whose silken ears she had held so softly in her hands, only that morning.   The last sunshine faded from the brown gable of the old homestead—the chickens began to gather in quiet groups and talk soberly of bedtime ; the turkeys to gobble their last news ; and the geese to waddle slowly homeward, when she looked down the lane the way Brindle was gone, knowing she would not see her, but feeling impelled to look she knew not why.   The dust was all settled on the path she had gone, and quiet stretched the long road as far as she could see—quiet, but not all deserted ; slowly and wearily as it seemed, she saw coming in the distance a foot traveller, his coat swung over one arm, and a bundle on his shoulder.   How often we look at our future fate, and suspect it not.   Certainly Nancy dreamed not that poor traveller was anything to her.

Tired, very tired, from his work in the field, and slow,

behind the plough which he held sideways, for he did not care to turn a furrow now, came Mr. Davidson—the chains of the harness dragged heavily and rattled noisily as he came; and the old work-horses walked soberly enough, for they were tired too. Perhaps the smoke going up from the homestead chimney looked pleasant to the young man, and doubtless the smile and salutation of the farmer were kindly as he overtook him and slackened his pace, to make some inquiry about the nearest inn, and the prospects of obtaining employment thereabouts.

"What work can you do?" asked Mr. Davidson, letting the plough fall to the ground as he spoke.

The young man raised it up and held it steadily aslant as he replied that he had been used to farm-work and could do anything that a farmer would be likely to require.

"Come in," said Mr. Davidson, "and we will talk further about the matter."

Nancy had seen him holding the plough for her father as they came along, and she waited and gave him a sweet smile as he entered the gate—a smile that brought a deeper color to his cheek than had ever been there before, for the youth was a poor, hard-working youth, and not much used to woman's smiles. Hannah gave him a careless nod, but did not break off her song for his coming. She did not see the heightened color of his cheek, nor the tenderness in his blue eyes. When it was milking time, Timothy Linley, for that was the young man's name, offered to do the milking.

"I will assist him," said Nancy, for she and Hannah were used to doing all; but Hannah made no such offer; on the contrary, she remained in the house teasing her mother for a new gown and bonnet.

When Mr. and Mrs. Davidson sat on the cool stones at the door, in the deep shadow of the twilight, she told him how good the girls had been—how they had stayed at home all summer, and spun and milked and churned and now it was coming fall, and they deserved a little leisure and reward—in short, she wanted them to have some money, what he could spare, and spend a week in town with their aunt Martha. Just as a good husband and father would have done, Mr. Davidson counted into his wife's hand half the price of the cow, saying—

"Will that do ?"

"We must not both leave mother for a week," said Nancy ; " you may go, Hannah, in my place, I shall be quite well satisfied with what you buy for me ; and as for visiting Aunt Martha, I will do that some other time."

Never once said Hannah, " we will both go and stay three days—that will make a nice little visit, and you must choose your new dress yourself."

Timothy said Nancy must go—he would help her mother all he could—he would churn and draw all the water, and make the fires, and do many other chores ; but Nancy made excuses, for she felt how ill she could be spared, and Hannah went alone.

When the market-day came round, and Mr. Davidson went to town with the expectation of bringing home Hannah, with all the new things, mother and daughter were very busy—baking in the brick oven was done, and the house all set in order as for a stranger guest ; it was quite an event for Hannah to come from town with so much to tell and so many new things. Towards nightfall, when all eyes were straining down the road to catch the first glimpse, the white faces of the horses were seen.

"There they come!" shouted Willie from the gate-post. Nancy raised herself on tiptoe, while the good mother hastened to lay the cloth—but no, only the father was there. Great anxiety prevailed, and the wagon seemed to be an hour coming through the hollow and over the hill. Nancy ran to the gate to learn what was the matter.

"Nothing, Nancy, nothing," said the old man, smiling; but it was a very sad smile, and he added, "Hannah has found better friends than any of us, that is all."

Seeing how sad Nancy looked, Timothy managed to milk all the cows except one—it was not hard work at all, he said, he always liked to milk; and when the last chores were done, it was not yet dark, and one of the mildest and sweetest of the October days—so mild and so sweet, that Timothy ventured to say, blushing bashfully, and looking down, that a walk in the orchard would be pleasant. So taking a basket as an excuse, Timothy and Nancy went to the orchard together. The knolls, cushioned softly with grass, beneath the trees, invited to repose, and the heavy and curtaining silence to confidence. Every heart knows its own sorrows, and every heart desires that some other heart shall know them, and as naturally as the leaves fell in their lap, fell their words of gentle complaint and appeal for sympathy—not in vain.

A few days after this, Hannah came home, riding in a fine carriage, and with a fine gentleman beside her. She was a girl of fresh impulsive feelings, of a showy style, and easily charmed by flattery. And she had given and received admiration, if not affection.

In her new bonnet, with its gay ribbons, and new dress, ruffled and flounced, the plainer mother and sister hardly knew Hannah.

I am sorry to say, that the disposition she had made of the money was not a little selfish—Nancy's dress and bonnet were not only less gay, but evidently a good deal less expensive than her own.

When the apples hung their red cheeks down another year, and the mists were like dim shadows along the yellow leaves of the woods, the old homestead had a quieter and soberer look—Nancy and Hannah were married. Timothy, a slender and delicate youth, was the husband of one, and a healthy, hale man, who counted his money by thousands—the same who brought Hannah home in the fine carriage—was her husband now. She was gone to live in a great city, to be surrounded by fashion and friends, and wear fine morning dresses and evening dresses, and forget her playmate and workmate, poor Nancy.

November midnight lay black over the town, and black over the country; spires gleamed faintly through the rain; roofs stretched wide and wet over the sleeping and waking multitude, and the street lamps, burning dimly, lighted only now and then some home-going coach or solitary wanderer. The lamps in the halls and at the doors of the great houses had been put out, and only here and there, through windows closed against the rain, shone a little light. Some exceptions there were, it is true; mirth will not always let the November rain put out its fires, and melancholy will have its lights and watchers, too—life will come to life in its time, and death will claim its own at midnight as well as at noon. So, here and there, in the rainy darkness, stood some, lighted from basement to chamber, but only with one have we to do. The lamps at the door blaze over the broad steps, and the glittering chandelier in the

hall shines up the broad and elegantly-furnished staircase.
Coaches wait at the door, and the silver mounting of the harness is gemmed with rain—there is no noise of music or dancing
within; and yet, from the quick-moving steps and variously
flashing lights, the occasion seems to be mirthful. Let us go in
and see. In the drawing-room the lights are not brilliant, but
the table in the refectory is spread as for a holiday, and we
hear voices, suppressed, but joyful. Ah, here in the softened
light of these rich and carefully drawn curtains, we learn the
secret—a child is born to wealth and honor, and friends are
come through the November rain to rejoice with the mother,
and to kiss the bright-eyed little one, who as yet knows nothing
of the quality of the new world into which it has come.

We will leave them now, for their lives have been "a cake
unturned," and have hardened in the perpetual sunshine of
prosperity.

The rainy clouds of that midnight stretched far beyond the
roofs of the city, over cultivated fields and dreary reaches of
woods; over warm sheltered homesteads; great farms, where
the housed cattle listened to the rain on the roof; along the
grass-grown and obscure road, where the mover had drawn up
his wagon beneath the sheltering beech-tree, and wakeful,
watched his log-fire struggling with the storm; and over the
settler's cabin and clearing—and this last chiefly interests us
now. Scarcely at all shines the light from the small window
against the great background of wet, black woods; and the
rain soaks noiselessly in the mellow ground of the small patch
of clearing where the house stands—if house, so small and rude
a habitation may be called. But its heavy beating is heard
distinctly by the anxious watchers by the bedside—for between

them and the clapboards of the roof there is no floor nor ceiling. In the rough stone fireplace some oak wood is burning, and two tallow candles on the mantel-shelf make the light, which is shaded from the bed by a temporary screen. No splendid draperies soften the light to the eyes, that for the first time have opened upon the pain and sorrow of the world. The country doctor sits dreamily by the fire, hearing imperfectly the neighing of his rain-beaten horse at the door; the murmured voices of the women, and the moans of the mother, who has come to a deeper than midnight darkness, and must enter it alone.

The crying of the little daughter beside her makes to her understanding no woeful picture of orphan struggles and sorrows —she hears it not; let us hope she hears the welcoming songs of the angels.

Gloomily and wet came the day, and the kind-hearted women trod softly about the bed—not that there was any fear of waking the sleeper—if the crying of her baby disturbed her not, how should the treading of their footsteps? Yet her smile was so like life, they could not but tread softly as they came near her—the hair was so bright and sunny, you could not believe the cheek beneath it was so hard and cold—the feet had been so quick to do good, it was hard to believe they were straightened for the last time; the eyes had but yesterday shone with such tenderness and love for every living thing— how, oh, how could they be darkened forever? So the women trod softly and folded the sheet softly down about the bosom that, beyond all other chilling, Death had chilled.

The brightest of the sun's light stayed behind the clouds, and the rain fell and fell—most dismally over the two men who had left all more cheerful work for the digging of a grave—the red brier-leaves clung about the mound, by the side of which they were digging—it had not been there long, for no grass was grown on it as yet, and not a bit of moss dimmed the lettering of the head-stone—"Timothy Lindley, aged twenty-five years," is all that is graven there—what need of more?—all his goodness was known to the soul that has gone to meet him; for it is the grave of poor Nancy the two men are making. No spot could be more gloomy than that where she was laid, a new and seldom-travelled road on the one side, and a thick wood standing in everlasting shadow on the other.

When the baby was a week old, a man and woman, a plain-looking and tearful pair, journeyed that way, and took her with them. Many times they kissed her, naming her Orpha, and in the old house where her mother had lived she grew to womanhood, a great comfort to them—her grand-parents—almost all the comfort they had, in fact, for Willie had gone out into the world, and quite—no, not quite, but nearly—forgotten he was ever a boy, and sat on the gate-post, with tears in his eyes, looking after old Brindle. He was a man, with all a man's aims and ambitions, and though he still loved and reverenced his parents—the love was no longer primary, and sometimes for months and months no letter came to inquire of their welfare, or say what were his own hopes and fears. And Hannah was living, and prosperous and happy, and yet so different was her life from theirs and so far had she grown away from them, that they thought almost as sadly of her as Nancy.

Her fine house was only a day's journey from the old homestead, and yet for seven years she had not made it a visit, so absorbed with travels otherwhere, and with the thick-crowding gayeties of her life, had she been. A sense, if not the feeling of filial affection, was not quite lost to her, however, and prompted, mostly by duty, she one day wrote a letter to the old folks, and with a tact which, in their simplicity, they interpreted as the spontaneous opening of her heart, spoke of the old life at the homestead, in terms of tender endearment, almost of regret—she began with "My much-loved parents," and closed with "Your ever-dutiful and affectionate child." She was careful to make no account of her present mode of living, further than to say they had been blessed and prospered abundantly, and lived very comfortably, thank Provdence. She did not say so in so many words, but the general tone of her letter implied that we were all poor suffering sinners together, travelling to the same goal, but not by precisely the same road. Her oldest daughter, Anna, who it was pretended was named for herself, was shortly to be married, she intimated, very advantageously, into one of the oldest and most respectable families in the country. She really wished she could see the dear faces of her good old father and mother again, but really her motherly duties were so stringent that she found herself still obliged to hold the pleasure in reserve. Upon what little chances fate seems to turn—when that letter was sealed and superscribed, Hannah threw it down with a yawn, mingled with a sigh of satisfaction, saying to herself, "Thank my stars, the dreaded task is done for another year!"

Could that good old father and mother have heard that exclamation, their cheeks would not have flushed with the happy glow of much younger men and women, as they did when sweet-voiced Orpha stood up before the candle, between the blessing and the meat of the supper-table, and read that letter aloud. Orpha had been to school a good deal more than they, and could read writing as well as print.

"Oh, isn't it strange," she exclaimed, when she had finished the reading, "that cousin Anna is to be married? Why, she is only just as old as I am;" and like the child she was, she wondered whether Anna could make bread and pies, and was thoroughly accomplished in the beautiful art of house-keeping. Aunt Hannah did not say, but she supposed that was to be taken for granted, for Anna was an accomplished singer, embroidered well, and could ride on horseback, and play chess admirably—all this Orpha knew, and of course the more necessary instruction of sewing and cooking had been given first. Her little head was quite turned with wonder as to what Anna would wear when she was married, and in what sort of fashion the dress would be made. She supposed her uncle could afford to give her a hundred dollars, if she wanted it, to buy wedding clothes with; but for her part, she could not well see how so much could be spent. Once, when her grandfather had given her twenty-five dollars, she went to the near village and bought everything she needed, and carried fifteen dollars home with her.

For a few moments she sat quietly, seeing the serious happiness in the faces of her grandparents, and then bursting into a merry laugh at the idea, she said—

"Wouldn't it be a pleasant surprise to Aunt Hannah, and all of them, to see me coming into their house some night, when they had not been told anything about it, and you, grandfather, and you too, grandmother? Oh, wouldn't it be delightful?"

And as she clapped her little brown hands in glee, her grandparents could not tell whether it were she or the candle that made the room so light.

"I suppose likely Anna will go away off somewhere," said Mrs. Davidson, "and we shall never have another chance of seeing them all together."

She said no more—there was no need that she should say more; and after a thoughtful silence, the good-hearted husband and grandfather said—

"If there should come a good snow, now—seems to me the air feels like it."

"Well, grandfather, suppose there should, what of it—say, grandfather?"

"Oh, nothing, pet," replied the old man, trying to look serious—"it would be nice sleigh-riding, that's all."

Orpha pouted a very little, and broke the piece of bread she held in her hand into small crumbs on her plate, till catching the reassuring glance of her grandmother, her pretty cheeks dimpled and blushed for shame—for well enough she knew what her grandfather was thinking about. A good girl was Orpha, petted a great deal, and spoiled a little, of course, but with a heart of unsuspecting innocence, and soft and warm as the sunshine. As she lay in bed two hours later, in her chamber next the roof, she held her eyes fast shut with her fingers, but in vain—they would not be sleepy. She kept saying to herself she did not see what was the reason, for useless as the effort is, we are always trying, all of us, to deceive ourselves; and though Orpha held her eyes so close, her ears were sensitive to every sound. She heard her grandparents talking by the fire below stairs, and thought it not improbable they were planning a visit to Aunt Hannah's. How she wanted to know what they said; to be sure, grandmother would tell her in the morning—but what of that, it was twenty years till morning. Presently, she became almost sure she heard the snow sifting against the windows in the wind. She raised her head on her hand, and looked out, and though she was almost sure it was snowing fast, she could not rest, and in another moment was pattering across the floor in her bare feet—never had snow heartier greeting, than when its white flakes fell in her hand. No little bird under its mother's wing ever felt more comfortable and happy than she that night in her own warm bed. Not selfishly happy—but how could she help being glad, when her grandparents and she were going to give Aunt Hannah and the young ladies such a surprise of pleasure. To be sure, she wanted to see Anna's wedding dresses and all her fine things, and felt a little curiosity to know what manner of husband she had chosen—whether his eyes were blue or black; if he wore his beard, and if he were worthy; but surely he was, for her Cousin Anna would never marry a man who was not both very wise and very good.

The voices of the old folks by the fire had been still a good while, and in the distance she heard the roosters crow for midnight, as she glided from dreams to dreams, the sleeping less delusive than the waking ones.

It was well for Orpha that she did not hear what the old folks said, as laying the embers together, they trimmed the candle, and spelled through Hannah's carelessly written letter— it was well she did not see the tears that wet it as they reproached themselves for their long neglect of their darling child—they had sent her presents of apples and potatoes and flour every year, but they had never once gone to her house;

14*

fifty miles seemed a great journey, and so the faces of their grandchildren were strange to them. They had thought (they were sorry for it now) that Hannah would not care about seeing her old-fashioned father and mother in her stylish house in town. They never once saw, as they spelled through the letter, that she did not say, " Come to me," after the " I cannot go to you; " nor did they notice that Orpha's name was not once in the letter. Hannah could not help wishing to see Orpha, and loving her when she knew how pretty and how good she was; they knew that; and to the dear child it would be like a journey to paradise—that they might well be assured of—so they said, as they folded the letter carefully and laid it next to the picture of little Samuel, between the leaves of the big Bible.

" We are growing old now, and if we ever go to see Hannah, there will not come a better time—it will be a tiresome day's ride; but for Orpha's sake we must make ourselves strong enough to endure the fatigue."

It was well Orpha did not see their tears, and learn that it was more for her sake than theirs the visit was planned.

How sleepy she was in the morning, when her grandmother said, " Come, Orpha ! " It seemed as if she had but just come to bed; she could hardly open her eyes, and the " Yes, grandmother," was a good deal fainter than common; but when " Come, Orpha," was repeated, with the added words, " it's time to get up, pet, if you want to go to Aunt Hannah's with your grandfather and me," she was wide awake, and sitting straight up in bed in a moment. She saw the snow piled against the window, white and high—the candle in her grandmother's hand, for it was not daylight yet, and her own fresh

and smoothly ironed clothes over her arm. "Oh, grandmother!" that was all she could say for the happy, happy
tears.

Redder than a clover field in June was all the east, when
having carefully secured the doors, and sprinkled the hickory
sticks in the fireplace with water, they set out, breaking and
ploughing their way through the deep snow, in the old wood-
sled. Nobody would notice that it was not the best sleigh in
the world, Orpha thought, for grandfather had tied the newly
painted wagon-body on the sled, and that was filled with straw,
and overspread with the nicest coverlet of all the house.

What a pretty pink the clouds made on the snow—she was
never weary of looking at it, and how strangely the cattle
looked in pastures of snow, and the haystacks, crusted like
pound-cakes. Grandfather's horses would be the admiration
of all the city, she was sure, so gay and fine they looked, their
manes loose in the wind, and their ears trembling with the
exhilaration of the snow-drive.

For the first seven miles the scene was quite familiar—she
had twice been that distance on the road—once with her
grandfather to mill, and once to a funeral; but the strange
country into which they went, after crossing the creek where
the mill was, afforded new and surprising interest. The sleigh-
ride, in itself, was a perfect delight,—to watch the snow dropping from the bent boughs, the birds dipping into it with such
merry twitters, and to lean down over the sled-side and plough
a tiny furrow with her hand, were a great joy, without the
crowning fact that it was to end in the evening by arrival at
Aunt Hannah's.

Now she came forward to the front of the sled and held

grandmother's hands in hers, wondering why they were so cold;
now she turned up the collar of grandfather's overcoat, brushing back the gray hair that the wind blew about his eyes; and
now, wrapping his hands in her woollen shawl, and taking the
reins for a little while, she could drive as well as he, she said;
upon which he smiled, patting her cheek, but not telling her
that the horses were so well trained, and so sobered now with
the distance already travelled, that they would go straight along
without any guiding at all. Now they went through a wide
brawling creek, where the water ran fast through brown sand-
stones and cakes of broken ice, and Orpha trembled a little as
grandfather walked out on the tongue of the sled and loosened
the bridle-rein so that the horses could drink. Cold as it was,
their sides were all wet, and they breathed very hard and fast
between the drinking. At length, grandfather pulled off his
blue mitten, and pulled out his big silver watch and said it was
two o'clock, and a little while after that, where a painted sign
erected at the forks of the road, and a curious old house, having
no fence in front of it, stood, they stopped to procure an hour's
rest and some refreshments for themselves and their horses.
There was a great fire in the big room into which they were
shown, before which sat half a dozen travellers, eating apples
and cakes, and drinking cider and whiskey; across the middle
of the floor a long table was spread, and, at one end of it, there
sat a young man, sipping tea and writing, alternately. He
looked up from the sheet before him, on the entrance of our
party, and having made a friendly salutation, such as country
folks, though strangers, are in the habit of giving one another,
resumed his pen and was presently quite absorbed; his heavy
black hair fell over and partly concealed a smooth fair fore-

head, as he wrote, and a smile of extreme sweetness played round the mouth, betraying no irresolution, but seeming rather the outward shining of firm and good principles. The healthful glow of his cheek was in fine contrast with the blackness of his full curling beard, and the pearly teeth, sound and even, with the ripe redness of the lips.

Orpha thought she had never seen so handsome a man in her life, and in verity, she never had seen beauty cultivated and matured under the refining influences of intellect and art. She could not tell why, but there was an indefinable air of superiority about him, that made even the schoolmaster and the village clergyman seem commonplace in comparison with him. When her thoughts reverted to her Cousin Annie, she could not imagine how she could have fallen in love with any one, not having seen the young traveller. But how much did his beauty increase in her eyes, when, looking up as he folded his letter, he made haste to offer her grandfather (who was sitting on a hard bench) the leather-cushioned chair in which himself had been sitting, and with a gesture and a word, not rude, but authoritative, caused the men at the fire to dispose themselves in half the room they had previously occupied, so giving her grandmother and herself a warmer feeling of the fire from which, till then, they had almost been shut out.

"How far is it to the town of——?" said the old man to the landlord, as he entered with hot doughnuts and a fresh pot of cider; but the question was too modestly low for that blustering personage to hear.

"It is twenty-two miles, sir," replied the young man, who had heard the question.

" Are you much acquainted there ? " Mr. Davidson ventured timidly to inquire.

The young man answered that he knew the city pretty thoroughly, and had indeed a large personal acquaintance with the inhabitants.

" Then, perhaps, you know or have heard of my son, Joseph C. Pettibone," suggested the old man, his face aglow with animation.

" Oh, yes, sir—no one in the whole city better—an admirable family.

" Why, isn't it strange !" exclaimed the father, turning to his wife. " This young man here knows Mr. Pettibone. I am glad I have met you," he continued, offering his hand to the stranger; and he went on ingenuously—" we are on our way to Mr. Pettibone's house—my wife here, and this little girl—we haven't seen any of them these twenty years, nor they us. Indeed, Orpha, our little granddaughter, has never seen her Aunt Hannah Pettibone at all, and you may be sure she is happy enough, having a sleigh-ride and a chance to see the town and her aunt and cousins;" and tenderly he patted the cheek of Orpha, already blushing painfully with the attention called to her. " And so you know Mr. Pettibone, and Hannah, and all of them "—a new thought seemed to strike the old gentleman—and he continued, " maybe you know a young man of the name of Hammond, who is shortly, Hannah writes me, to be married to her daughter Annie."

There was a confused heightening of color in the cheek of the handsome stranger, and he bit his lip, to which, however, the accustomed smile came back with unwonted brightness as he replied that he had some acquaintance with the young man, and was just returning from a visit to his father's family, but that he was quite ignorant of the proposed marriage.

"A family of position and influence, I suppose, from what Hannah says," mused the grandfather aloud; "she seemed to think it would be a fine match for her girl—what do you think? Was the young man at home when you were at his father's?"

"Why, yes," replied the stranger, "he was there, but in fact I did not converse with him much."

"Well, do you think Annie is going to do pretty well?" continued the grandfather, perseveringly; "great fathers don't always have great sons, nor even good ones."

The young man replied that he hardly knew what to think, and hastened to interrupt the conversation by inquiring of the landlord what time the coach would arrive.

That personage raised himself on tiptoe, and looking from the window, said the coach was just coming in sight; and taking out his watch, he continued in a tone that indicated especial felicity—

"She is making good time to-day—that coach is; but, young man, your chance of getting aboard is slim, mighty slim, sir—black as she can be with passengers on the outside;" and this additional fact evidently gave him increased happiness.

"I have provided against that," said the young man (a shadow crossing his face as he spoke), "in part, at least;" and giving a letter into the landlord's hand he begged that he would see it forwarded.

"You are designing to reach the city to-night?" said Mr. Davidson, again addressing the young traveller.

"Yes," he replied, "Mrs. Pettibone has a kind of birthnight

merrymaking at her house to-night, and I had promised myself the pleasure of being with them;" and he went on to say his horse had fallen lame that day, and he had proposed leaving him in the landlord's care, and going forward in the coach.

"You are very welcome, sir, to a seat with us," said the grandfather, cordially; and surveying the fashionable exterior of the young man he added: "we have only a sled; but our horses are in good order, and we move pretty fast and very comfortably."

Half an hour after this, the horses having been regaled with oats and an hour's rest, our party, with the accession of the young man, were gliding briskly through the snow.

The variedly amusing talk of the young man kept the old people from feeling the cold as they did in the morning; and then he was so kind, taking his fine comforter from his neck and wrapping it about that of the old farmer, and quite forcing Mrs. Davidson to wear his plaided shawl, and taking the reins for an hour when the hands of the old man became numb.

Not one word spoke Orpha, but such smiles dimpled the cheeks that were nestled among brown curls and almost hid in her deep hood, with every attention bestowed on her grand-parents, that no words were needed to assure the young man of her goodness of heart. The old folks grew tired after a while, and sat silent, wishing the journey at an end, and the stranger singing—it may have been to himself, it may have been to Orpha—

> "It may be for years, and it may be forever,
> Then why art thou silent, thou bride of my heart."

They moved on and on, and at last to its lullaby sound, Orpha nestled down in the coverlet and fell asleep.

When she awoke it was night, and the sled standing still before the finest house she had ever seen—all brilliant with lights and musical with voices. Lamps were shining down the street, carriages and beautiful sleighs moving to and fro, and houses and people as far as she could see.

"Well, petty, we have got there," said the grandfather; and taking the handkerchief from her face, she sat up; and, in her bewilderment, said almost sadly:

"I am sorry; I wish it was further."

"So do I," said the young stranger, "from my heart;" and he almost lifted Orpha out of the sled.

"I wonder whether Mr. Pettibone has any stable?" asked Mr. Davidson of the young man; adding, as he patted the neck of his horses caressingly—"poor fellows, you are tired, aint you?"

"I know where he keeps his horses," replied the young man; "go right in, and I will attend to them, if you will trust me," and he ran up the steps and gave the bell a vigorous pull.

"See they don't drink while they are so warm, if you please," said the careful farmer, availing himself of the young man's kindness; "and that they have plenty of meal and oats, and I will see you by and by here, at my son's house, and thank you."

"I guess we have got to the wrong place, like enough," he said, looking inquiringly at his wife, as he saw the grin in the face of the negro who opened the door, and the number of black men and women moving through the great hall.

"Does Mr. Pettibone live here?" he inquired.

"Yes, sah."

"Joseph C. Pettibone?" repeated the old man, still in doubt.

"Yes, sah; who shall I announce?"

"Why, I will announce myself," said Mr. Davidson, indignantly; "Mrs. Pettibone is my daughter. Will we find her in here where the frolic seems to be?" And with his good wife beside him, he made his way to the open door of the brilliant drawing-room, poor Orpha, trembling like a frightened bird, nestling close to her grandmother's skirts.

A stylish and richly dressed woman advanced as their shadows crossed the threshold, and started, retreating slightly, and a kind of blank surprise taking the place of the welcoming smile she had assumed, when she saw the persons who came behind the shadows.

The mother's heart, rather than her eyes, told her that it was Hannah, and with the sobbing cry of "My daughter!" she would have taken her in her arms; but the white-gloved hand of the lady motioned her back—the lights dazzled, and the wonderstruck faces repelled her; staggering, rather than walking, she retreated.

"Hannah, Hannah," said the old man, giving one reproachful look, and with his head dropping on his bosom, and the tears making everything dim in spite of the much light, he retraced solemnly and slowly the way he had come.

At the door they were overtaken by Mr. Pettibone, whose strong common sense had been outraged by his wife's reception of her parents, though perhaps his feelings had little to do with his manner, which was cordial enough.

He reminded them how long it was since they had met, adding that a child might be forgiven for forgetting even her mother, in the course of twenty years. Hannah would be as rejoiced as himself when she knew it was her own father and mother were come. All they could do, however, the old folks could not feel what the man's words implied. " And this little body," he said, shaking the trembling hand of Orpha, " who is she?"

" Nancy's child, to be sure," answered the old man.

" Nancy, Nancy; who is she? Oh, I remember now, the one who went to the new country," for Mr. Pettibone felt it incumbent on him to remember something, and believing he had struck the right vein, continued: " I was under the impression that Nancy's children were all boys. Well, how does she like the new country?"

" We don't know," the father said, wiping his eyes; " poor Nancy has gone to the country from whence no traveller returns."

Half believing and half disbelieving that Hannah had in truth failed to recognize them, the old folks suffered themselves to be conducted to one of the chambers, furnished so luxuriously and warmed and lighted so comfortably, that if anything could have made them forget the chilly air which rustled out of Hannah's brocade, they would have forgotten it.

In the second meeting with her parents, she hid her face for a moment in her lace handkerchief, but the tears, if she shed them, left her eyes dry; and though she said she was never so happy, she looked distressed and mortified, and seemed not to know what to do or say.

Her children were brought and introduced to their dear grandpapa and grandmamma, and to pretty cousin Orpha, and having kissed the cheeks of the old folks, retired very properly—

gay butterflies that they were. Orpha, in her close-fitting woollen frock, feared they would catch cold with bare neck and arms, but she dare not say so; as with admiring eyes (for they looked very pretty) she watched them leaving the room.

Annie, a tall, slender girl, with a colorless and expressionless face, and thin, flaxen hair, insisted that Orpha should wear one of her dresses and accept the services of her maid—she could easily be dressed before midnight, and that was quite early enough.

Mrs. Pettibone could not leave her guests—Mr. Hammond would of course be greatly annoyed by Annie's absence, her dear parents must excuse them—they would hasten to join them the earliest moment at which they were at liberty. Some wine, sweetmeats and cake were sent up, very unlike the substantial supper they had hoped to take with their dear children and children's children.

Orpha was not hungry, she said; but climbing to her grandfather's knee, smoothed his long, silver hair, and nestling her cheek against his home-made coat, than which she had thought, till that night, nothing could be finer, she fell asleep, thinking in her heart she did not care what anybody said, her grandfather was just as good as any one. And she was right —good little Orpha.

Having seen the sled and horses of his new friend properly cared for, our young traveller made haste to present himself at Mr. Pettibone's, wondering how those dimpled cheeks would look outside the muffling hood.

To his surprise, he neither saw nor heard anything of the country people—he feared it was all a dream, and seating himself apart in the shadow of a curtain, recalled minutely all the circumstances of the afternoon. Surely he was not mistaken; we come so much nearer guileless natures, the impression they leave upon us is deeper than all the artificial devices in the world are able to leave. He could almost hear the voice of the grandfather and see his benignant smile, and no matter at what beauty he looked, his eyes could not see it for the dimples of Orpha. He was not long left to his quiet meditations—Mrs. Pettibone soon joined, and having rallied him on the sentimental seriousness of his mood, protested that it quite baffled her powers to dissipate; and, having deputed her daughter, Anna, whose skill she hoped would be more effective, she playfully, let us hope not designedly, retired.

To any one except the young lady addressed, Mr. Hammond would have been delightfully entertaining; but to her he was particularly unsatisfactory—he said not, in short, what she had expected him to say.

When Orpha awoke in the morning and looked about the fine chamber, she could not at first tell where she was, and with memory came a strange, sad, home-sick feeling that she had never in her life known till then. When she was dressed in her brown flannel frock, she looked at herself in the great looking-glass, before her, with painful dissatisfaction. Afterwards she seated herself at the window and looked into the cold, dreary street. Few persons were stirring yet, for it was early; the snow was driving before the wind in dismal gusts—all looked strange and dreary, dreary; despite all she could do, the tears kept dropping and dropping on her little brown hands, folded together in her lap. When the first sunshine touched the window, she held up her handkerchief to dry the tears in its light. Why did she blush and smile and tremble all at once? it is not her own name wrought with black silk thread that she sees—Richard Hammond is written there in clear black characters. How came she by it? Ah, she remembers now that when she awoke from sleep in the sled last night, she found her face covered with a handkerchief—could this have been the one?

Richard Hammond rose early too—it was not his habit, but that morning he could not sleep—of course he could not imagine why, and the thought came to him that a little exercise before breakfast might be beneficial, and with no defined plan or motive, he bent his steps in the direction of Mr. Pettibone's house; he saw those tearful eyes at the window, and intuition told him why they had grown so dim since yesterday, and his heart knocked tumultuously to get out of his bosom and go up to that window and comfort her.

Two hours later, he was ringing the bell, and inquiring for Mr. Davidson. It was his duty to tell the old gentleman how well his horses were doing and where they were.

"I am glad you have come," said the old man, "our folks think they have been in town long enough;" but the light which beamed in his face said very plainly how pleased he, too, was with the prospect of going home.

"Not to-day, surely," said the young man; but the farmer thought he would get up the horses, drive about a little and show his folks the town, and then start home—they would have a full moon to light them, he said, and if they were a little late in getting there, why no matter.

Mr. Hammond knew the town well; everything that was worth seeing he would be happy to show his new friends, if they would accept his guidance.

They could not think of making him such trouble, the old man said; but it was evidently not a trouble, and when, some minutes later, the horses came prancing up to the door, it was Richard Hammond who was driving them.

Neither Mrs. Pettibone nor Anna came near the front door to see their guests go away—they were afraid of the chilly air of morning; but what was their astonishment and confusion when, on looking from the window, they saw Richard Hammond almost lifting Orpha into the sled, and with a tenderness of manner which they had never seen till then.

He saw them—smiled and kissed his hand gaily as they drove off, and the last their wonder-struck vision saw of him he was carefully wrapping the coverlet about the young girl's feet. No, not the last they saw of him—the following winter, looking handsomer and happier than ever, they chanced to see him at the opera, and beside him, the sunny lengths of her hair rippling over her dimples and half down her snowy cloak, a young woman whose beauty was evidently the admiration of the house.

"I wonder what Hannah and her proud daughters think of their country cousin now!" said Grandfather Davidson, as he snuffed the candles, and heaped high the fire, the while his wife polished the silver tea-pot, and adjusted the pound-cake and custard cups, on the evening "the children" were expected home from their bridal visit in town.

The two pins in the sleeve of the grandmother's black silk dress, were not straighter and brighter than everything else about the house; and the hearts of the old folks were not happier their own marriage-day than when the joyous barking of the watch-dog at the door told them "the children" were come.

AN OLD MAID'S STORY.

I WAS sitting one summer afternoon in the shadow of a grape-vine and cherry-tree—for the one running through the top of the other cast a shadow on the short, thick grass beneath, through which scarcely a sunbeam found way. I was sitting there with an open book on my knee, but I was not reading; on the contrary, two or three thicknesses of the cloth which I had been sewing at intervals lay on the open page, and on this rested my idle hands. I was not working, nor thinking of work. On the side of the hill, behind me, the mowers were wading through billows of red clover—they were not whistling nor singing that I remember of—they had no grape-vines nor cherry-tree limbs between their bent backs and the sunbeams that fell straight and hot upon them—and yet, perhaps, they were happier than I with all my cool shadows, for we have to pay to the uttermost farthing for the enjoyments of this life. The water was nearly dried up in the run that went crookedly across the hollow, and the sober noise it made I could not hear. The grey, dry dust was an inch deep along the road, which was consequently almost as still as the meadows. Now and then a team went by, taking a little cloud with it; and now and then a young woman trotted along on the old mare, which at home did nothing but switch flies, and was evidently averse to any other employment. Two or three young women I remember to have seen go along with bundles on their saddle-horns, and a little cloud of dust, similar to that in which they moved, half a mile, perhaps, behind them, in which trotted the colt, after its mother. I had seen, without especially noticing them, and yet it was an unusual thing that two or three young women should ride along on the same afternoon.

Immediately above my head, and fronting me, there was a porch, level with the second floor of the house, and on this porch a young, rosy-cheeked girl was spinning wool. She was running up and down as gaily as if it were gold and not common wool she held in her hand, and her face was beaming as though the rumble of her wheel were pleasantest music. Her thoughts run little further than the thread she spun, good simple girl, and, therefore never became so tangled as to vex and puzzle her ; and so it was easy to spin and smile, and smile and spin, all day. Once in a while the high well-sweep came down and down, and then went up and up—the iron hoops of the bucket rattled against the curb—some mower drank his fill, and with a deep breath of satisfaction went away, never wondering how or why half the clover along his path drew so bright a red from the black ground, and the other so sweet a white ; and it was well he did not wonder, for had he done so ever so much all would have ended in the fact that there was red and white clover, and that the same ground produced both.

A little shower of dust blew over me and settled in the green grass and the white dying roses about me, and Surly.

our dapple-nosed house-dog, dashed by me and gave noisy welcome to the visitor then about unlatching the gate. I hastened to conceal my book under the rosebush at hand, and to shake the dust from my work preparatory to using my needle, for to be found reading or idle would have been considered alike disgraceful in the estimation of our neighbors. When the visitor appeared, I recoguized Miss Emeline Barker, and at the same time became aware that she was bent on holiday pleasure. She had been riding on horseback, but her white dress showed scarcely a wrinkle, so well had she managed it— a sash of pink ribbon depended from the waist, and the short sleeves were looped up with roses—her straw hat was trimmed with flowers and ribbon, and her boots were smoothly laced with tape instead of leather strings. But more than her dress, her face betrayed the joyous nature of the errand she was bent on. "Somebody is going to be married," was my first thought, "and Emeline has come to invite me to the wedding," and I was confirmed in this when she declined the seat I offered, with the assurance that she had not tine to stay a moment. Expectation was on tiptoe, and when I said " how do they all at home?" I had no doubt she would tell me that Mary Ann, who was her elder sister, was to be married ; but she answered simply that all were very well, and went on to tell about the harvest, the heat of the day, and other commonplaces, just as if she wore her every-day calico dress and not a white muslin one, looped up at the sleeves with roses.

Directly she bid me good bye without having said anything extraordinary at all, and then, as if suddenly recollecting it, she exclaimed, "Oh ! I want to see Jane a moment." I pointed to the porch where Jane Whitehead was spinning, and with my heart drawing strangely into itself took the banished book from its place of concealment, quite careless of what Emeline Barker might think of me.

I felt dissatisfied and unhappy. I knew not why; the shadow of an unseen sorrow had fallen over me, and I could not escape it—in truth, I did not try. If I had taken a few steps I should have found the sunshine, but I did not, and the vague discomfort took a more definite shape.

I lifted the book to conceal my face, which it seemed to me must reflect my unhappy mind, but I did not read any more than before. Another book was opened which seemed to me the Book of Fate, and to be illustrated with one picture—that of an unloved old maid. We might be made wiser sometimes, perhaps, if it were permitted us to see ourselves as others see us, but we should rarely be made more comfortable.

There were whispers and laughter, and laughter and whispers, on the porch, but the rumble of the wheel so drowned the voices that for some time I heard not one word; but the first that reached me confirmed my feeling—myself was the subject of conversation.

"I should have thought they would have asked her," said Jane, half piteously, and turning her wheel slowly as she spoke, but not spinning any more. After a moment she continued, " suppose, Em, you take it upon yourself to invite her."

"Fie!" exclaimed Emeline, "if I were an old maid, I should not expect to be invited to young parties. Let old folks go with old folks, I say; and I am sure we would not be mad if all the old maids in the county should make a frolic and leave us out, would we, Jenny?"

"Why no," replied Jane ; "but then this seems like another case, and I can't help liking Miss "——

"So do I like her well enough in her way," said Emeline, "but I would not like her at a party of young folks. She must be as old as the hills, and the dear knows she has no beauty to recommend her."

"Oh, she is not so very old—past getting married to be sure, or being cared for in that way, but she could help sew, you know, and be amused by our fun in the evening. Suppose we ask her to go with us ?"

"I tell you she would be in the way," persisted Emeline, "and I suppose if Mrs. Nichols had cared to have her she would have invited her."

"Perhaps she forgot it," insisted Jenny.

"No, she didn't," replied Emeline. "Didn't I hear her talking all about who she wanted and who she did not, and who she felt obliged to ask ; and she said if she asked Miss—— there were two or three others a good deal older and less desirable that would think themselves entitled to invitations, and she must stop somewhere, and on the whole might better not begin."

"Well, then, you tell her," pleaded Jane, evidently receiving, and sorry to receive, the stubborn facts.

When I became aware that I was the " old maid," so compassionated and dreaded, I was as one stunned by some dreadful blow. I felt it due to myself to remove from where I sat, but I had no strength to go ; I seemed not to be myself. I saw myself by the new light whereby other people saw me. I began to count up my years. I was twenty-five the May past, but my life had been entirely confined to the old homestead, and no special, peculiarly interesting, or peculiarly sorrowful events had broken its monotony, so that I found it hard to realize the truth. I was young in knowledge—young in experience, and one year had been drawn into another without the visible separation of even a New Year's dinner. I had never thought of dividing myself from the younger people of the neighborhood, and till now I had never suspected that they desired to divide themselves from me. Directly Jenny sliped the bands, set by her wheel, and whispering and laughing the two girls came down and essayed to make some explanation which should not be wholly false, and yet soften the truth. Emeline was to remain a little while and assist Jenny, after which the two were to go together to Mrs. Nichols' to help with some sewing she was busy about.

So the old mare was led into the door-yard, Emeline hung her gay hat on a low limb of the cherry-tree, and tying on one of Jenny's aprons the happy pair set busily to work.

My task was much harder than theirs, for I must keep close the misery that was in my heart, and not suffer one single pang to break the expression of quietude in my face. The hat swinging gaily in the wind—the laughter of the girls, smothered away from my participation, seemed like injuries to my insulted sorrow. I could have lifted myself above hatred. Against a false accusation I could have proudly defended myself, but my crime was simply that of being an old maid, whom nobody cared to see, and against that there was nothing I could interpose. For the first time in my life I felt a sort of solemn satisfaction in the white and dying roses, and in the yellow leaves that fell from the cherry-tree over my head and into my lap.

Sometimes, when the girls came near me, they would lift up their voices as if in continuance of a conversation previously going forward, but I understood very well that these clear-toned episodes were put in for the occasion.

When the heart is light the hands are nimble, and the work was soon done, and Jenny ready to make her toilet—a task for which a country girl, at the time and place I write of, would have been ashamed to require more than ten minutes. The shadow of the cherry-tree was stretching far to the east when the old mare, quite used to "carry double," was led to the fence-side, and Emeline and Jane mounted and rode away.

I put my hands before my face when they were gone, but I did not cry. It was a hard, withered feeling in my heart, that tears could not wash away. In all the world I could see no green and dewy ground. There was nothing I could do— nothing I could undo. There was no one I blamed, no special act for whch I blamed myself, unless it were for having been born. The sun went down under a black bank of clouds, and the winds came up and began to tell the leaves about a coming storm.

Pattering fast through the dust a little boy passed the gate, climbed into the meadow, and was soon across the hollow, and over the hill. The men were very active now, pitching the mown hay into heaps, turning their heads now and then towards the blackening west, and talking earnestly and loud. The boy drew close to them and seemed to speak, for all the workmen stood silent, and the rake dropped from the hand of the foremost and his head sunk down almost to his bosom. Presently one of the men took up the rake, another brought the coat and hat of the foremost laborer, who had been work-

ing bareheaded, and assisted him to put them on, for he seemed as one half dead, and quite unable to help himself—then the
little boy took his hand and led him away, and I noticed that
he walked with staggering steps, and often passed his hand
across his eyes as he went. The men left in the field resumed
work directly, but though a deep silence fell with the first
shadows I could not hear a word, so lowly they spoke to one
another. Till long after dark they kept rolling and tumbling
the hay into heaps, but at last I heard them gathering water
pails and pitchers together, and soon after they crossed the
meadow towards the house—not noiselessly, as they came generally, but speaking few words and the few in low and kindly
tones. The black bank of clouds had widened up nearly half
the sky, and a blinding flash of lightning showed me their
faces as they drew near the well and paused—not so much because they wished to drink, as because they felt reluctant to
separate and go their different ways. While one of the men
lowered the bucket, another approached me, and wiping his
sunburnt face with his red silk handkerchief, said—"One
of our hands has had bad news this evening."

I felt what it was before he went on to say, " his youngest
child died about five o'clock, and will be buried to-morrow
morning, I suppose."

Poor, poor father—no wonder the rake had fallen from his
hands, and that he had suffered himself to be led away like a little child. What anguish must be the mother's, thought I, when
the sterner and stouter-hearted father so bows himself down,
and forgets that there is anything in the world but the cold
white clay that is to be buried to-morrow.

I forgot Mrs. Nichols and the gay people she had about

her ; forgot that I had been forgotten, and remembered only our common humanity and our common need.

The sky was black overhead and the lightning every few minutes illuminated the grey dust before me, that was beginning to be dotted with drops of rain, falling at intervals, as I hurried through the darkness to the humble home where last year a babe had been born, and where the last day it had died. Two or three living children were left, and yet it seemed as if all were gone, the room was so still and gloomy. The little mouth had never spoken, and the little hands had never worked for food or for clothing, yet how poor the parents felt, having the precious burden laid from off their bosoms.

Close by the window, where the morning-glories grew thick, dressed in white and as if quietly asleep, lay the little one, waking not when the flowers dropped on its face, nor when the mother called it by all the sweetest names that a mother's fondness can shape.

"You must not grieve—the baby is better off than we," said a tall woman, dressed in black, and she led the poor mother from the white bed where it lay. After some further words of admonition and reproof, she proceeded to light the candles and to arrange the table preparatory, as I supposed, for morning service.

The rain came plashing on the vines at the window, and the mother's grief burst out afresh as she thought of the grave it would fall upon in the morning. A step came softly along the rainy grass, and a face whose calm benignity seemed to dispel the darkness, drew my eyes from the sleeping baby to itself. But the voice--there was in it such sweetness and refinement—

such a mingling of love and piety, that I was blessed, as I had never been blessed, in being permitted to listen to it.

I recognized the visitor for the village clergyman who had lately come among us, and whom I had only seen once, when he gave baptism to the little one that was now returned to dust.

I recognized not only the form and features, but I also recognized, or thought I did, a spiritual kindred—the desolation that had divided me from the world an hour past was gone—heaven came down near to me, so near that earth was filled with the reflection of its glory and happiness.

All the night we were together. There were few words spoken. There was nothing to do but to listen to the rain and the beating of my heart. There was nothing to see but the baby on its white bed, the dimly-burning candle and the calm soul-full eyes of the clergyman—now bent on the sacred page before him, now on the leaves that trembled in the rain, and now, as something told me, for I scarcely dared look up, upon myself.

I wished there were something I might do for him, but I could think of nothing except to offer the rocking-chair which had been given me on my coming, and which was all the luxury the poor man's house afforded. In my over-anxiety to serve, I forgot this most obvious service I could render, and when it occurred to me at last my unfortunate forgetfulness so much embarrassed me that I knew not how to speak or stir. If there had been any noise—if any one had been present but our two selves—if he would speak to me—but as it was, I could not for a long while find courage for that proffer of my simple courtesy. There he sat silent, as far from me as he could well be, and as more time went by, looking at me more and more earnestly, I thought. At last the steadfast gaze became so painful that I felt that any change would be relief, and mastering my embarrassment as I best could, I offered the rocking-chair to the clergyman, whose name was Wardwell, with the energetic haste with which one touches the lion he would tame.

"No, my child," he said, very calmly, "you have most need of it."

I know not what I said, but in some vehement way, which I afterwards feared expressed all I was most anxious to conceal, made my refusal.

He smiled and accepted the chair, I thought in pity of my confusion, and rather to place me at ease, than for the sake of his own comfort.

He asked me directly whether I had ever been far from the village—a natural question enough, and asked doubtless for the sake of relieving the tedium of silence—but I saw in it only the inference of my rusticity and want of knowledge, and replied with a proud humility that I was native to the village —had scarcely been out of sight of it, and had no knowledge beyond the common knowledge of its common people.

With a changed expression—I could not tell whether of pain or annoyance—Mr. Wardwell moved his position slightly nearer me, but the habitual smile returned presently, and he rocked quietly to and fro, saying only, "well, well."

There was nothing in the tone or the manner to give force to the words. They might indicate that it was as well to live in the village as any other place. They might indicate that he had no interest in the inquiry—and none in the answer—or it might be that they expressed the fixedness of a foregone conclusion. I chose to receive the last interpretation, and leaned my head on the hard sill of the open window to conceal the tears with which, in spite of myself, my eyes were slowly filling.

All the time the clergyman had remained silent I had longed with a sincere and childish simplicity to be noticed or spoken to, and now if I could have unsaid the few words he had directly addressed to me a tormenting weight would have been lifted from my bosom.

The wet leaves shook almost in my face, and now and then some cold drops plashed on my head; but I would not manifest any inconvenience. I felt as if Mr. Wardwell were responsible for my discomfort, and I would be a patient martyr to whatever he might inflict.

"My child, you are courting danger," he said, at last; "the chill air of these rainy midnights is not to be tampered with by one of your susceptible organization."

Ah, thought I to myself, he is trying to pour oil on the wound he has made, but doubtless he thinks no amount of chill rain could injure me, for all of his soft speaking. So I affected to sleep, for I was ashamed to manifest the rudeness I felt, though my position was becoming seriously uncomfortable, to say nothing of its imprudence. My heart trembled, audibly, I feared, when Mr. Wardwell approached, and stooping over me, longer I thought than need were, softly let down the window. I would have thanked him, but to do so would have been to betray my ill-nature, which I was now repentant, and ashamed of. He passed his hand over my wet hair, and afterwards brought the cushion of the rocking-chair and placed it stealthily beneath my head. Soothed from my sorrow, and unused to watching, I was presently fast asleep. I dreamed I was at home, and that some one was walking across and across my chamber, and so close to my bedside that I felt a distinct fear. So strong was the impression I could not rid myself of it, even when, fully conscious, I unclosed my eyes and saw the still baby before me, and the clergyman apparently dozing in his chair. Was it he who had been walking so near me, in forgetfulness of me and simply to relieve the monotony of the time? Yes, said probability, even before my eyes fell upon a handkerchief of white cambric, lying almost at my feet, and which I was quite sure was not there when I took my seat at the window.

I took it up, partly from curiosity, partly for the want of other occupation, examined the flowers in the border, and read and re-read the initial letters, worked in black in one corner—C. D. W. I fancied the letters had been wrought by a female hand, and with a feeling strangely akin to jealousy, and which I should have blushed to own, tossed the handkerchief on the table and took my own from my pocket, more aware of its coarseness and plainness than I had ever been till then. It was as white as snow, neatly folded, and smelling of rose-leaves; but for all that I felt keenly how badly it contrasted with that of the clergyman.

I wished he would wake, if he were indeed asleep—move ever so slightly, look up, or speak one word, no matter what; but for all my wishing he sat there just the same—his eyes closed, and his placid face turned more to the wall than to me.

From the roost near by, and from across the neighboring hills, sounded the lusty crowing—it might be midnight or daybreak ; I could not tell which, for the night had been to me unlike any other night. I arose softly, and taking the candle which burned dimly now, held it before the white face of the skeleton of a clock, to tell the hour, but the clock had been forgotten and was " run down."

I crossed the room on tiptoe and reseated myself without noise, but had scarcely done so when Mr. Wardwell, evidently aware of my movements and wishes, took from his vest an elegant watch and named the time, which was but half an hour after midnight. I sighed, for I felt as if the morning would never come.

" The time is heavy to you, my dear child," he replied, as if in answer to my sigh, and replacing the cushion, he offered me the easy-chair, blaming himself for having deprived me of it so selfishly and so long—and professing to be quite refreshed by the sleep which I suspected he had not taken.

I tried to decline, for in my heart I wished him to have the best chair, but when he took my hand with what I felt to be rather gallantry than paternal solicitude, I could no longer refuse, and in affectation of a quietude I did not feel, took up the hymn-book which lay at hand, and bent my eyes on the words I did not read.

" Will you read the poem that interests you ?" asked Mr. Wardwell, coming near, and turning his bright, blessed face full upon me.

I trembled, for it seemed to me that my heart was open before my companion, and even if it were not I knew my cheek was playing the tell-tale, but in some way I stammered an answer to the most obvious sense of the words, and replied that it was the hymn-book I held.

"I know it," replied my pleasing tormentor; "but it is a *poem* you are reading for all that."

I said there were some hymns which were also most ennobling and beautiful poetry, and I went on to instance a few which I regarded as such. He seemed not to hear my words, but said, rather as if musing aloud than speaking to me,—

"Yes, yes, my dear child,"—(he said *dear* child now, and not child as 'at first)—"at your time of life there are many sweet poems for the heart to read, which it does read without the aid of books."

He looked on me as he spoke with a sort of sorrowful compassion, I thought, and yet there was something tenderer and deeper than compassion, which I could not define.

He was greatly my senior, but it was not a filial feeling that caused me to say, I was past the time when frivolous fancy most readily turns evanescent things to poetry, and I mentioned myself as twenty-six the May coming, and not twenty-five the May past, as most women would have done.

"To me that seems very young!" replied my companion, solemnly, "I am"— he hesitated, and went on hurriedly and confusedly I thought, "I am much older than you are."

He went away from me as he spoke, and passed his hand along his deeply-lined forehead and whitening hair, as if in contemplation of them.

I could not bear the solemn gladness that came like a soft shadow over the dewier glow that had lighted his face awhile past, and hastened to say, though I had never thought of it before, that the best experience and the truest poetry of life should come to us in the full ripeness of years. He shook his

head doubtfully, smiled the old benignant smile, as he replied :

"It is quite natural, my dear child, that you should think so."

I had no courage to say more, especially as his thoughts
seemed to return to their more habitual channels ; but oh, how
much I wished he could feel this life as richly worth living as
I did.

He raised the sash, and leaned his head close to the wet
vines, though he had reproved me for doing the same thing,
and before I could find courage to remind him of it, or to say
anything, he was fast asleep.

I recalled every word I had spoken, and conscious of an
awakening interest that I had never before experienced for
man or woman, I thought I had betrayed it, and the betrayal
had produced the sleepy indifference, which, in spite of myself,
mortified me to the quick. I read the hymn-book till I was
weary of hymns ; and afterwards thought till I was weary of
thinking, then read again, and at last, to keep the place which
I had no interest in keeping, I placed my handkerchief between
the leaves of the book, and so turning my face as to see just
that part of the wall which Mr. Wardwell had looked at an
hour previously, I forgot him and myself and all things.

It was not the noise of the rain that woke me—nor the
crowing of the morning cocks, nor the sun's yellow light that
struggled through the room, nor yet the mother calling in her
renewed anguish to the baby that smiled not for all her calling, nor lifted its little hands to the bosom that bent above it
in such loving and terrible despair—it seemed to me it was
none of these, but a torturous premonition of solitude and
desolation.

Mr. Wardwell was gone, and the night was gone—but there was a pleasant voice in my ear, and a serene smile, kindling now and then in transient enthusiasm, whichever way I turned.

O night of solemn joy, O humble room, made sacred by the presence of death—O dream, whose sweet beginning promised so beautiful a close, how often have I gone back to you, and hewed out cisterns that I knew must break!

Surely in the mysterious providences that wrap themselves around us and which to our weak apprehensions seem so dark and so hard, there are true and good meanings, if we could but find them out.

Help us to be patient, oh, our Father, and give us the trusting hearts of little children, and the faith that mounts higher and brighter than the fire.

In the southern suburb of the village, and in sight of my own chamber window, is a low, gloomy stone church, which stood there before I was born, and which had scarcely changed any within my remembrance. All the long summer afternoons I used to sit at this window, looking up often from my sewing or my book, and always in one direction—that of the dark little church. I could see the oak trees that grew in different parts of the churchyard, and made deep shadows over the green mounds below, and it pleased me not a little to think Mr. Wardwell might be looking on them at the same moment with myself, for the parsonage, or "preacher's house," as it was called, stood in the same inclosure with the church building.

I could not see the parsonage itself, but I could see the smoke drifting from its chimneys, and know when a fire was being made, and could guess at the probable work that was going on indoors—whether dinner or tea, or whether it were the day for scrubbing or for baking, for I took the liveliest interest in such faint and far-away observations of Mr. Wardwell's household affairs, as I was able to make. Sometimes I would see a white fluttering among the trees, and know it had been washing day at the preacher's house, and then I would imagine the discomfort that had reigned in the kitchen all day, and the scouring of the ash floor, and the brightening of the hearth, that came afterward. I never made my seat under the grape-covered cherry tree, after the day that solemnized my destiny with the appellation of " old maid," and the evening' that saw our first hand led away.

The night that followed had opened a new page in my life— a page where I saw my future reflected in colors brighter than my spring flowers, that were all dead now. I did not regret them. Often came Emeline and talked and laughed with Jenny as she spun on the porch, and I praised the pink and blue dresses she wore, and the roses that trimmed her hat, and said I was too old for pink dresses and roses, without a sigh on my lips, or a pang in my heart. I lived in a world of my own now ; on Sunday eve we went to church together, and yet not to the same church—we sat in the same pew, but the face of the preacher turned not to the faces of my companions as it sometimes turned to mine, and for me there were meanings in his words which they could not see nor feel.

When he spoke of the great hereafter, when our souls that had crossed their mates, perhaps, and perhaps left them behind or gone unconsciously before them—dissatisfied and longing and faltering all the time, and of the deep of joy they would enter into, on recognizing fully and freely the other self, which, in this world, had been so poorly and vaguely comprehended, if at all—what delicious tremor, half fear and half fervor, thrilled all my being, and made me feel that the dust of time and the barriers of circumstance—the dreary pain of a life separated from all others—death itself—all were nothing but shadows passing between me and the eternal sunshine of love. I could afford to wait—I could afford to be patient under my burdens and to go straight forward through all hard fates and fortunes, assured that I should know and be known at last, love and be loved in the fullness of a blessedness, which, even here, mixed with bitterness as it is, is the sweetest of all. What was it to me that my hair was black, and my step firm, while his hair to whom I listened so reverentially was white, and his step slow, if not feeble. What was it that he had more wisdom, and more experience than I, and what was it that he never said, " you are faintly recognized, and I see a germ close-folded, which in the mysterious processes of God's providence may unfold a great white flower." We had but crossed each other in the long journey, and I was satisfied, for I felt that in our traversing up the ages, we should meet again.

How sweet the singing of the evening and the morning service used to be. Our voices met and mingled then, and in the same breath and to the same tune we praised the Lord, for his mercy, which endureth forever.

One afternoon Emeline and Jenny teased me to join them on the porch—they pitied me, perhaps, shut up in the dim old chamber, as we often pity those who are most to be envied, and finding they would not leave me to my own thoughts, I allowed myself to be drawn from my favorite position

Emeline was cutting some handkerchiefs from a piece of linen, and she asked me for one of mine as a measure. I opened a drawer where my nicest things were, sprinkled over with dried rose-leaves, and took up a white apron with a ruffled border, which I had worn the most memorable night of my life, and folded away just as I wore it—I took it up, thinking of the night, drew a handkerchief from the pocket and laid it across the lap of Emeline.

What laughter and clapping of hands and accusations of blushes followed, and true enough, the blushes made red confusion in my face when Emeline held up, not my own coarse, plain handkerchief, but a fine one with a deep purple border, and marked with the initial letters of Mr. Wardwell's name.

In vain I denied all knowledge of how I came by it; they were merrily incredulous, and asserted that if I knew nothing of the handkerchief I of course cared nothing for it—they would keep it and return it to the owner, who had no doubt dropped it by accident—just as I had taken it up.

I said it must be so, and spoke of the watch we had kept together, which gave the utmost probability to their suggestion, and which involved me in a serious dilemma. In the early twilight, they said we would walk together to the preacher's house—return him the lost handkerchief, and in return for our good office receive some of the red pears that grew at his door.

I could not bear that Mr. Wardwell should be mentioned in the same sentence with red pears—just as I would have mentioned any other person, and yet for the world I would not have had them see him as I saw him. I could not bear the thought of parting with my treasure which I had unconsciously possessed so long ; I would speedily have folded it just as I found it and as he had folded it, and replacing it in the pocket of my apron, have kept it forever shut in the drawer among the rose-leaves.

But how to evade the plan of my young friends without betraying my own secret I could not discover. Having forced myself to comply, for they insisted that they would go without me if not with me, I tried to reconcile myself by the light of judgment and the cold probabilities of the case. Between dreaming and waking I must have taken up the handkerchief instead of my own. But convinced against my will, I was of the same opinion still. I remembered very distinctly placing the handkerchief on the table before me, and of seeing it there when I placed my own between the leaves of my hymn-book—and I remembered too, right well, that Mr. Wardwell was gone when I awoke—how then could the accident have occurred ? And yet, if not by accident, how came I by the handkerchief ? I could not tell, but one thing I was forced to do, to give it back. If it must be done, it should not be the hand of Emeline or of Jenny that did it, but my own. When it was time to go I folded my treasure neatly, and hid it under my shawl and next my heart. It was autumn now and there were no flowers but the few deep red ones that were left on the rose of Sharon that grew by my window. I gathered a green spray that held two bright ones, and hiding my heart as carefully as I did my treasure, I seemed to listen to what my young friends said as we went along.

A little way from the door, in a rustic seat, beneath the boughs of an apple-tree Mr. Wardwell sat reading—as he looked up, the expression of a young and happy heart passed across his face, and gave way to a more sober and paternal one. He laid the book he had been reading in the rustic chair and came forward to meet and welcome us. He called me dear child again and laid his hand upon my head with a solemn and tender pressure, that seemed to me at once a promise and a benediction.

I said why we were come, and in my confusion offered the handkerchief with the hand that held the flowers. He smiled sadly as we sometimes do when we are misunderstood, and pointing my friends to the pears that were lying red on the ground, he took the handkerchief, the flowers and the hand that held them in both his own, and for a moment pressed them close to his bosom. When my hand was restored to me the handkerchief was in it, but not the flowers.

"I want the roses," he said, "and will buy them with the handkerchief, for we must pay for our pleasures whether we will or no."

I knew not how to understand him, and was yet holding my treasure timidly forth, when, seeing my friends approach, he put my hand softly back, and I hastened to conceal it as before—next my heart. The youthful expression, that dewy-rose-look of summer and sunshine, came out in his face again —my heart had spoken to his heart, and we felt that we were assuredly bound to the same haven.

The aprons of my young friends were full of red pears, and their faces beaming with pleasure, and I, whom they compassionated as an old maid, hid my sacred joy deep in my bosom, and turned aside that their frivolous and frolicsome mirth might not mar it. Involuntarily I turned towards the rustic chair, and with an interest which I felt in everything belonging to Mr. Wardwell, opened the book he had left there. It was the well-remembered hymn-book, and my handkerchief was keeping the place of the hymn I had read so often on the most memorable of the nights of my life. How happy I was, and what dreams I dreamed after that. The blessed handker-chief is shut up with rose-leaves in my drawer, but the giver I never spoke with but once again.

It was years after I had learned that my treasure was not an accident, and when Jenny and Emeline were each the happy mother of more than one pretty baby—still liking me a little, and pitying me a great deal because I was an old maid, when one snowy night, the old woman, who kept house at the parsonage, came for me. I must make haste, she said, for good Mr. Wardwell had been that day seized with a fit, and seemed to be slowly dying. It was true, as she said, he seemed but to wait for me. The Bible and hymn-book were by his bedside ; the plain linen handkerchief was between the leaves of the latter, and placing his hand on it, he whispered—

" Put this over my face when I am dead and the flowers"—

He could not say more, but I understood him and softly placing my hand on the heart where the life-tide was ebbing, I bent my face down close and kissed the cheek that was already moistening with death-dew. All the face brightened with that sweet, sweet expression that was manhood and angelhood at once—then came the terrible shadow, and the eyes that had known me, knew me no more—the lips gave up their color, but the habitual smile fixed itself in more than mortal beauty. As I unfolded the handkerchief two roses fell from it, which we buried with him.

His grave is at the south of the old church, and a rose-tree, grown from the slip of the one at my window, blooms at his head. Nothing now would tempt me away from the hills I was born among—from the old grey church, and the grave near which I hope to be buried.

"Come see my treasure ;" and Abbie Morrison (for that was the story-teller's name) unlocked the drawer, where, folded among rose leaves, almost scentless now, was the handkerchief with dark border, and marked with the initials, C. D. W.

To her neighbors Abbie Morrison is only an old maid in whose praise there is not much to be said. If any one is sick she is sent for, but in seasons of joy nobody has a thought of her. What does she know of pleasure? they say, or what does she care for anything but singing in the church and cutting the weeds from the graveyard?

The children love her sweet voice, and stop on the way to school if she chances to sing in the garden, and, as she gives them flowers, wonder why their sisters call her old and ugly. It may be that angels wonder too.

THE END.